FAIRY IDOL Kanon 3

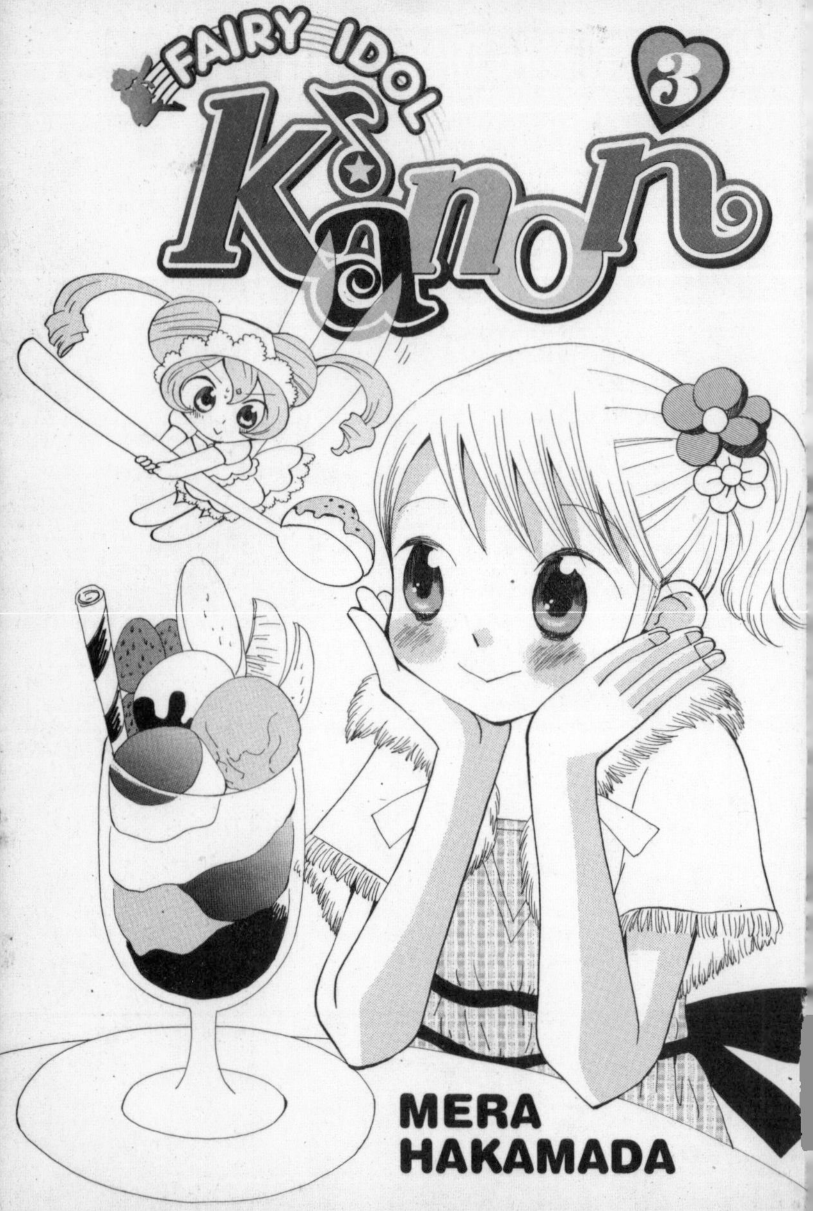

MERA HAKAMADA

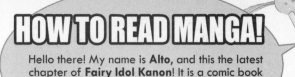

HOW TO READ MANGA!

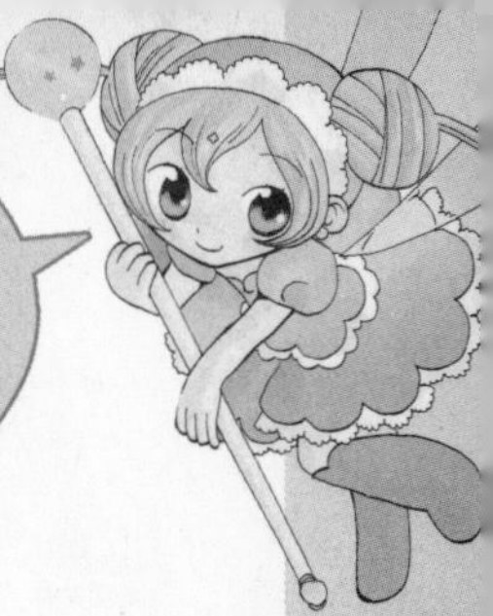

Hello there! My name is **Alto,** and this the latest chapter of **Fairy Idol Kanon**! It is a comic book originally created in the country of **Japan,** where comics are called **manga.**

A manga book is read from **right-to-left,** which is **backwards** from the normal books you know. This means that you will find the first page where you expect to find the last page! It also means that each page begins in the top right corner.

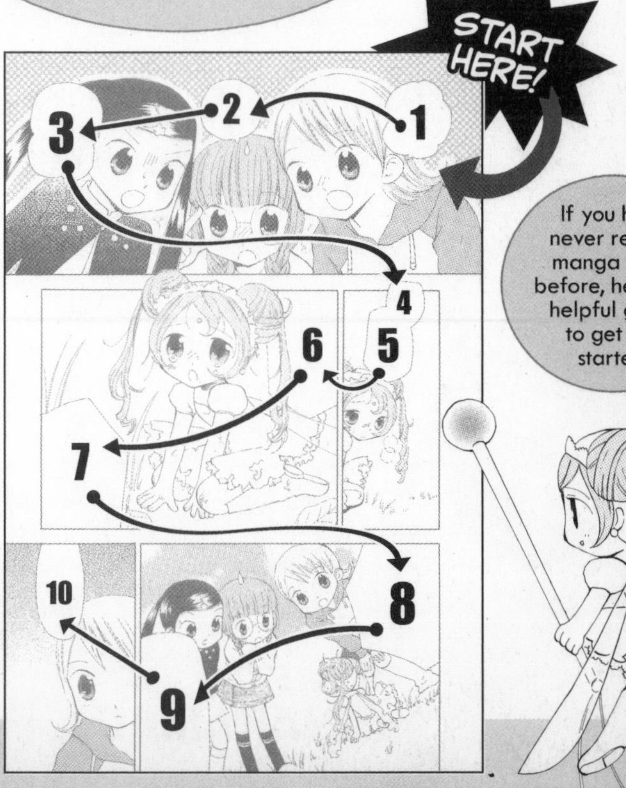
START HERE!
1
2
3
4
5
6
7
8
9
10

If you have never read a manga book before, here is a helpful guide to get you started!

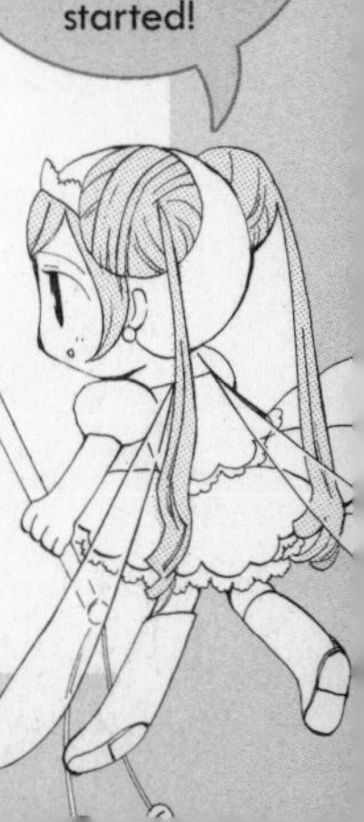

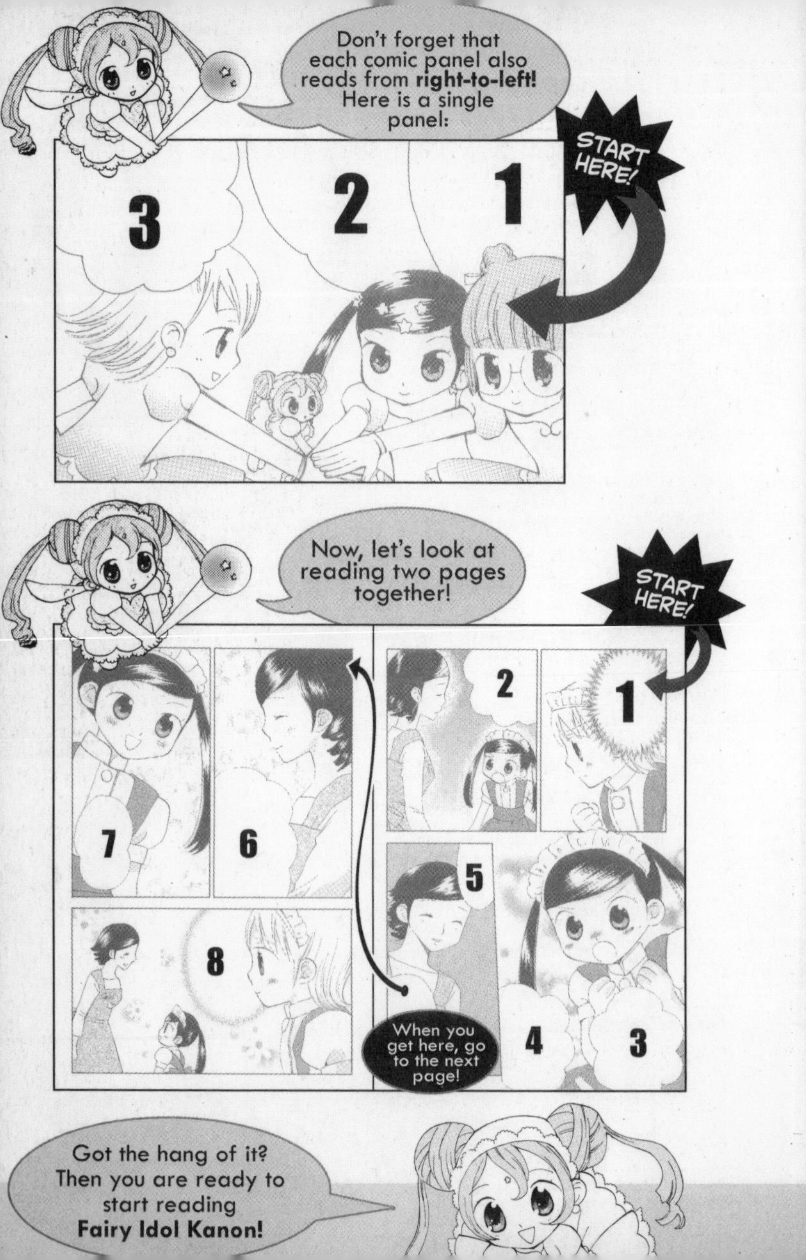
Don't forget that each comic panel also reads from **right-to-left!** Here is a single panel:
START HERE!
1
2
3
Now, let's look at reading two pages together!
START HERE!
1
2
3
4
5
6
7
8
When you get here, go to the next page!
Got the hang of it? Then you are ready to start reading **Fairy Idol Kanon!**

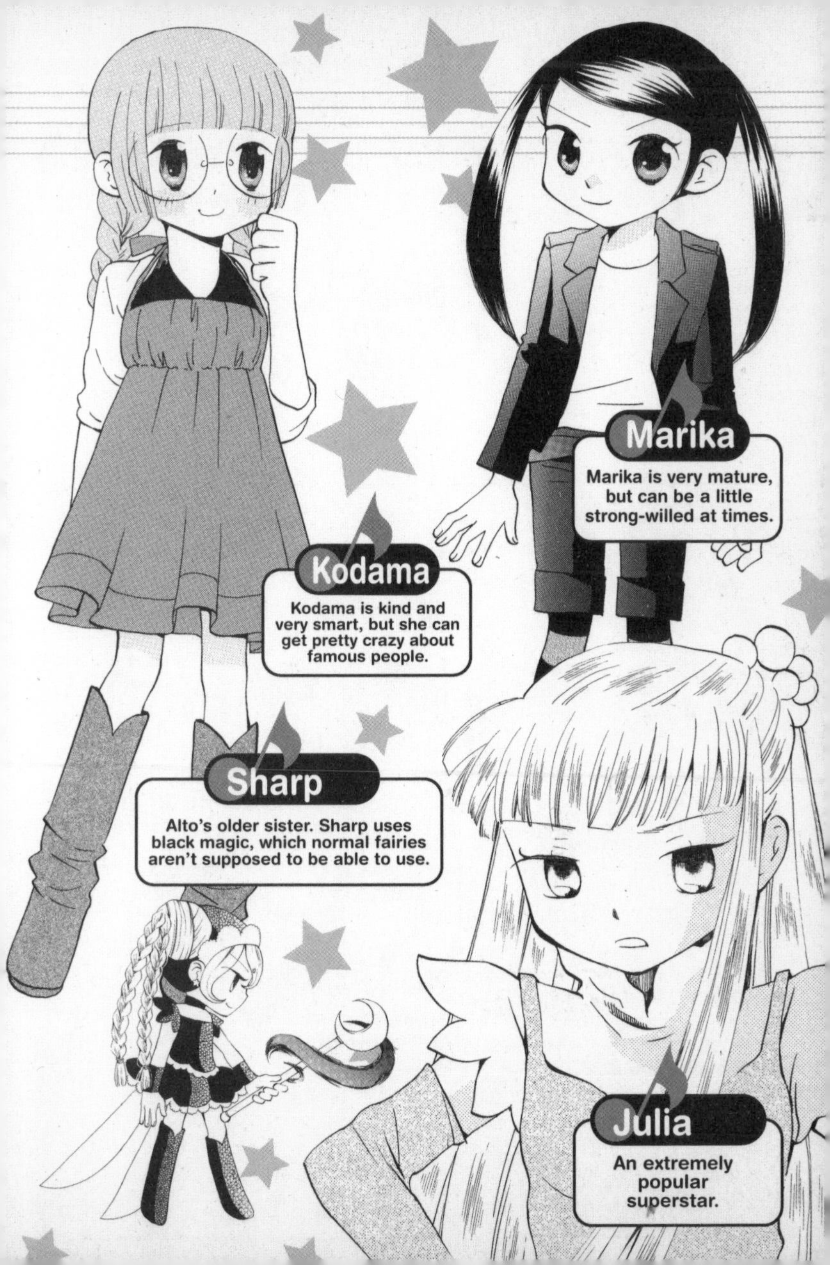
Marika
Marika is very mature, but can be a little strong-willed at times.
Kodama
Kodama is kind and very smart, but she can get pretty crazy about famous people.
Sharp
Alto's older sister. Sharp uses black magic, which normal fairies aren't supposed to be able to use.
Julia
An extremely popular superstar.

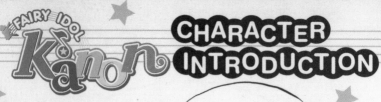

Fairy Idol Kanon
Character Introduction

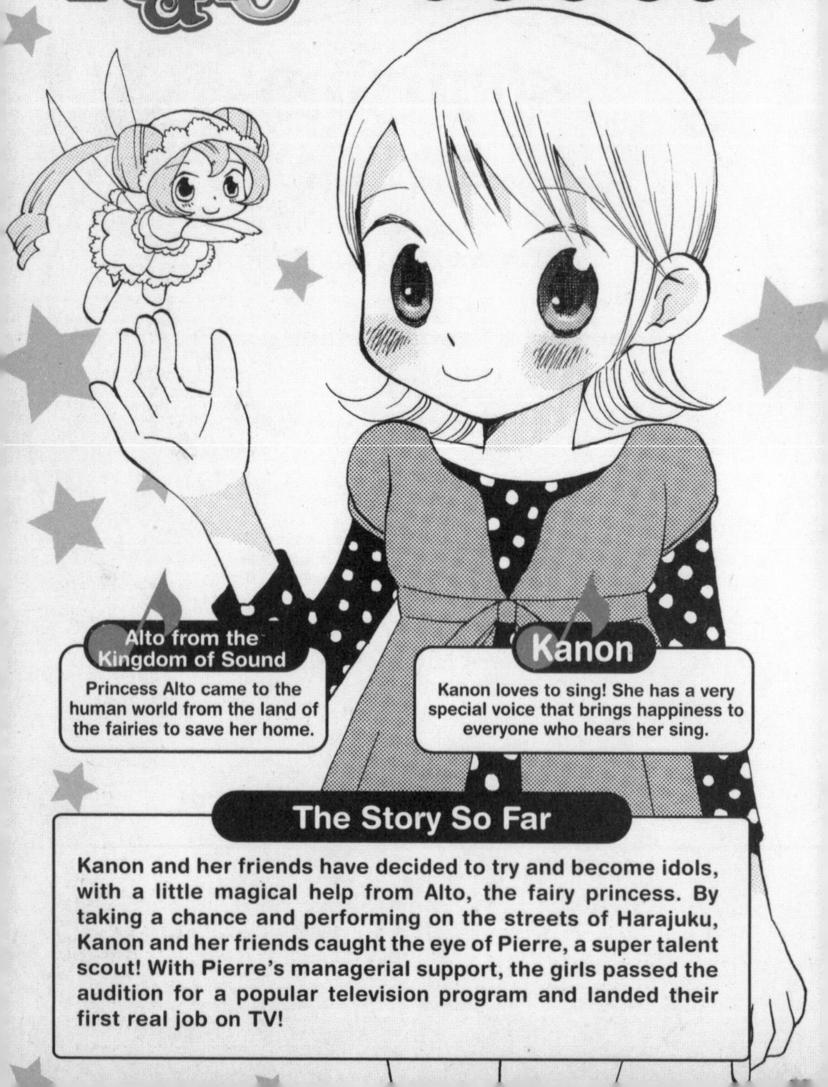

Alto from the Kingdom of Sound

Princess Alto came to the human world from the land of the fairies to save her home.

Kanon

Kanon loves to sing! She has a very special voice that brings happiness to everyone who hears her sing.

The Story So Far

Kanon and her friends have decided to try and become idols, with a little magical help from Alto, the fairy princess. By taking a chance and performing on the streets of Harajuku, Kanon and her friends caught the eye of Pierre, a super talent scout! With Pierre's managerial support, the girls passed the audition for a popular television program and landed their first real job on TV!

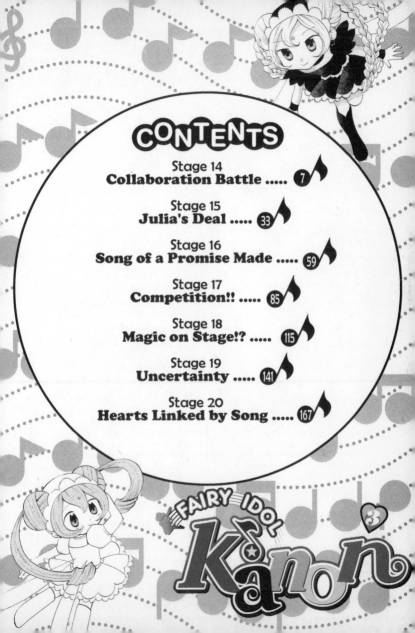

CONTENTS

FAIRY IDOL

Kanon 3

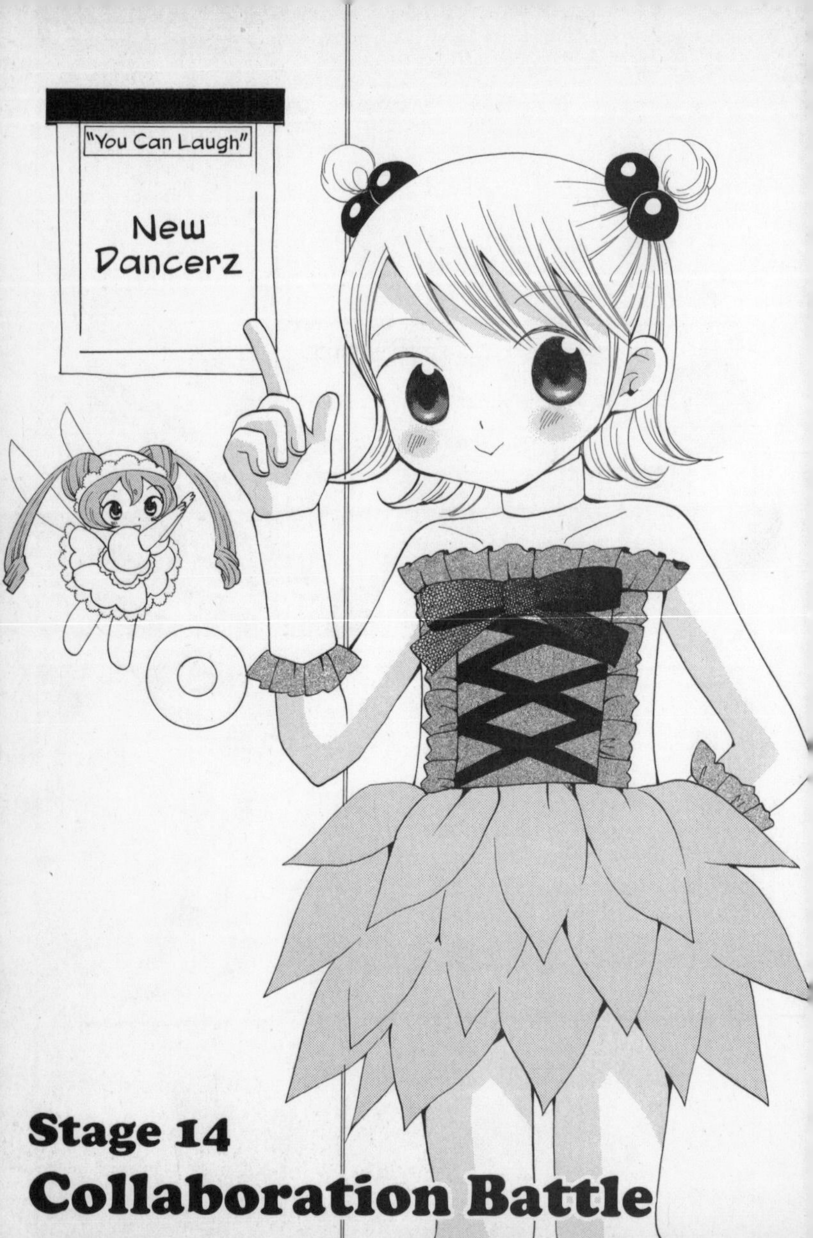

"You Can Laugh"
New Dancerz

Stage 14
Collaboration Battle

Read this way

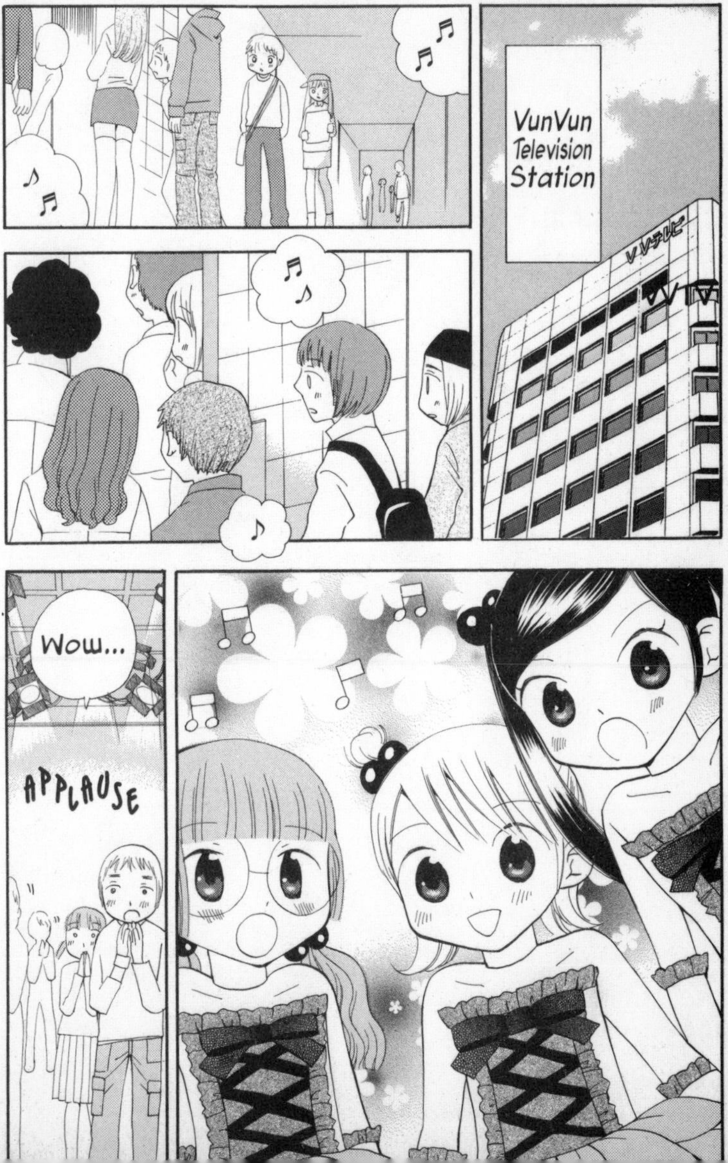
VunVun Television Station
Wow...
APPLAUSE

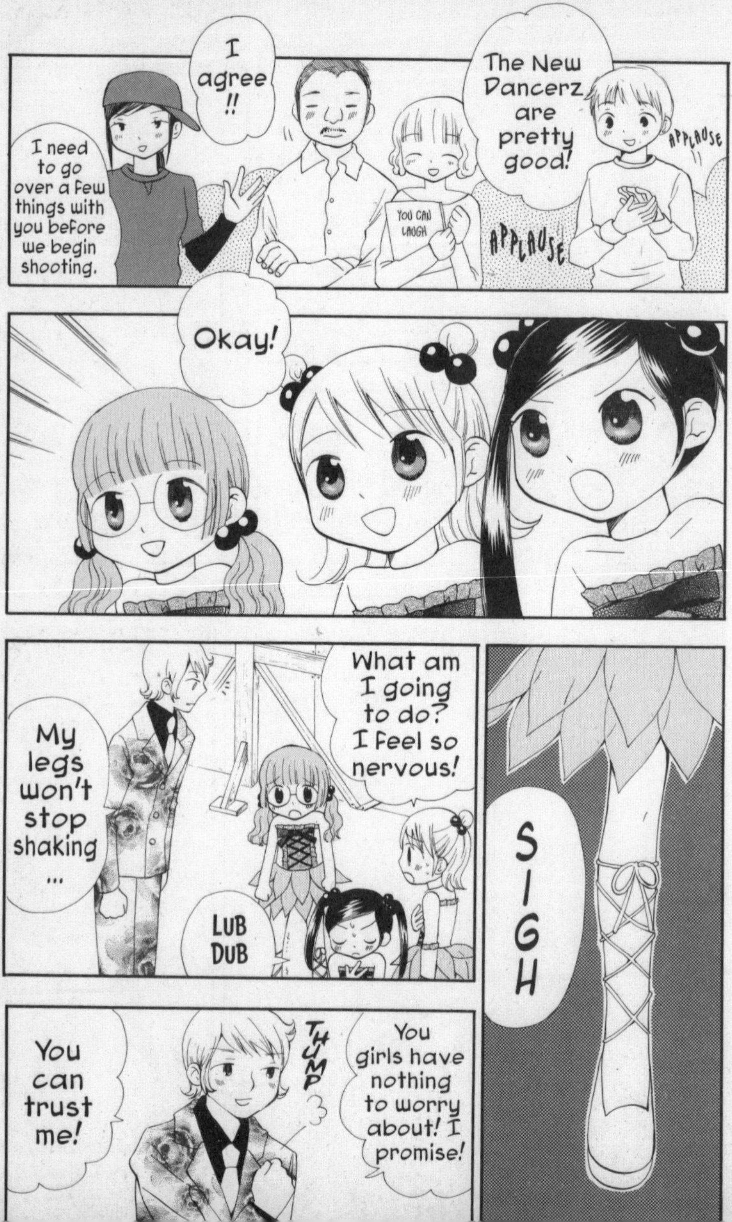
The New Dancerz are pretty good!
APPLAUSE
I agree!!
APPLAUSE
YOU CAN LAUGH
I need to go over a few things with you before we begin shooting.
Okay!
SIGH
What am I going to do? I feel so nervous!
My legs won't stop shaking ...
LUB DUB
You girls have nothing to worry about! I promise!
THUMP
You can trust me!

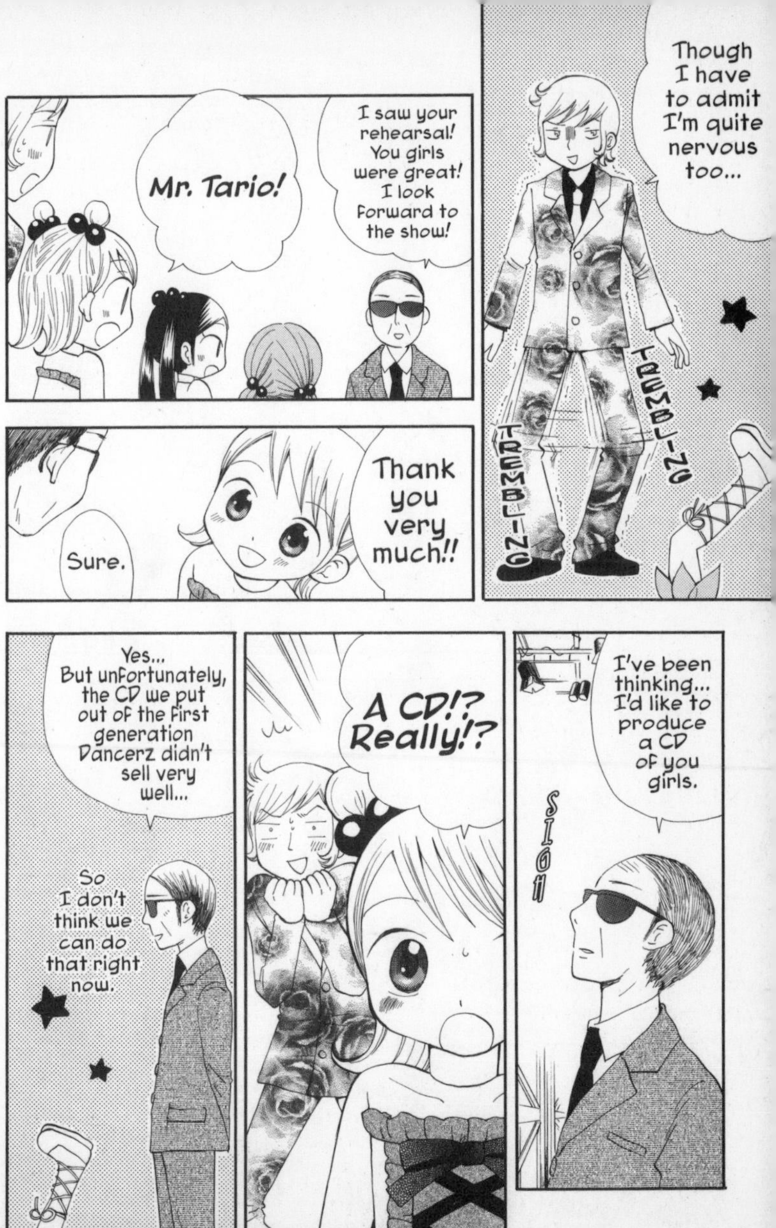
Though I have to admit I'm quite nervous too...
TREMBLING
TREMBLING
I saw your rehearsal! You girls were great! I look forward to the show!
Mr. Tario!
Thank you very much!!
Sure.
I've been thinking... I'd like to produce a CD of you girls.
SIGH
A CD!? Really!?
Yes... But unfortunately, the CD we put out of the first generation Dancerz didn't sell very well...
So I don't think we can do that right now.

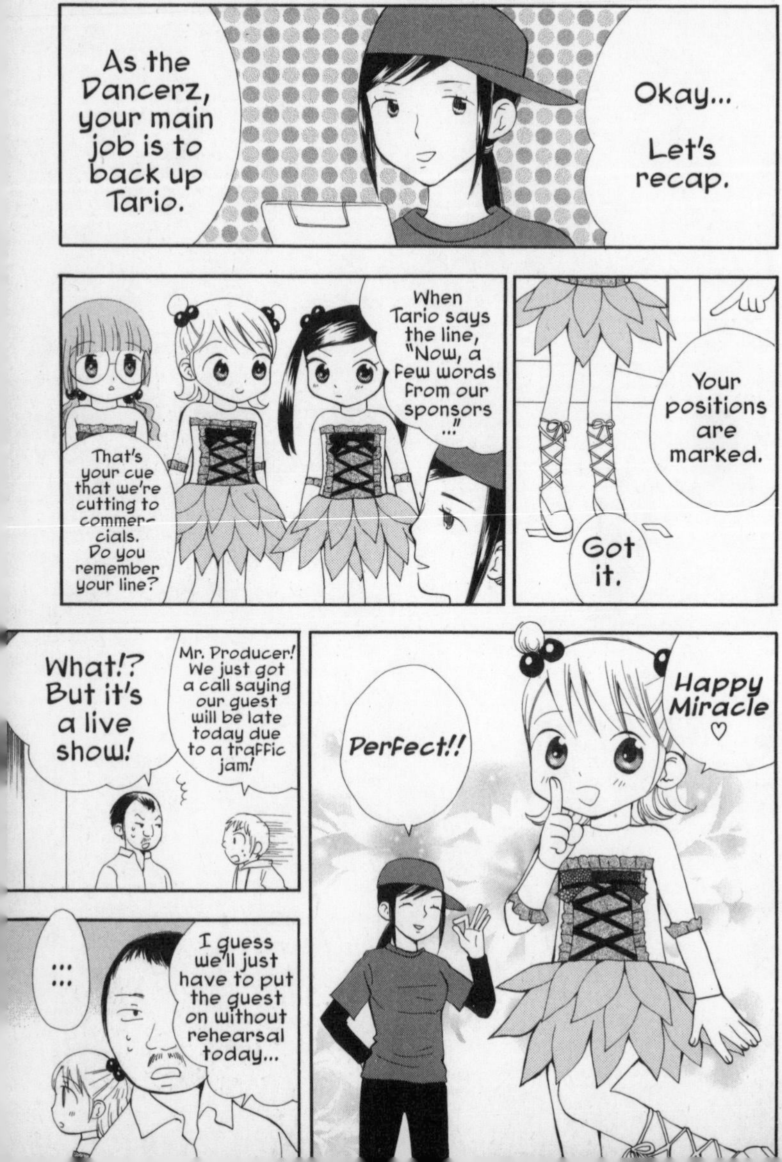
Okay... Let's recap.
As the Dancerz, your main job is to back up Tario.
Your positions are marked.
Got it.
When Tario says the line, "Now, a few words from our sponsors..."
That's your cue that we're cutting to commercials. Do you remember your line?
Happy Miracle ♡
Perfect!!
Mr. Producer! We just got a call saying our guest will be late today due to a traffic jam!
What!? But it's a live show!
I guess we'll just have to put the guest on without rehearsal today...
......

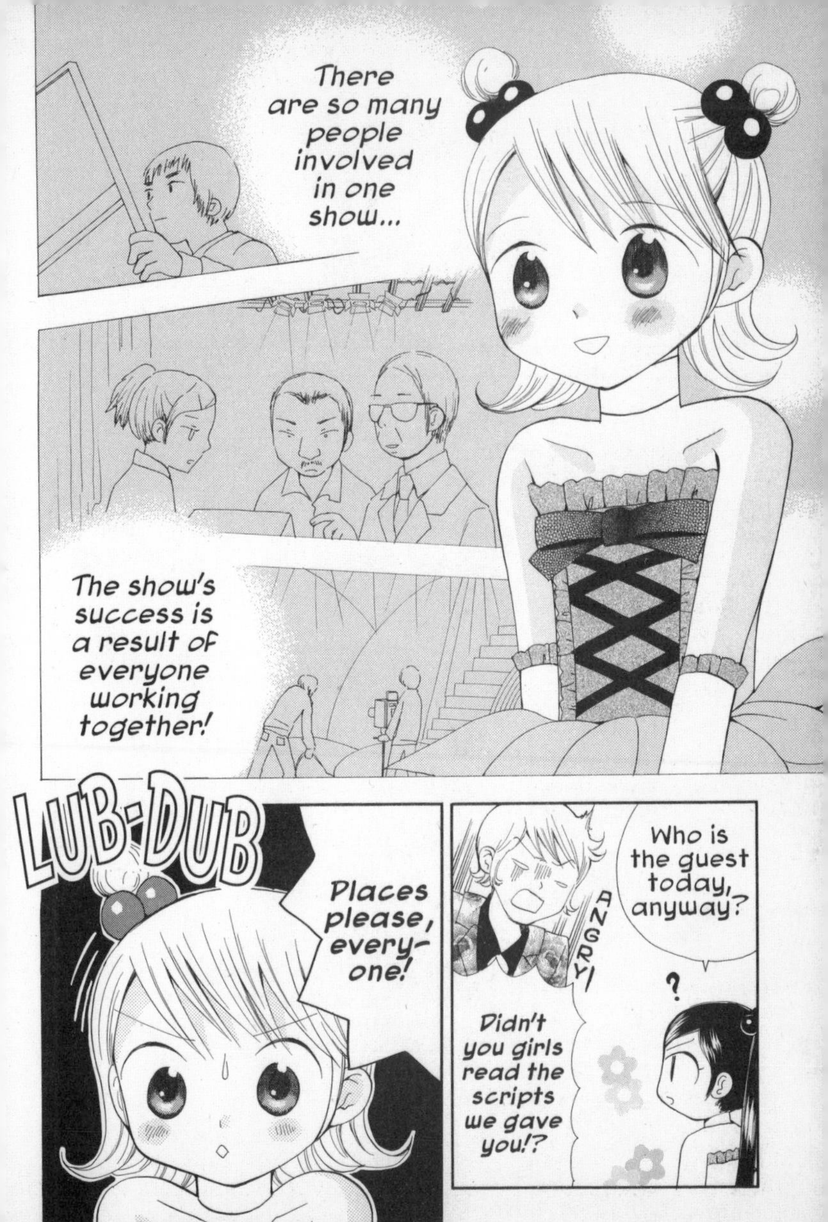
There are so many people involved in one show...
The show's success is a result of everyone working together!
Who is the guest today, anyway?
ANGRY!
?
Didn't you girls read the scripts we gave you!?
LUB-DUB
Places please, every-one!

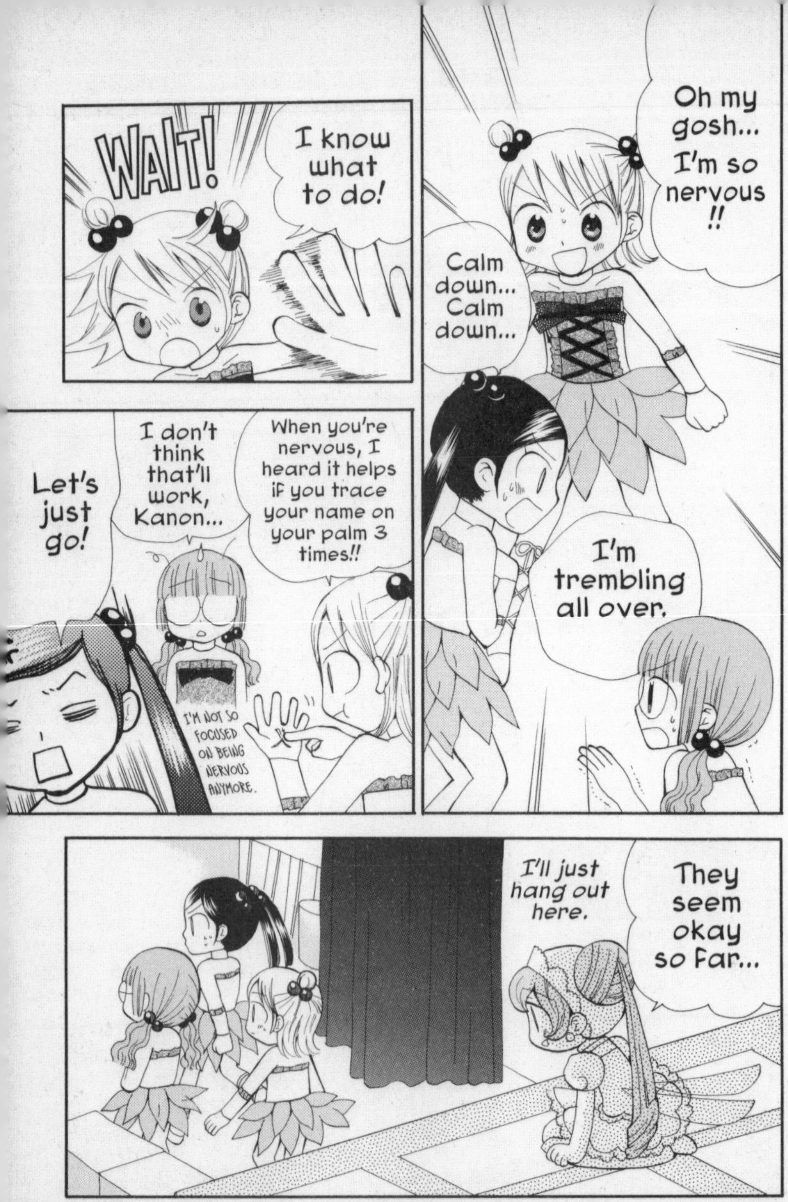
Oh my gosh... I'm so nervous !!
Calm down... Calm down...
I'm trembling all over.
I know what to do!
WAIT!
When you're nervous, I heard it helps if you trace your name on your palm 3 times!!
I don't think that'll work, Kanon...
Let's just go!
I'M NOT SO FOCUSED ON BEING NERVOUS ANYMORE.
They seem okay so far...
I'll just hang out here.

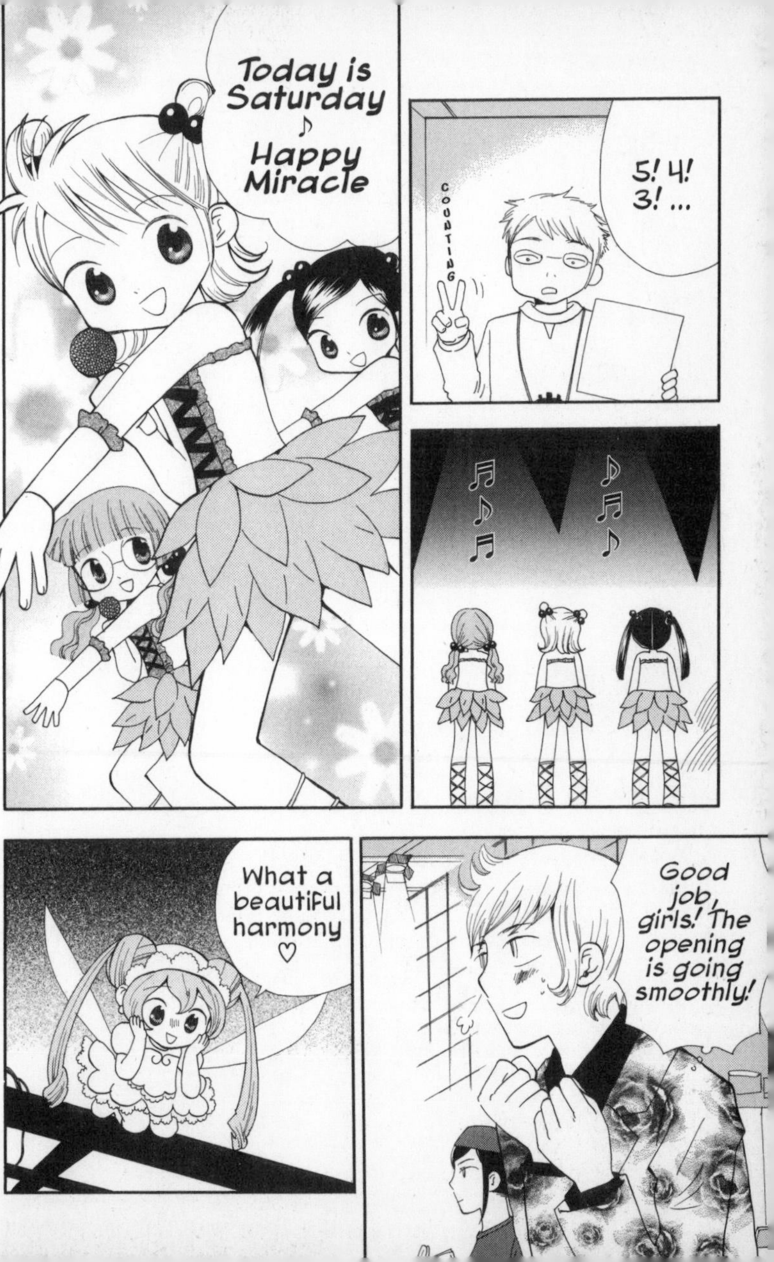
5! 4! 3! ...
COUNTING
Today is Saturday ♪ Happy Miracle
Good job, girls! The opening is going smoothly!
What a beautiful harmony ♡

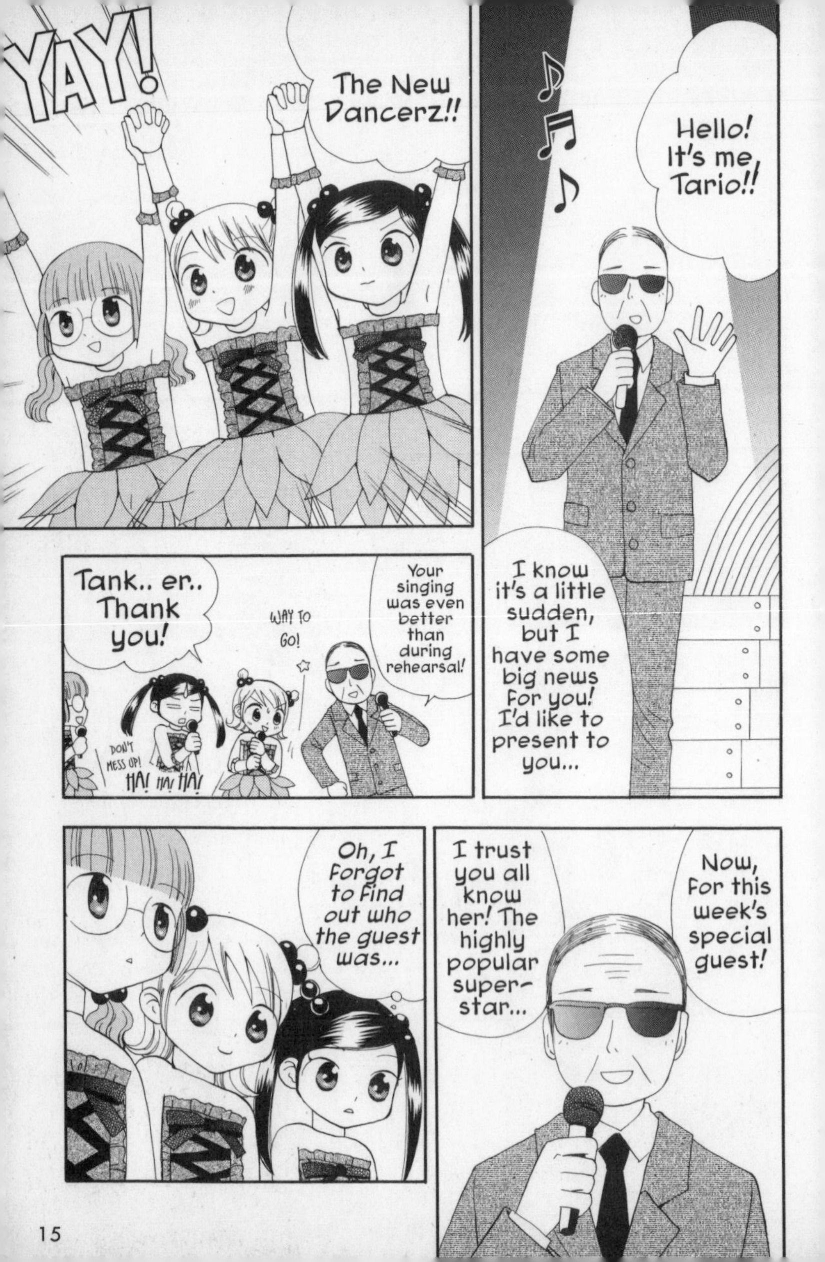
Hello! It's me, Tario!!
I know it's a little sudden, but I have some big news for you! I'd like to present to you...
The New Dancerz!!
YAY!
Your singing was even better than during rehearsal!
WAY TO GO!
Tank.. er.. Thank you!
DON'T MESS UP!
HA! HA! HA!
Now, for this week's special guest!
I trust you all know her! The highly popular super-star...
Oh, I forgot to find out who the guest was...

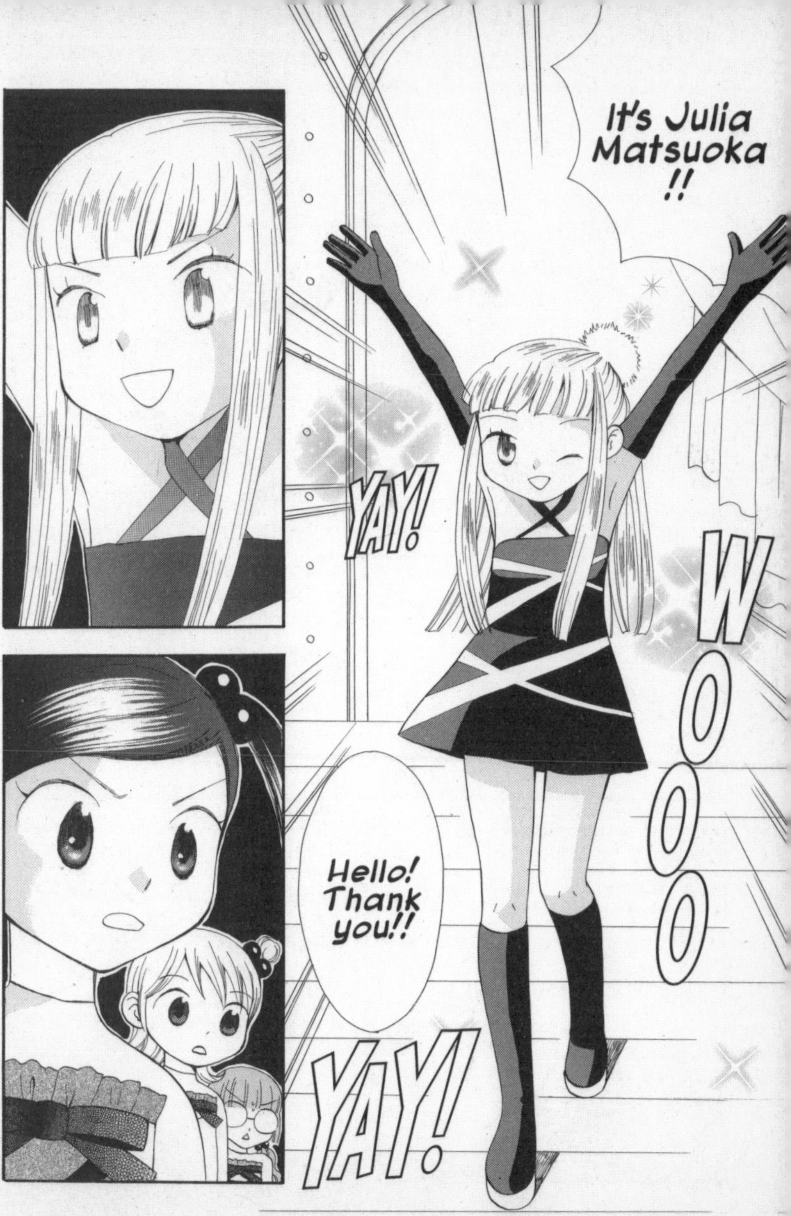
It's Julia Matsuoka !!
WOOOO
YAY!
Hello! Thank you!!
YAY!

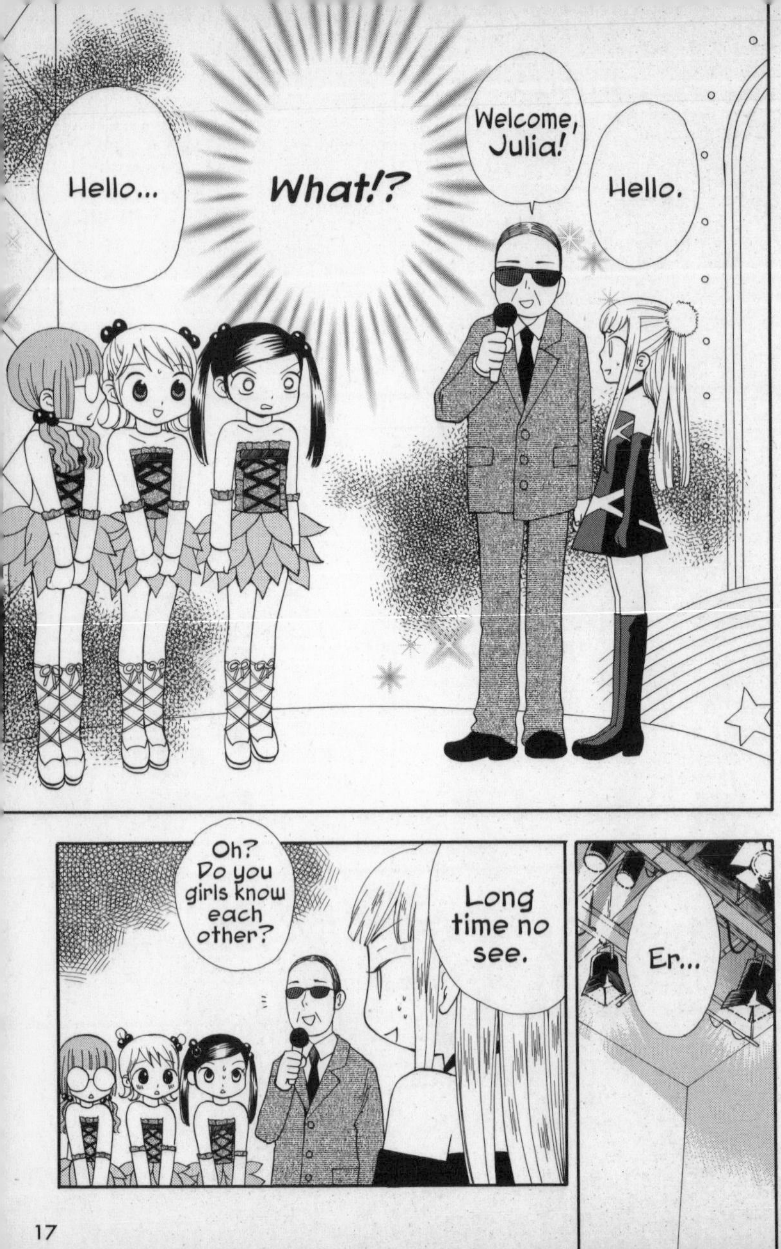
Hello.
Welcome, Julia!
What!?
Hello...
Er...
Long time no see.
Oh? Do you girls know each other?

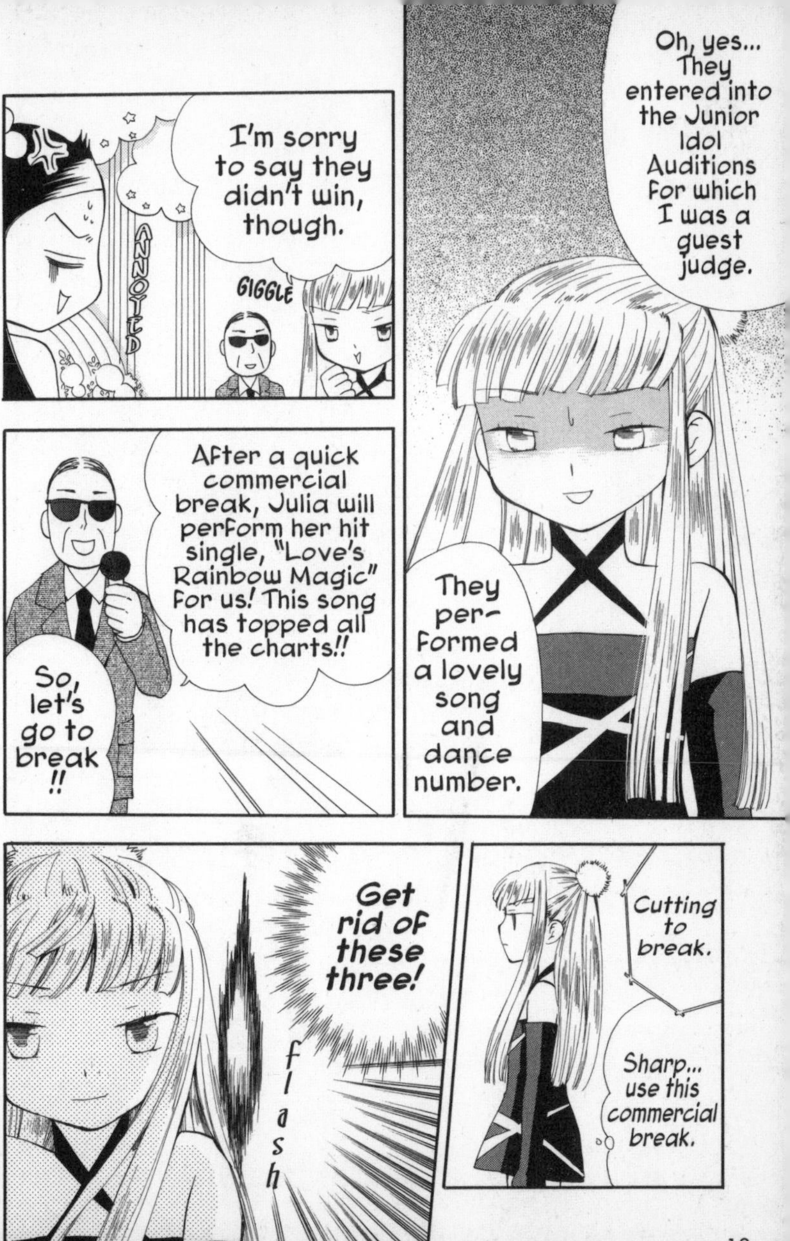
Oh, yes... They entered into the Junior Idol Auditions for which I was a guest judge.
They performed a lovely song and dance number.
I'm sorry to say they didn't win, though.
GIGGLE
ANNOYED
After a quick commercial break, Julia will perform her hit single, "Love's Rainbow Magic" for us! This song has topped all the charts!!
So, let's go to break!!
Cutting to break.
Sharp... use this commercial break.
Get rid of these three!
flash

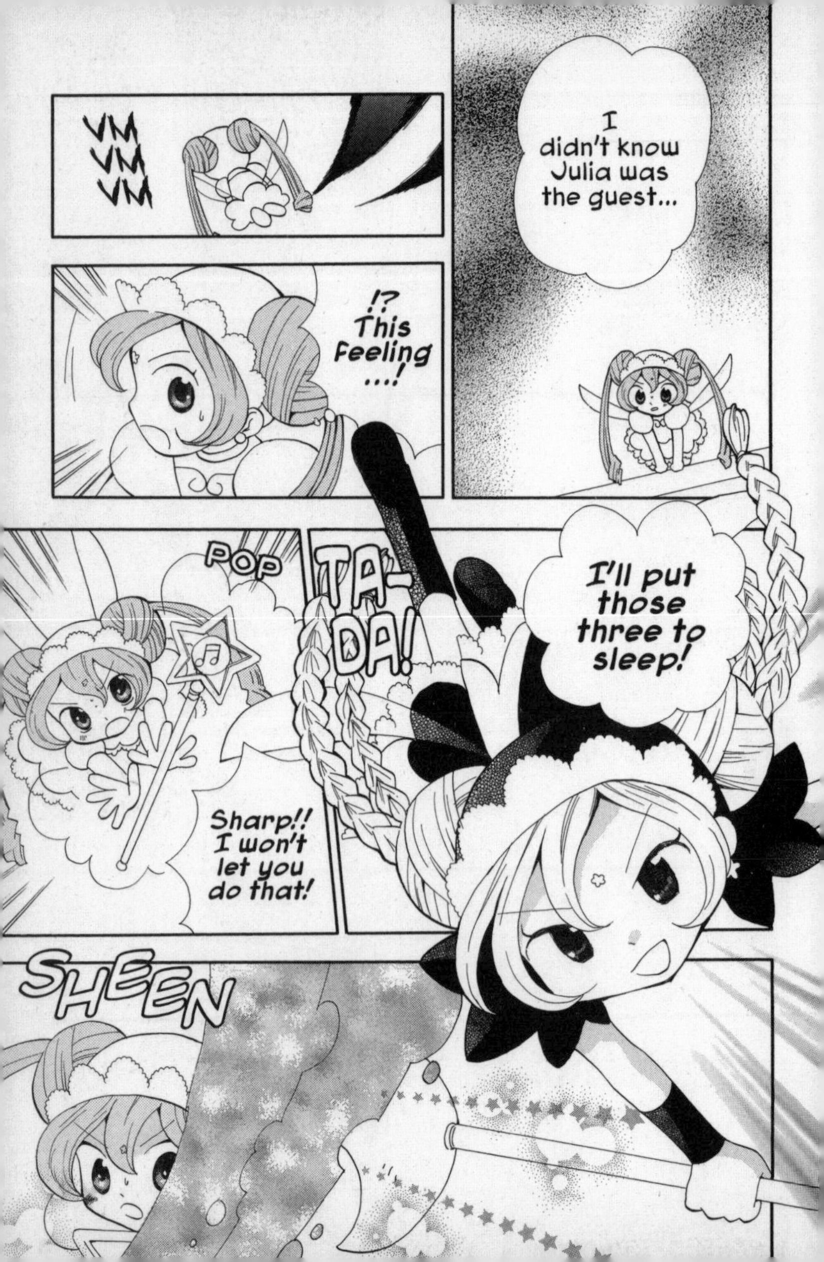

I didn't know Julia was the guest...
VM VM VM
!? This feeling ...!
TA-DA!
I'll put those three to sleep!
POP
Sharp!! I won't let you do that!
SHEEN

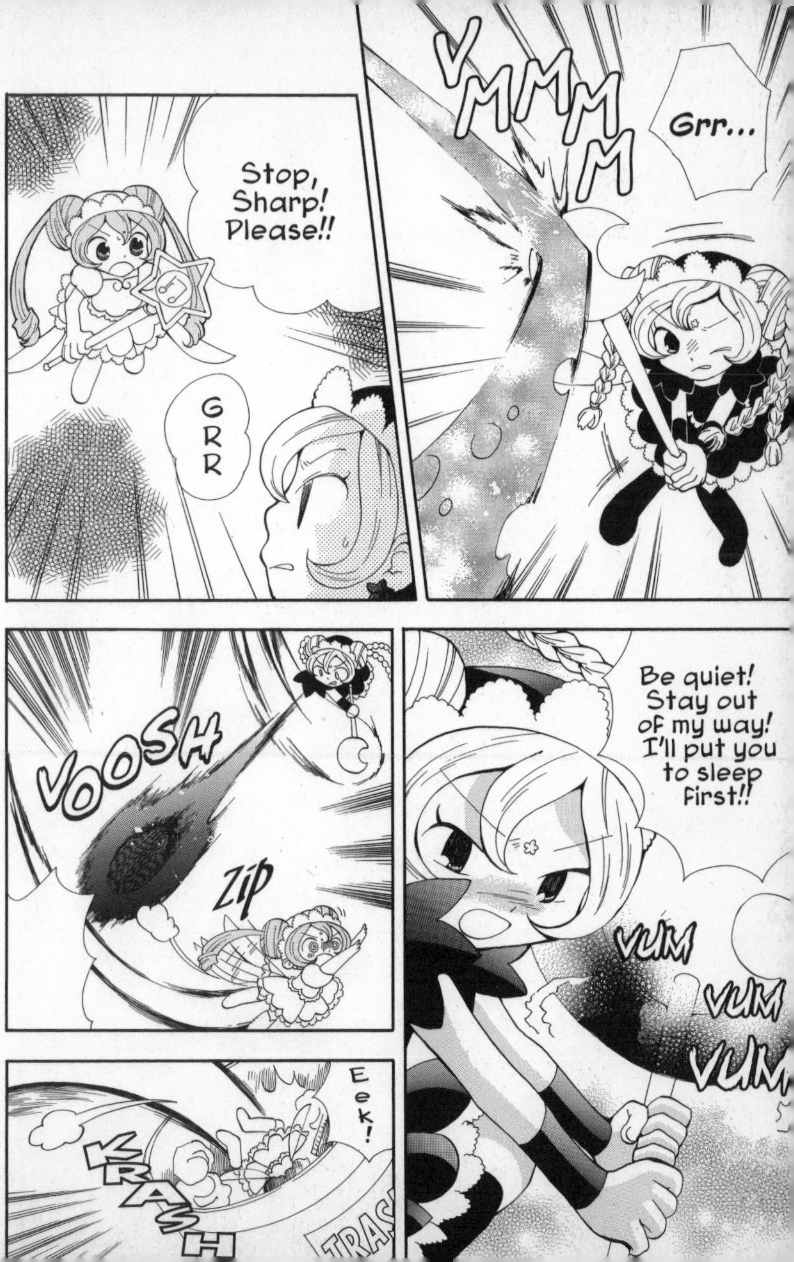

Grr...
VMMMM
Stop, Sharp! Please!!
GRR
Be quiet! Stay out of my way! I'll put you to sleep first!!
VUM
VUM
VUM
VOOSH
Zip
Eek!
KRASH

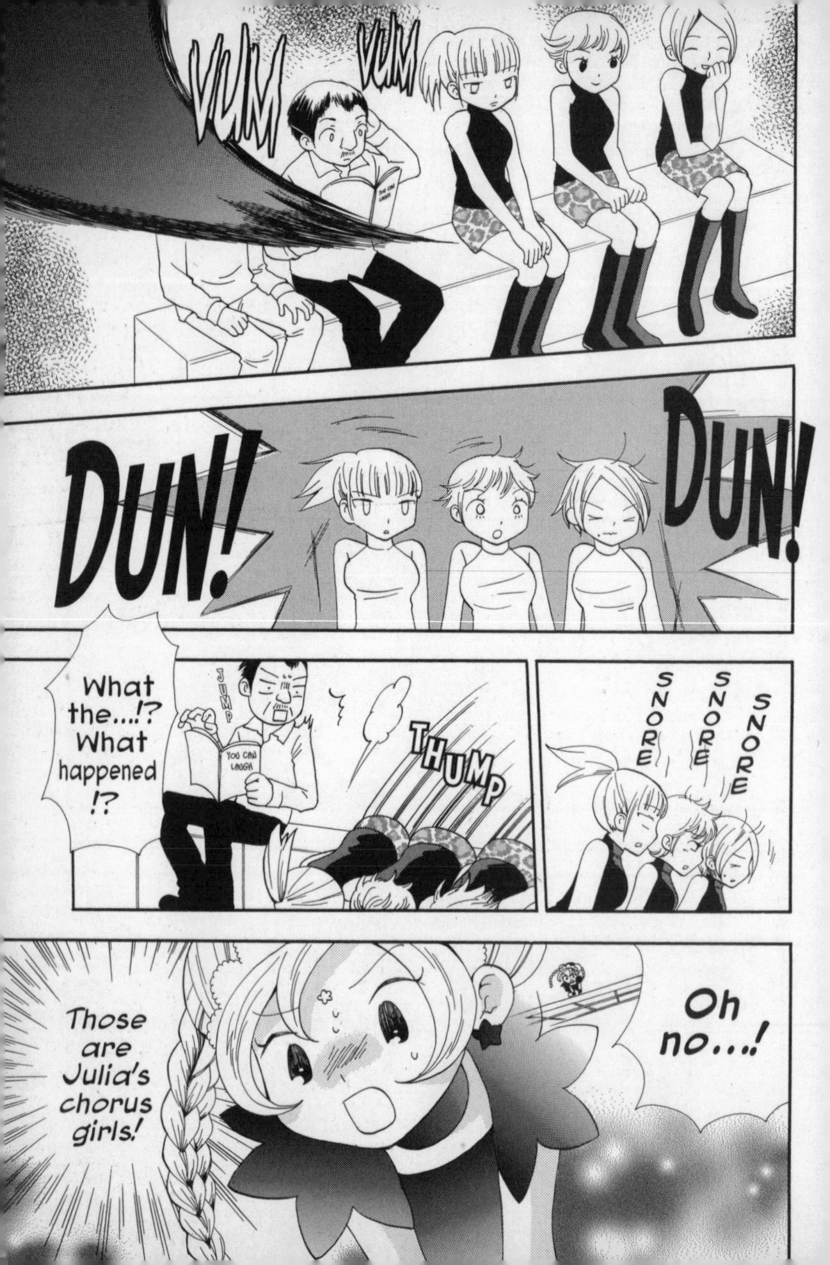

VUM
VUM
DUN!
DUN!
SNORE
SNORE
SNORE
THUMP
JUMP
What the...!? What happened!?
YOU CAN LAUGH
Oh no...!
Those are Julia's chorus girls!

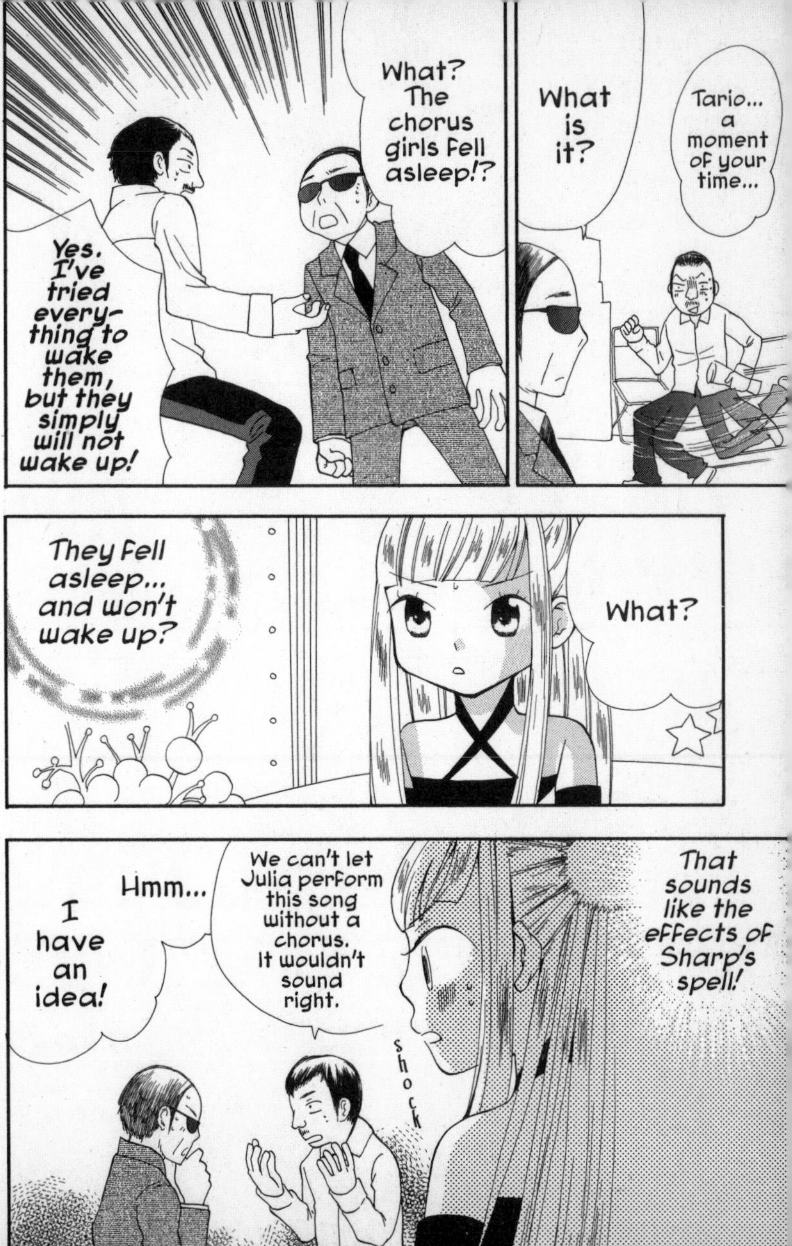
Tario... a moment of your time...
What is it?
What? The chorus girls fell asleep!?
Yes. I've tried everything to wake them, but they simply will not wake up!
What?
They fell asleep... and won't wake up?
That sounds like the effects of Sharp's spell!
shock
We can't let Julia perform this song without a chorus. It wouldn't sound right.
Hmm...
I have an idea!

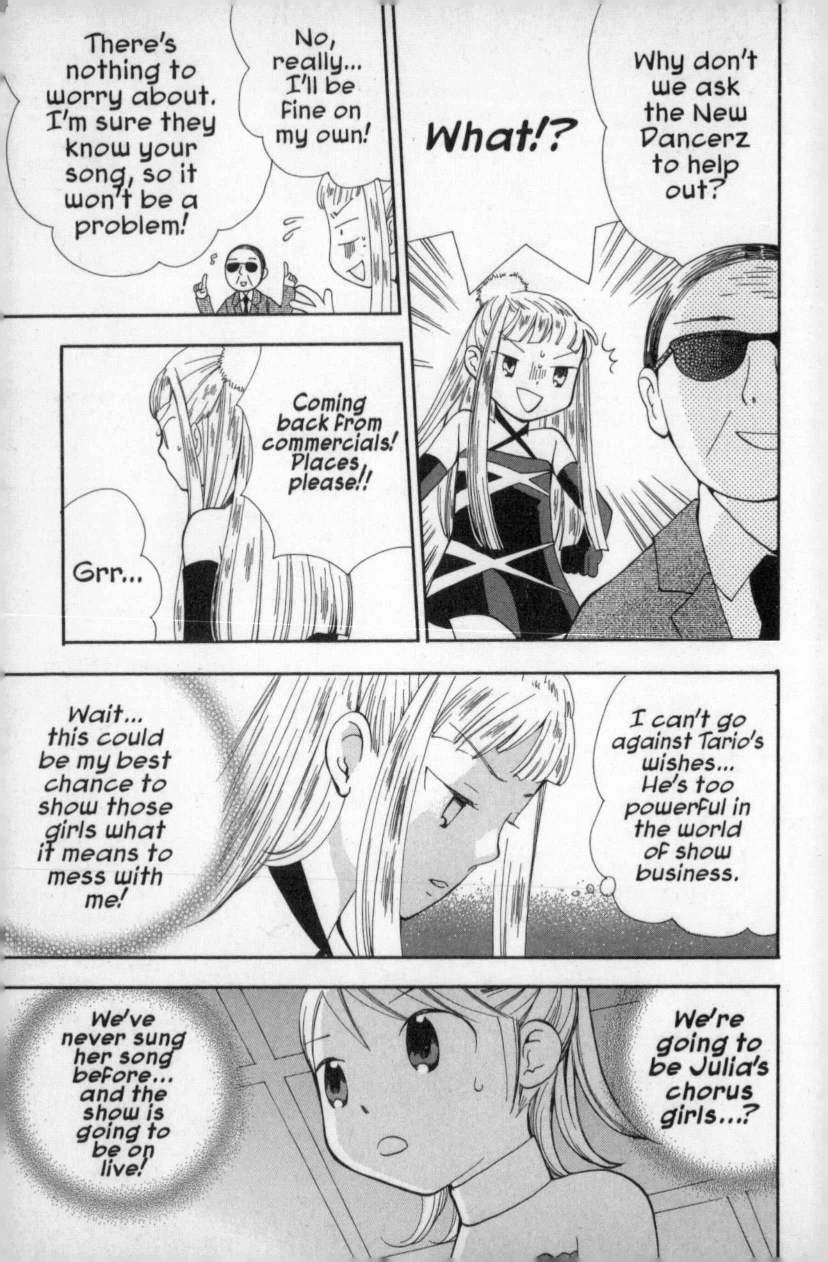
Why don't we ask the New Dancerz to help out?
What!?
No, really... I'll be fine on my own!
There's nothing to worry about. I'm sure they know your song, so it won't be a problem!
Coming back from commercials! Places please!!
Grr...
I can't go against Tario's wishes... He's too powerful in the world of show business.
Wait... this could be my best chance to show those girls what it means to mess with me!
We're going to be Julia's chorus girls...?
We've never sung her song before... and the show is going to be on live!

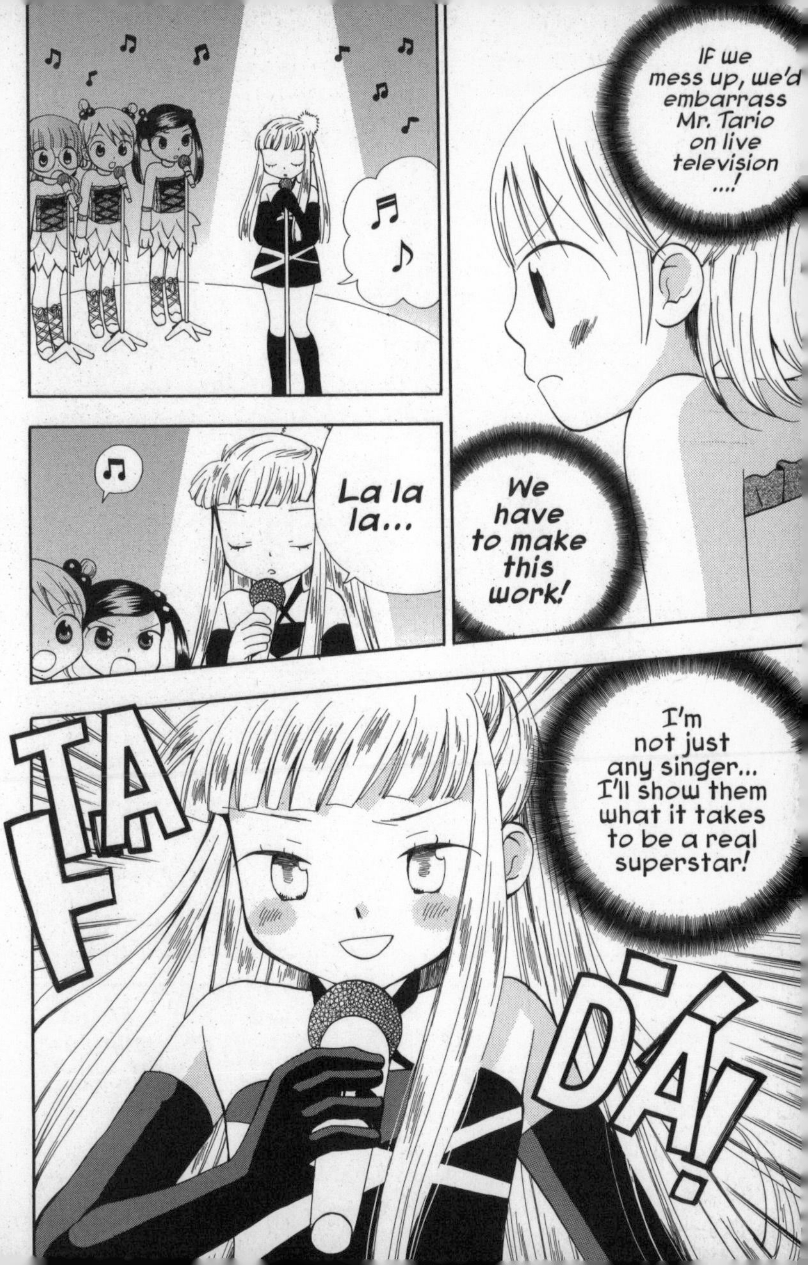
If we mess up, we'd embarrass Mr. Tario on live television ...!
We have to make this work!
La la la...
I'm not just any singer... I'll show them what it takes to be a real superstar!
TA
DA!

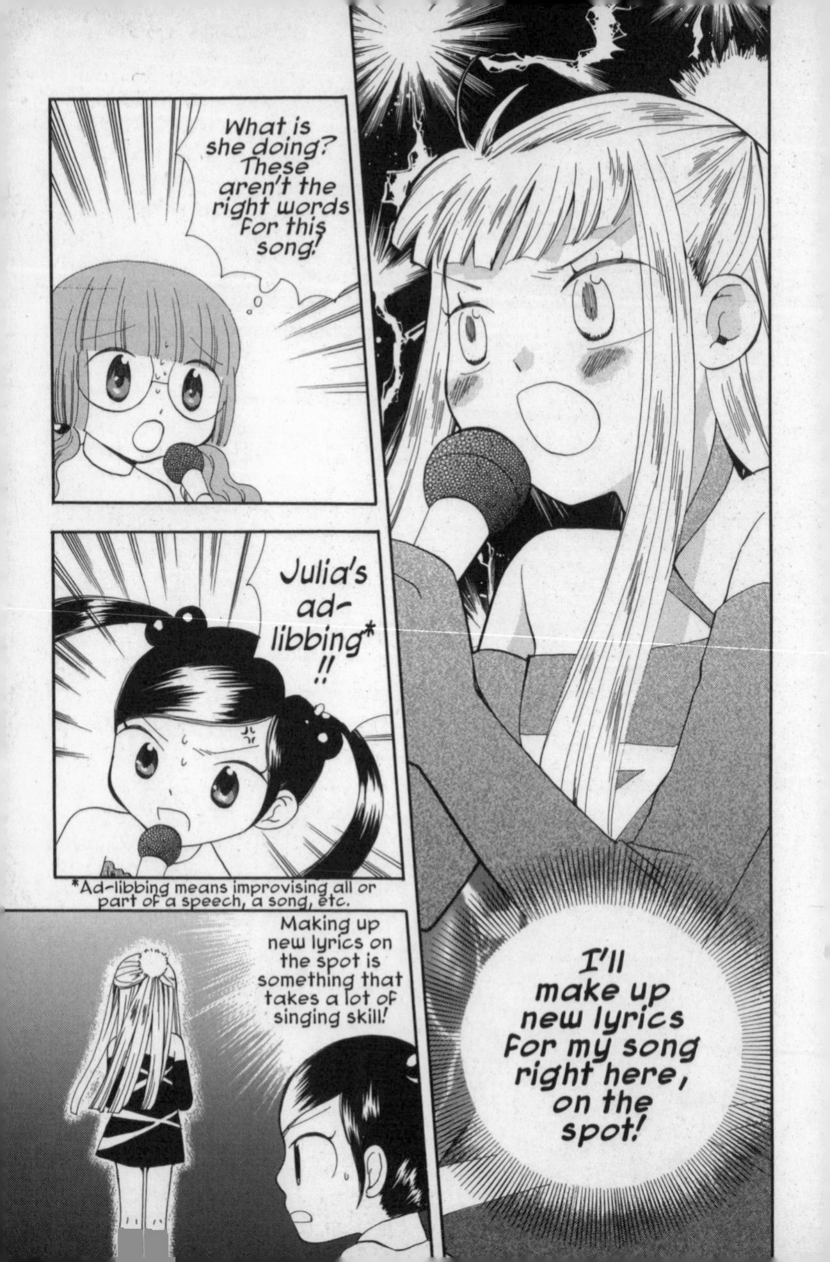
I'll make up new lyrics for my song right here, on the spot!
What is she doing? These aren't the right words for this song!
Julia's ad-libbing* !!
*Ad-libbing means improvising all or part of a speech, a song, etc.
Making up new lyrics on the spot is something that takes a lot of singing skill!

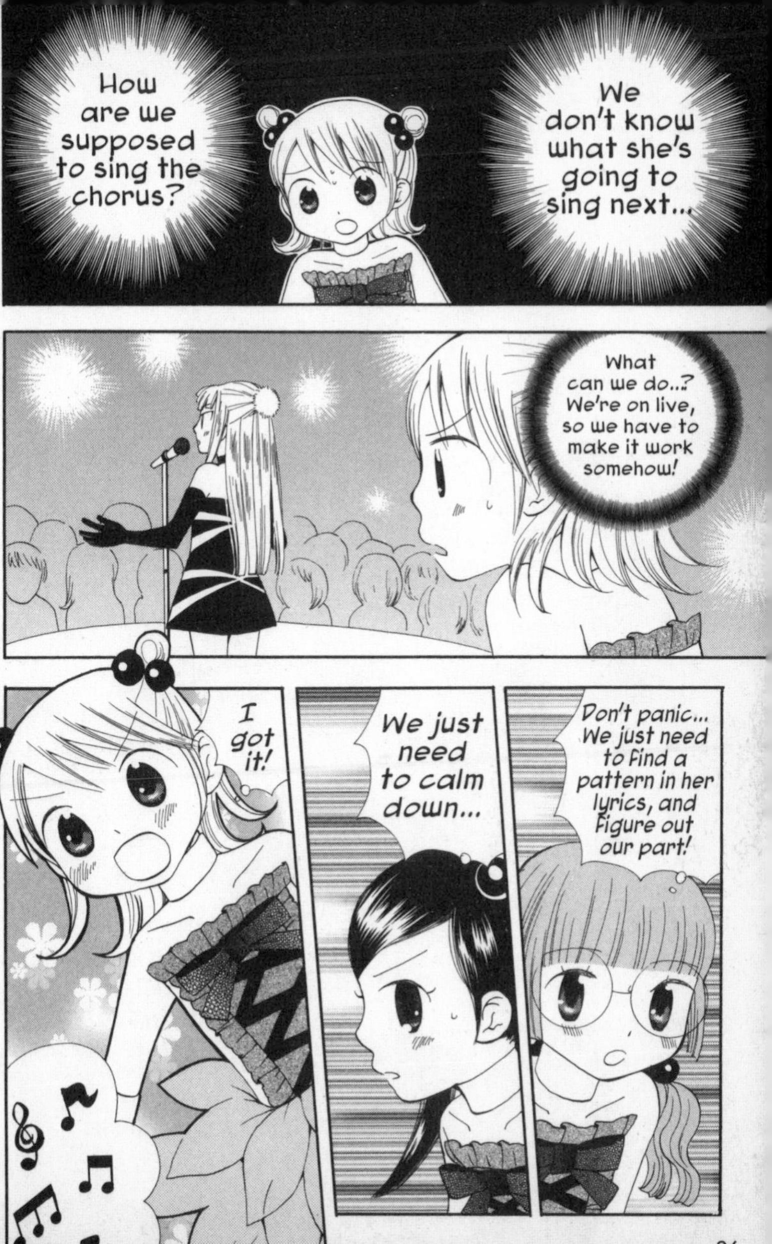
We don't know what she's going to sing next...
How are we supposed to sing the chorus?
What can we do...? We're on live, so we have to make it work somehow!
Don't panic... We just need to find a pattern in her lyrics, and figure out our part!
We just need to calm down...
I got it!

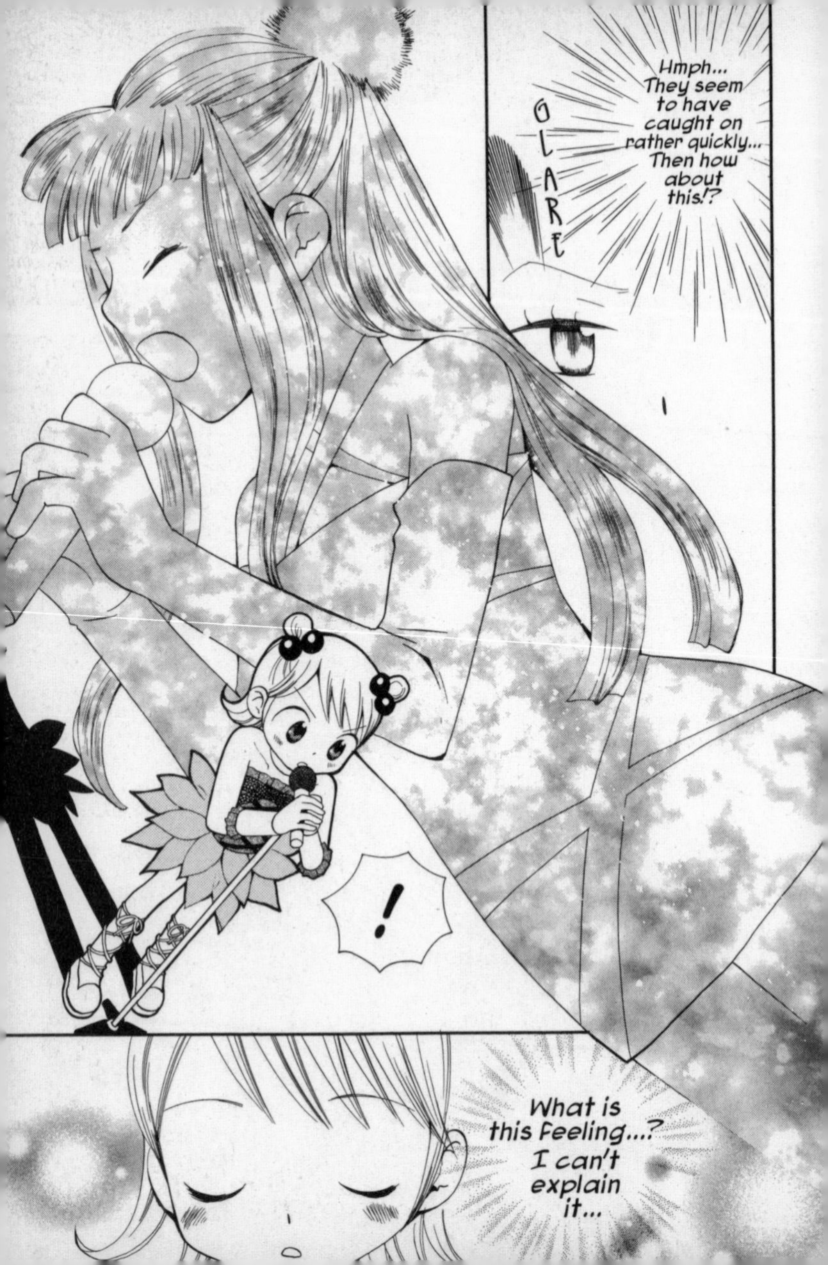
Hmph... They seem to have caught on rather quickly... Then how about this!?
GLARE
!
!
What is this feeling...? I can't explain it...

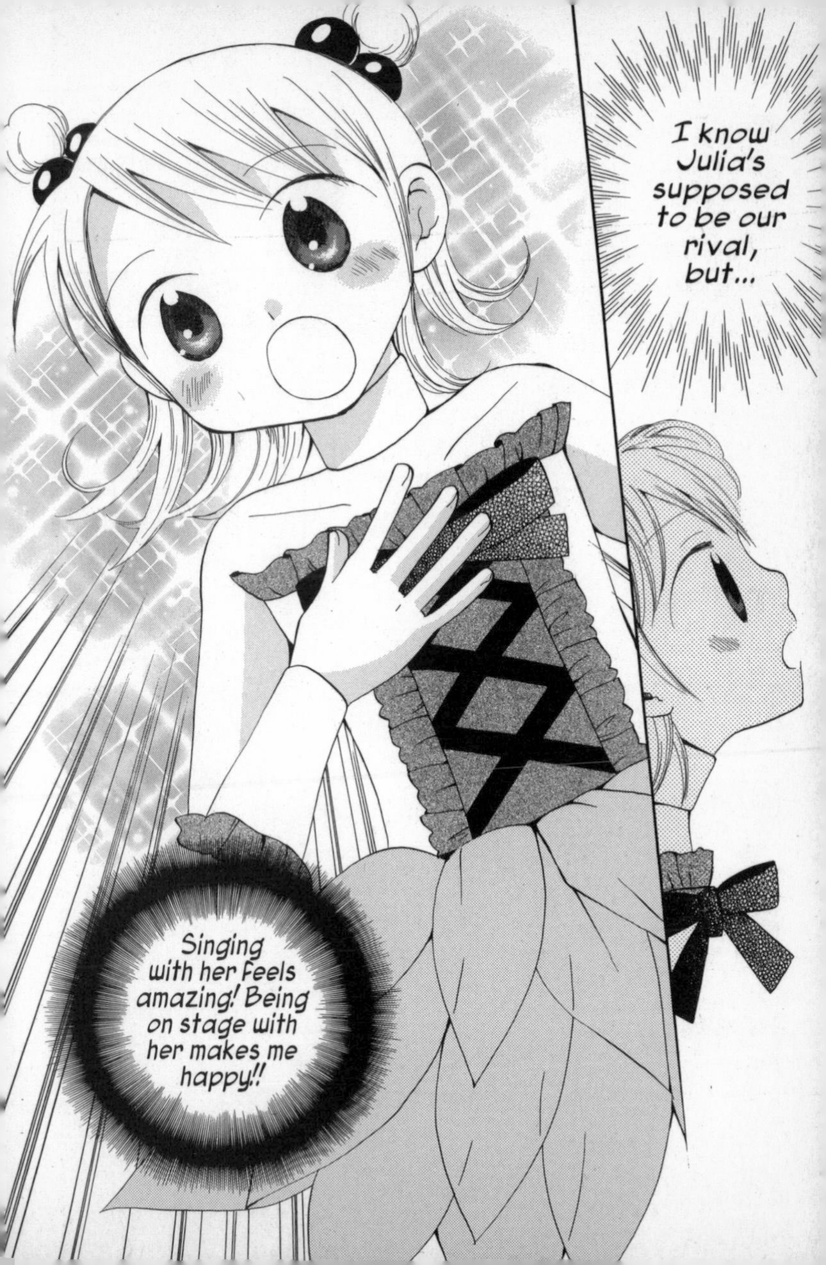
I know Julia's supposed to be our rival, but...
Singing with her feels amazing! Being on stage with her makes me happy!!

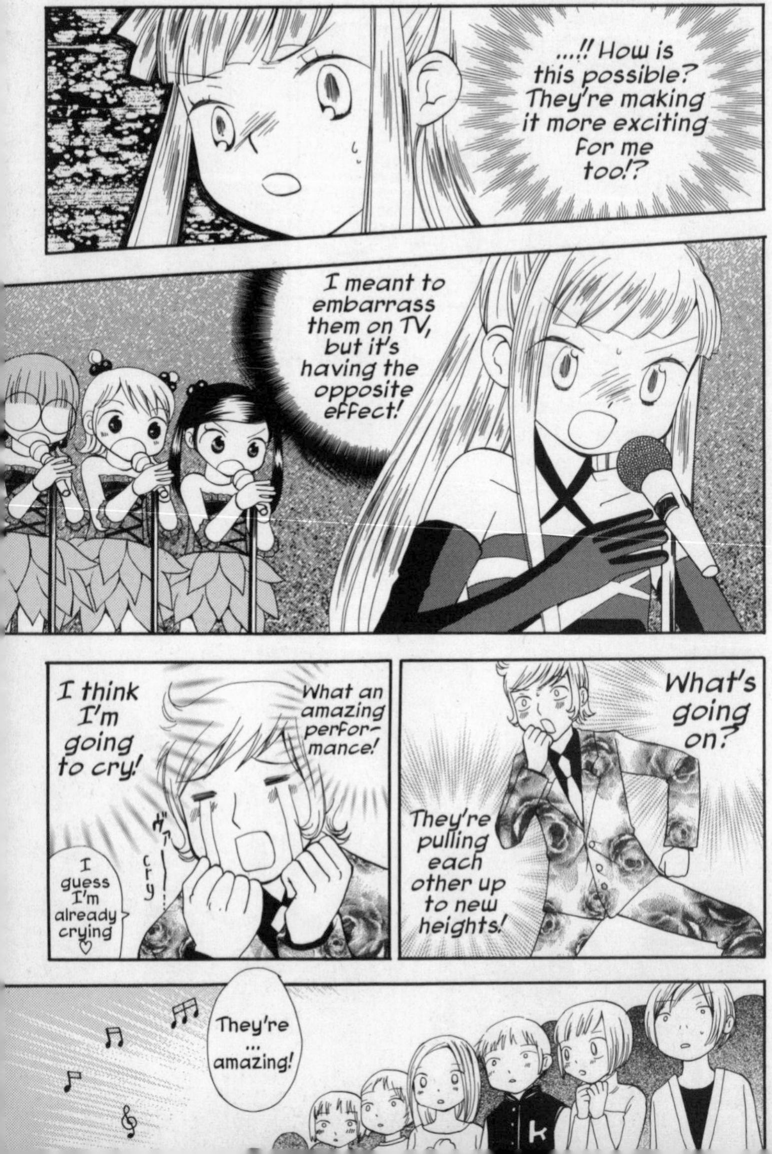

...!! How is this possible? They're making it more exciting for me too!?
I meant to embarrass them on TV, but it's having the opposite effect!
What's going on?
They're pulling each other up to new heights!
What an amazing perfor-mance!
I think I'm going to cry!
cry
I guess I'm already crying ♡
They're ... amazing!

Read this way

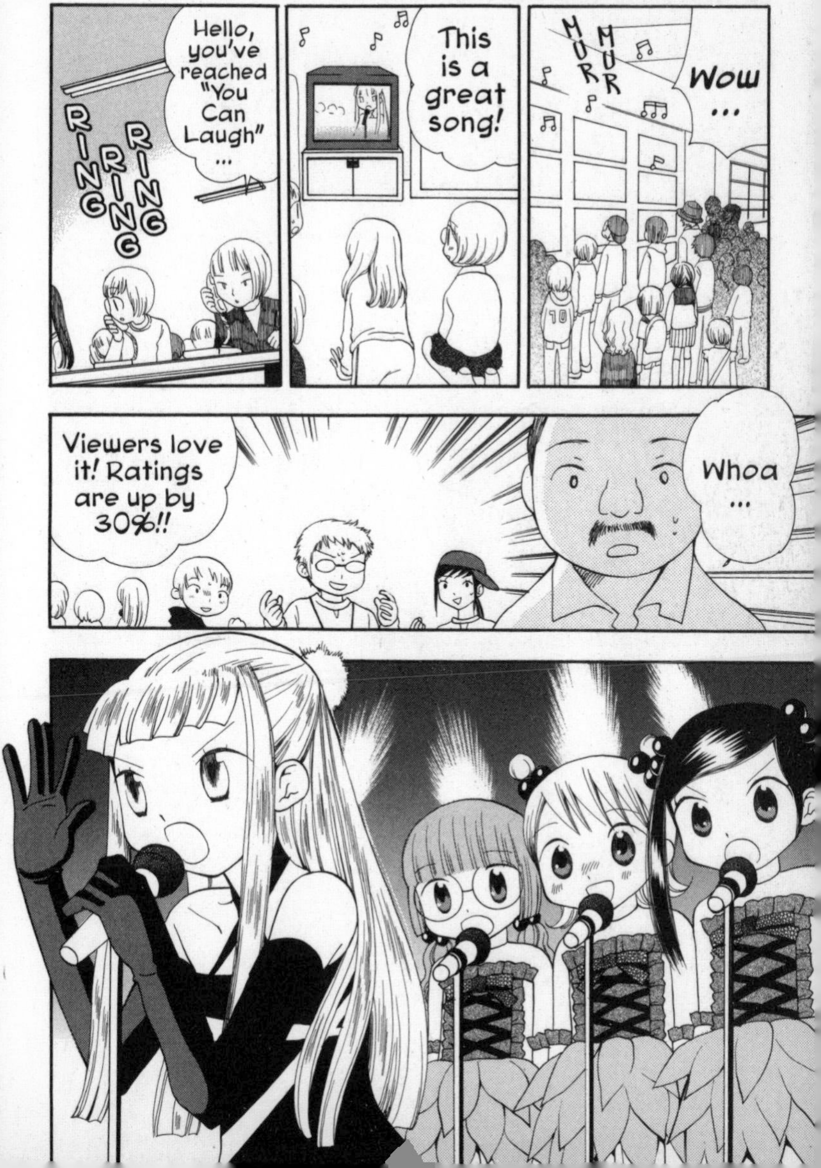
MUR MUR
Wow ...
This is a great song!
RING RING RING
Hello, you've reached "You Can Laugh" ...
Whoa ...
Viewers love it! Ratings are up by 30%!!

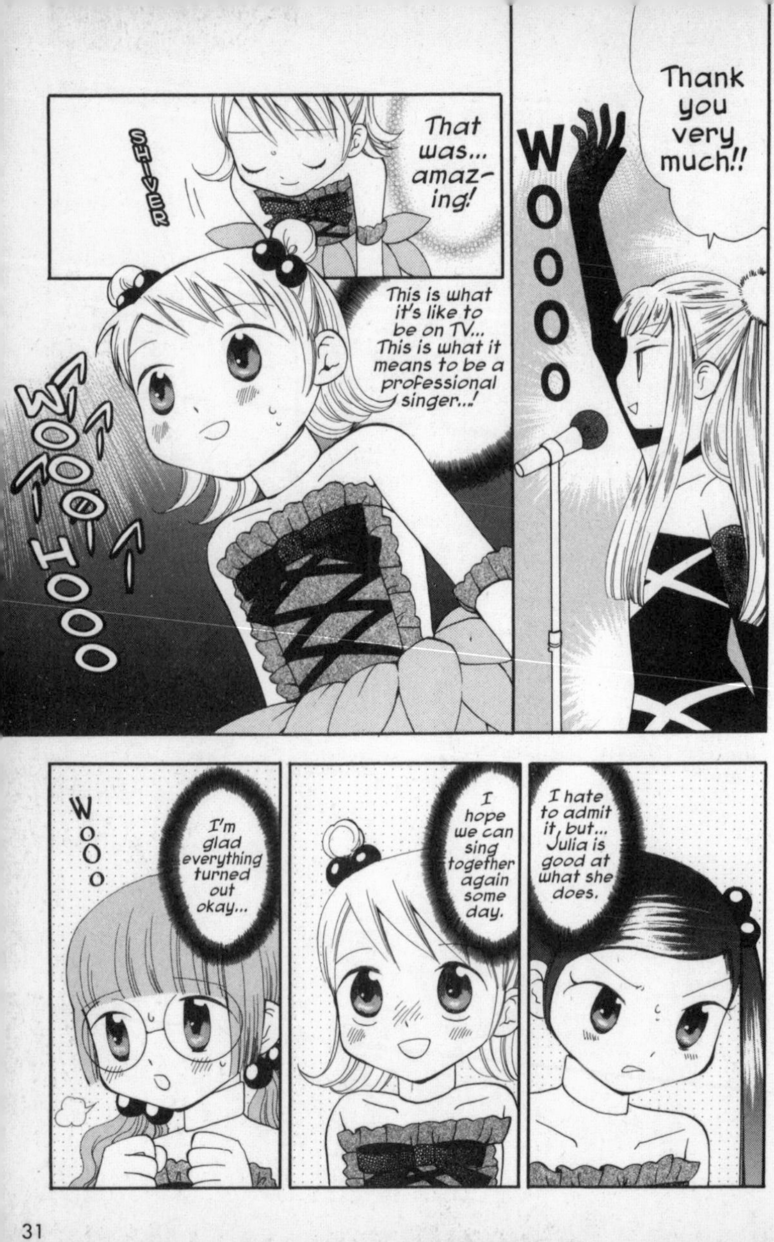
Thank you very much!!
WOOOO
That was... amazing!
SHIVER
This is what it's like to be on TV... This is what it means to be a professional singer...!
WOOOO HOOOO
I hate to admit it, but... Julia is good at what she does.
I hope we can sing together again some day.
I'm glad everything turned out okay...
WOOo

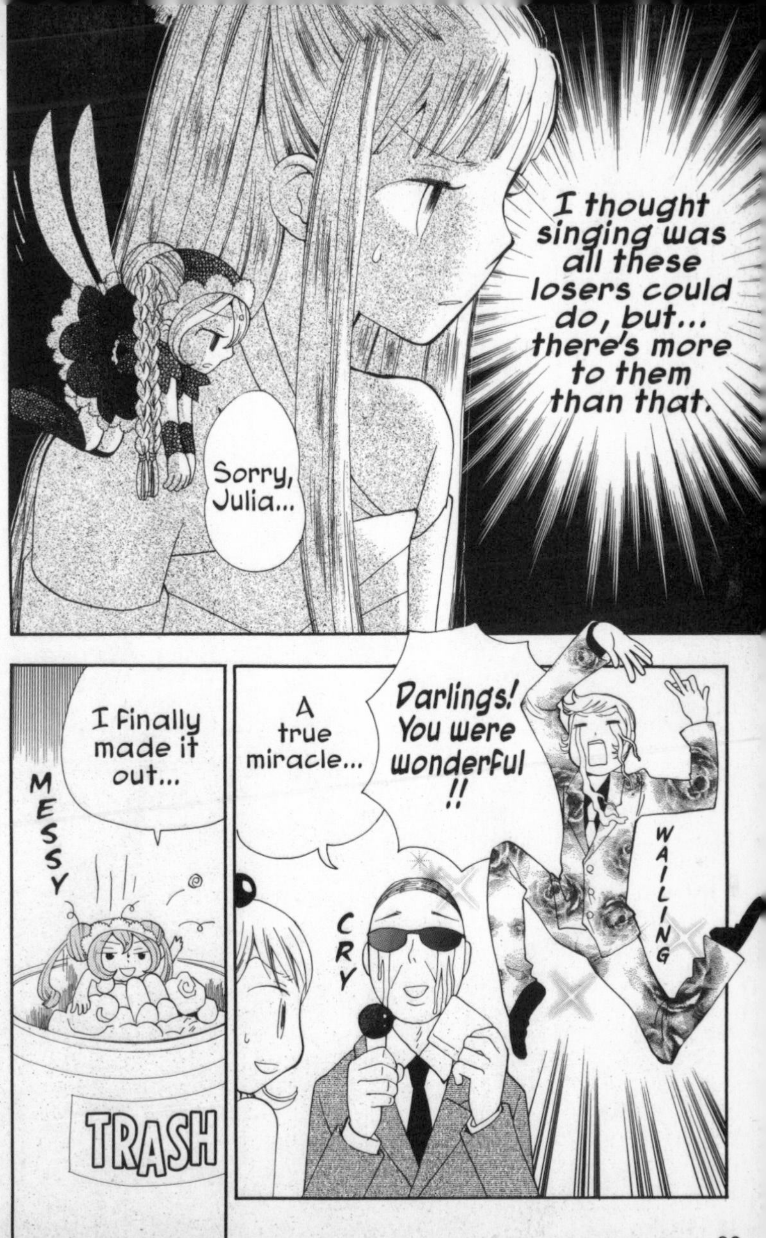
I thought singing was all these losers could do, but... there's more to them than that.
Sorry, Julia...
Darlings! You were wonderful !!
A true miracle...
WAILING
CRY
MESSY
I finally made it out...
TRASH

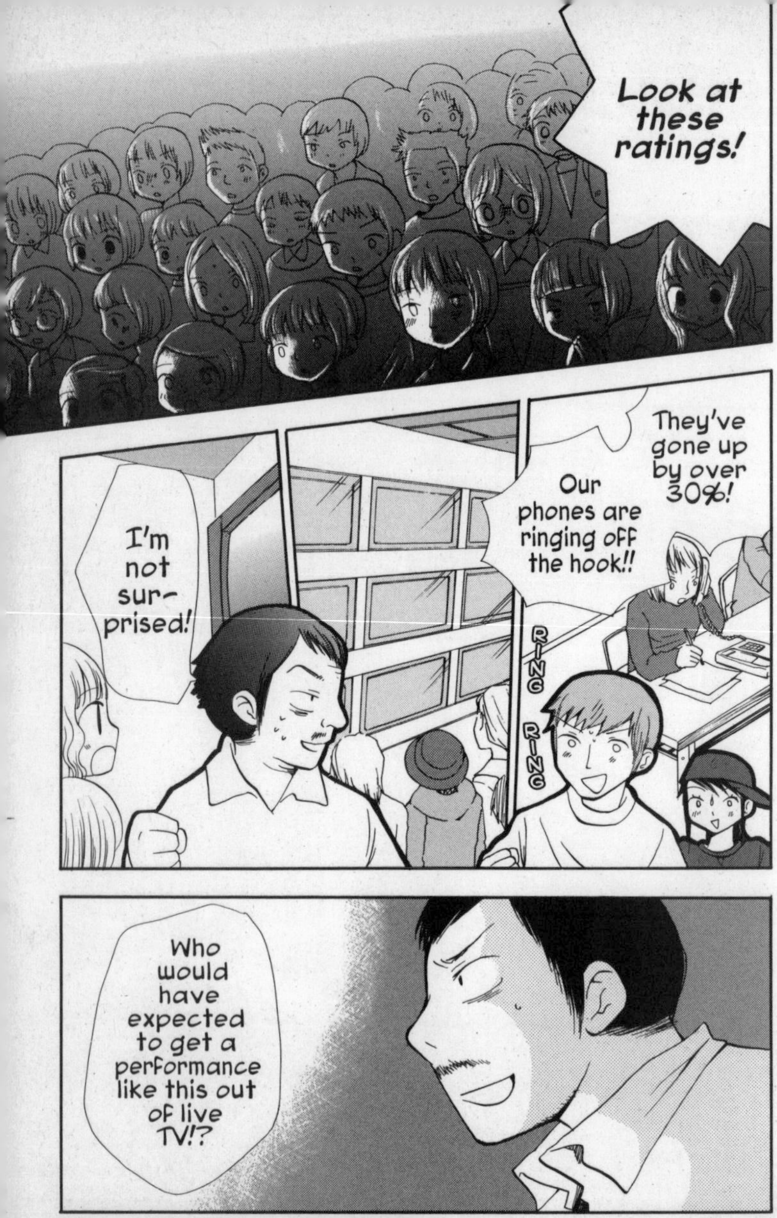
Look at these ratings!
They've gone up by over 30%!
Our phones are ringing off the hook!!
RING RING
I'm not surprised!
Who would have expected to get a performance like this out of live TV!?

Stage 15 Julia's Deal

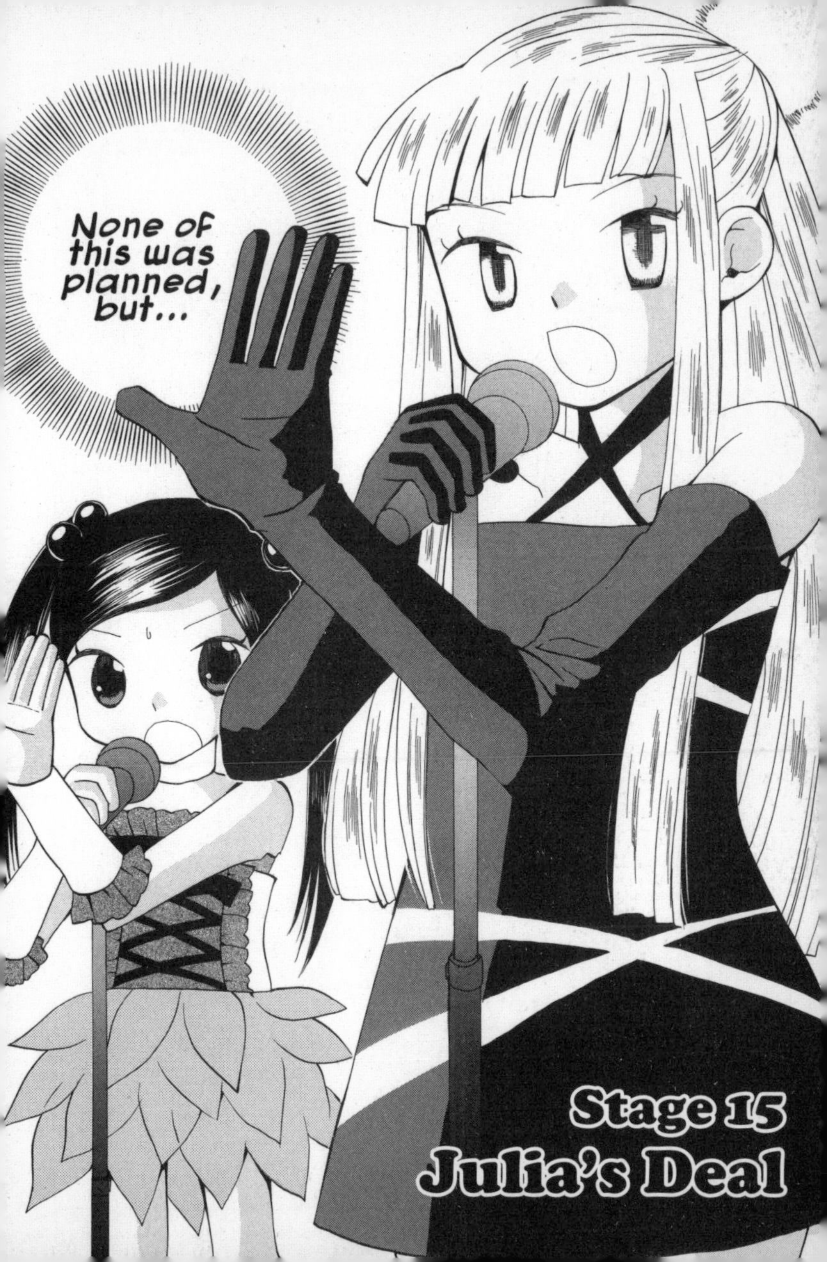
None of this was planned, but...
Stage 15
Julia's Deal

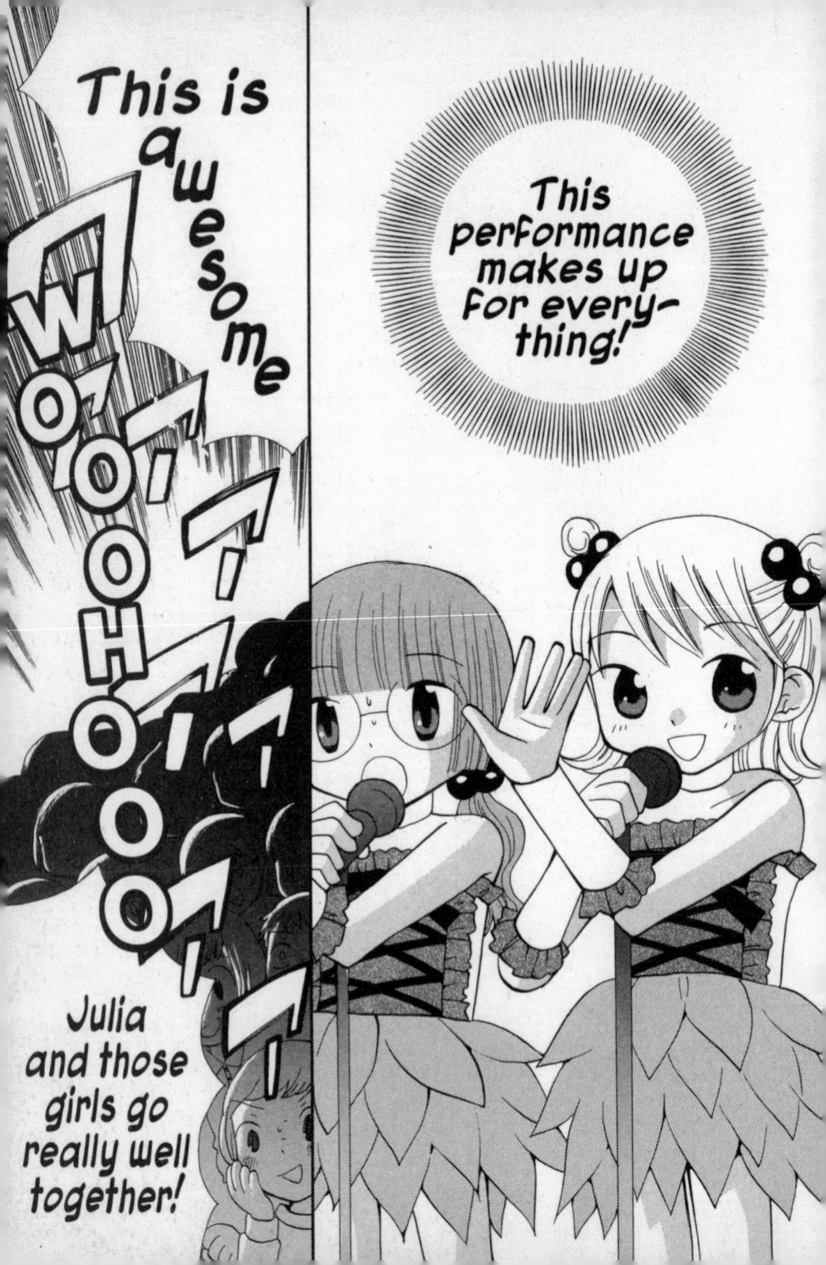
This performance makes up for every-thing!
This is awesome
WOOOHOOO
Julia and those girls go really well together!

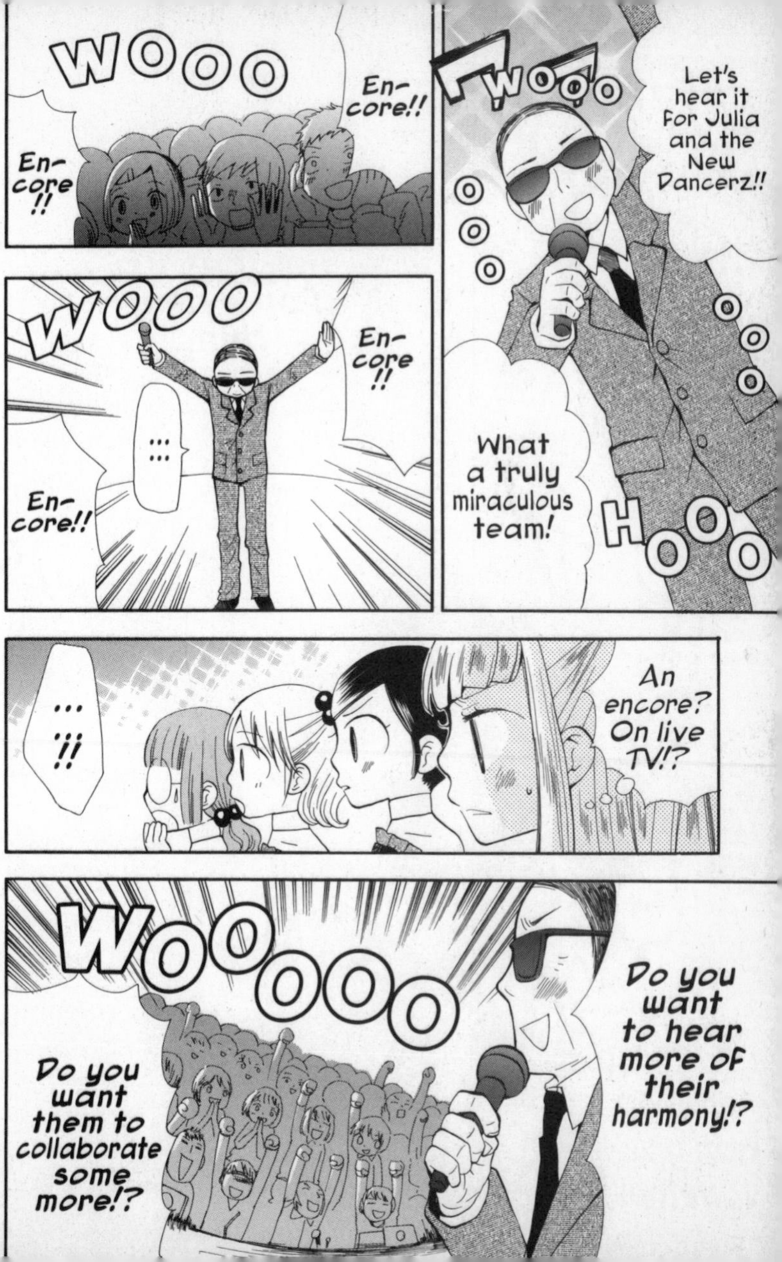
Let's hear it for Julia and the New Dancerz!!
WOOOO
OOO
OOO
What a truly miraculous team!
HOOOO
En-core!!
WOOO
En-core!!
En-core!!
WOOO
......
En-core!!
An encore? On live TV!?
...!!
Do you want to hear more of their harmony!?
WOOOOOO
Do you want them to collaborate some more!?

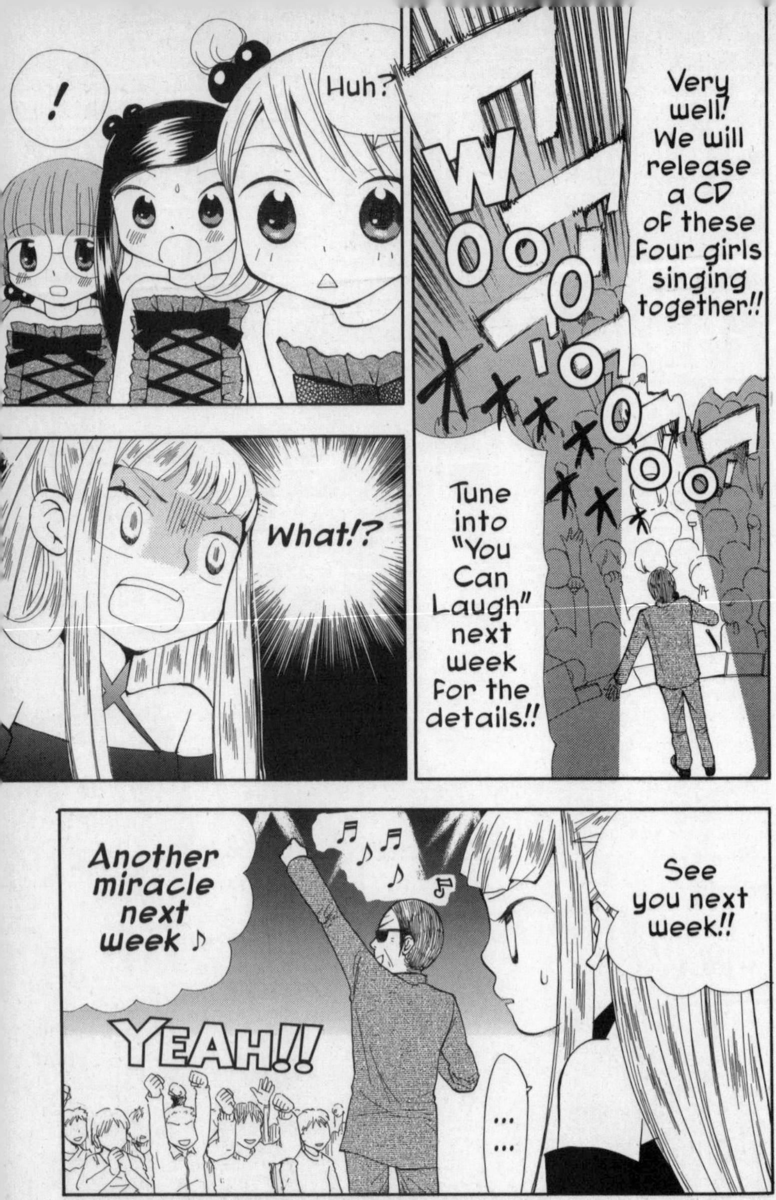
Very well! We will release a CD of these four girls singing together!!
WOOOOOOO!
Tune into "You Can Laugh" next week for the details!!
Huh?
!
What!?
See you next week!!
... ...
Another miracle next week ♪
YEAH!!

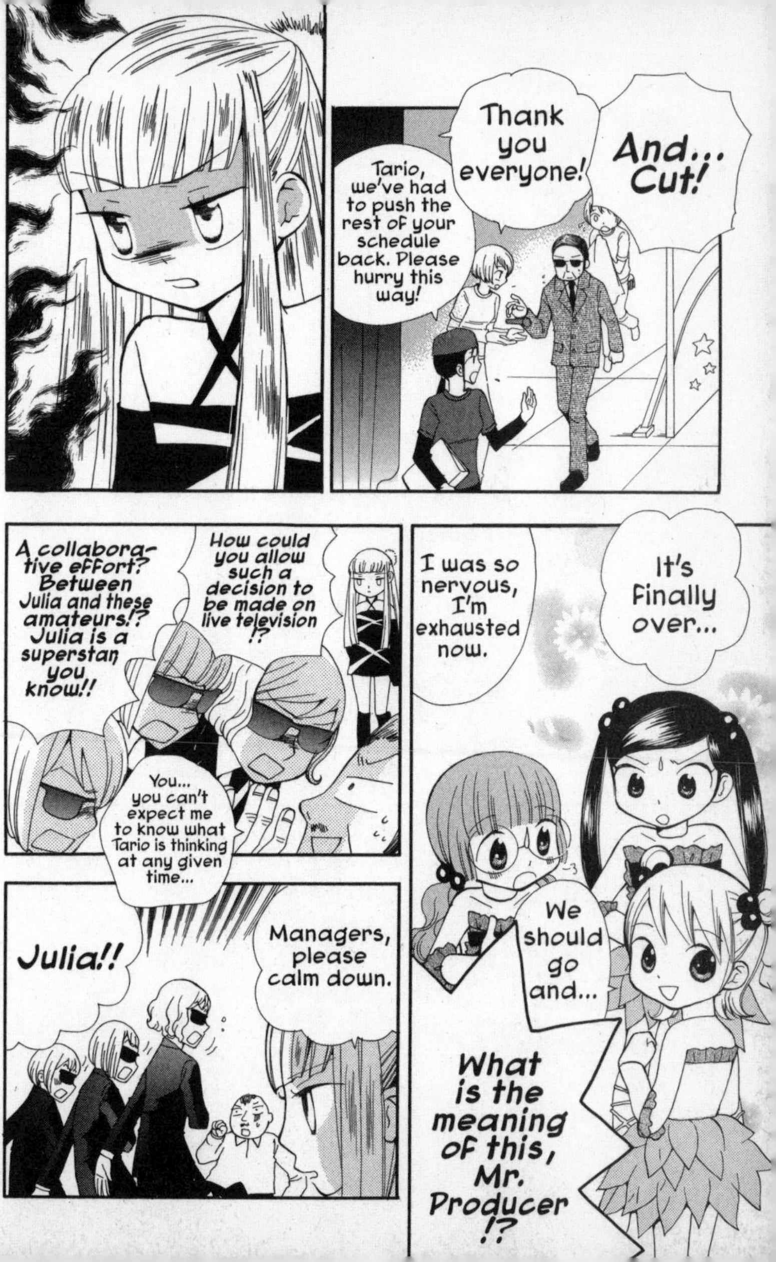
And... Cut!
Thank you everyone!
Tario, we've had to push the rest of your schedule back. Please hurry this way!
It's finally over...
I was so nervous, I'm exhausted now.
We should go and...
What is the meaning of this, Mr. Producer!?
How could you allow such a decision to be made on live television!?
A collabora-tive effort? Between Julia and these amateurs!? Julia is a superstar, you know!!
You... you can't expect me to know what Tario is thinking at any given time...
Managers, please calm down.
Julia!!

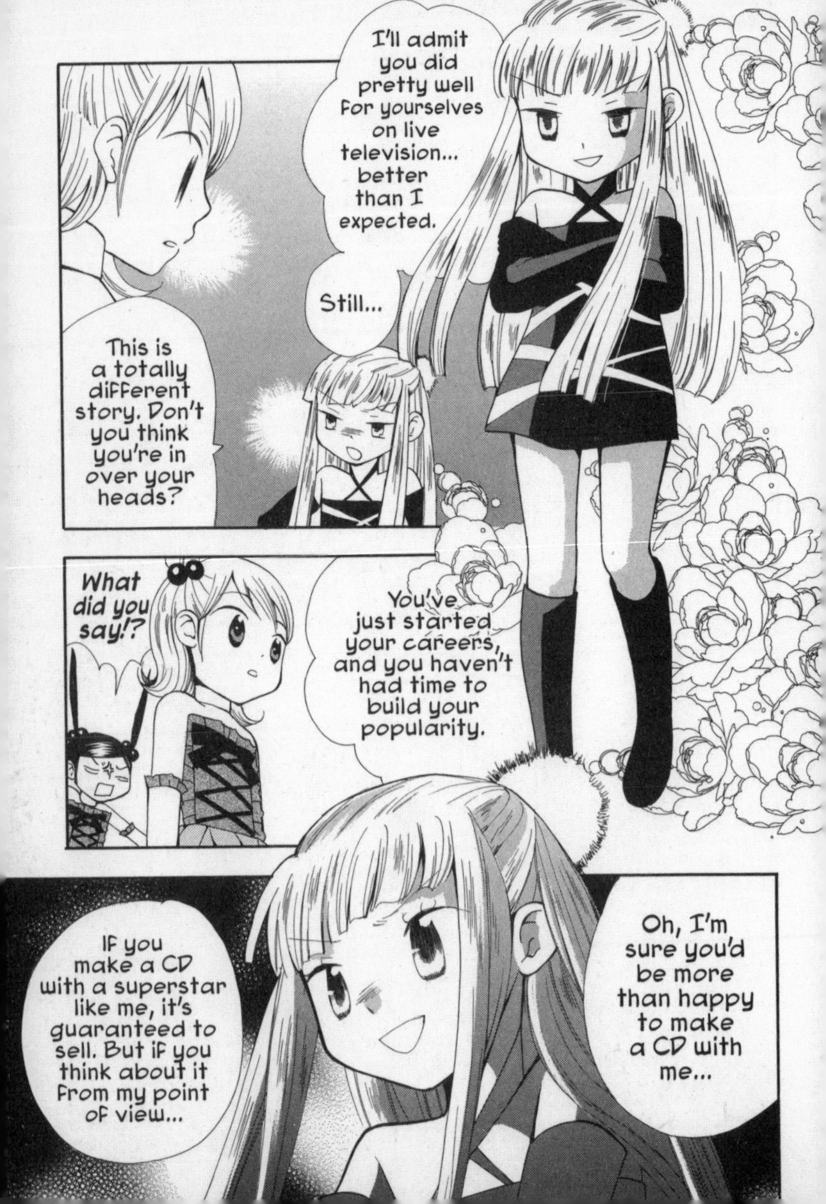
I'll admit you did pretty well for yourselves on live television... better than I expected.
Still...
This is a totally different story. Don't you think you're in over your heads?
You've just started your careers, and you haven't had time to build your popularity.
What did you say!?
Oh, I'm sure you'd be more than happy to make a CD with me...
If you make a CD with a superstar like me, it's guaranteed to sell. But if you think about it from my point of view...

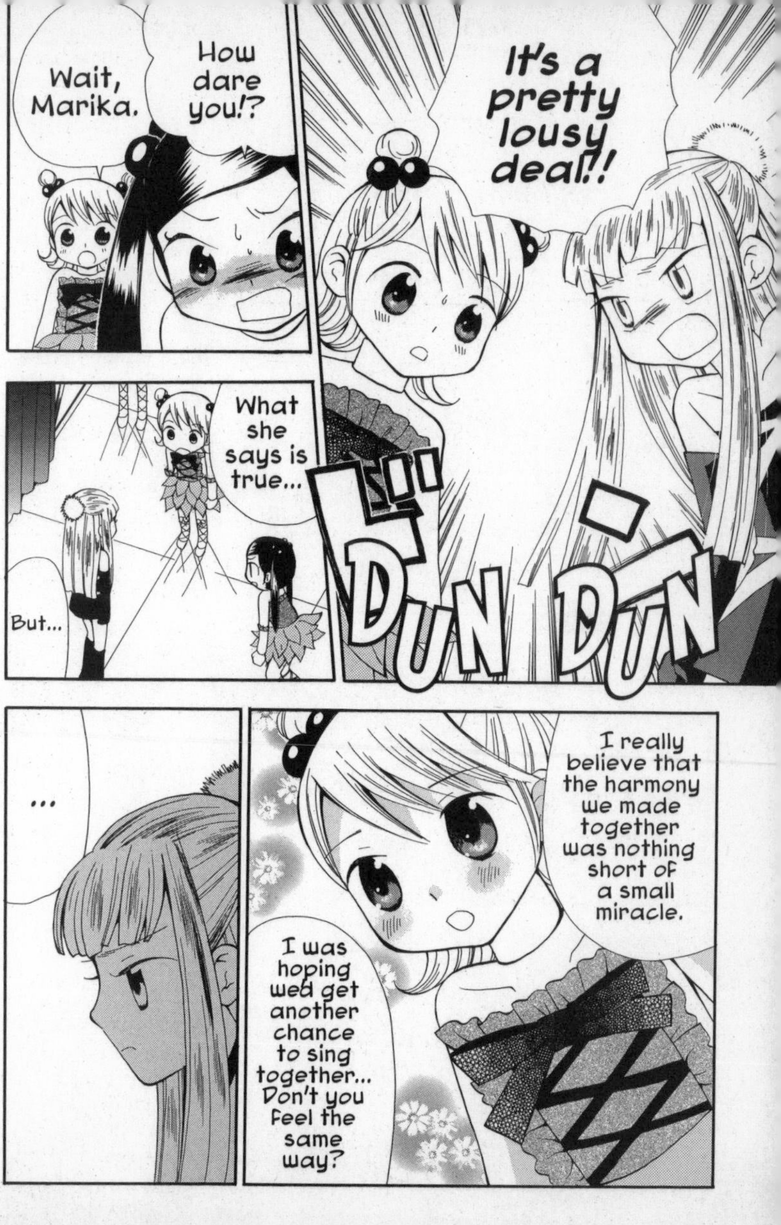
It's a pretty lousy deal!!
DUN DUN
How dare you!?
Wait, Marika.
What she says is true...
But...
I really believe that the harmony we made together was nothing short of a small miracle.
I was hoping we'd get another chance to sing together... Don't you feel the same way?
...

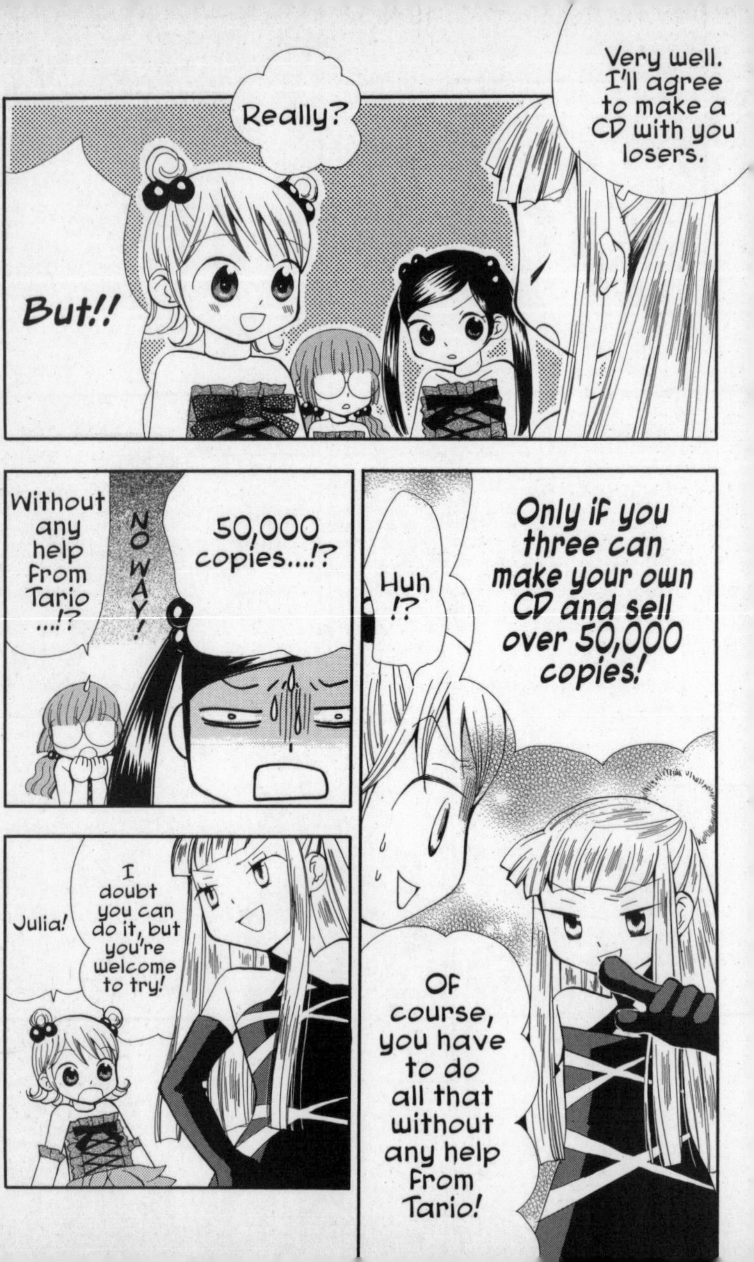
Very well. I'll agree to make a CD with you losers.
Really?
But!!
Only if you three can make your own CD and sell over 50,000 copies!
Huh!?
Of course, you have to do all that without any help from Tario!
50,000 copies...!?
NO WAY!
Without any help from Tario...!?
I doubt you can do it, but you're welcome to try!
Julia!

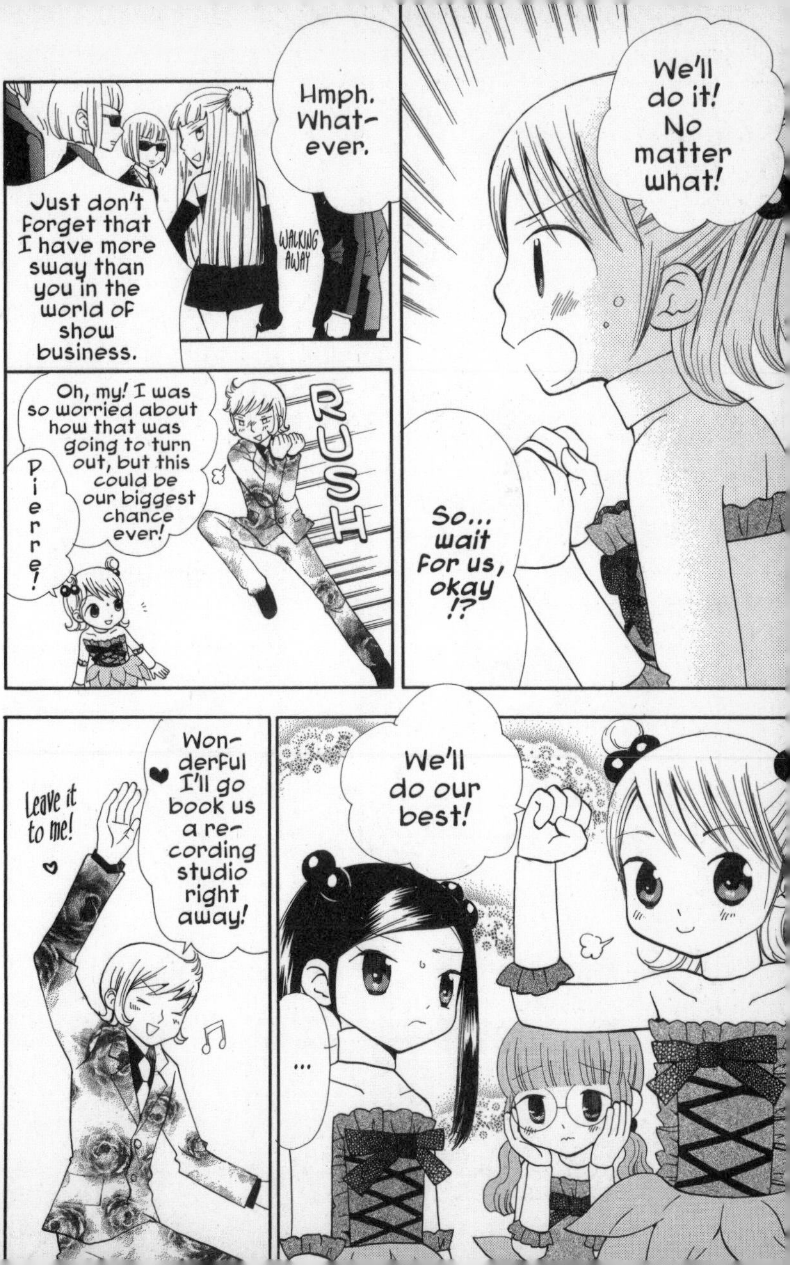
We'll do it! No matter what!
So... wait for us, okay!?
Hmph. Whatever.
WALKING AWAY
Just don't forget that I have more sway than you in the world of show business.
RUSH
Oh, my! I was so worried about how that was going to turn out, but this could be our biggest chance ever!
Pierre!
We'll do our best!
...
Wonderful I'll go book us a recording studio right away!
Leave it to me!

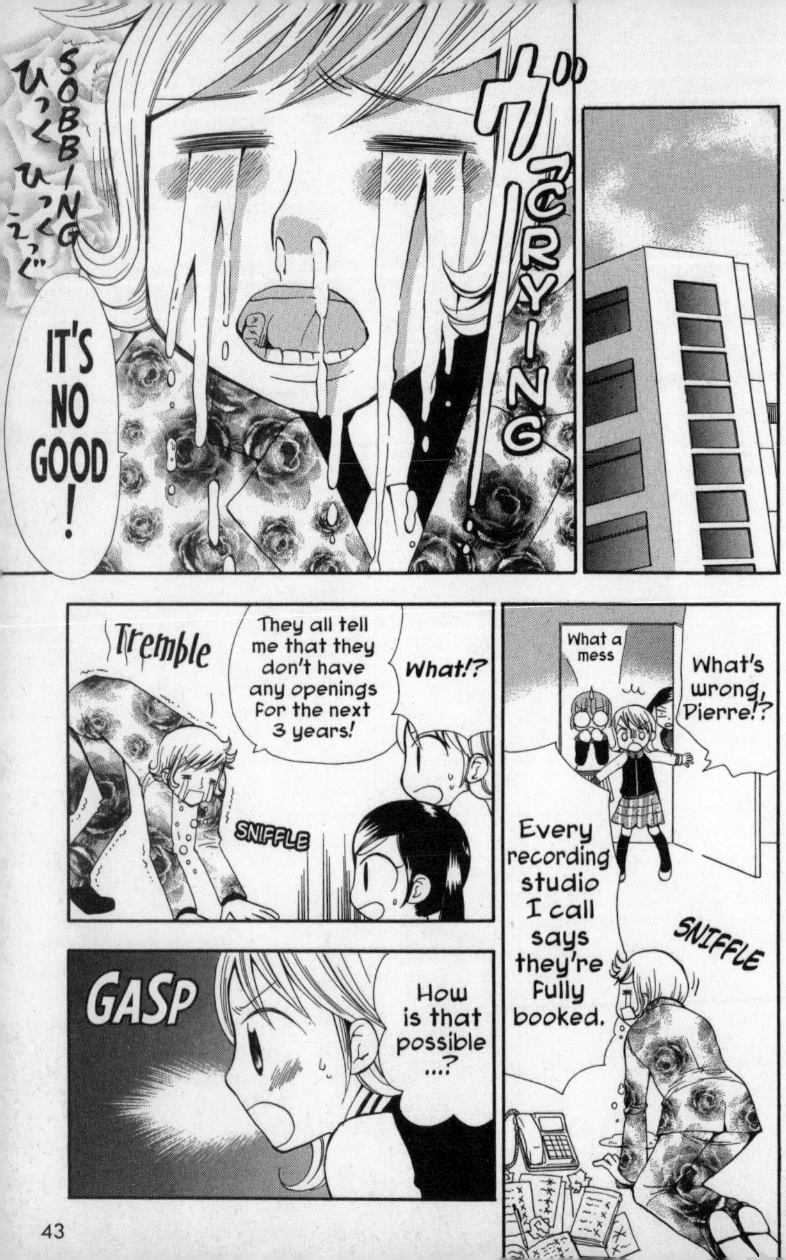

ウー
CRYING
SOBBING
ひっくひっくえっぐ
IT'S NO GOOD!
What's wrong, Pierre!?
What a mess
Every recording studio I call says they're fully booked.
SNIFFLE
What!?
They all tell me that they don't have any openings for the next 3 years!
Tremble
SNIFFLE
How is that possible ...?
GASP

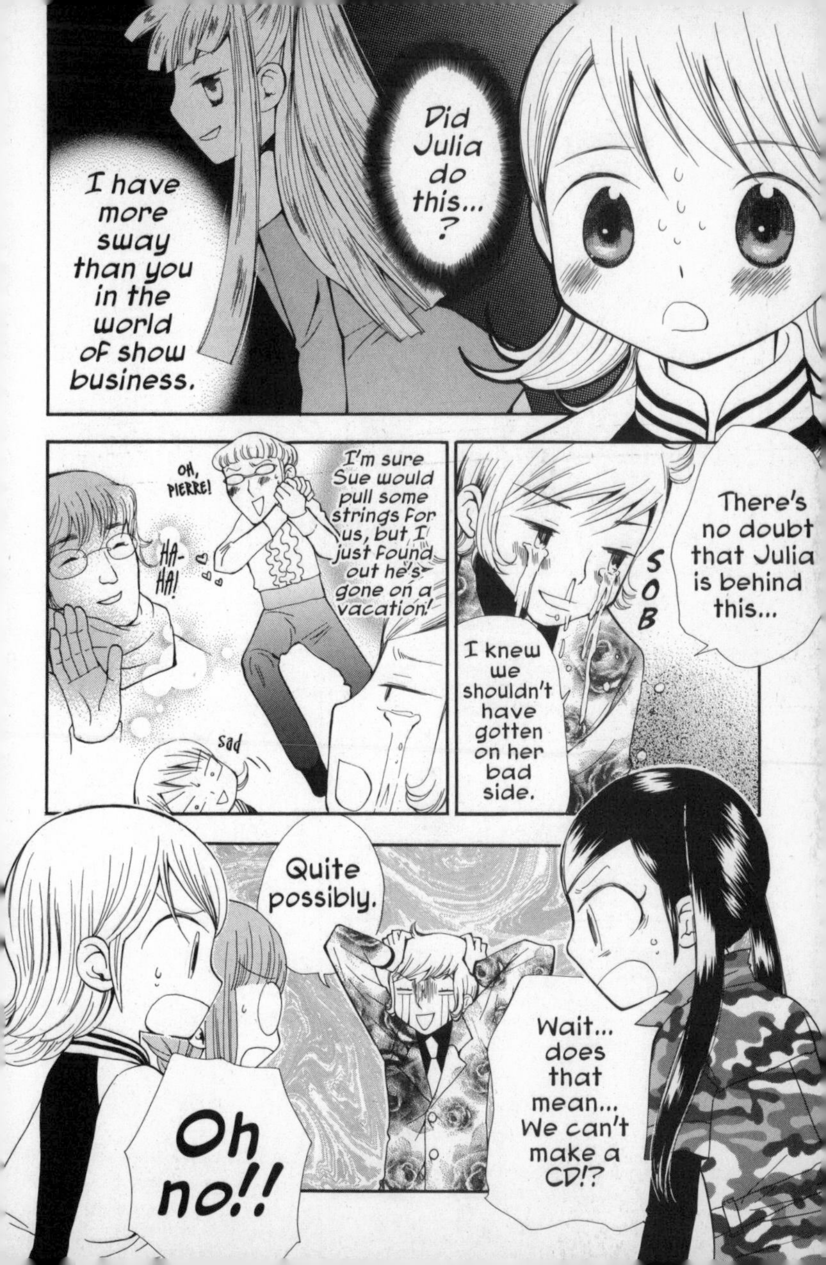
Did Julia do this...?
I have more sway than you in the world of show business.
There's no doubt that Julia is behind this...
SOB
I knew we shouldn't have gotten on her bad side.
I'm sure Sue would pull some strings for us, but I just found out he's gone on a vacation!
OH, PIERRE!
HA-HA!
sad
Wait... does that mean... We can't make a CD!?
Quite possibly.
Oh no!!

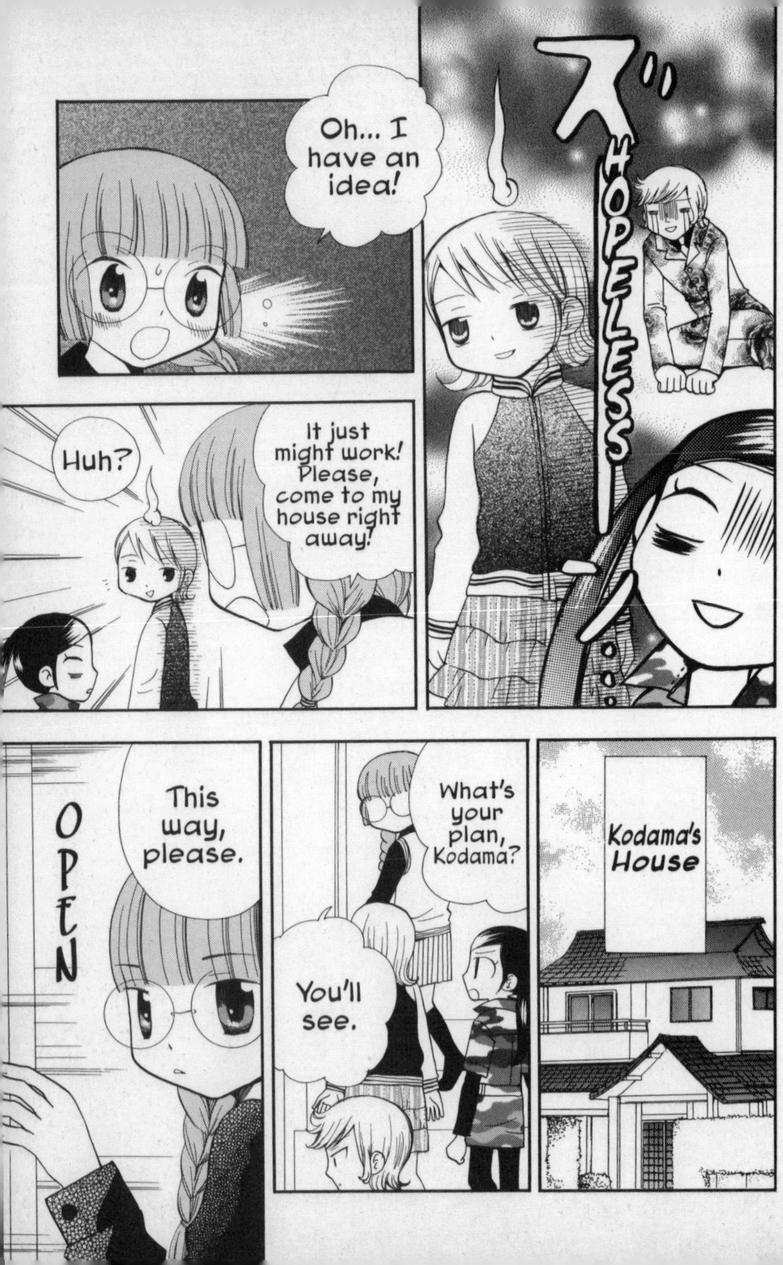
HOPELESS
Oh... I have an idea!
It just might work! Please, come to my house right away!
Huh?
Kodama's House
What's your plan, Kodama?
You'll see.
This way, please.
OPEN

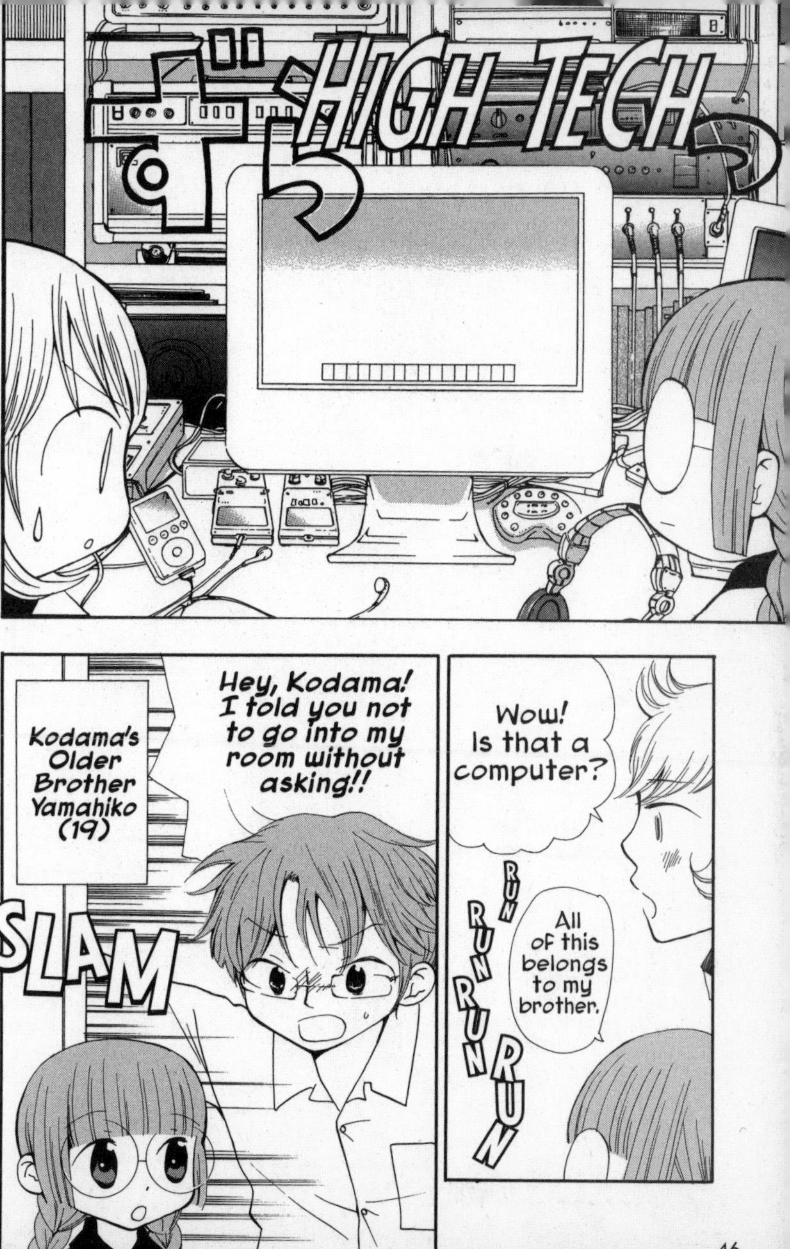
HIGH TECH
Wow! Is that a computer?
All of this belongs to my brother.
RUN RUN RUN RUN RUN RUN
Hey, Kodama! I told you not to go into my room without asking!!
Kodama's Older Brother Yamahiko (19)
SLAM

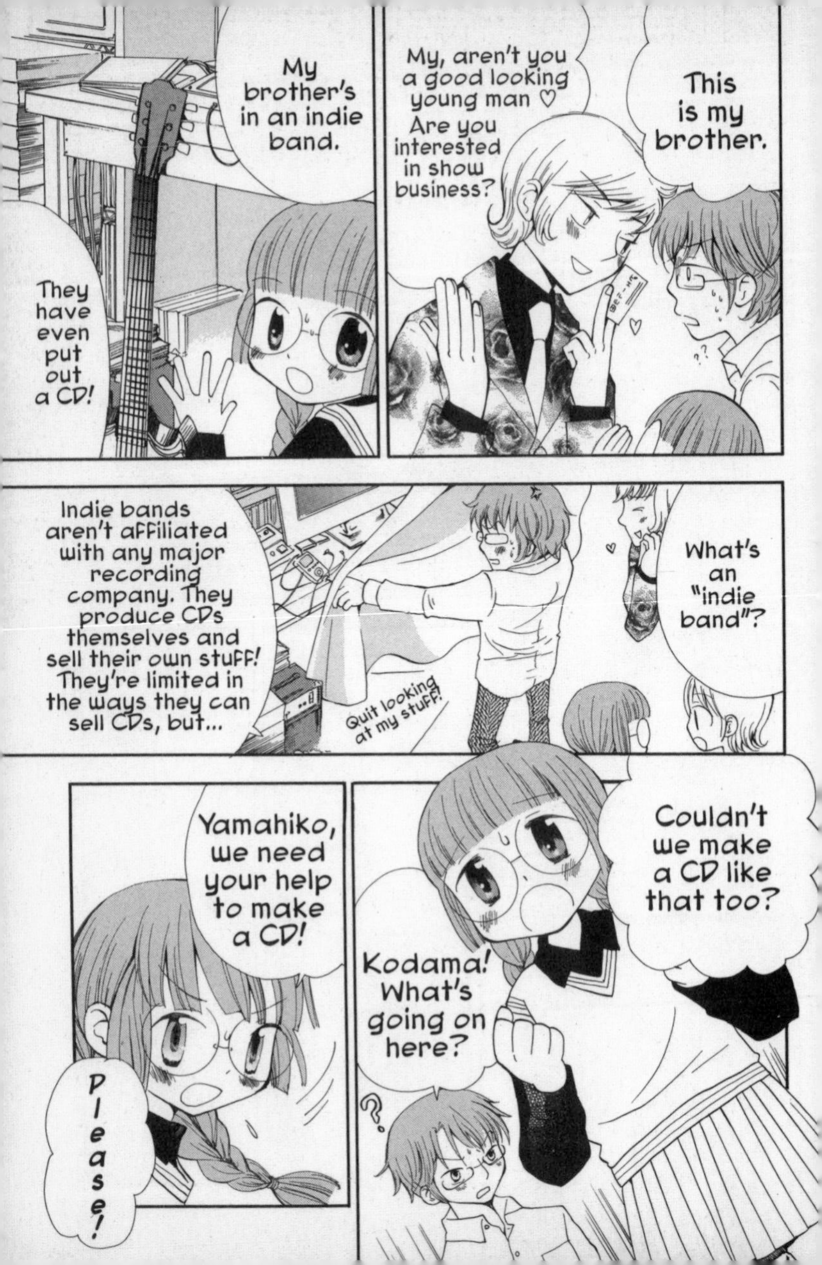
This is my brother.
My, aren't you a good looking young man ♡ Are you interested in show business?
My brother's in an indie band.
They have even put out a CD!
What's an "indie band"?
Quit looking at my stuff!
Indie bands aren't affiliated with any major recording company. They produce CDs themselves and sell their own stuff! They're limited in the ways they can sell CDs, but...
Couldn't we make a CD like that too?
Kodama! What's going on here?
Yamahiko, we need your help to make a CD!
Please!

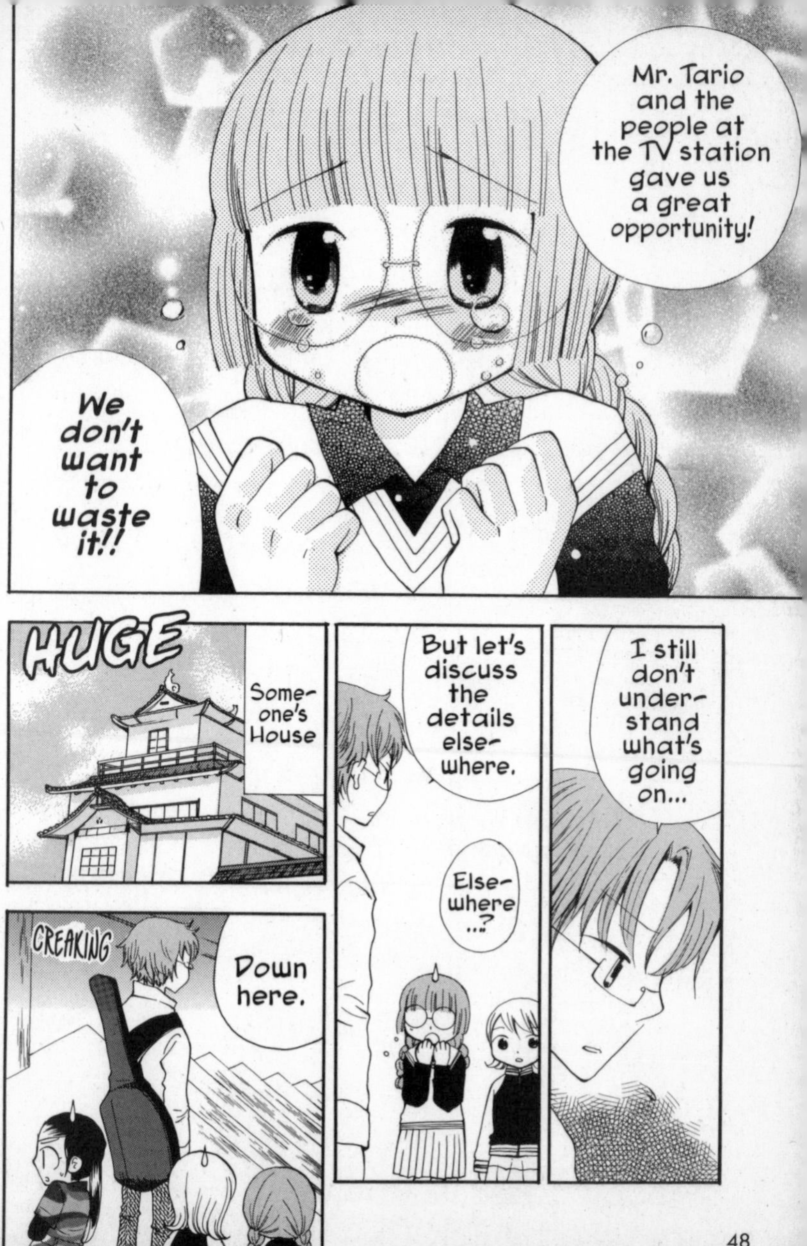
Mr. Tario and the people at the TV station gave us a great opportunity!
We don't want to waste it!!
I still don't under-stand what's going on...
But let's discuss the details else-where.
Else-where...?
HUGE
Some-one's House
CREAKING
Down here.

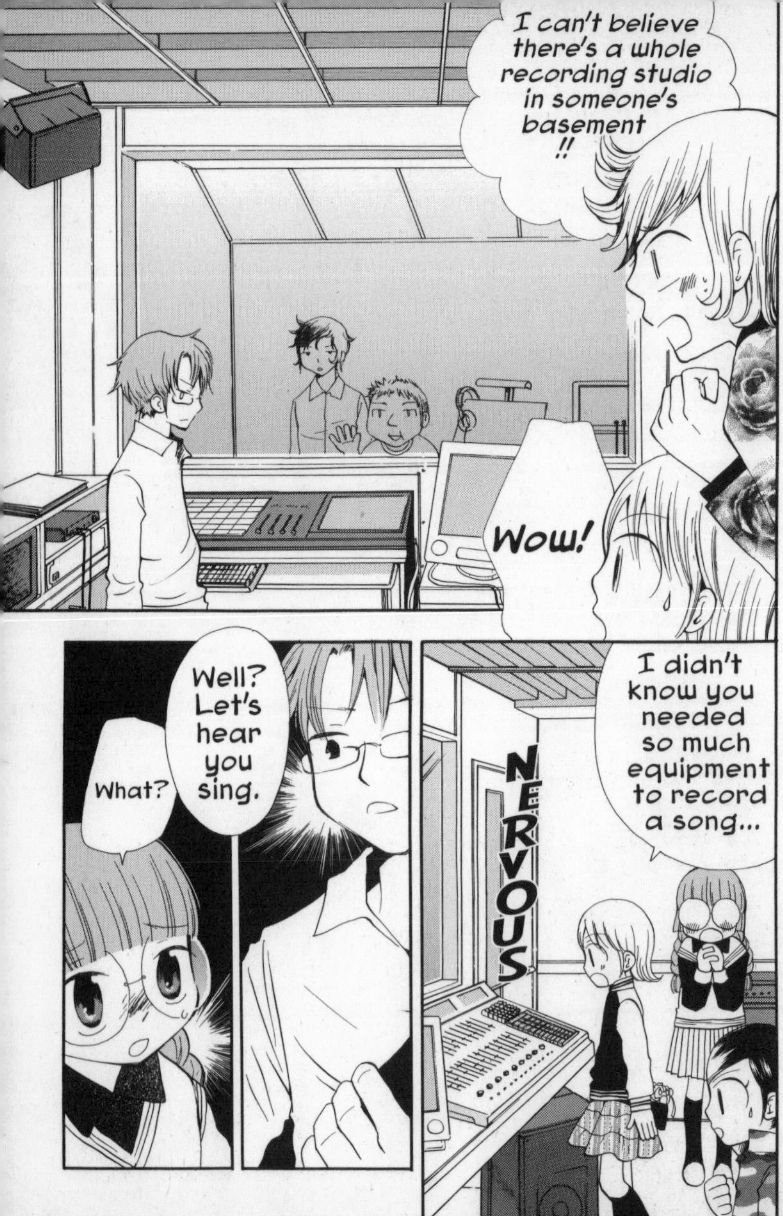
I can't believe there's a whole recording studio in someone's basement !!
Wow!
I didn't know you needed so much equipment to record a song...
NERVOUS
Well? Let's hear you sing.
What?

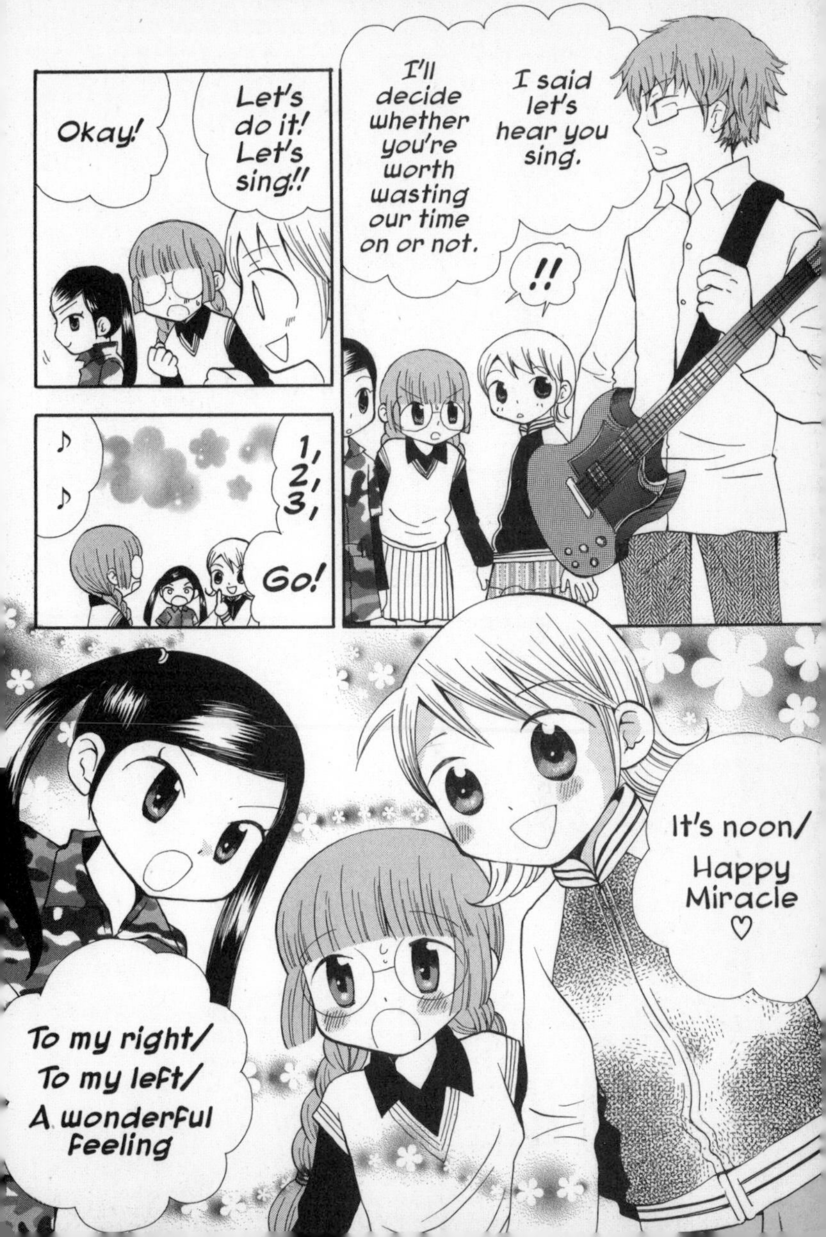
I said let's hear you sing.
I'll decide whether you're worth wasting our time on or not.
!!
Let's do it! Let's sing!!
Okay!
1, 2, 3, Go!
♪ ♪
It's noon/ Happy Miracle ♡
To my right/ To my left/ A wonderful feeling

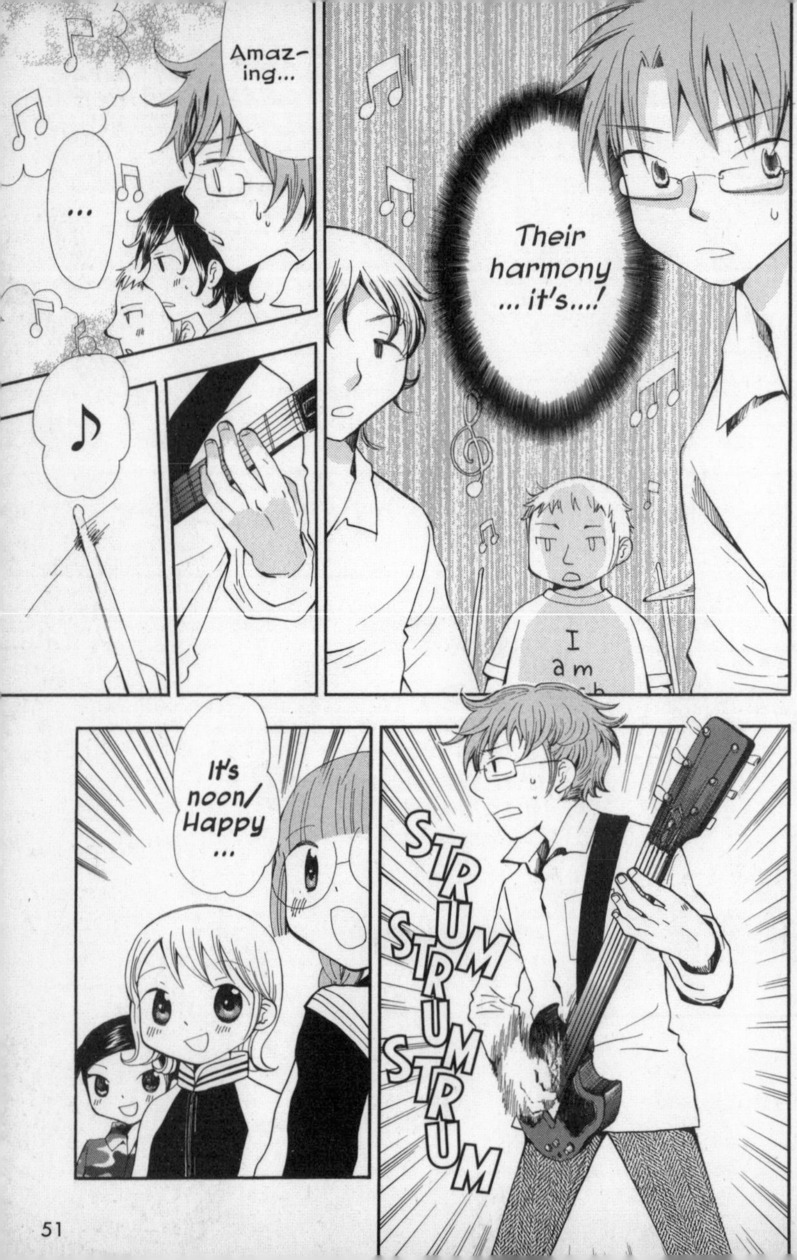
Their harmony ... it's....!
I am
Amaz-ing...
...
♪
STRUM STRUM STRUM STRUM
It's noon/ Happy ...

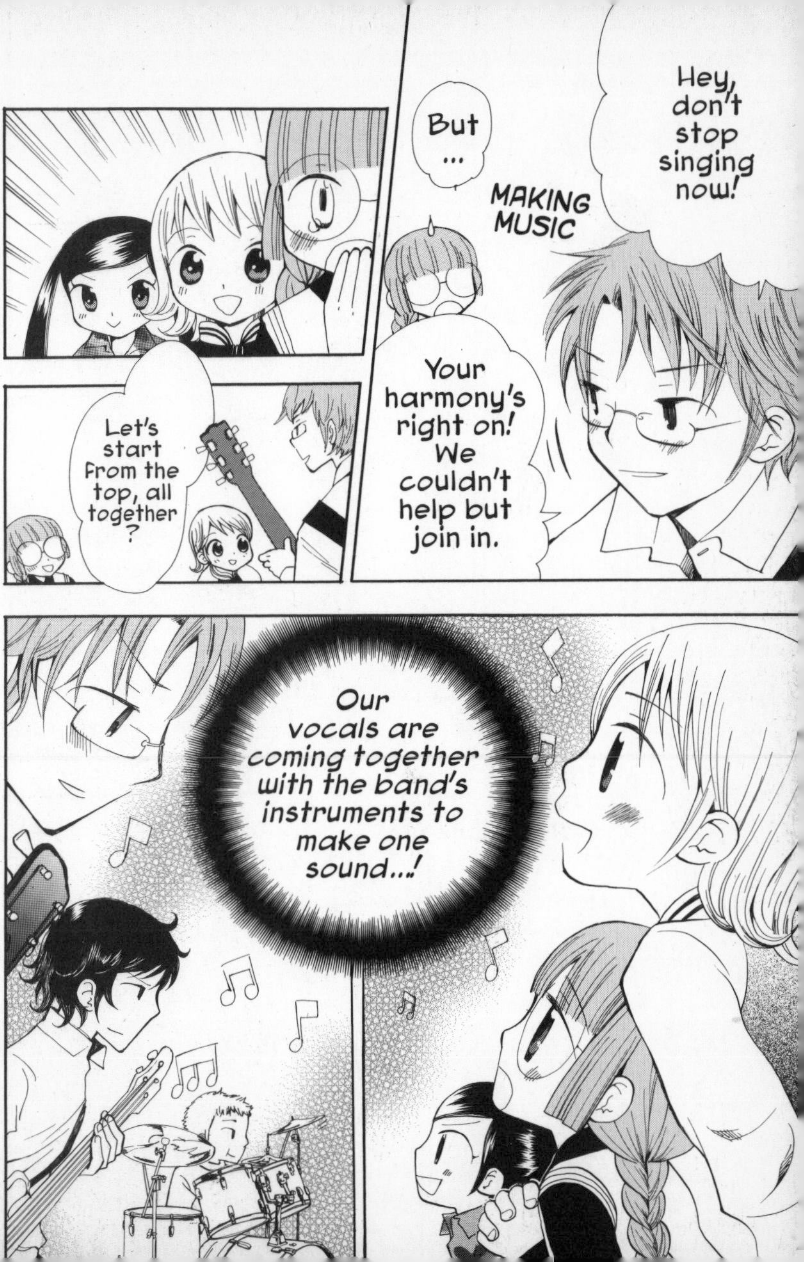

Hey, don't stop singing now!
MAKING MUSIC
But ...
Your harmony's right on! We couldn't help but join in.
Let's start from the top, all together?
Our vocals are coming together with the band's instruments to make one sound...!

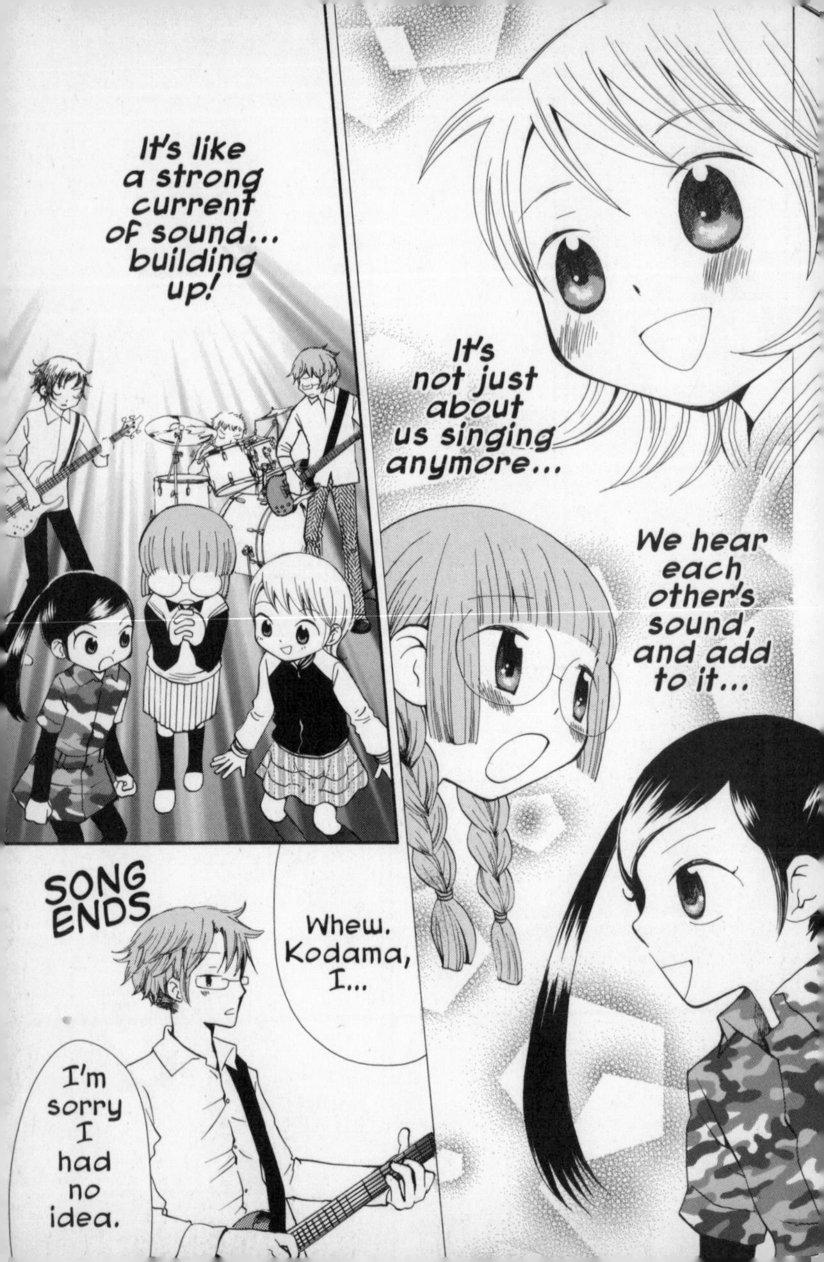

It's not just about us singing anymore...
We hear each other's sound, and add to it...
It's like a strong current of sound... building up!
SONG ENDS
Whew. Kodama, I...
I'm sorry I had no idea.

Read this way

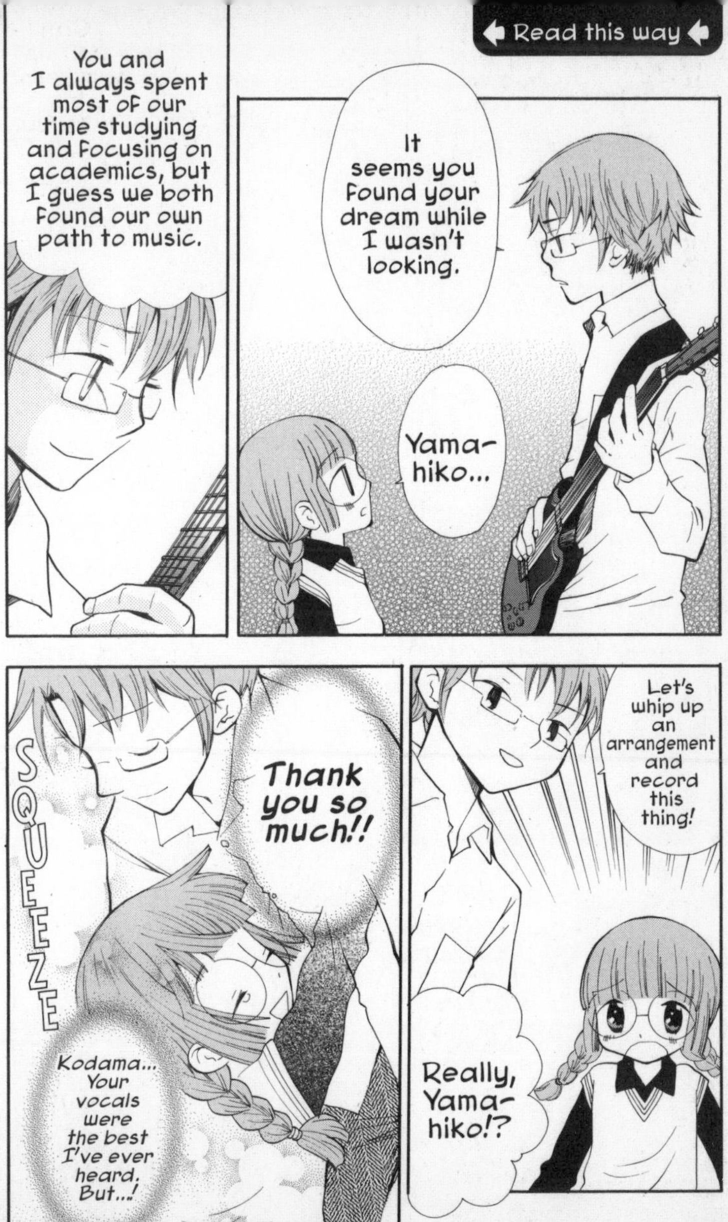
It seems you found your dream while I wasn't looking.
Yama-hiko...
You and I always spent most of our time studying and focusing on academics, but I guess we both found our own path to music.
Let's whip up an arrangement and record this thing!
Really, Yama-hiko!?
Thank you so much!!
SQUEEZE
Kodama... Your vocals were the best I've ever heard. But...!

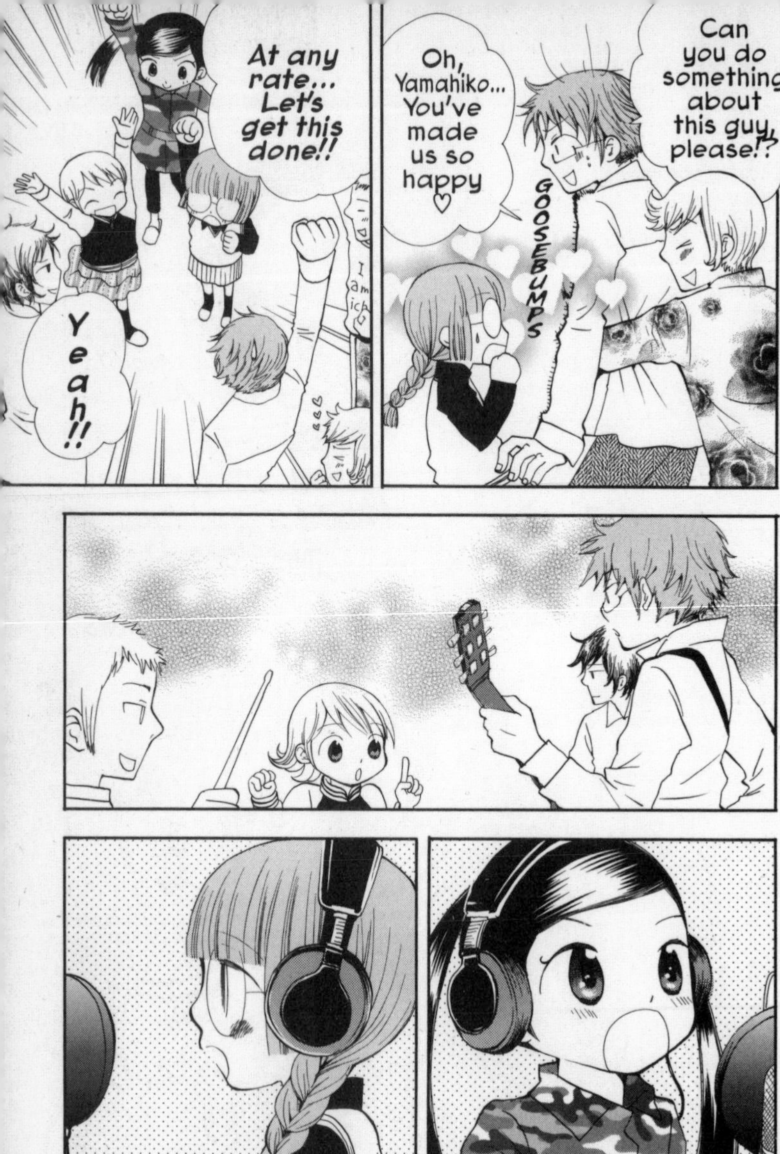
Can you do something about this guy, please!?
Oh, Yamahiko... You've made us so happy ♡
GOOSEBUMPS
At any rate... Let's get this done!!
Yeah!!

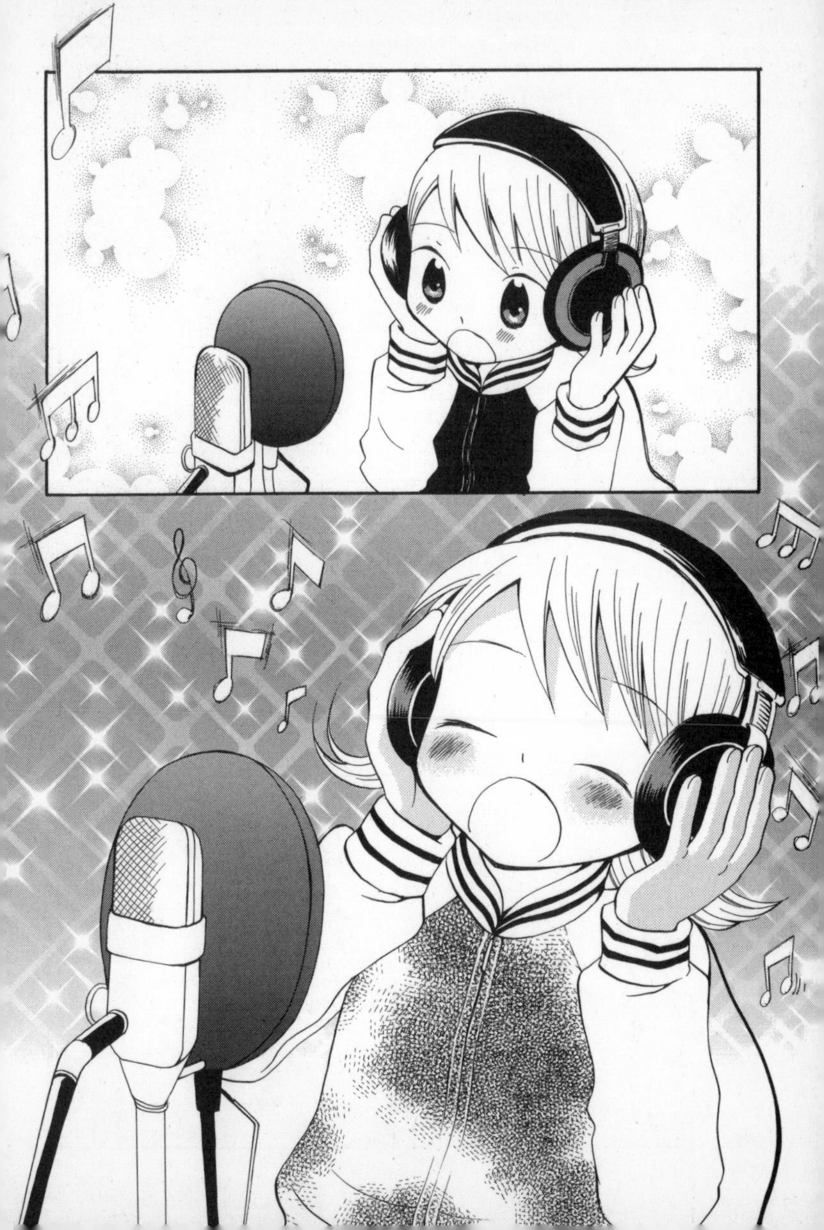

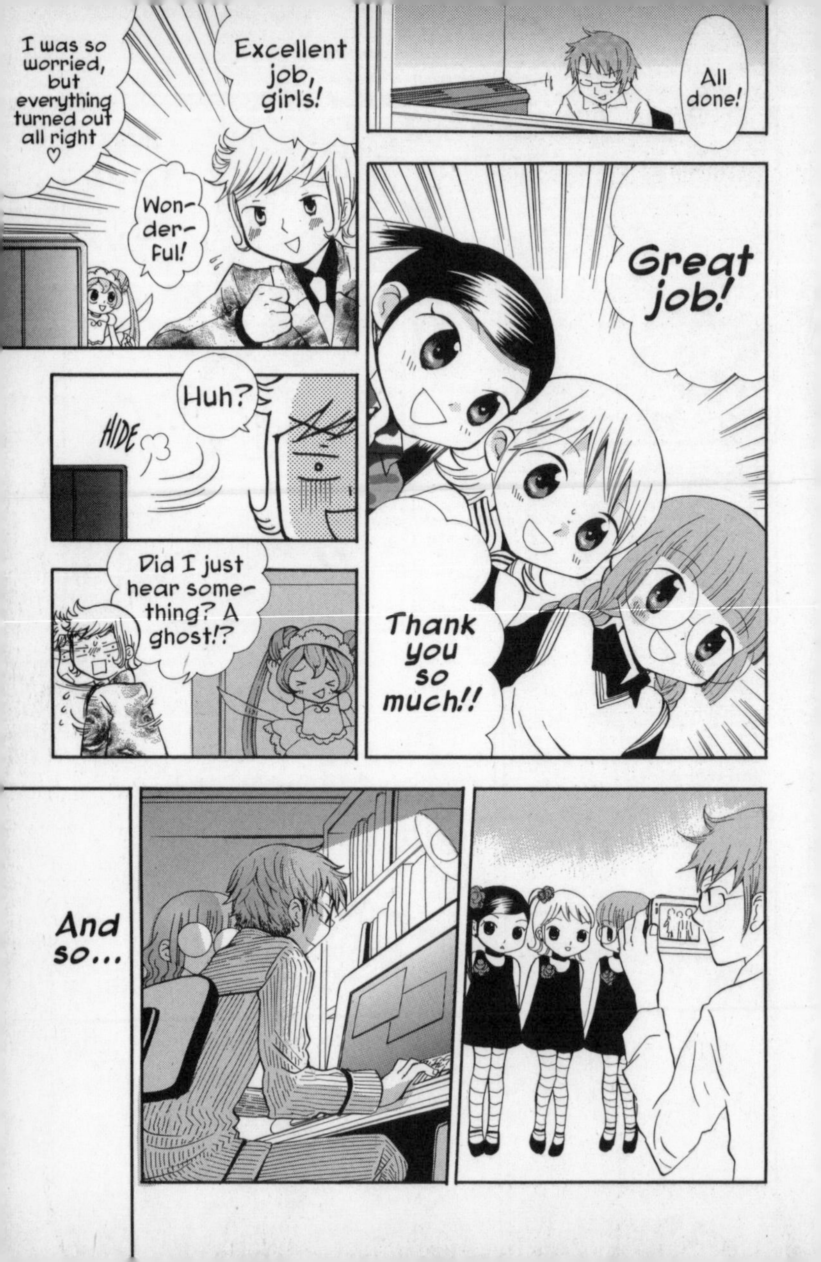
All done!
Great job!
Thank you so much!!
Excellent job, girls!
I was so worried, but everything turned out all right ♡
Won-der-ful!
Huh?
HIDE
Did I just hear some-thing? A ghost!?
And so...

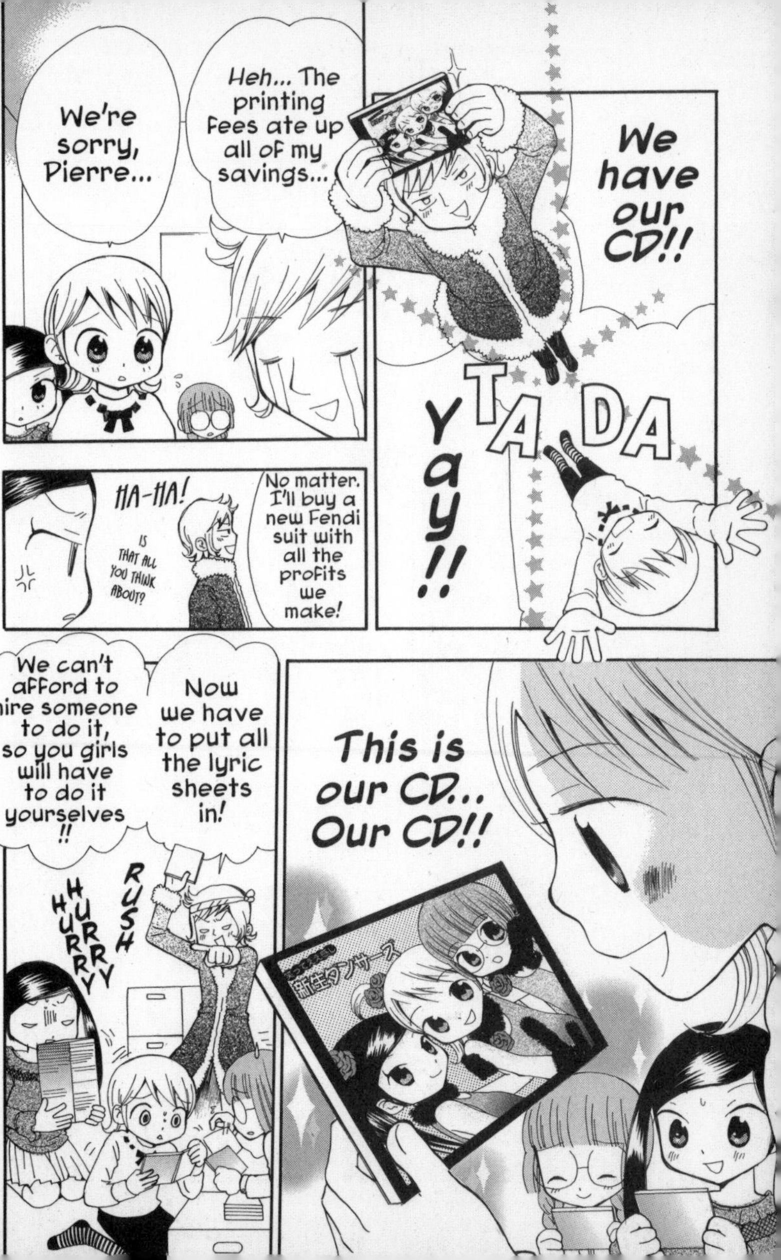

We have our CD!!
TA DA
Yay!!
Heh... The printing fees ate up all of my savings...
We're sorry, Pierre...
No matter. I'll buy a new Fendi suit with all the profits we make!
HA-HA!
IS THAT ALL YOU THINK ABOUT?
This is our CD... Our CD!!
Now we have to put all the lyric sheets in!
We can't afford to hire someone to do it, so you girls will have to do it yourselves!!
RUSH
HURRY HURRY

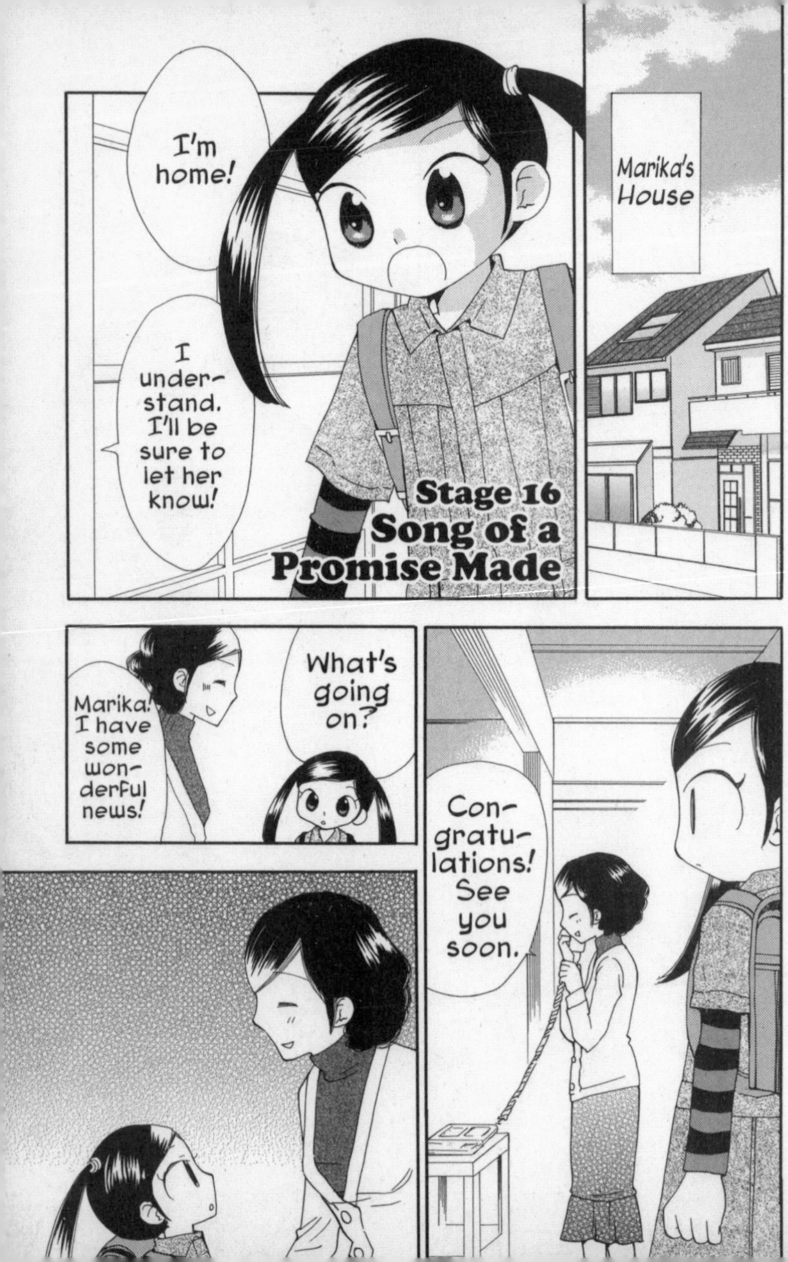
Marika's House
I'm home!
I understand. I'll be sure to let her know!
Stage 16 Song of a Promise Made
Congratulations! See you soon.
What's going on?
Marika! I have some wonderful news!

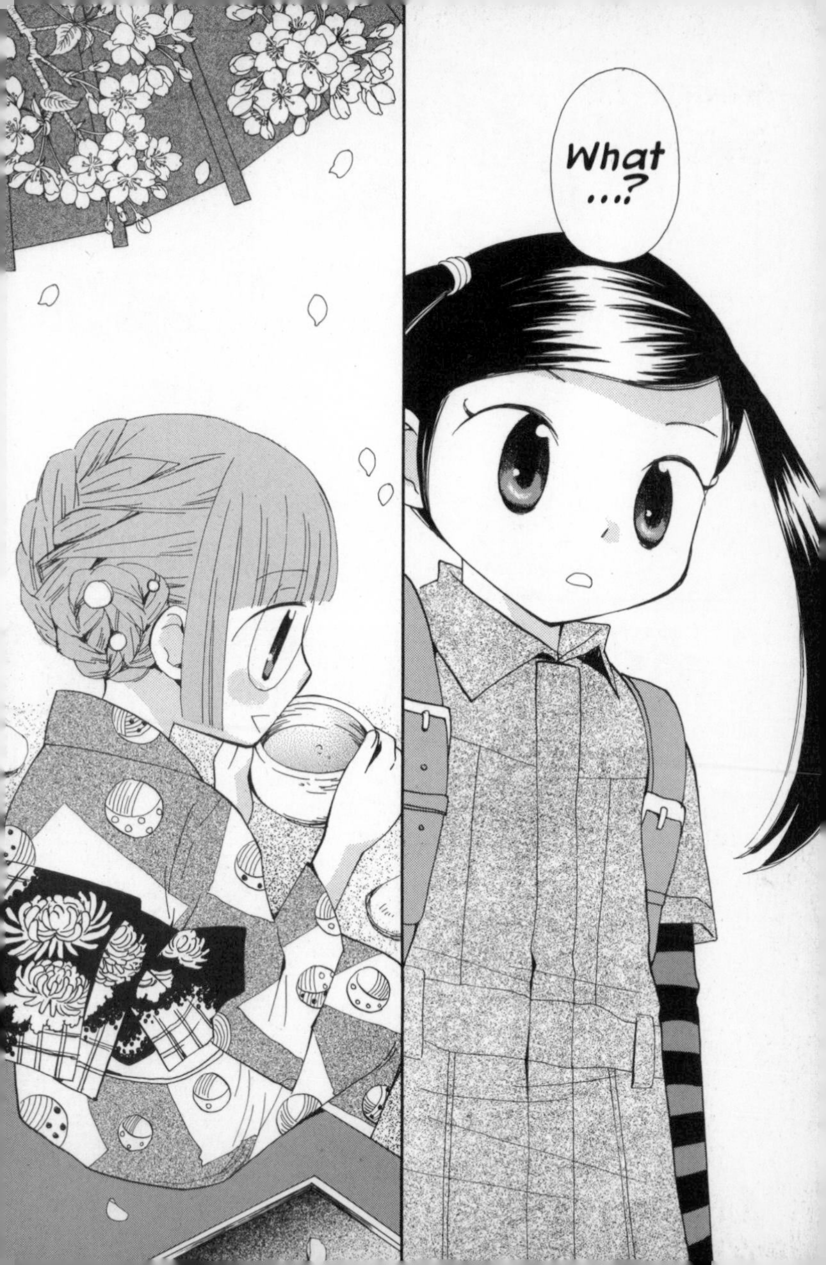
What ...?

Stage 16
Song of a Promise Made

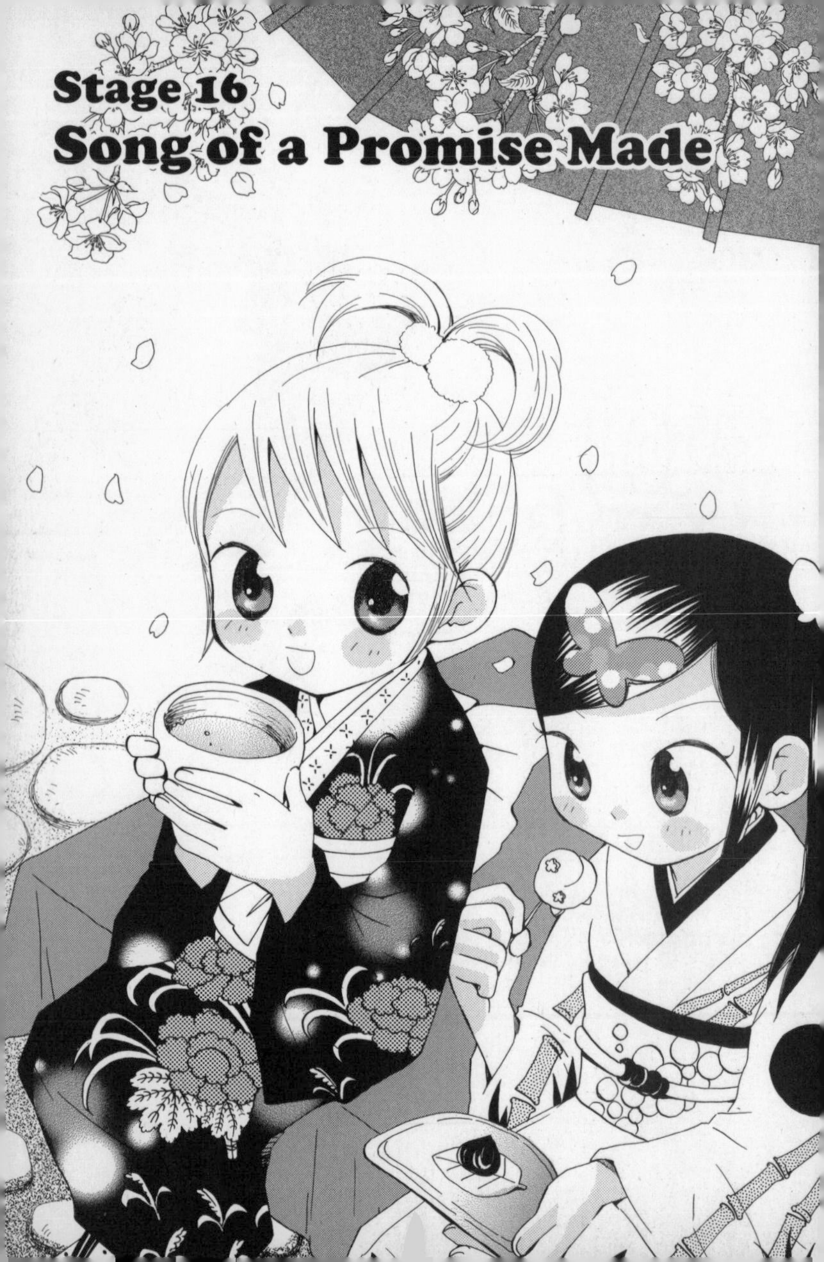

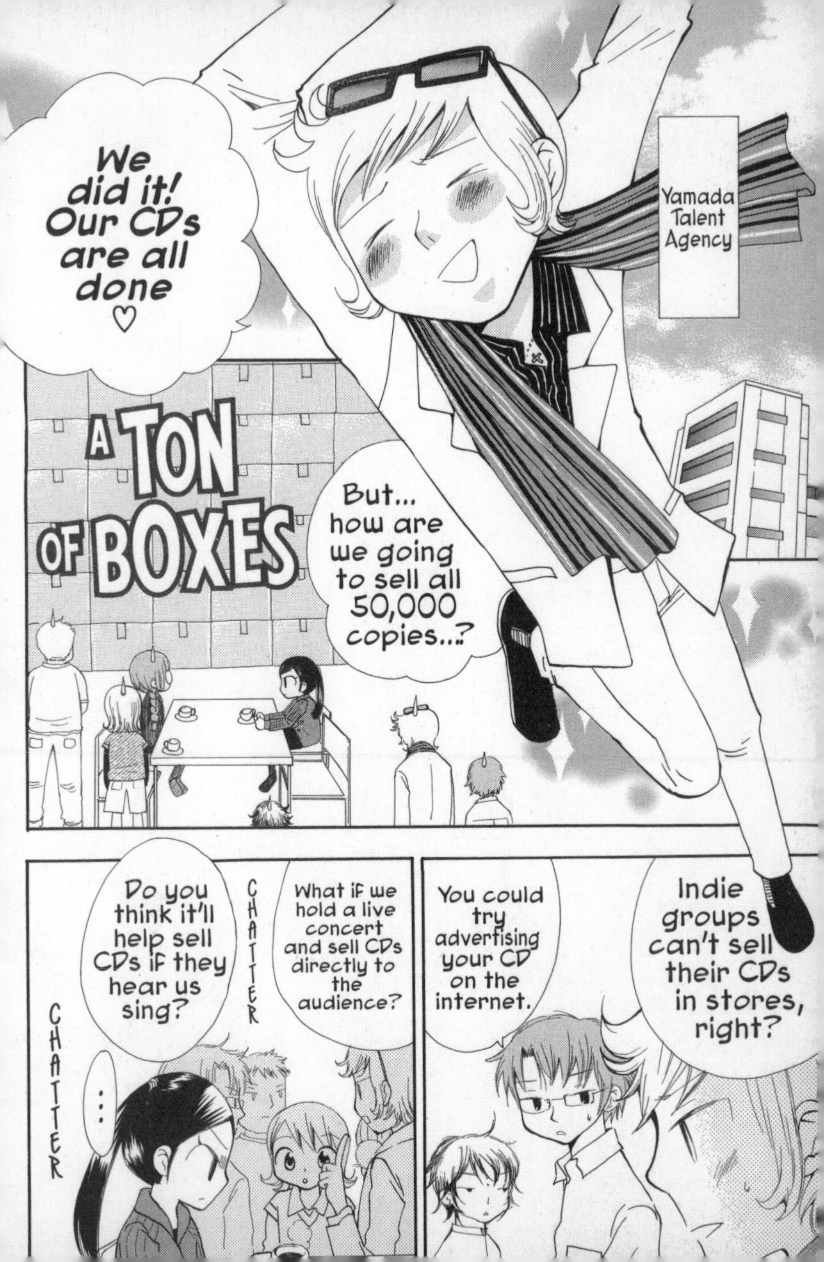
Yamada Talent Agency
We did it! Our CDs are all done ♡
A TON OF BOXES
But... how are we going to sell all 50,000 copies...?
Indie groups can't sell their CDs in stores, right?
You could try advertising your CD on the internet.
What if we hold a live concert and sell CDs directly to the audience?
CHATTER
Do you think it'll help sell CDs if they hear us sing?
CHATTER
...

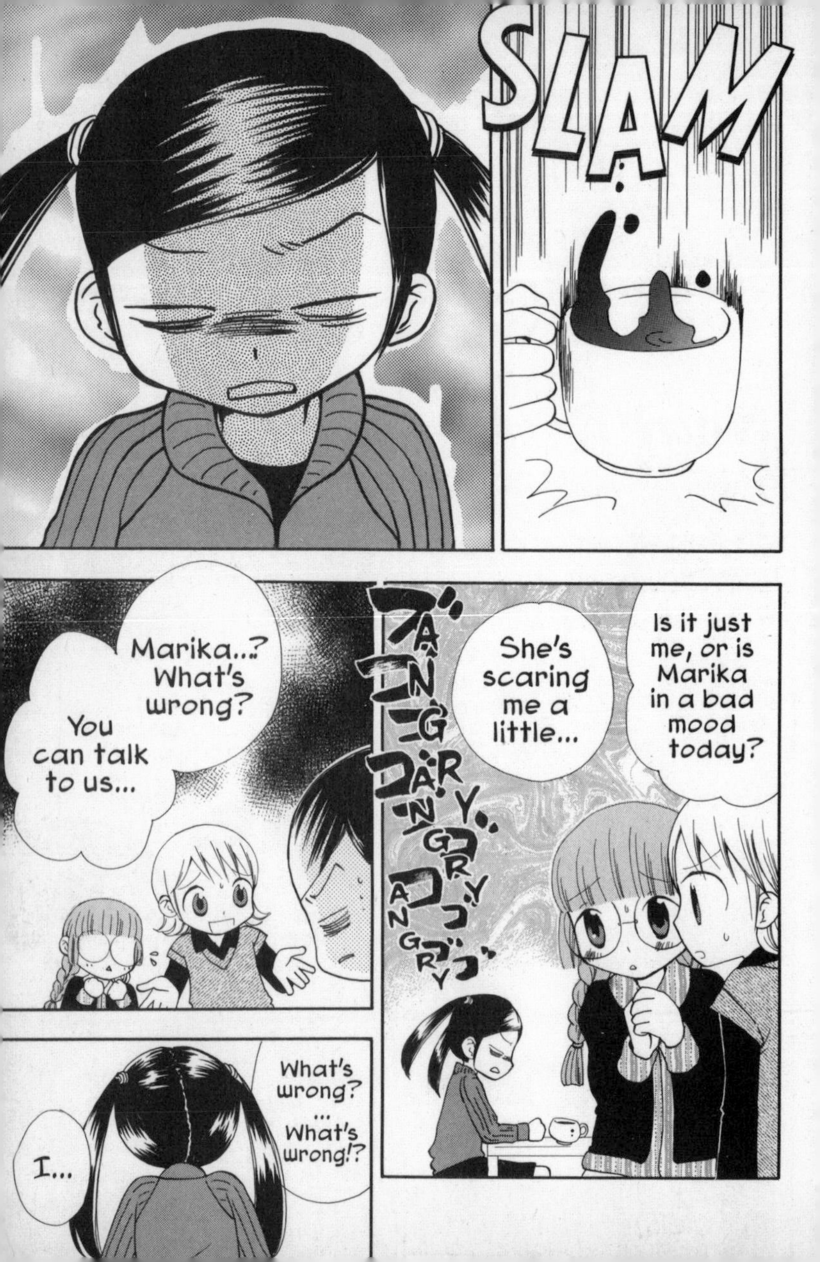
SLAM
Is it just me, or is Marika in a bad mood today?
She's scaring me a little...
ANGRY ANGRY ANGRY ANGRY
Marika...? What's wrong?
You can talk to us...
What's wrong? ... What's wrong!?
I...

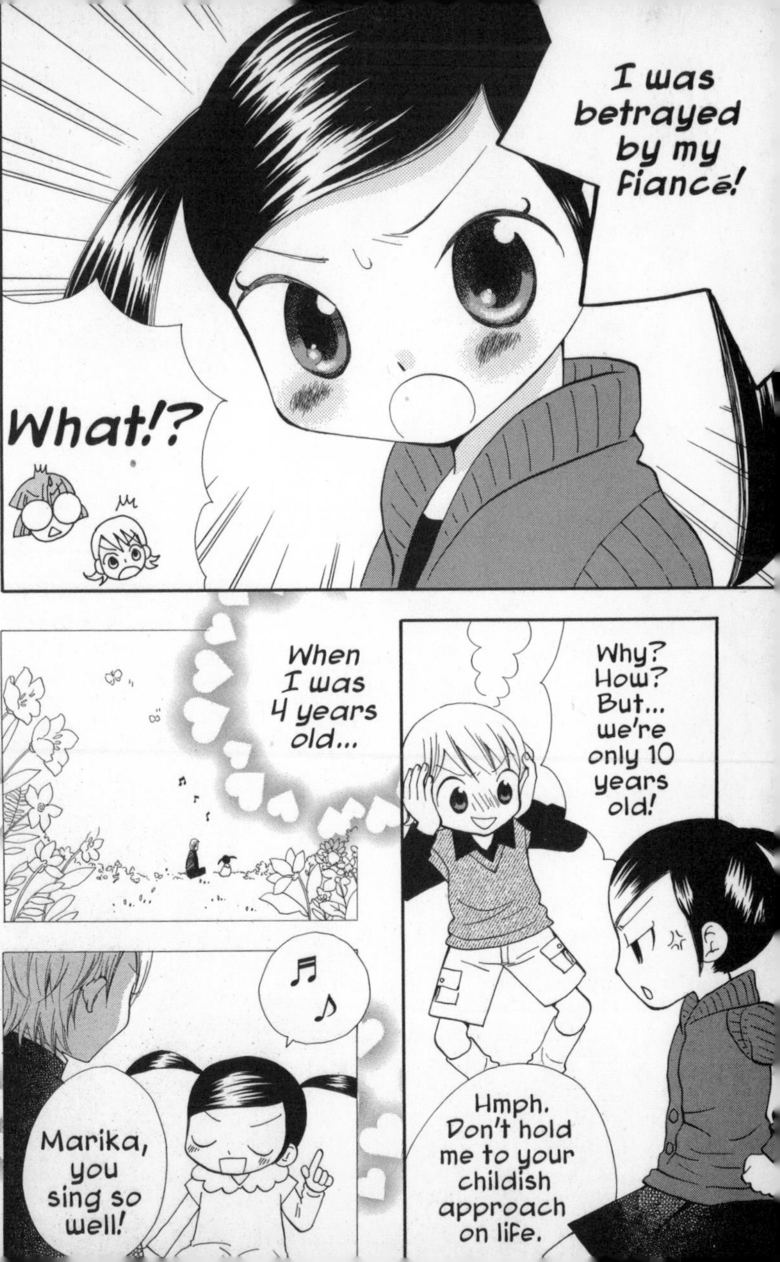
I was betrayed by my fiancé!
What!?
Why? How? But... we're only 10 years old!
Hmph. Don't hold me to your childish approach on life.
When I was 4 years old...
Marika, you sing so well!

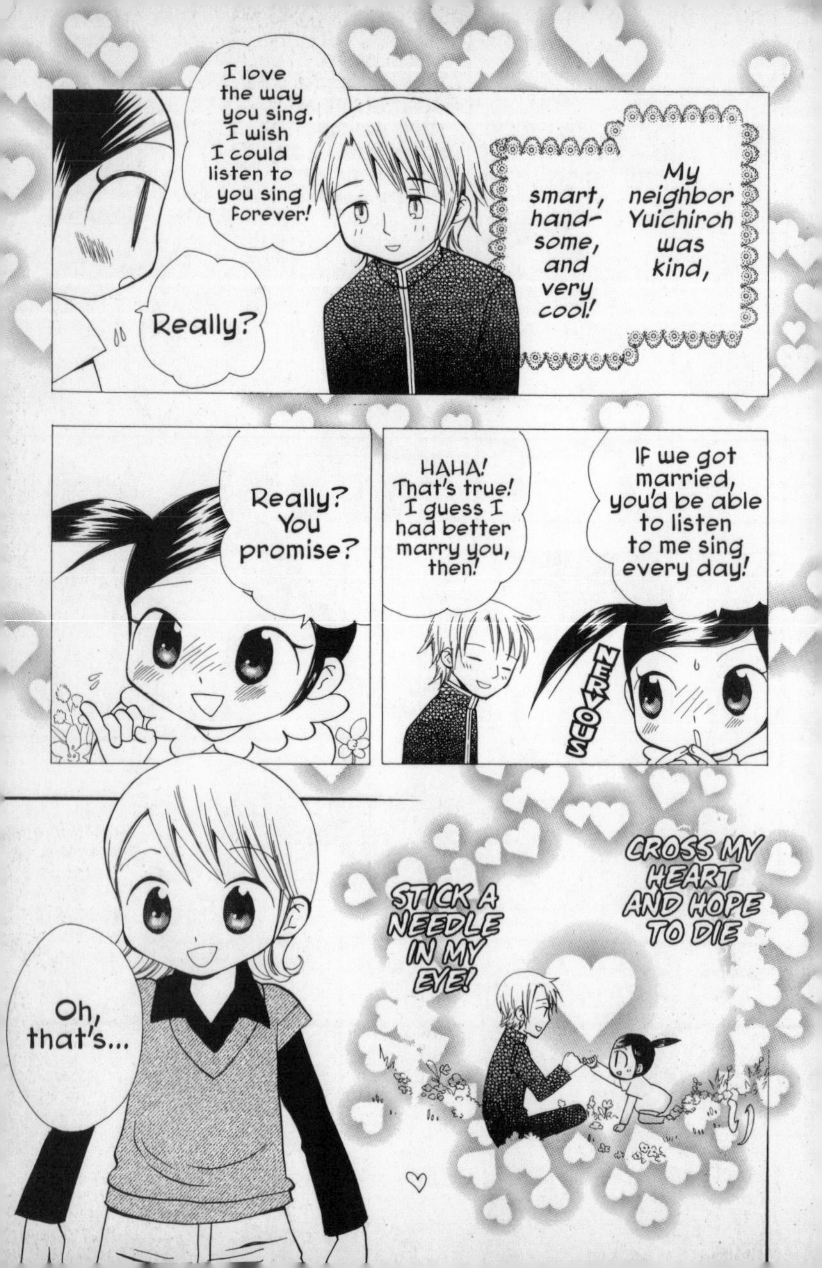
My neighbor Yuichiroh was kind, smart, hand-some, and very cool!
I love the way you sing. I wish I could listen to you sing forever!
Really?
If we got married, you'd be able to listen to me sing every day!
HAHA! That's true! I guess I had better marry you, then!
NERVOUS
Really? You promise?
CROSS MY HEART AND HOPE TO DIE
STICK A NEEDLE IN MY EYE!
Oh, that's...

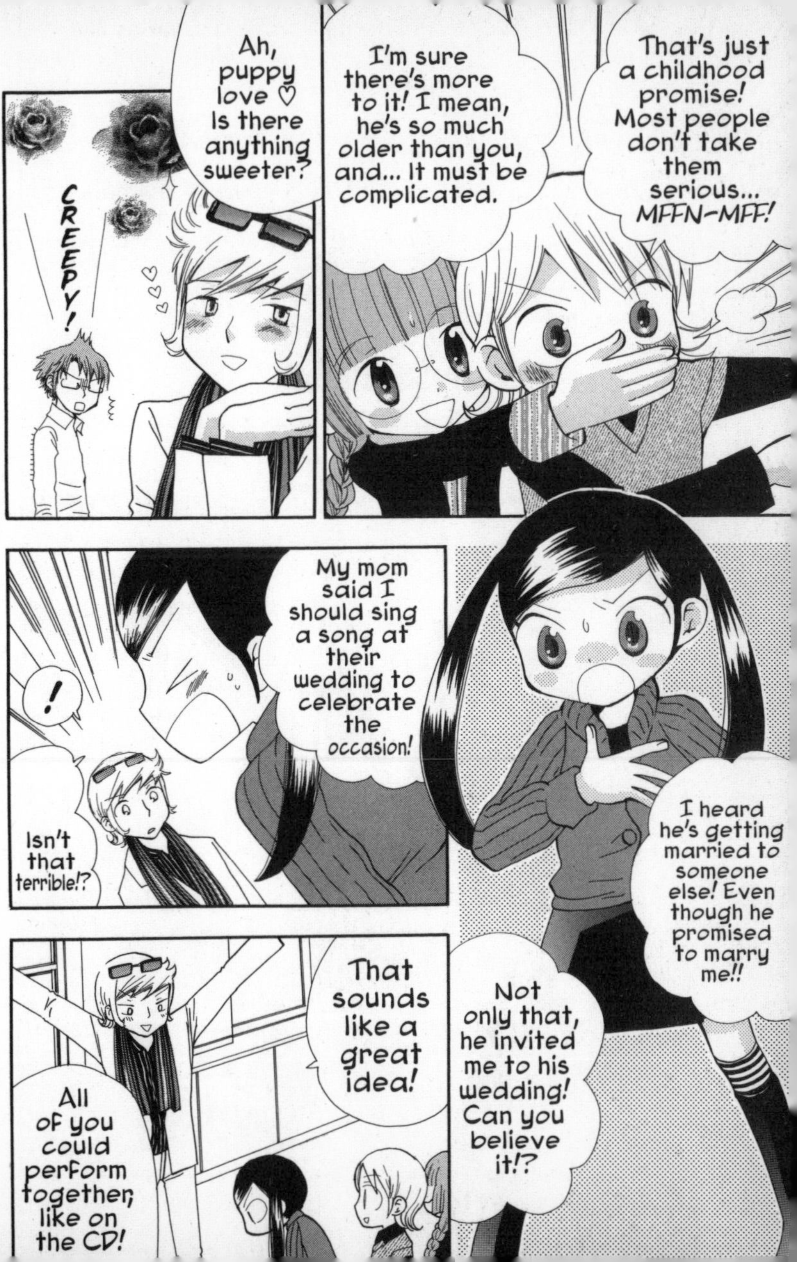

That's just a childhood promise! Most people don't take them serious... MFFN-MFF!
I'm sure there's more to it! I mean, he's so much older than you, and... It must be complicated.
Ah, puppy love ♡ Is there anything sweeter?
CREEPY!
I heard he's getting married to someone else! Even though he promised to marry me!!
Not only that, he invited me to his wedding! Can you believe it!?
My mom said I should sing a song at their wedding to celebrate the occasion!
!
Isn't that terrible!?
That sounds like a great idea!
All of you could perform together, like on the CD!

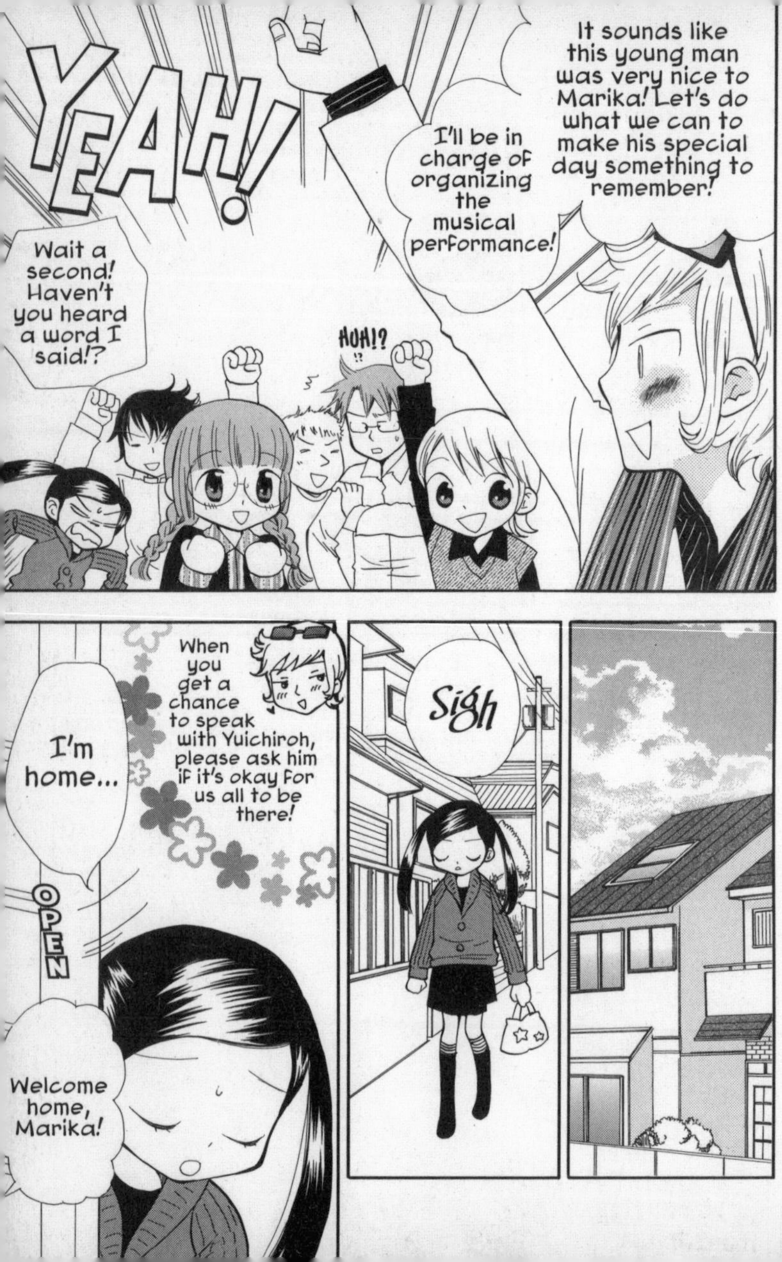
It sounds like this young man was very nice to Marika! Let's do what we can to make his special day something to remember!
I'll be in charge of organizing the musical performance!
YEAH!
HUH!?
Wait a second! Haven't you heard a word I said!?
Sigh
When you get a chance to speak with Yuichiroh, please ask him if it's okay for us all to be there!
I'm home...
OPEN
Welcome home, Marika!

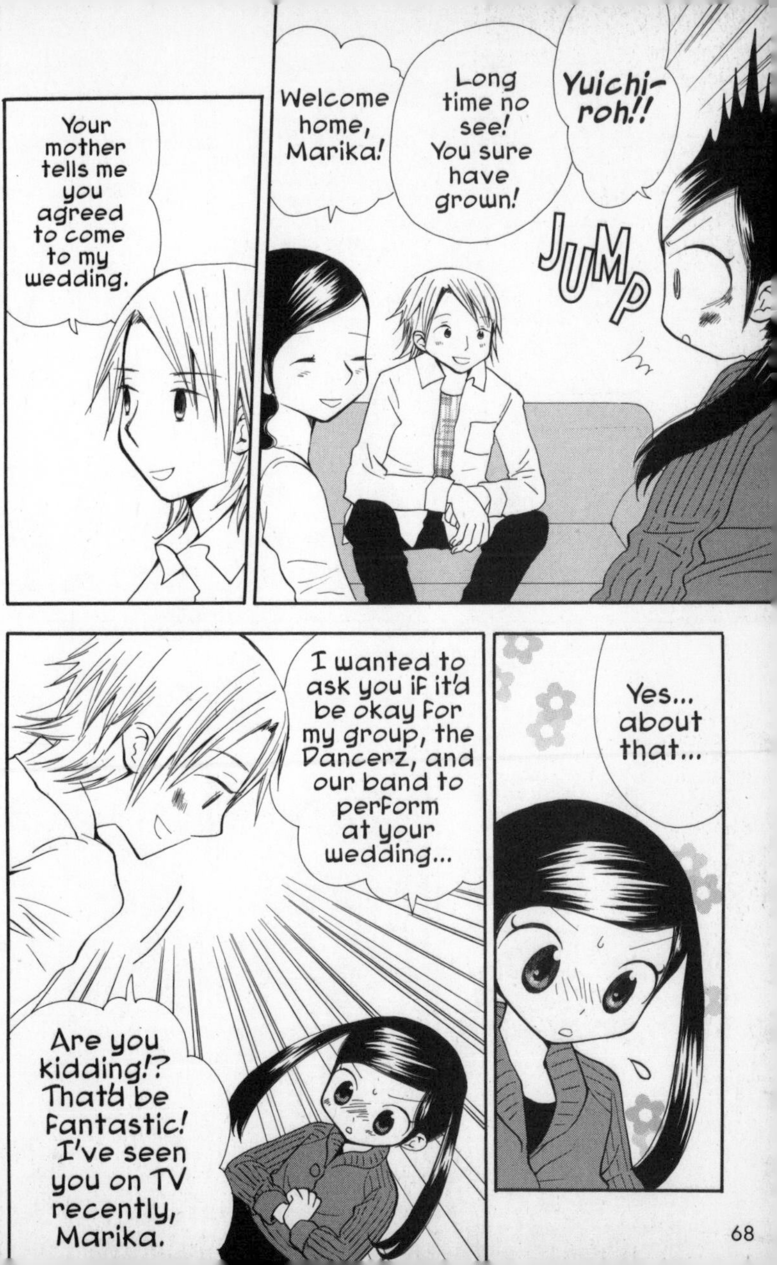

Yuichi-roh!!
JUMP
Long time no see! You sure have grown!
Welcome home, Marika!
Your mother tells me you agreed to come to my wedding.
Yes... about that...
I wanted to ask you if it'd be okay for my group, the Dancerz, and our band to perform at your wedding...
Are you kidding!? That'd be fantastic! I've seen you on TV recently, Marika.

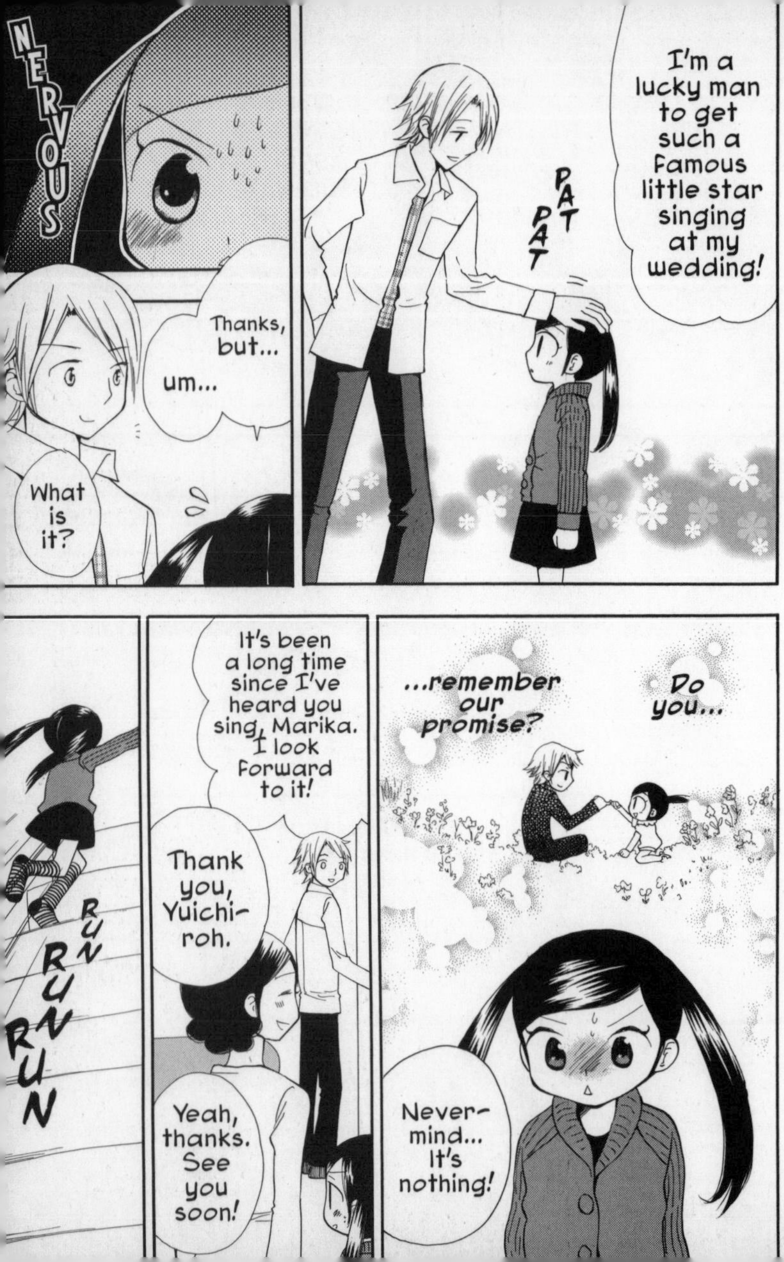
I'm a lucky man to get such a famous little star singing at my wedding!
PAT PAT
NERVOUS
Thanks, but...
um...
What is it?
Do you...
...remember our promise?
Never-mind... It's nothing!
It's been a long time since I've heard you sing, Marika. I look forward to it!
Thank you, Yuichi-roh.
Yeah, thanks. See you soon!
RUN RUN RUN

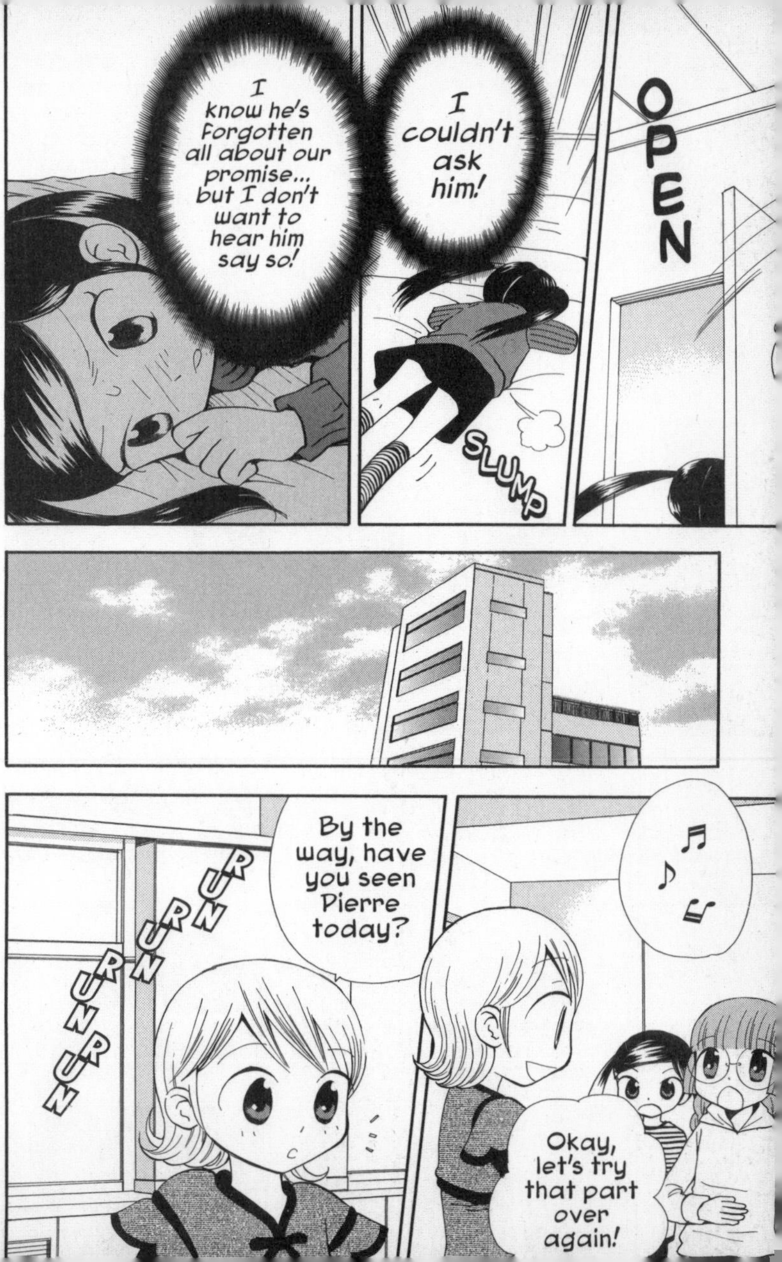
OPEN
I couldn't ask him!
SLUMP
I know he's forgotten all about our promise... but I don't want to hear him say so!
Okay, let's try that part over again!
By the way, have you seen Pierre today?
RUN RUN RUN RUN RUN

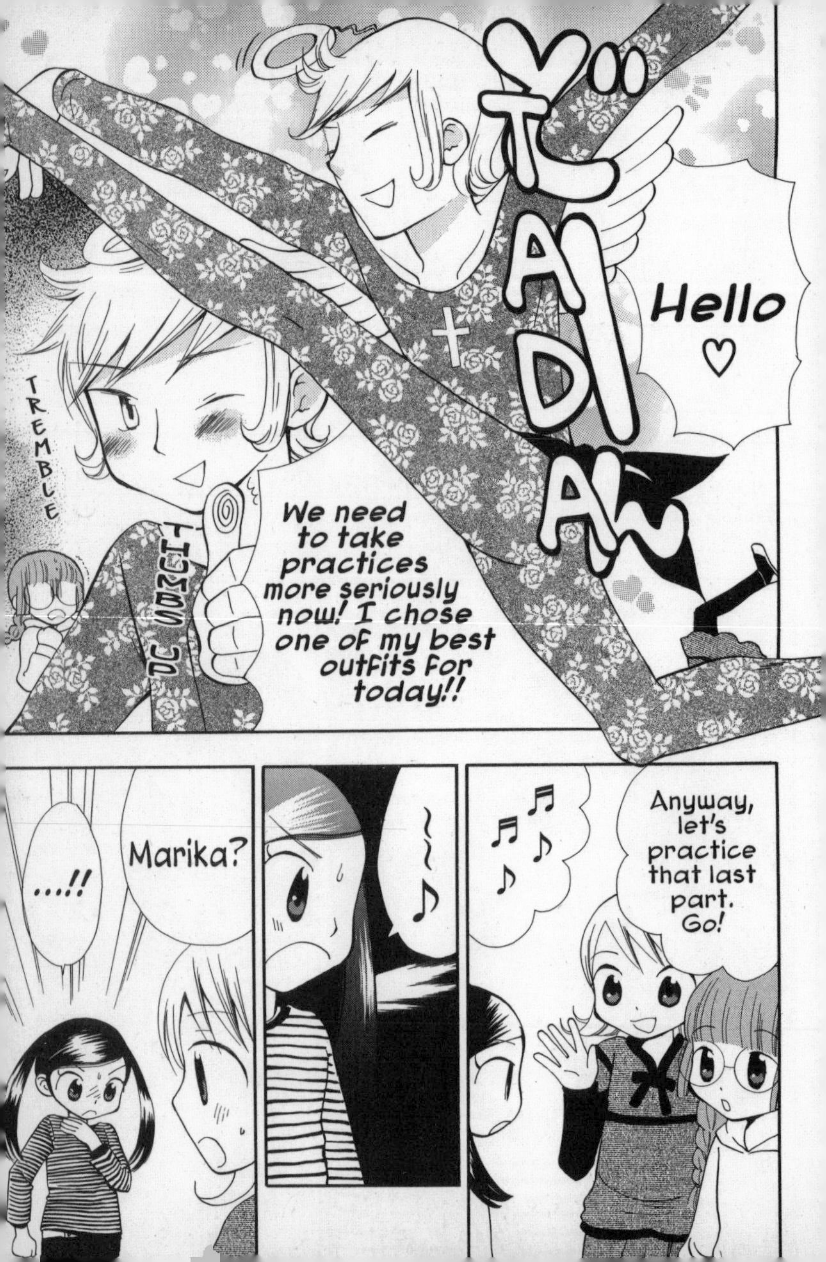
♥TADA
Hello ♥
We need to take practices more seriously now! I chose one of my best outfits for today!!
THUMBS UP
TREMBLE
Anyway, let's practice that last part. Go!
♪ ♪ ♪ ♪
~~♪
Marika?
...!!

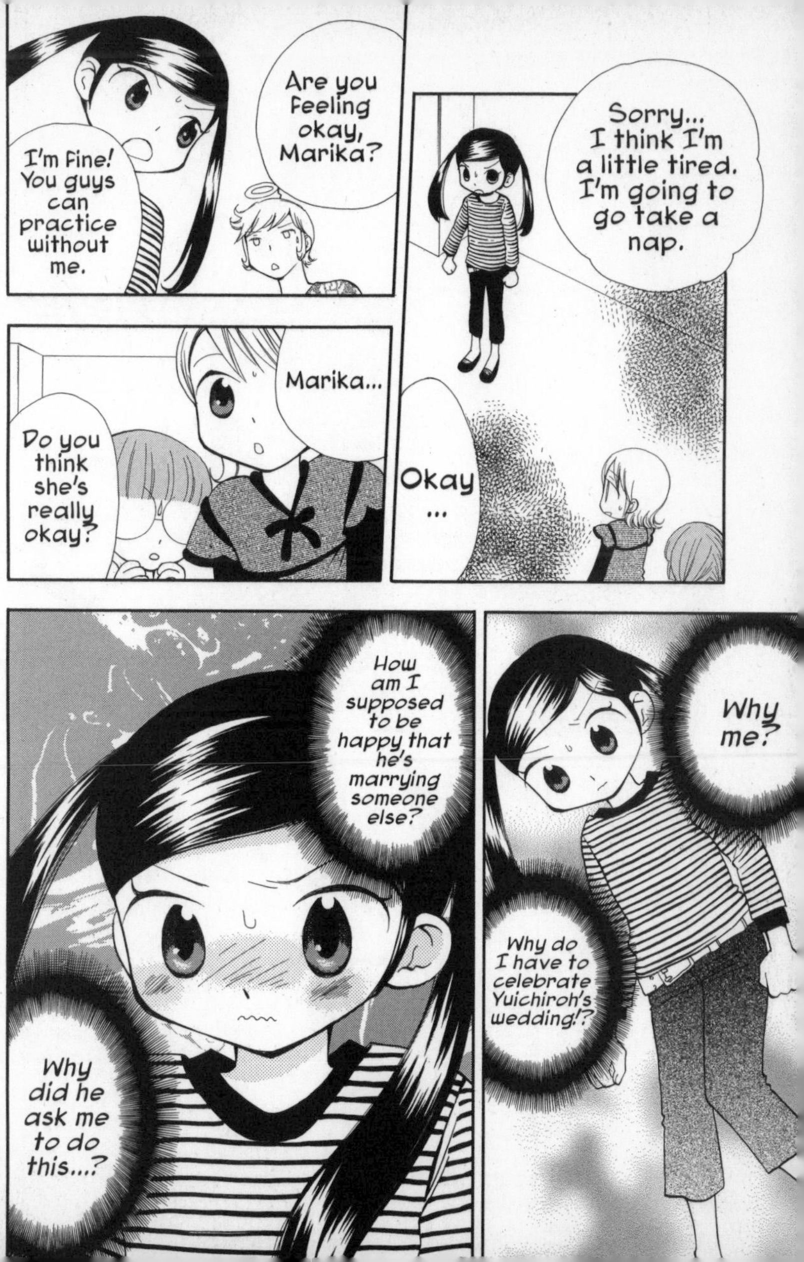
Sorry... I think I'm a little tired. I'm going to go take a nap.
Okay ...
Are you feeling okay, Marika?
I'm fine! You guys can practice without me.
Marika...
Do you think she's really okay?
Why me?
Why do I have to celebrate Yuichiroh's wedding!?
How am I supposed to be happy that he's marrying someone else?
Why did he ask me to do this...?

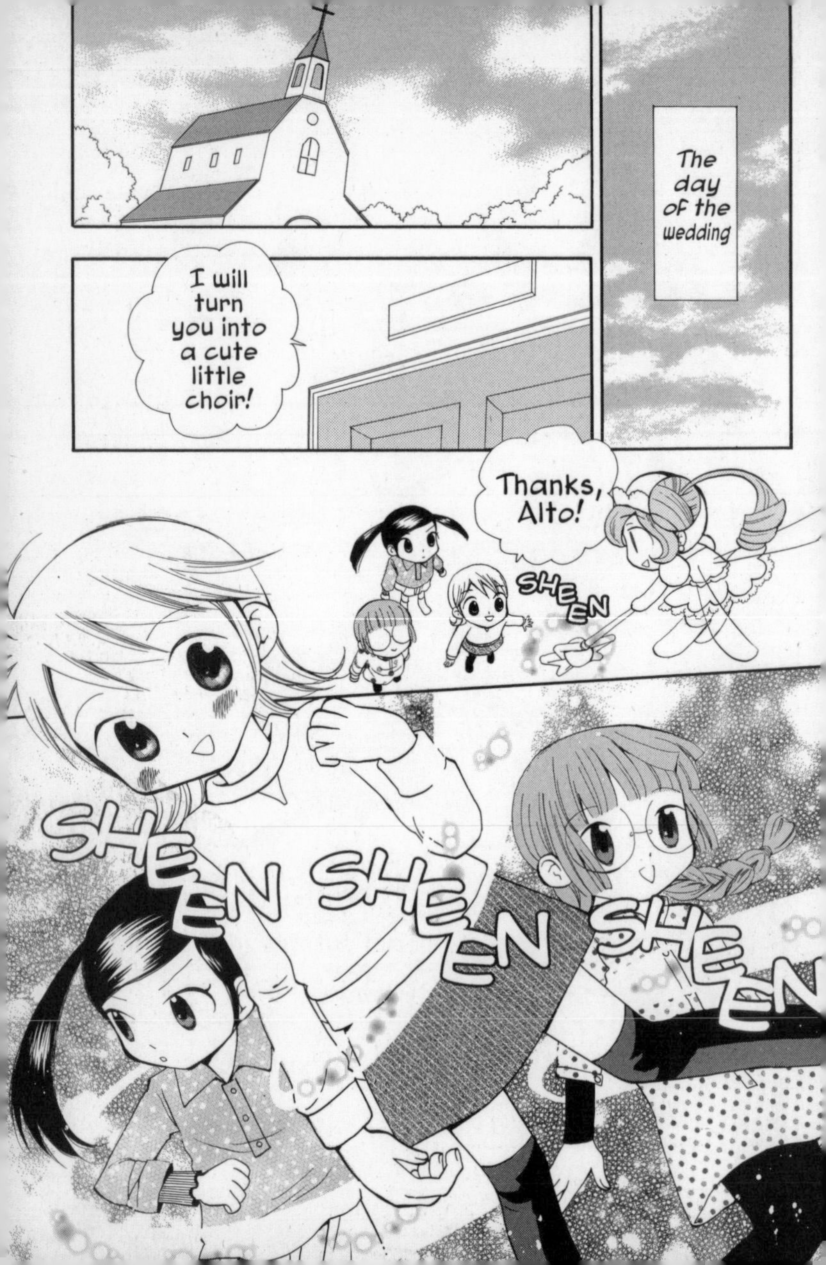
The day of the wedding
I will turn you into a cute little choir!
Thanks, Alto!
SHEEN
SHEEN
SHEEN
SHEEN

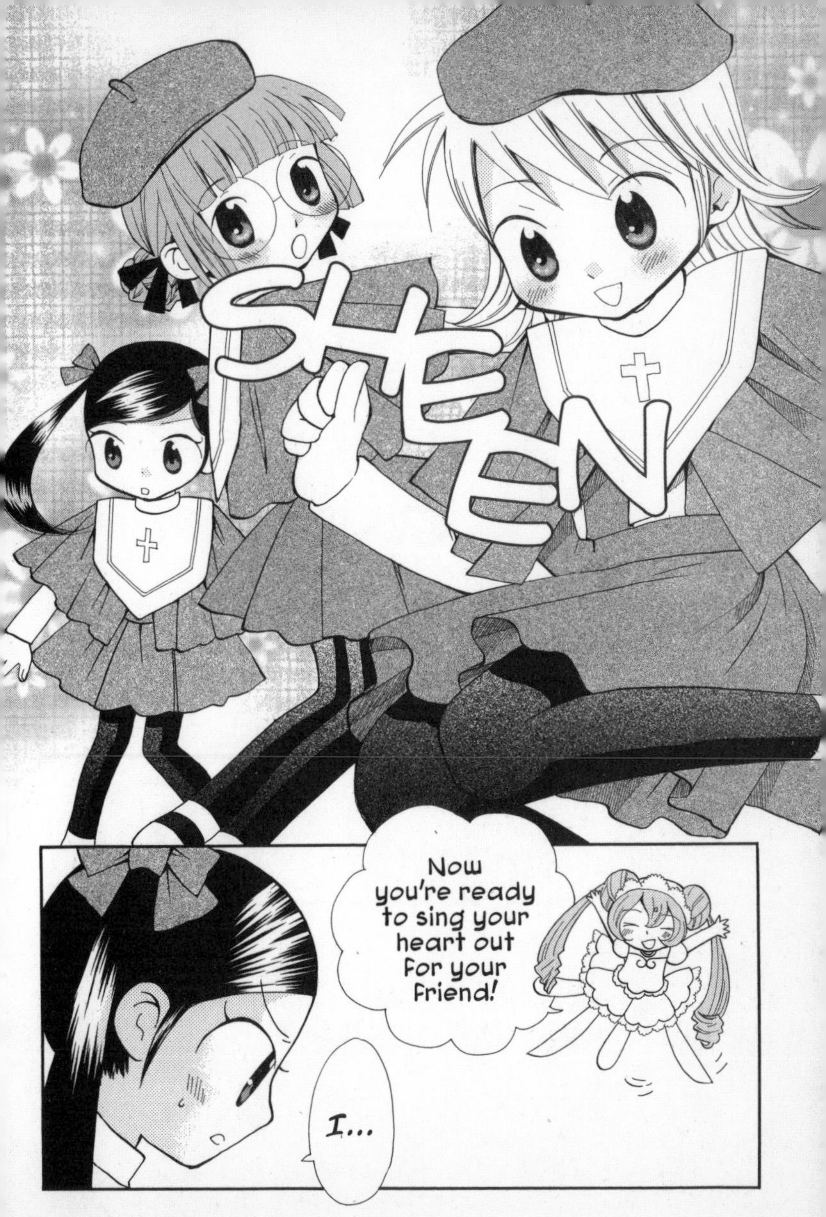
SHEEN
Now you're ready to sing your heart out for your friend!
I...

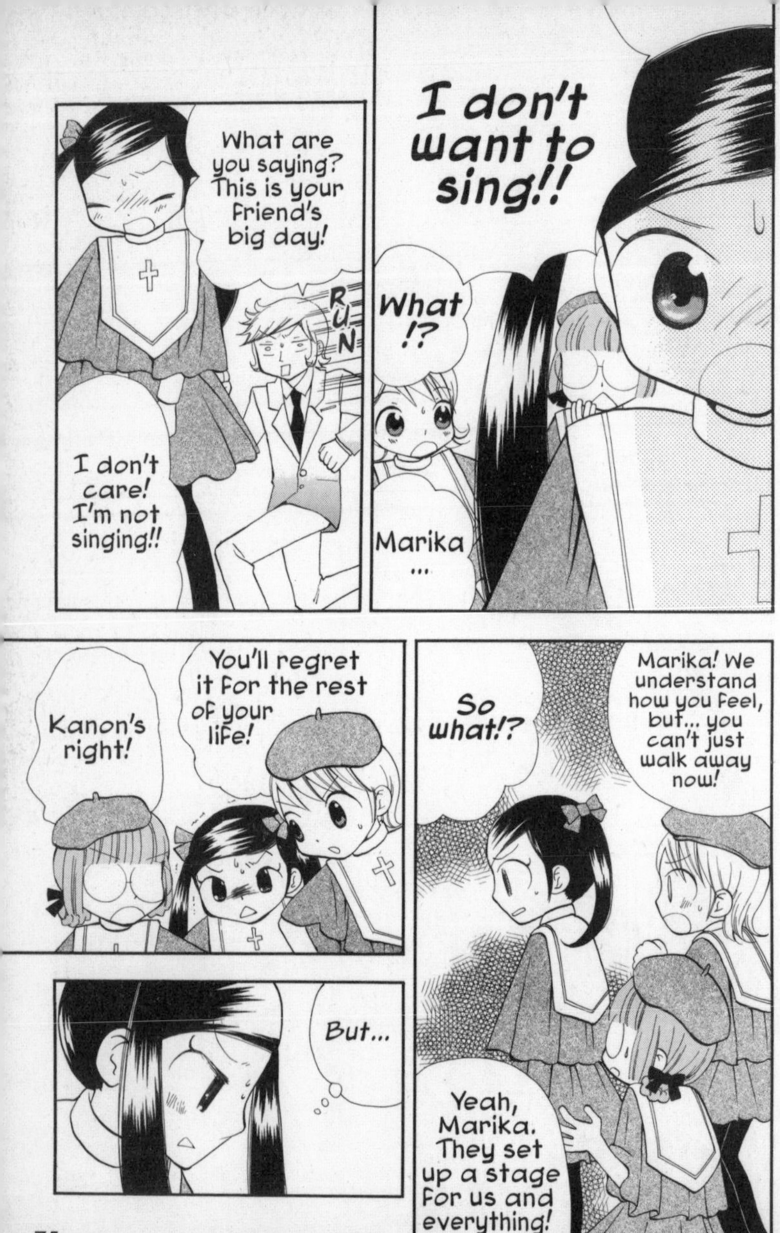
I don't want to sing!!
What !?
Marika ...
What are you saying? This is your friend's big day!
RUN
I don't care! I'm not singing!!
Marika! We understand how you feel, but... you can't just walk away now!
So what!?
Yeah, Marika. They set up a stage for us and everything!
You'll regret it for the rest of your life!
Kanon's right!
But...

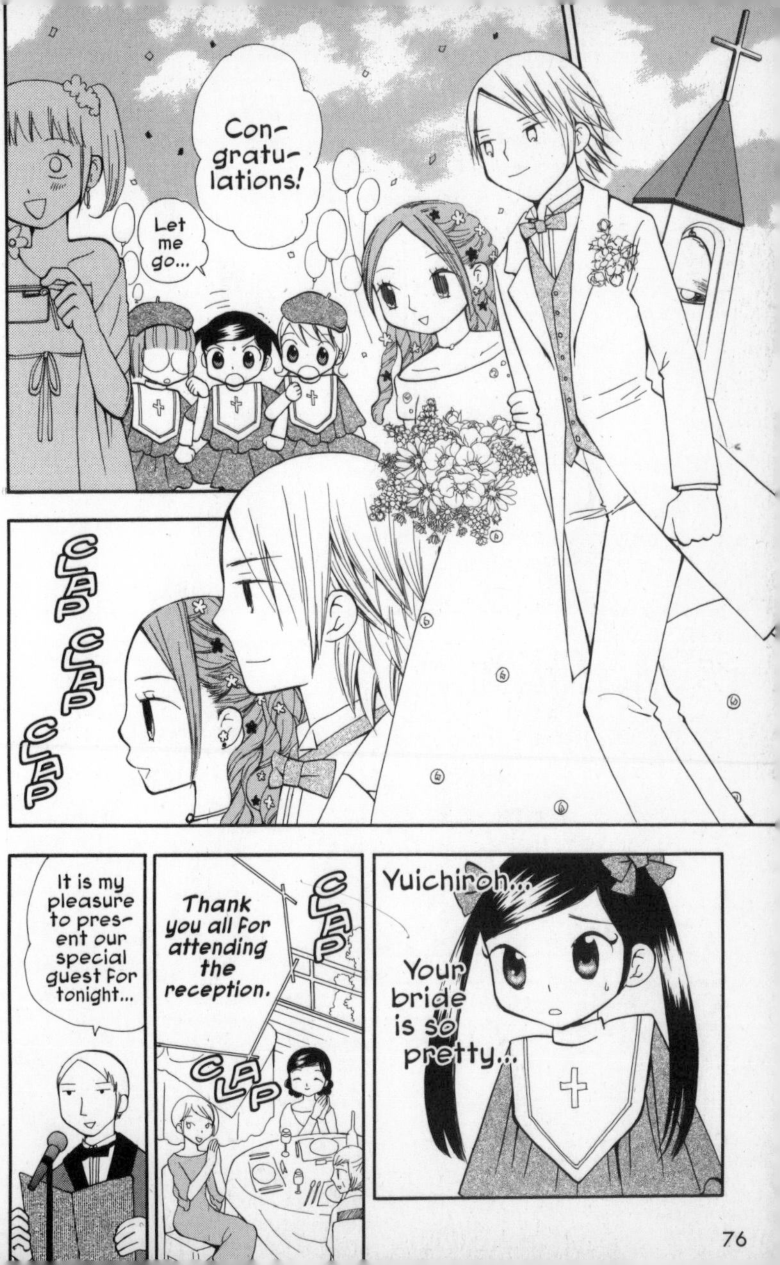
Con-gratu-lations!
Let me go...
CLAP CLAP CLAP
Yuichiroh...
Your bride is so pretty...
CLAP
Thank you all for attending the reception.
CLAP
It is my pleasure to present our special guest for tonight...

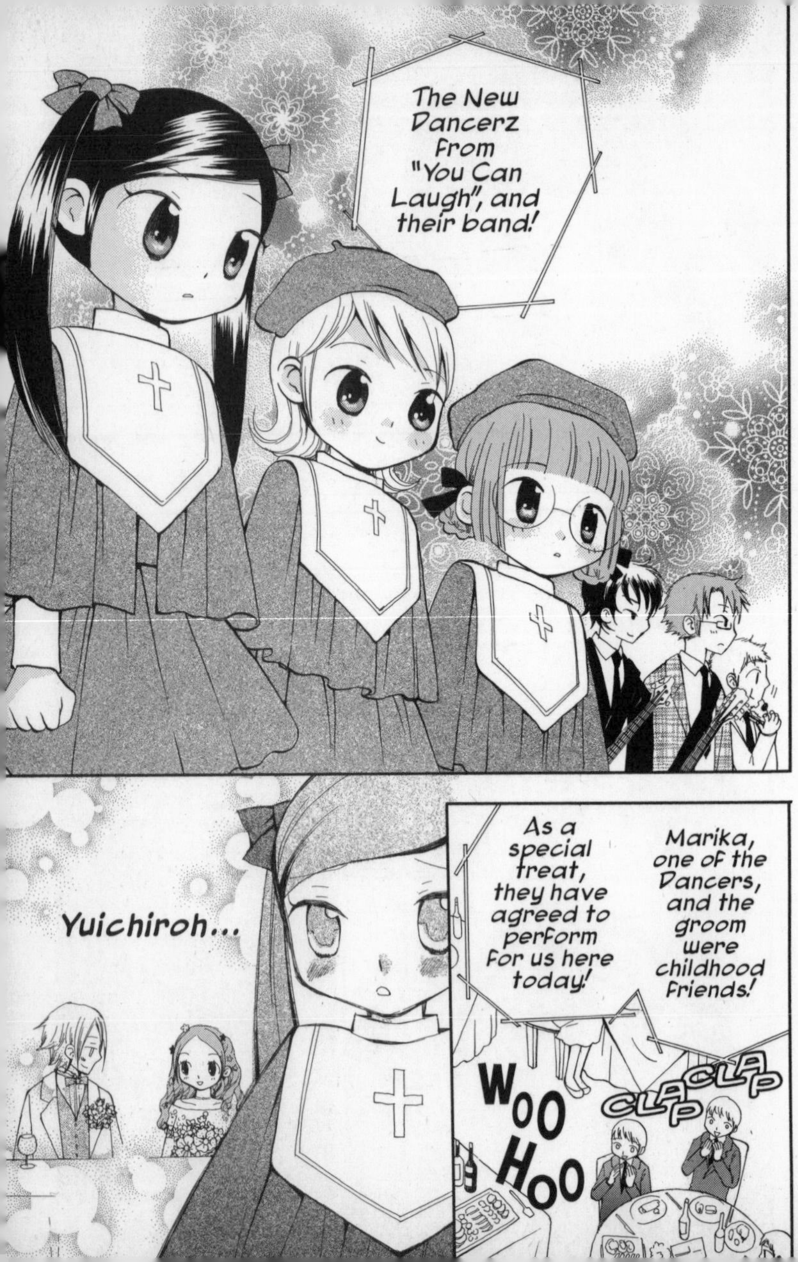
The New Dancerz from "You Can Laugh", and their band!
As a special treat, they have agreed to perform for us here today!
Marika, one of the Dancers, and the groom were childhood friends!
WOO HOO
CLAP CLAP
Yuichiroh...

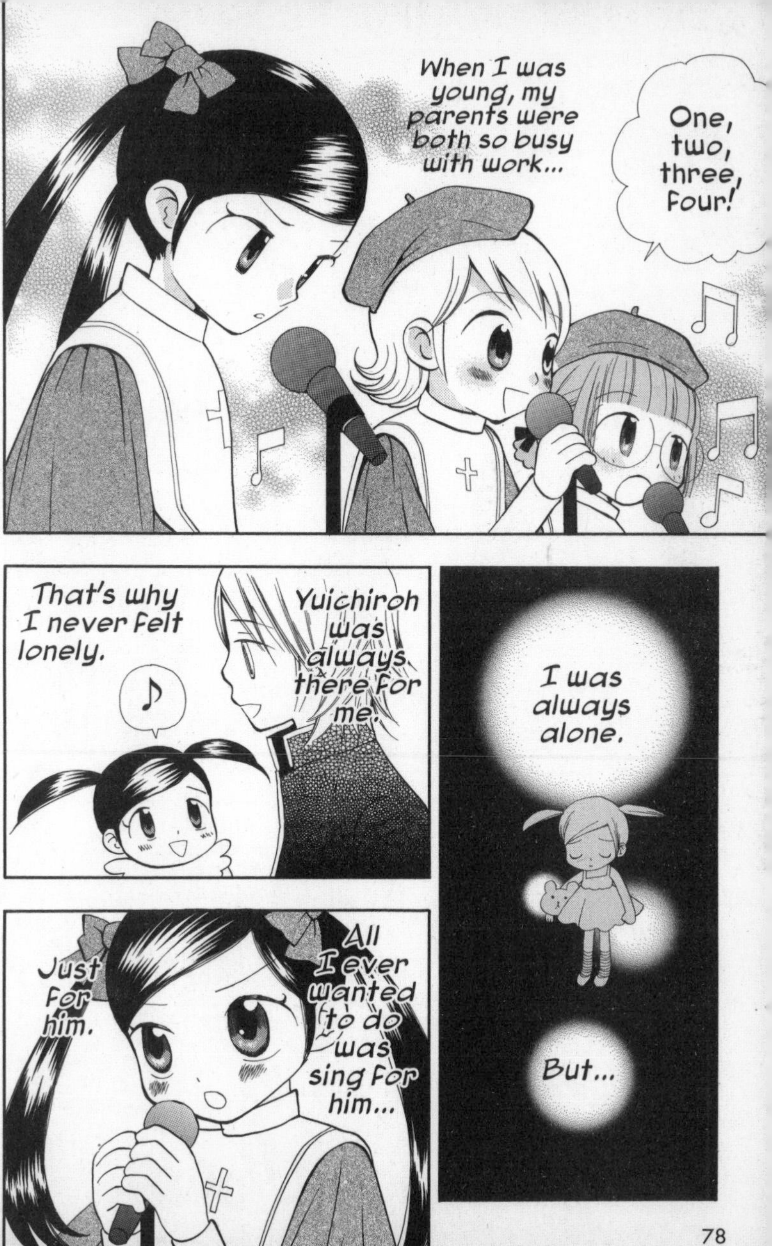
One, two, three, four!
When I was young, my parents were both so busy with work...
I was always alone.
But...
Yuichiroh was always there for me.
♪
That's why I never felt lonely.
All I ever wanted to do was sing for him...
Just for him.

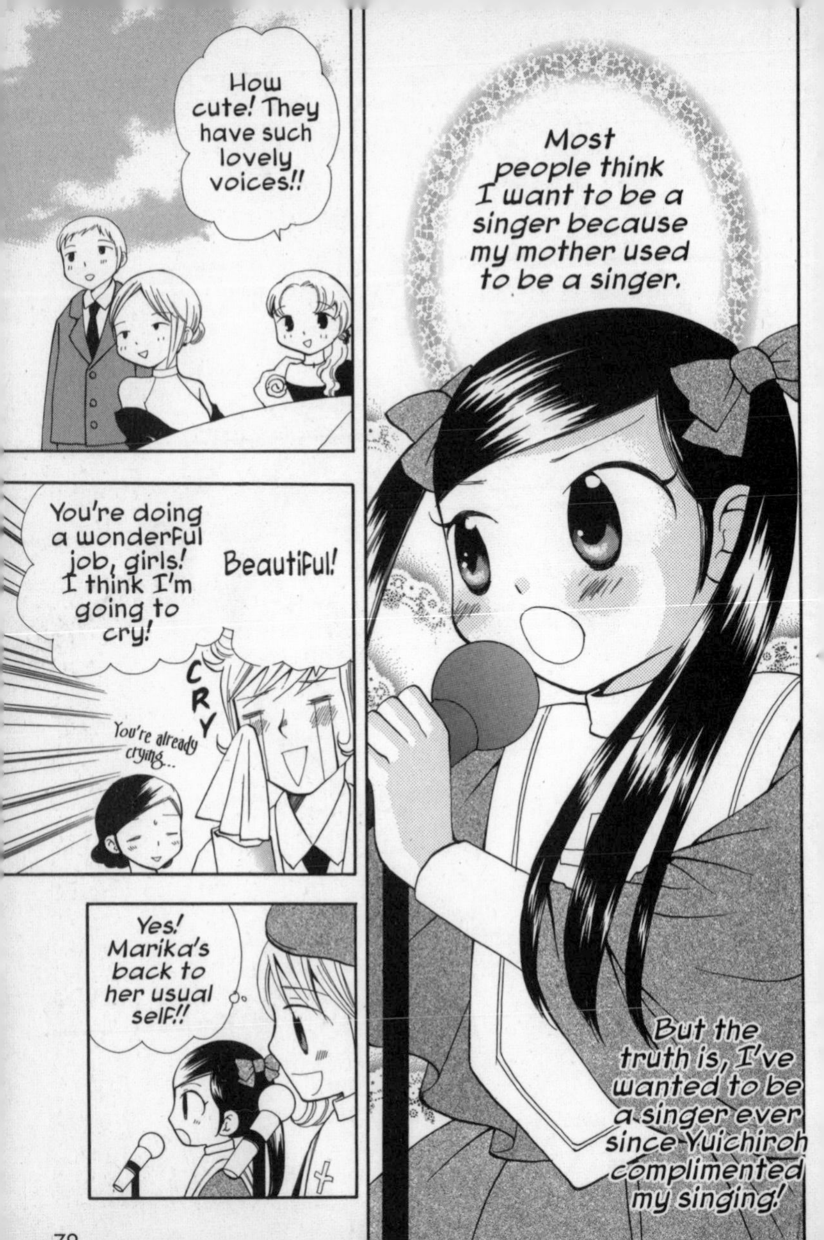
Most people think I want to be a singer because my mother used to be a singer.
But the truth is, I've wanted to be a singer ever since Yuichiroh complimented my singing!
How cute! They have such lovely voices!!
Beautiful!
You're doing a wonderful job, girls! I think I'm going to cry!
CRY
You're already crying...
Yes! Marika's back to her usual self!!

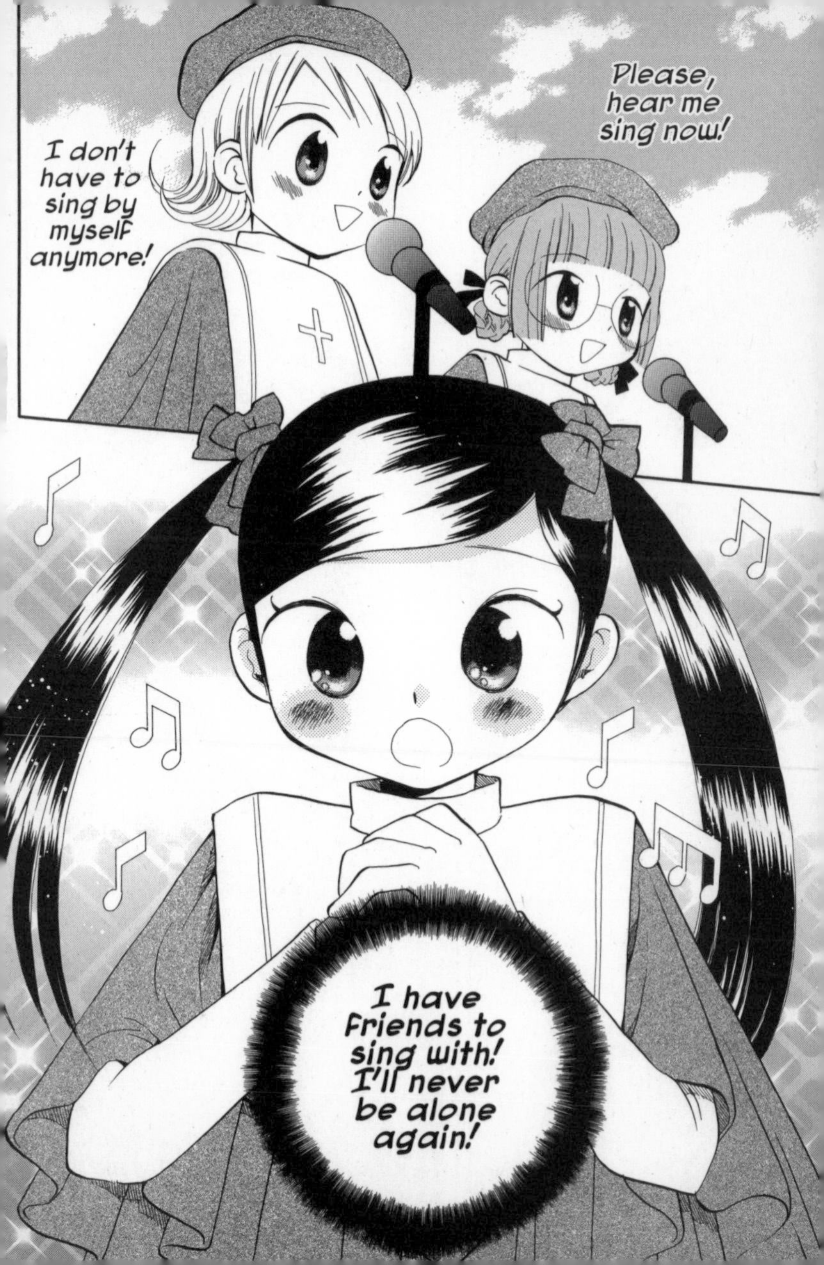
Please, hear me sing now!
I don't have to sing by myself anymore!
I have friends to sing with! I'll never be alone again!

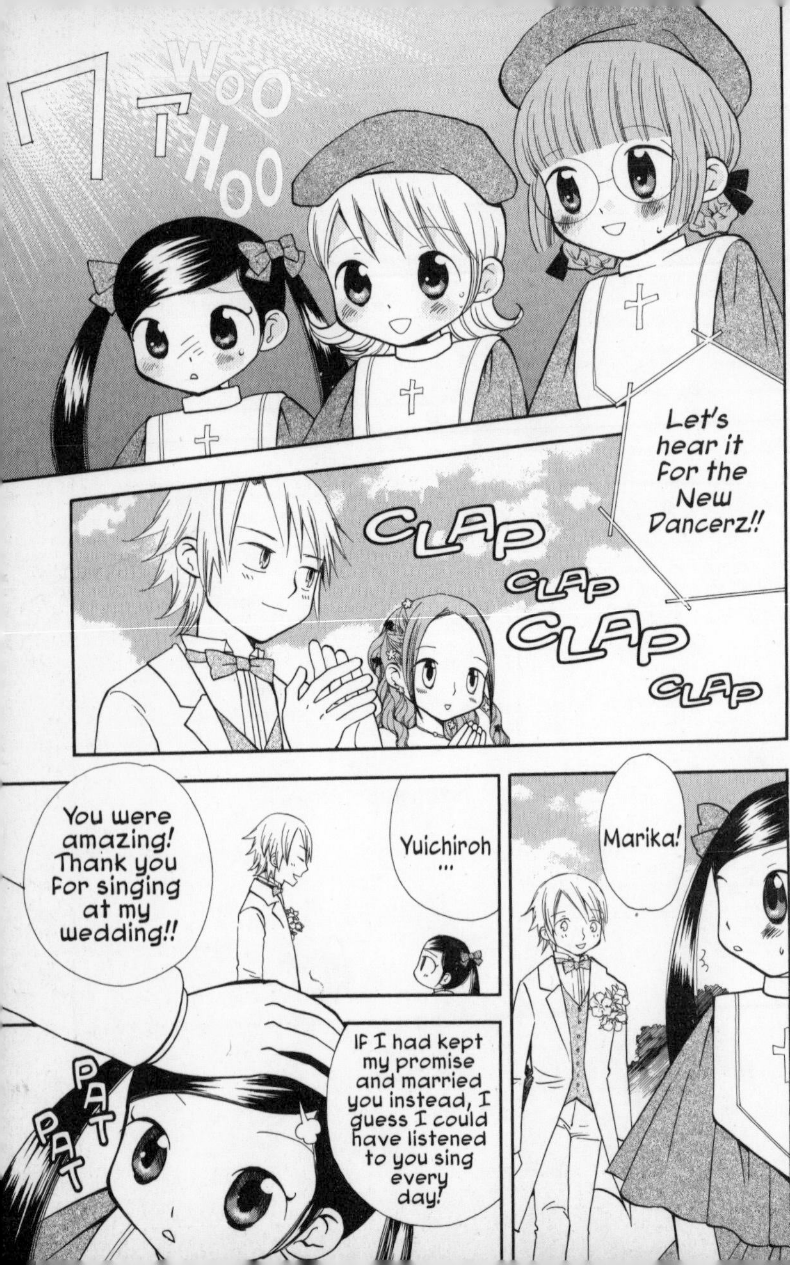
WOO HOO
Let's hear it for the New Dancerz!!
CLAP
CLAP
CLAP
CLAP
Marika!
Yuichiroh ...
You were amazing! Thank you for singing at my wedding!!
If I had kept my promise and married you instead, I guess I could have listened to you sing every day!
PAT PAT

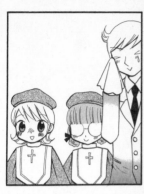

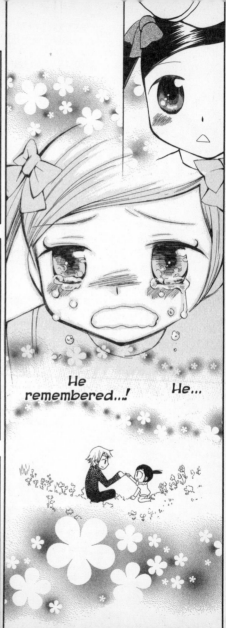

He... He remembered...!

You're going to be a big star one day.

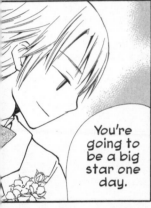

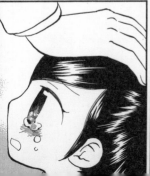

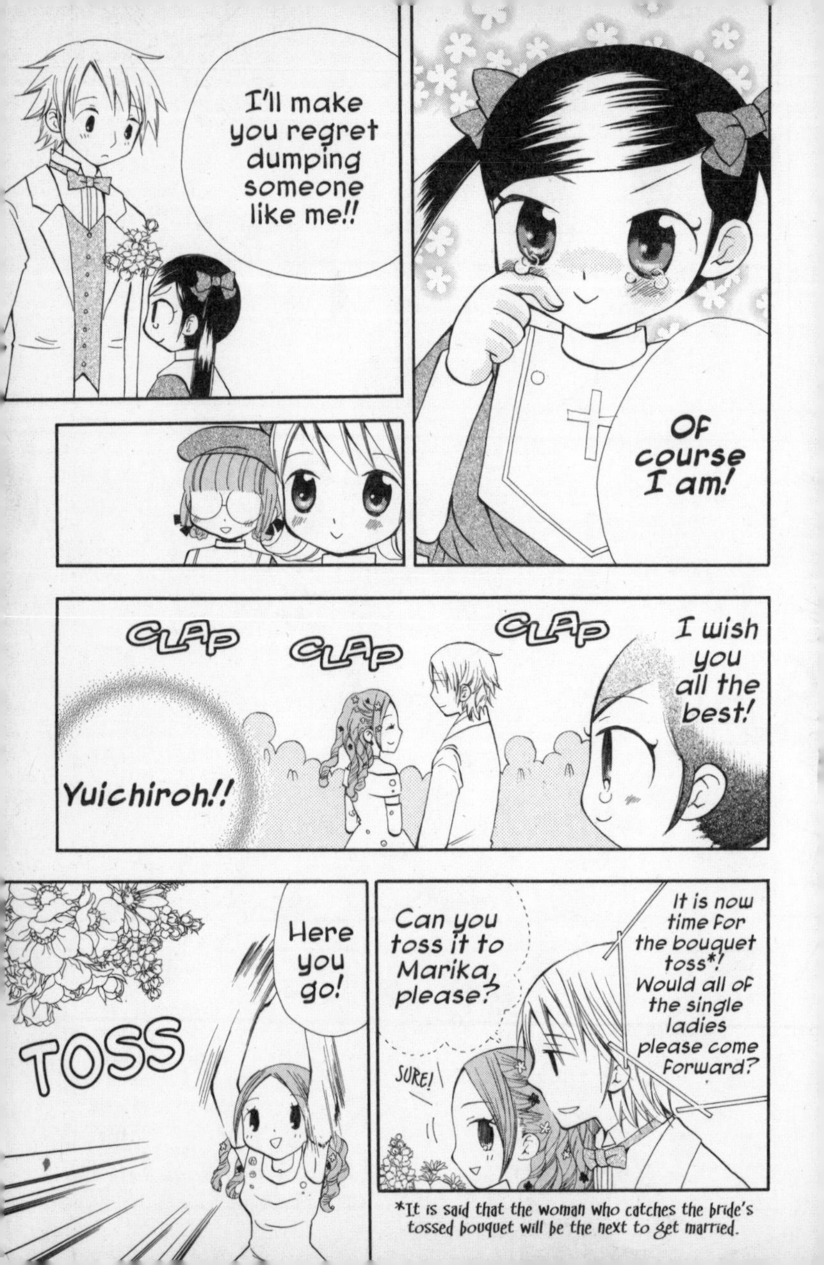
Of course I am!
I'll make you regret dumping someone like me!!
I wish you all the best!
CLAP
CLAP
CLAP
Yuichiroh!!
It is now time for the bouquet toss*! Would all of the single ladies please come forward?
Can you toss it to Marika, please?
SURE!
Here you go!
TOSS

*It is said that the woman who catches the bride's tossed bouquet will be the next to get married.

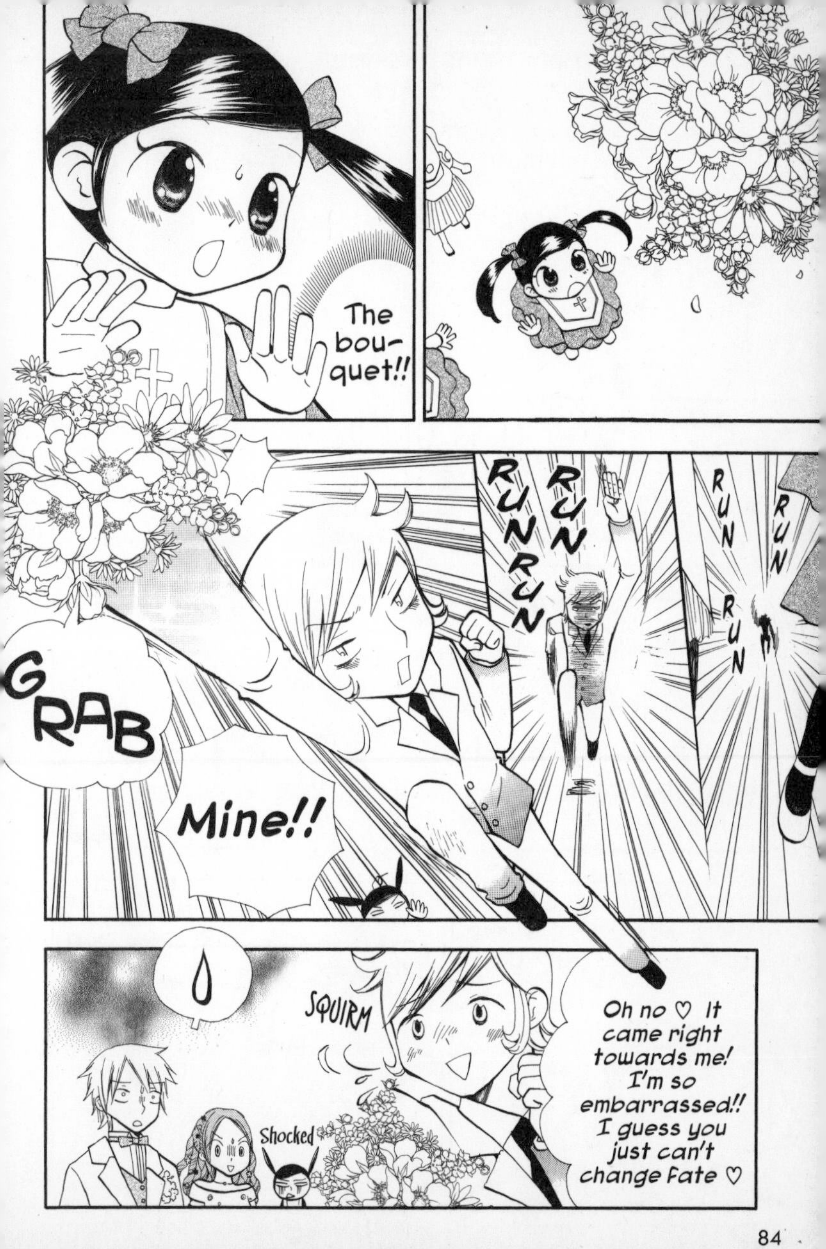
The bou-quet!!
RUN RUN RUN RUN
RUNRUNRUN RUN
GRAB
Mine!!
Oh no ♡ It came right towards me! I'm so embarrassed!! I guess you just can't change fate ♡
SQUIRM
Shocked

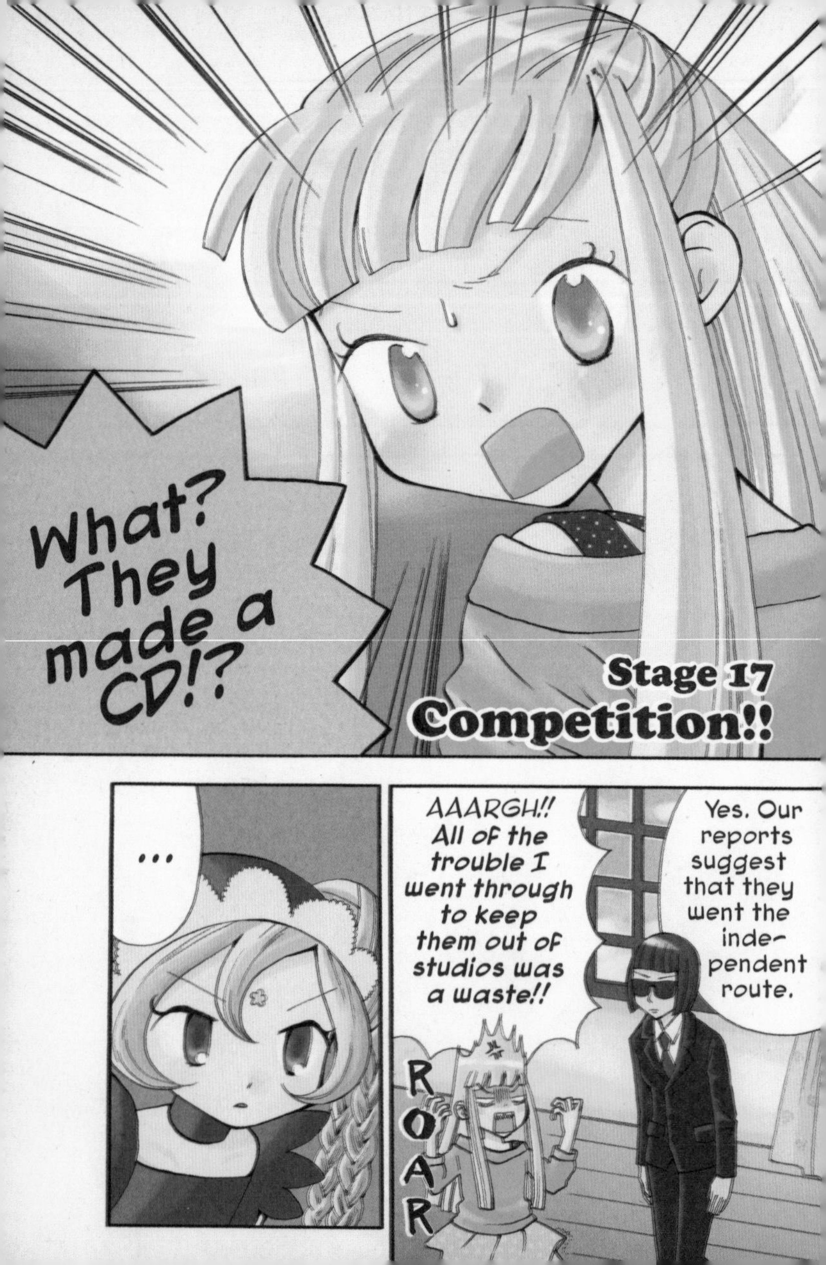
What? They made a CD!?
Stage 17
Competition!!
Yes. Our reports suggest that they went the inde-pendent route.
AAARGH!! All of the trouble I went through to keep them out of studios was a waste!!
ROAR
...

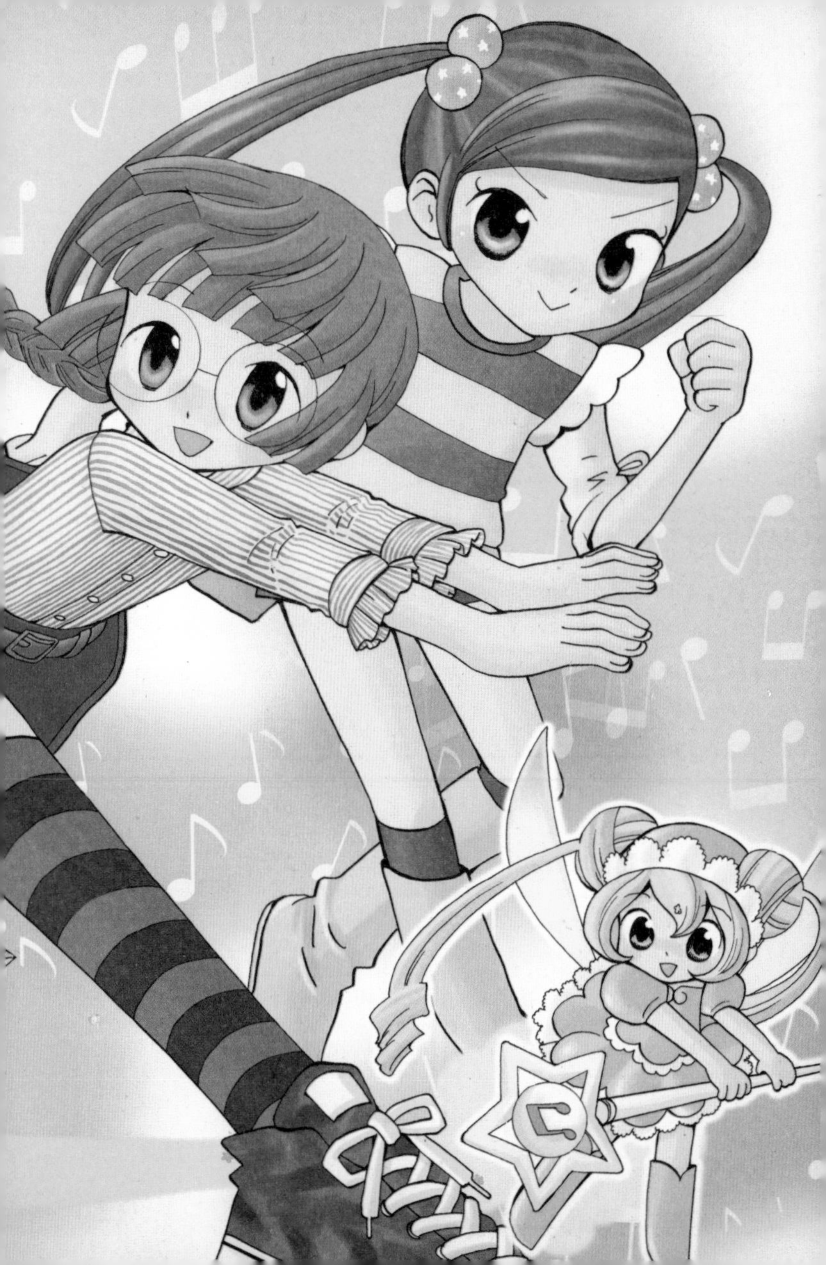

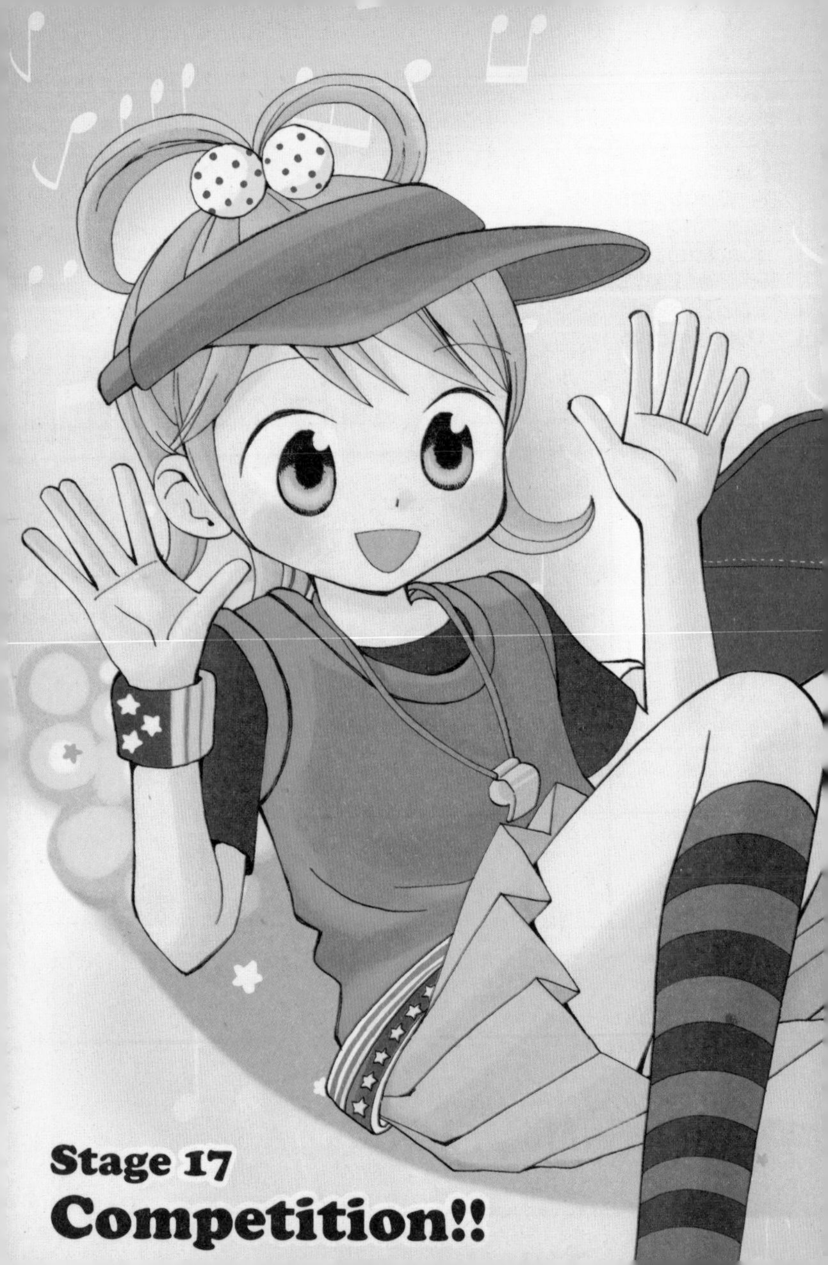

Stage 17
Competition!!

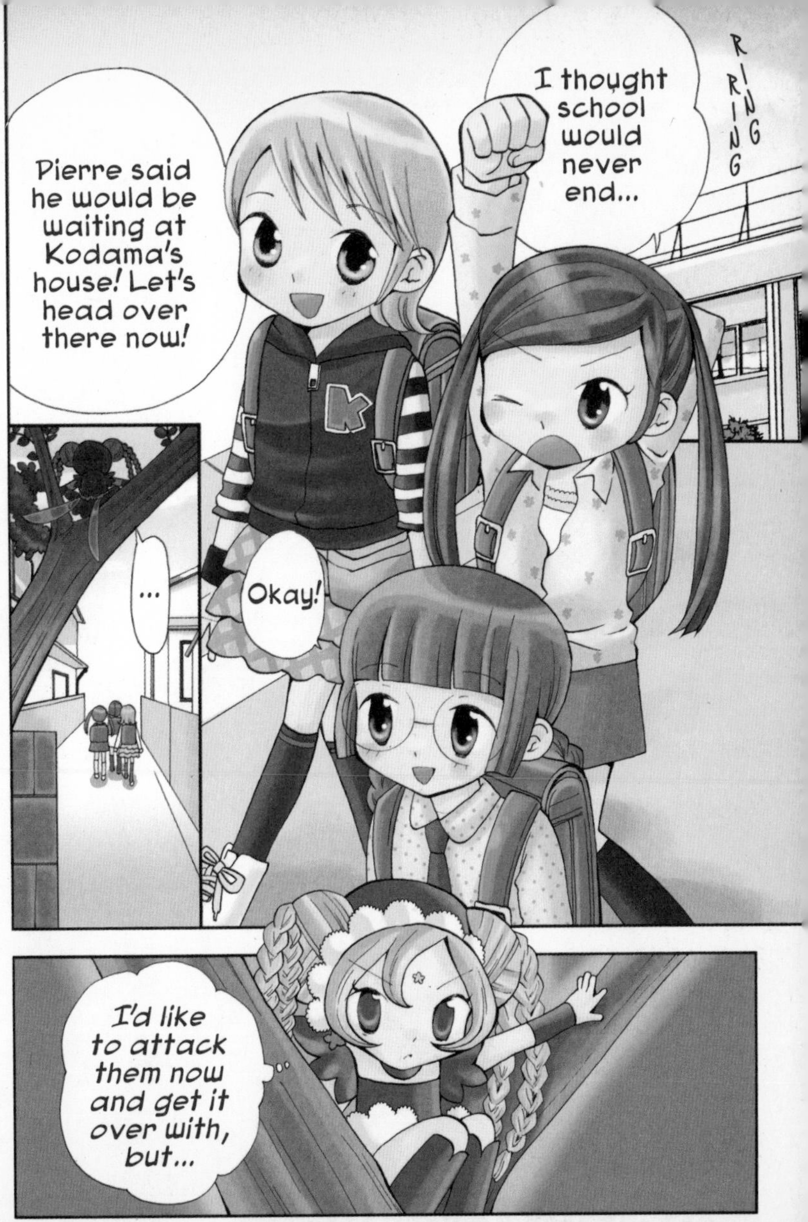
RING RING
I thought school would never end...
Pierre said he would be waiting at Kodama's house! Let's head over there now!
Okay!
...
I'd like to attack them now and get it over with, but...

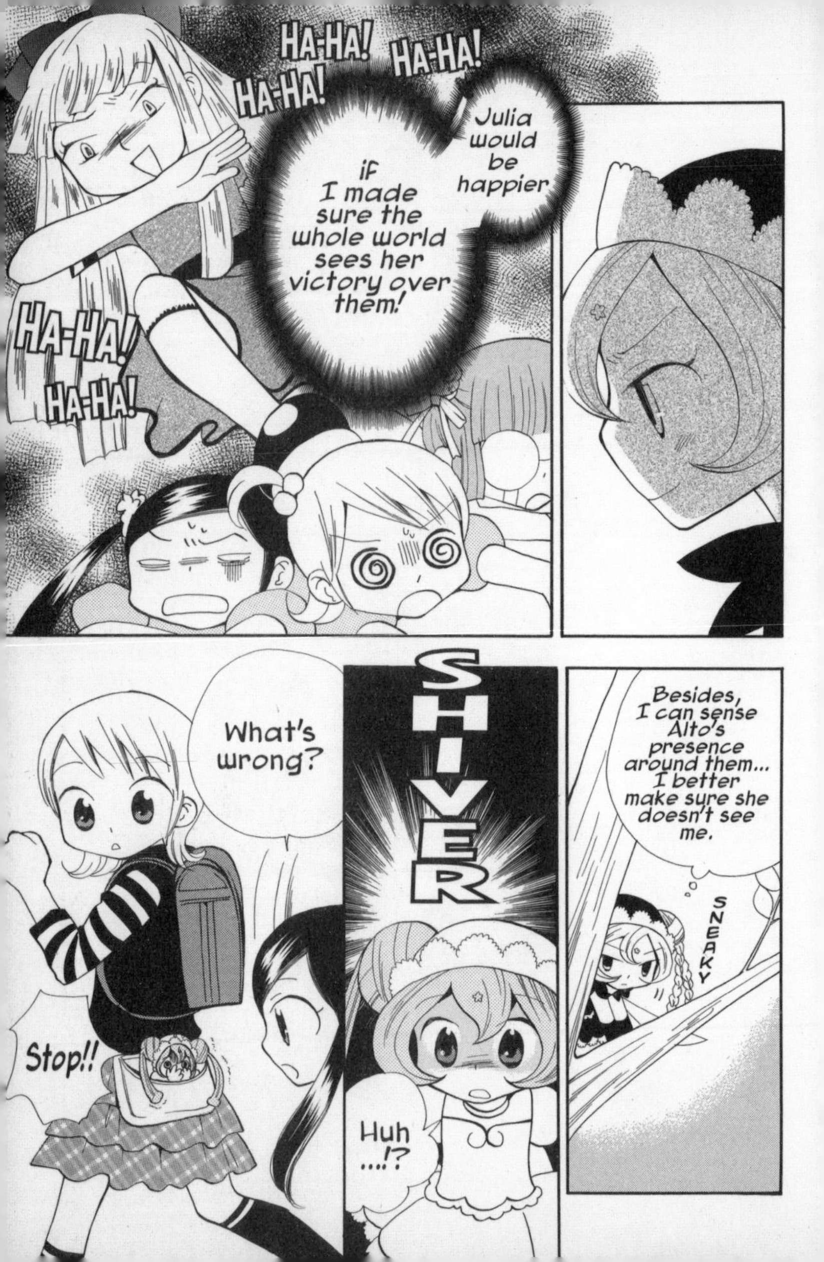
HA-HA!
HA-HA!
HA-HA!
Julia would be happier if I made sure the whole world sees her victory over them!
HA-HA!
HA-HA!
Besides, I can sense Alto's presence around them... I better make sure she doesn't see me.
SNEAKY
SHIVER
Huh ...!?
What's wrong?
Stop!!

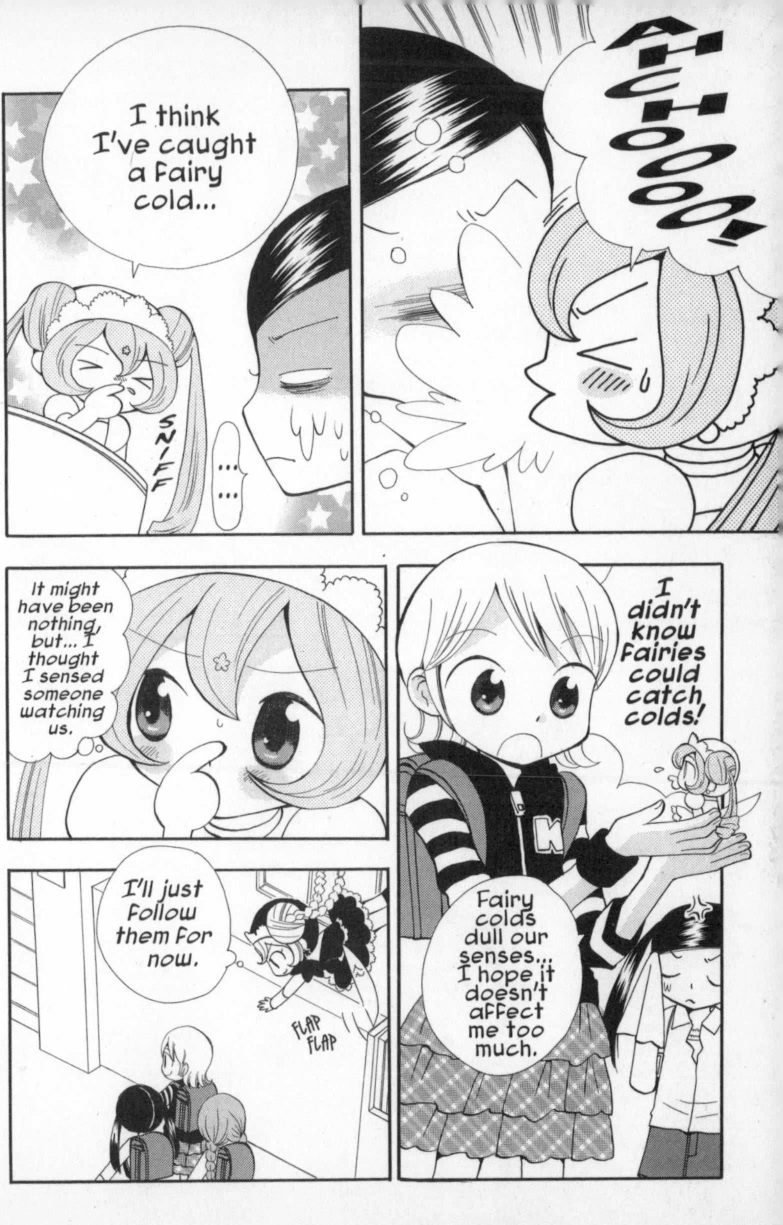

ACHOOOOO!
I think I've caught a fairy cold...
SNIFF
......
I didn't know fairies could catch colds!
Fairy colds dull our senses... I hope it doesn't affect me too much.
It might have been nothing, but... I thought I sensed someone watching us.
I'll just follow them for now.
FLAP FLAP

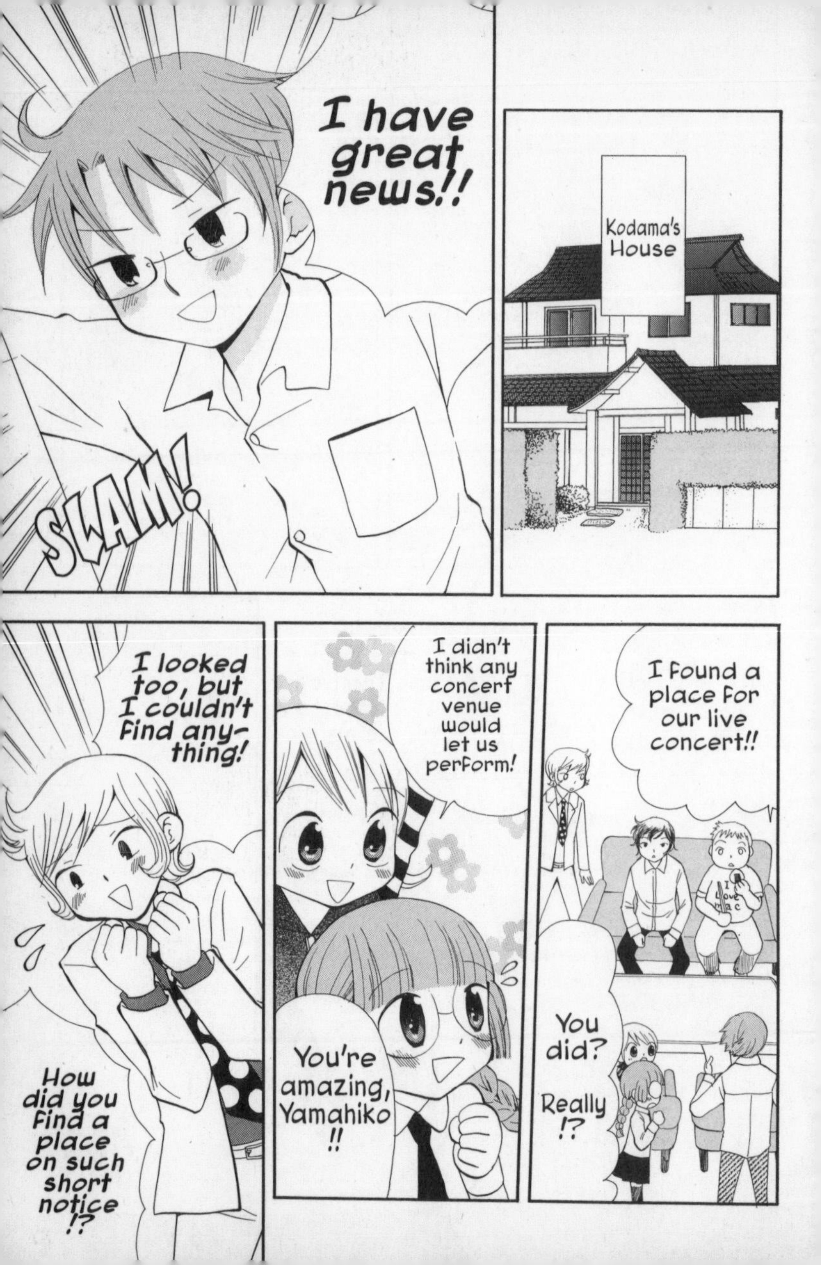
Kodama's House
I have great news!!
SLAM!
I found a place for our live concert!!
You did?
Really!?
I didn't think any concert venue would let us perform!
You're amazing, Yamahiko!!
I looked too, but I couldn't find any-thing!
How did you find a place on such short notice!?

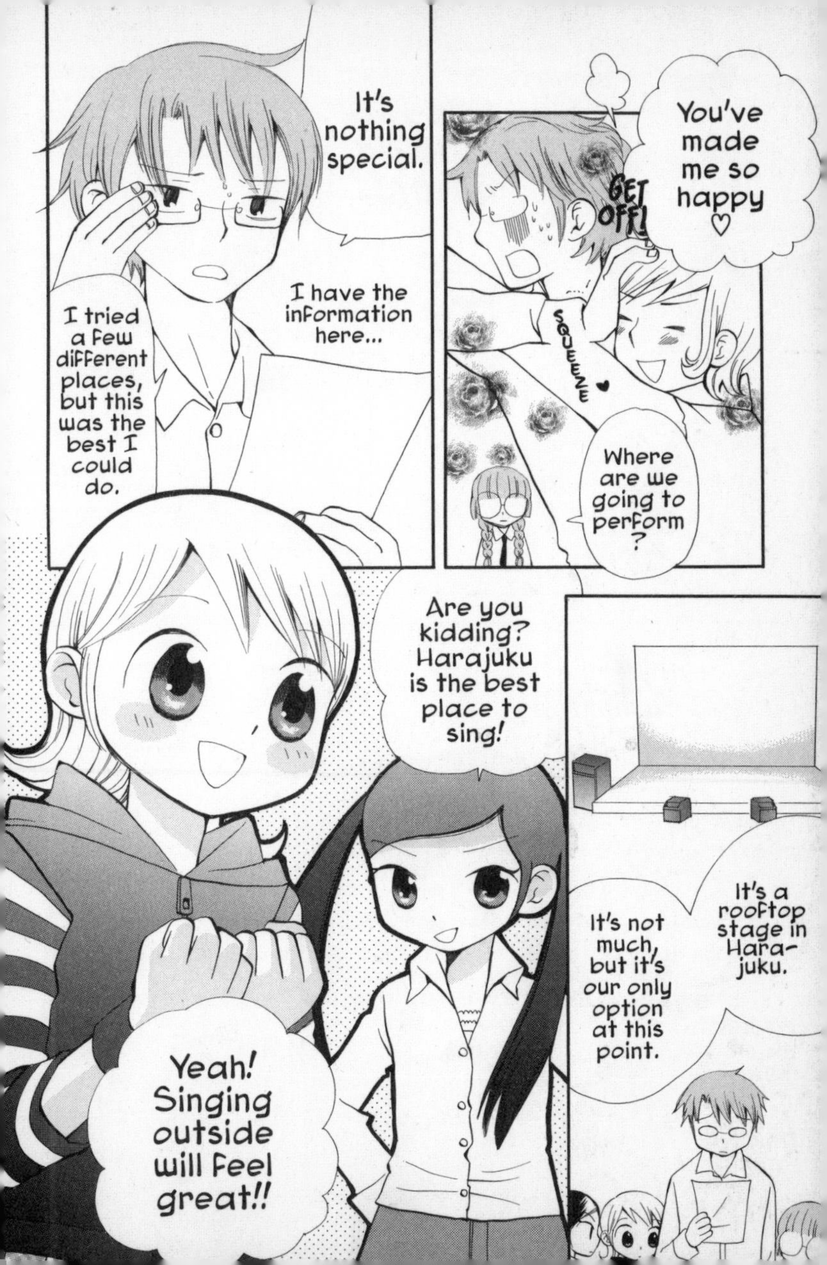

You've made me so happy ♡
GET OFF!
SQUEEZE ♥
Where are we going to perform?
It's nothing special.
I have the information here...
I tried a few different places, but this was the best I could do.
It's a rooftop stage in Hara-juku.
It's not much, but it's our only option at this point.
Are you kidding? Harajuku is the best place to sing!
Yeah! Singing outside will feel great!!

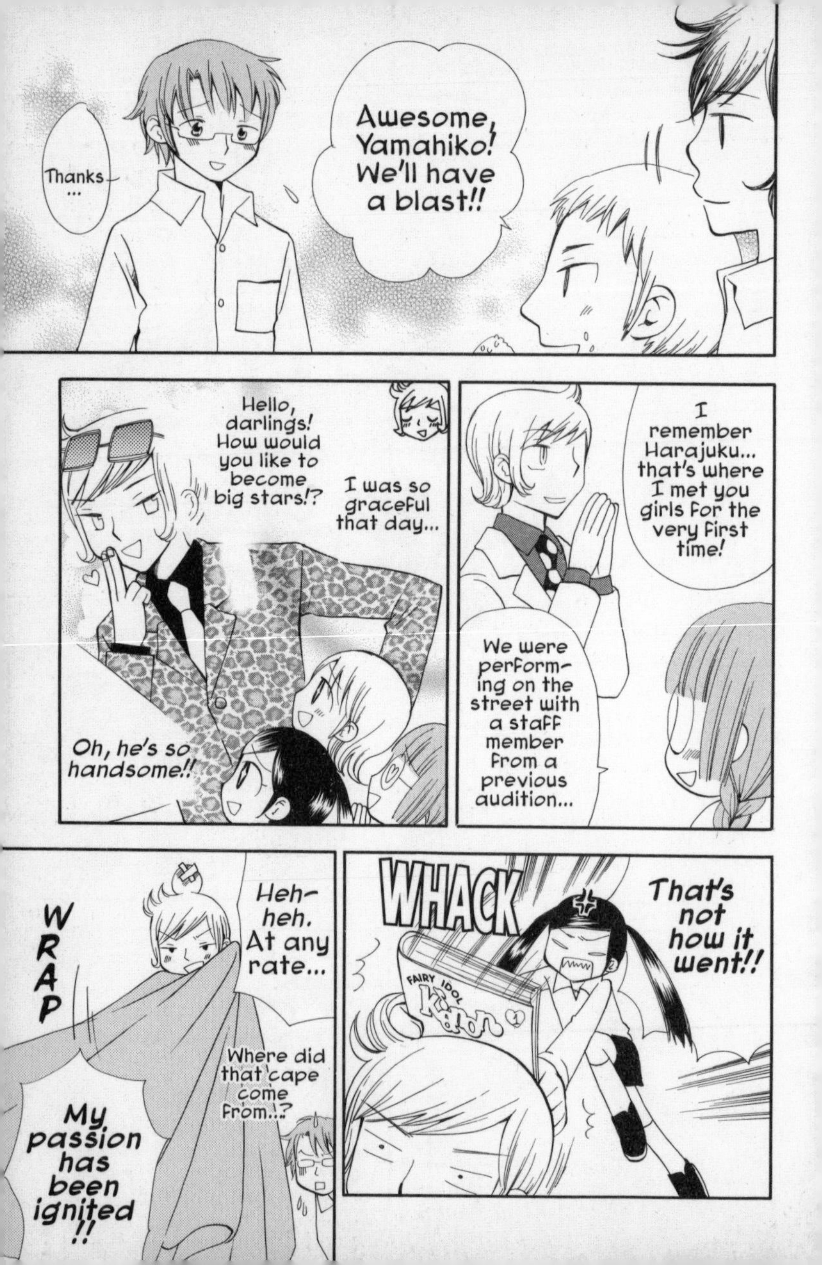

Awesome, Yamahiko! We'll have a blast!!
Thanks...
I remember Harajuku... that's where I met you girls for the very first time!
We were performing on the street with a staff member from a previous audition...
Hello, darlings! How would you like to become big stars!?
I was so graceful that day...
Oh, he's so handsome!!
WHACK
That's not how it went!!
FAIRY IDOL
1
Heh-heh. At any rate...
WRAP
Where did that cape come from...?
My passion has been ignited!!

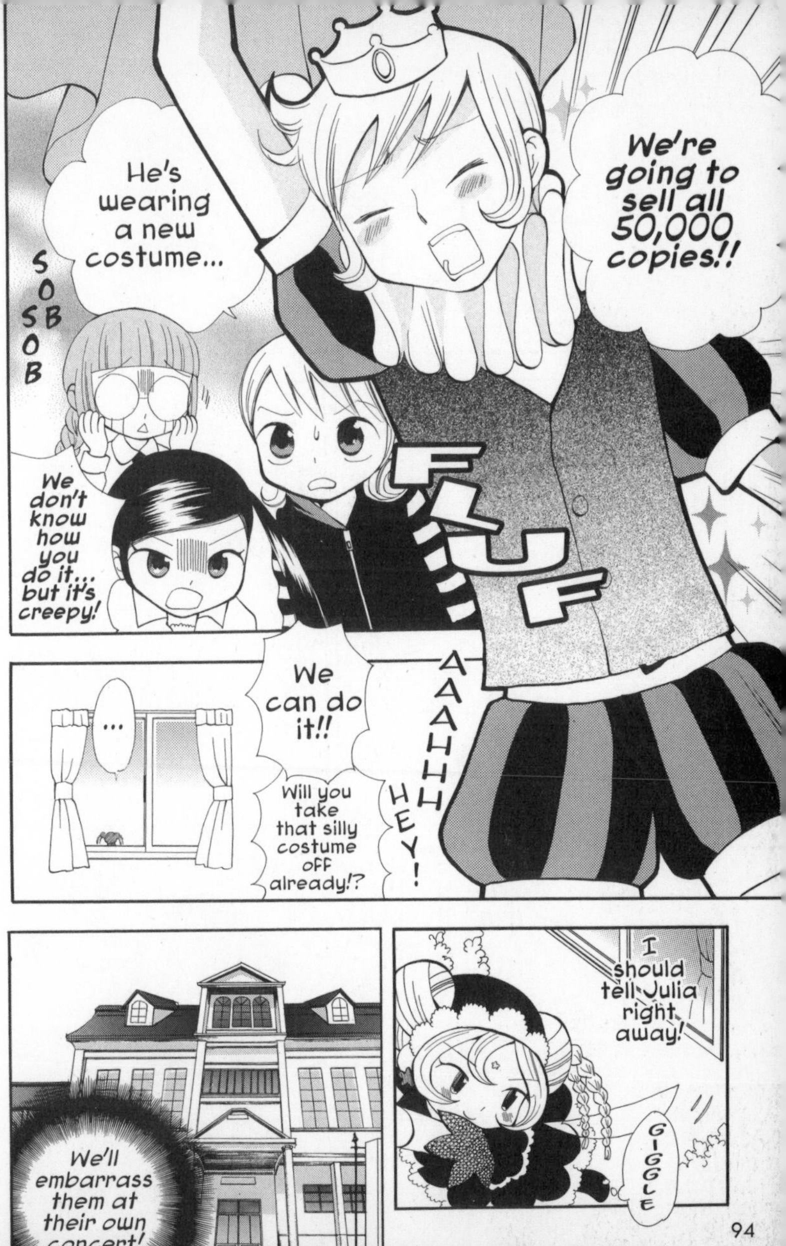
We're going to sell all 50,000 copies!!
He's wearing a new costume...
SOB SOB
FLUF
We don't know how you do it... but it's creepy!
AAAAHHH
We can do it!!
HEY!
Will you take that silly costume off already!?
...
I should tell Julia right away!
GIGGLE
We'll embarrass them at their own concert!

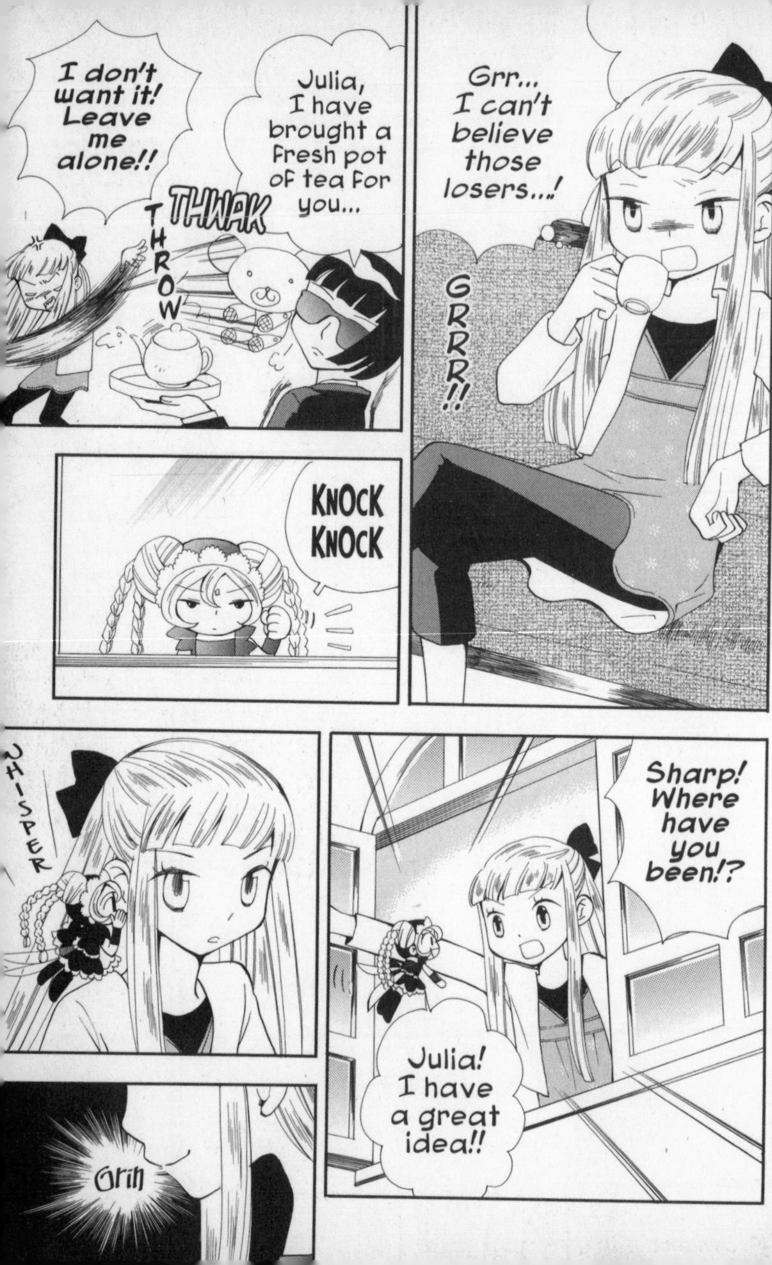
Grr... I can't believe those losers...!
GRRR!!
Julia, I have brought a fresh pot of tea for you...
I don't want it! Leave me alone!!
THWAK
THROW
KNOCK KNOCK
Sharp! Where have you been!?
Julia! I have a great idea!!
WHISPER
Grin

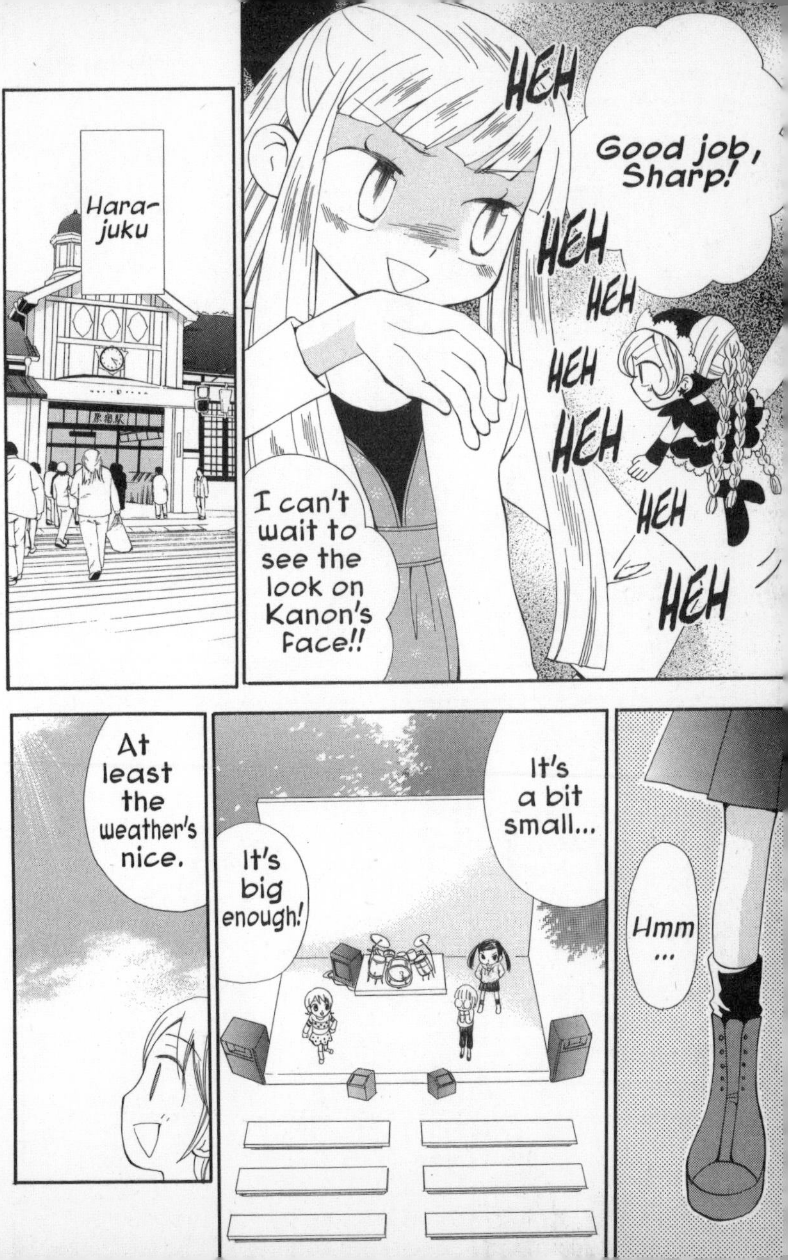

HEH
Good job, Sharp!
HEH
HEH
HEH
HEH
HEH
HEH
I can't wait to see the look on Kanon's face!!
Hara-juku
Hmm ...
It's a bit small...
It's big enough!
At least the weather's nice.

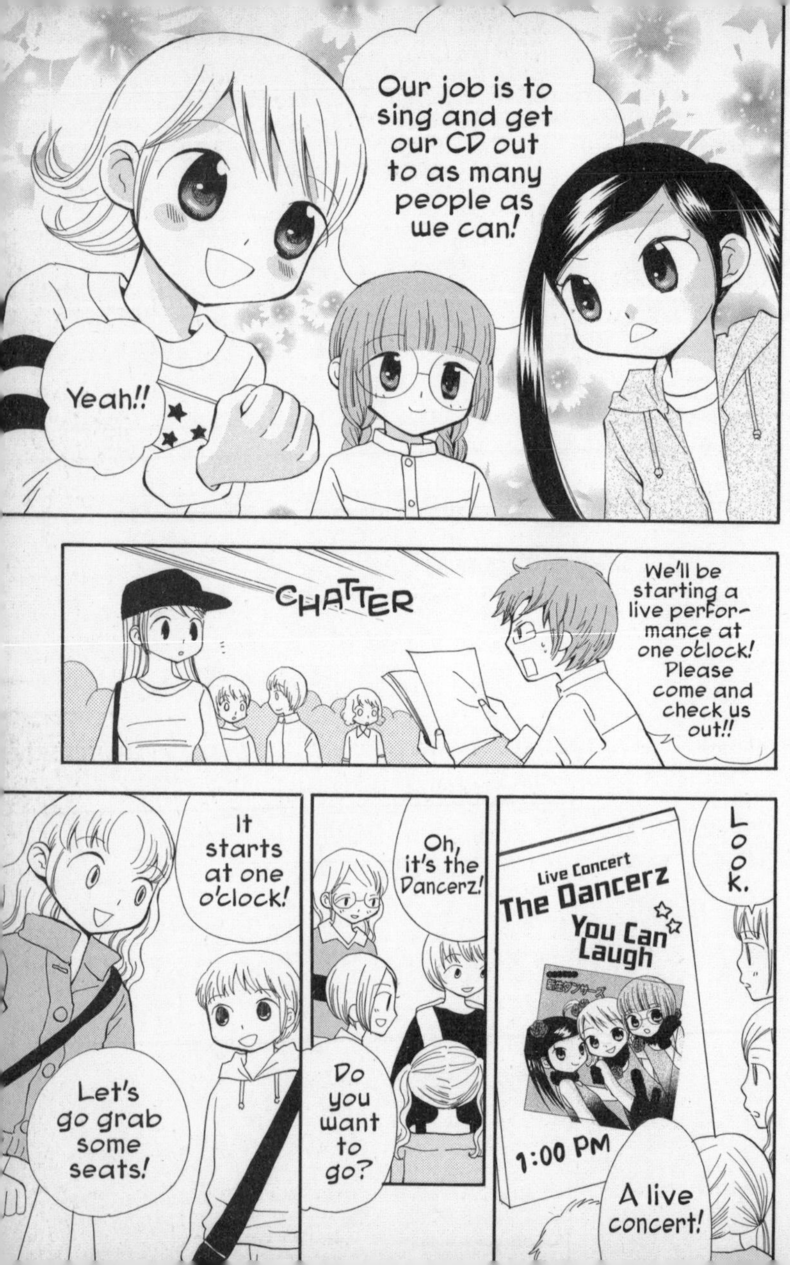
Our job is to sing and get our CD out to as many people as we can!
Yeah!!
We'll be starting a live performance at one o'clock! Please come and check us out!!
CHATTER
LOOK.
Live Concert
The Dancerz
You Can Laugh
1:00 PM
A live concert!
Oh, it's the Dancerz!
Do you want to go?
It starts at one o'clock!
Let's go grab some seats!

Read this way

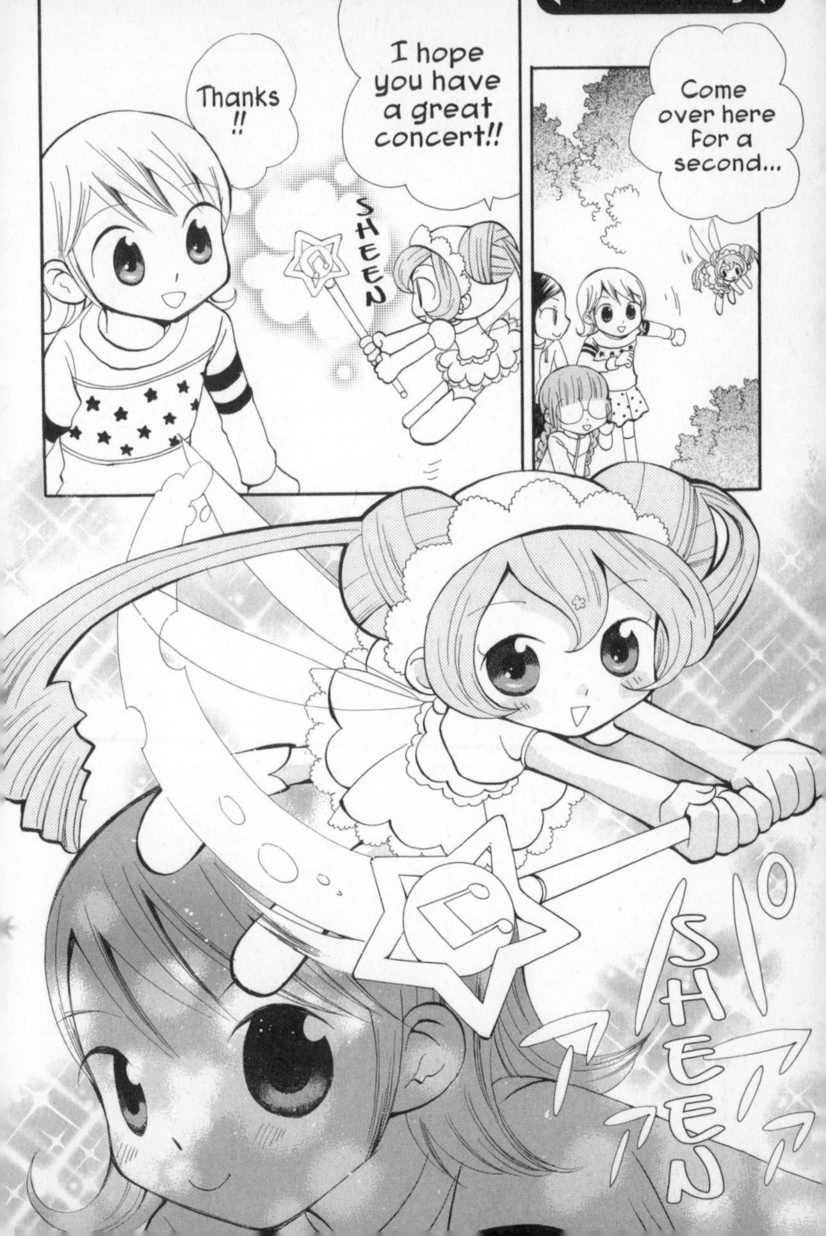
Come over here for a second...
I hope you have a great concert!!
SHEEN
Thanks!!
SHEEN

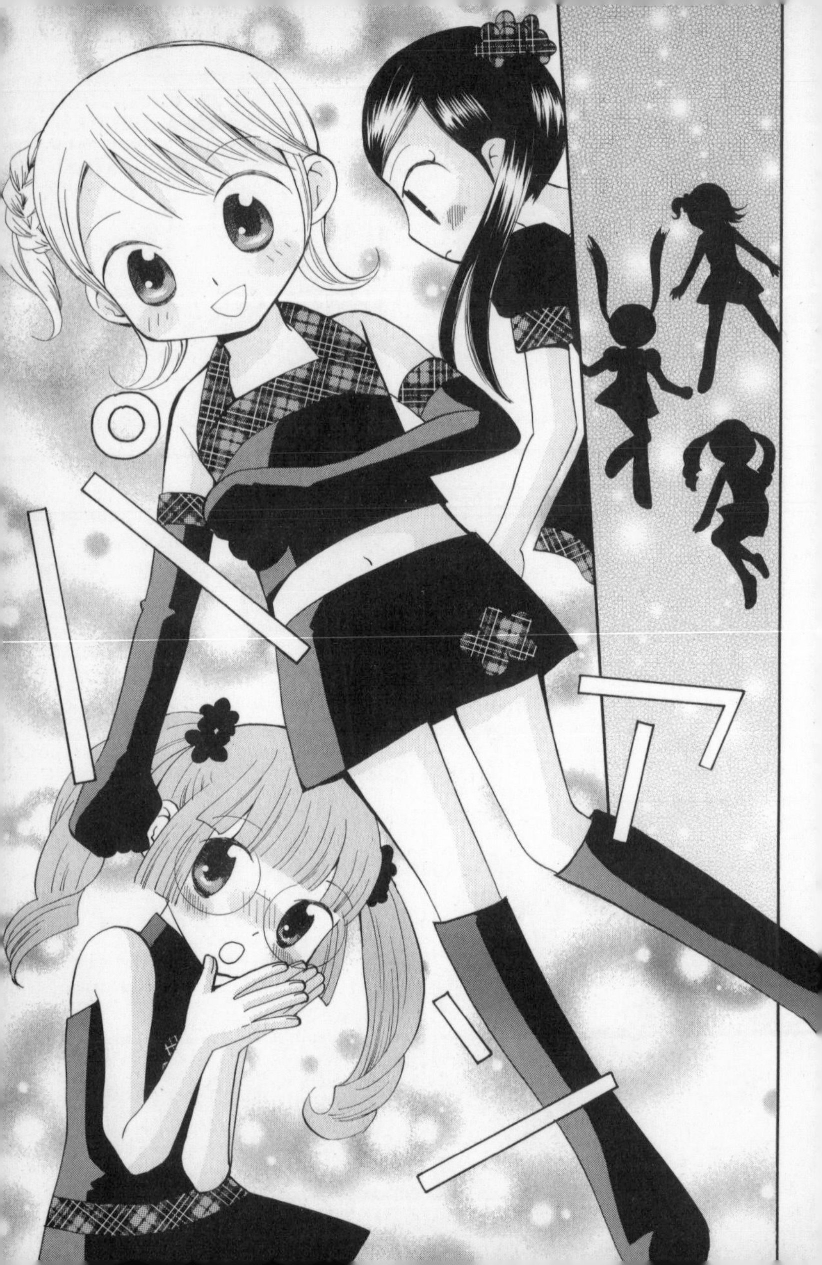

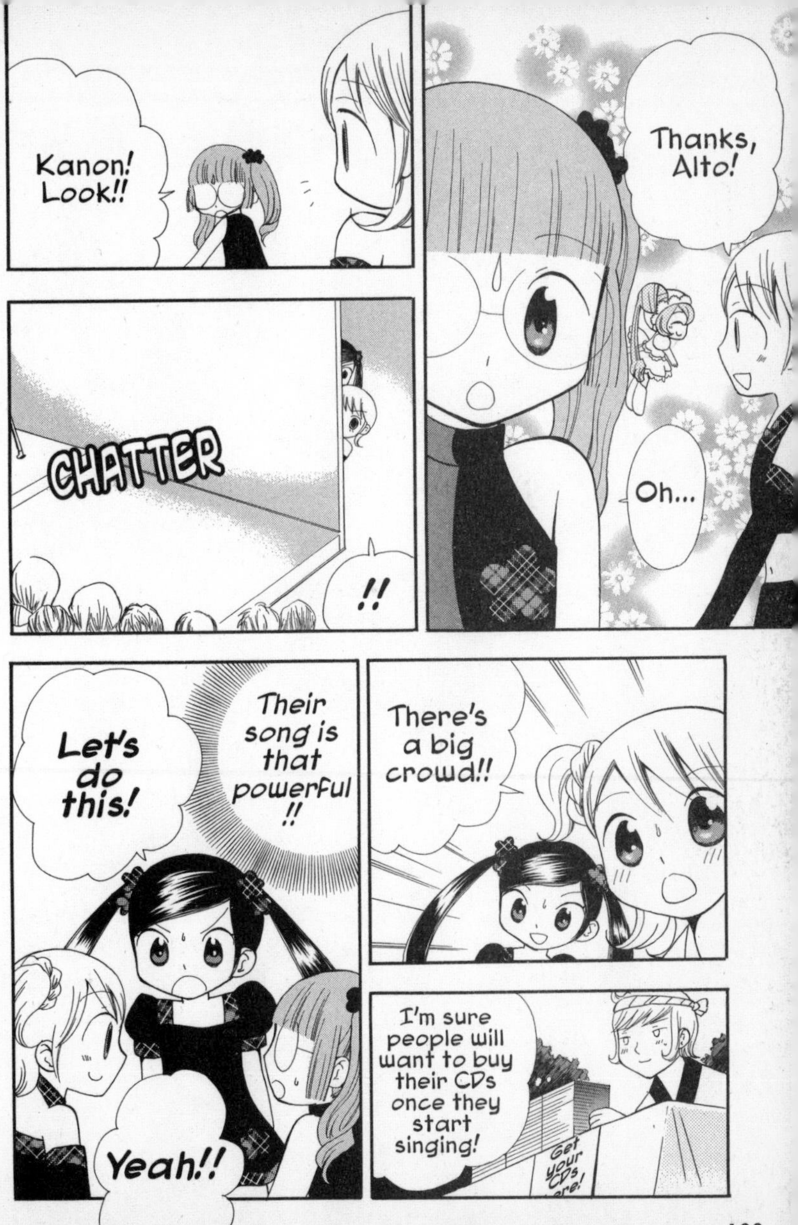

Thanks, Alto!
Oh...
Kanon! Look!!
CHATTER
!!
There's a big crowd!!
I'm sure people will want to buy their CDs once they start singing!
Get your CDs
Their song is that powerful!!
Let's do this!
Yeah!!

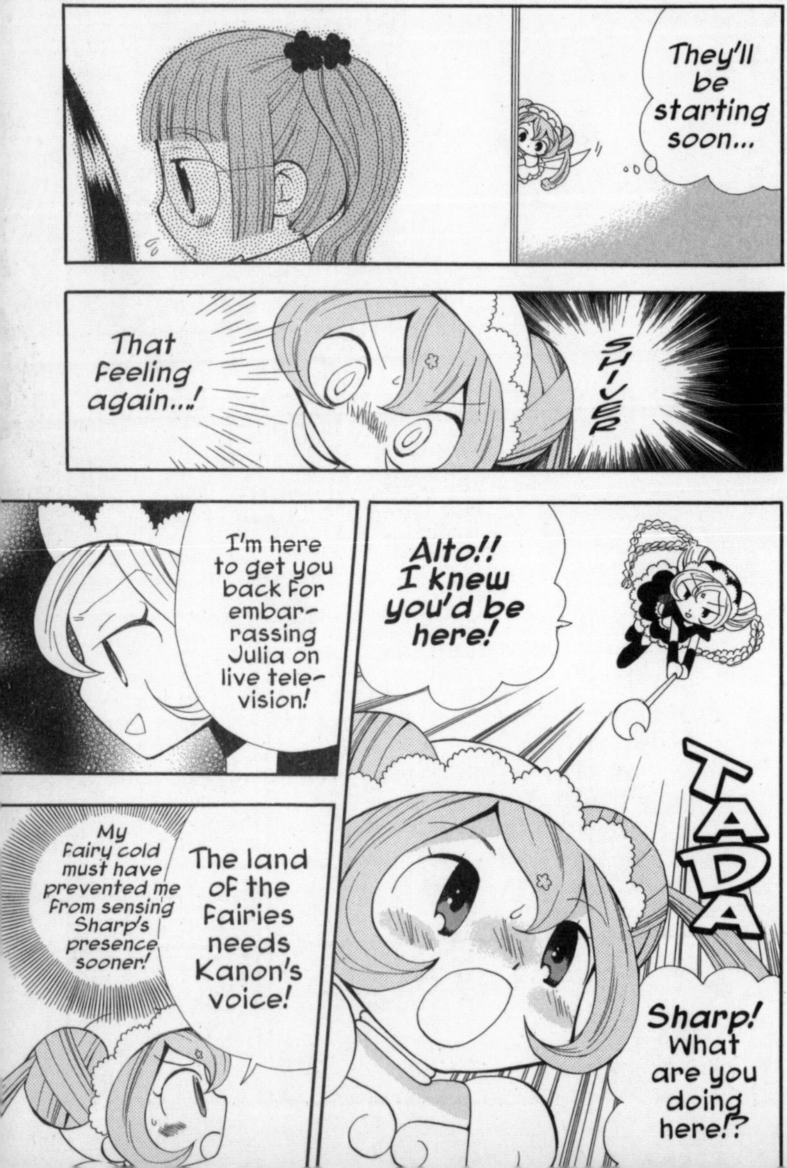
They'll be starting soon...
SHIVER
That feeling again...!
Alto!! I knew you'd be here!
TADA
Sharp! What are you doing here!?
I'm here to get you back for embarrassing Julia on live television!
The land of the Fairies needs Kanon's voice!
My fairy cold must have prevented me from sensing Sharp's presence sooner!

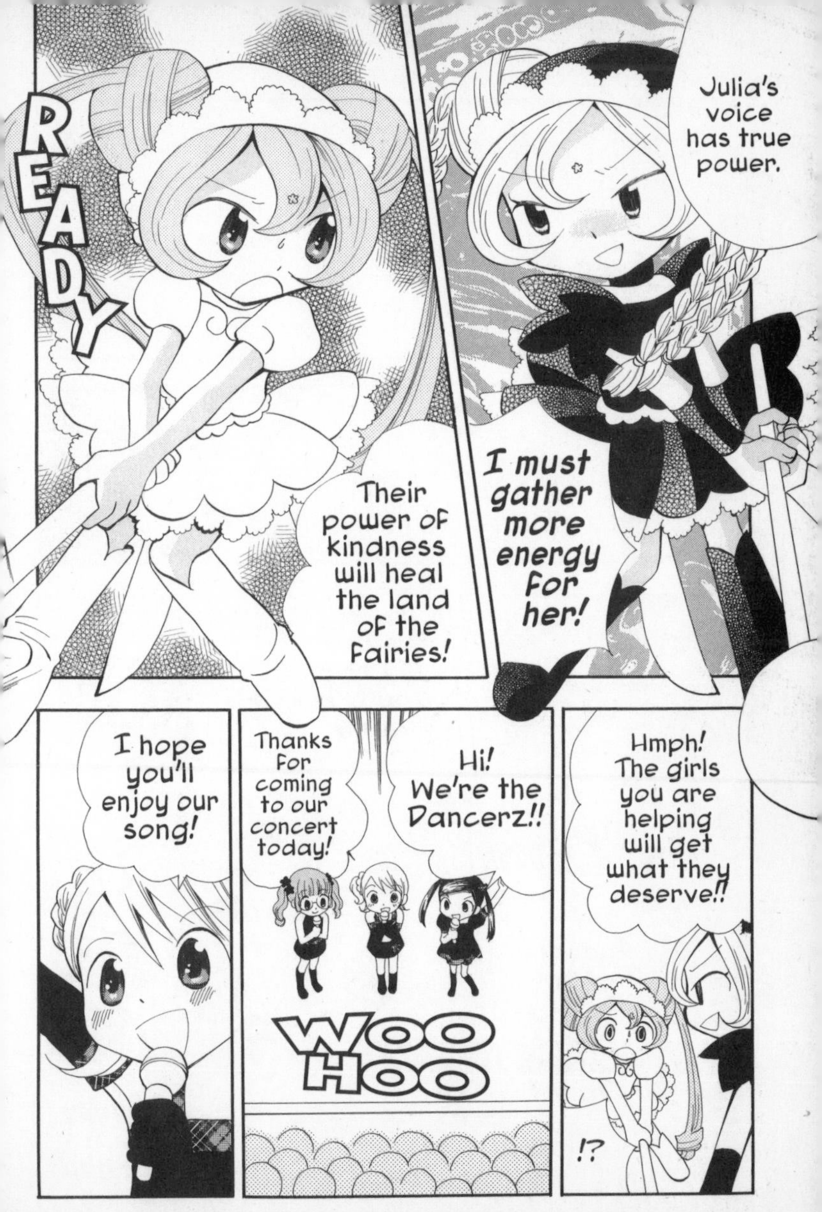
Julia's voice has true power.
I must gather more energy for her!
READY
Their power of kindness will heal the land of the fairies!
Hmph! The girls you are helping will get what they deserve!!
!?
Hi! We're the Dancerz!!
Thanks for coming to our concert today!
WOO HOO
I hope you'll enjoy our song!

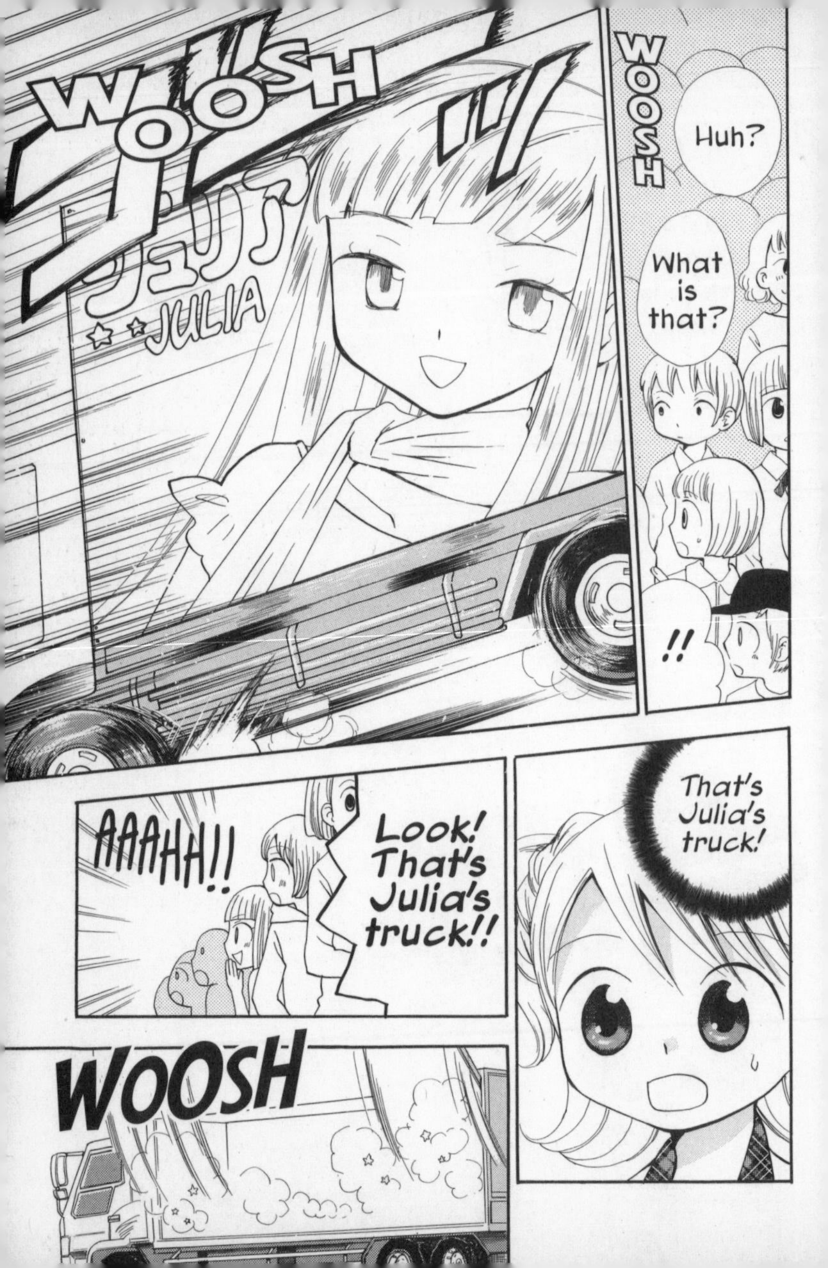

WOOSH
Huh?
What is that?
!!
WOOSH
ジュリア
JULIA
That's Julia's truck!
Look! That's Julia's truck!!
AAAHH!!
WOOSH

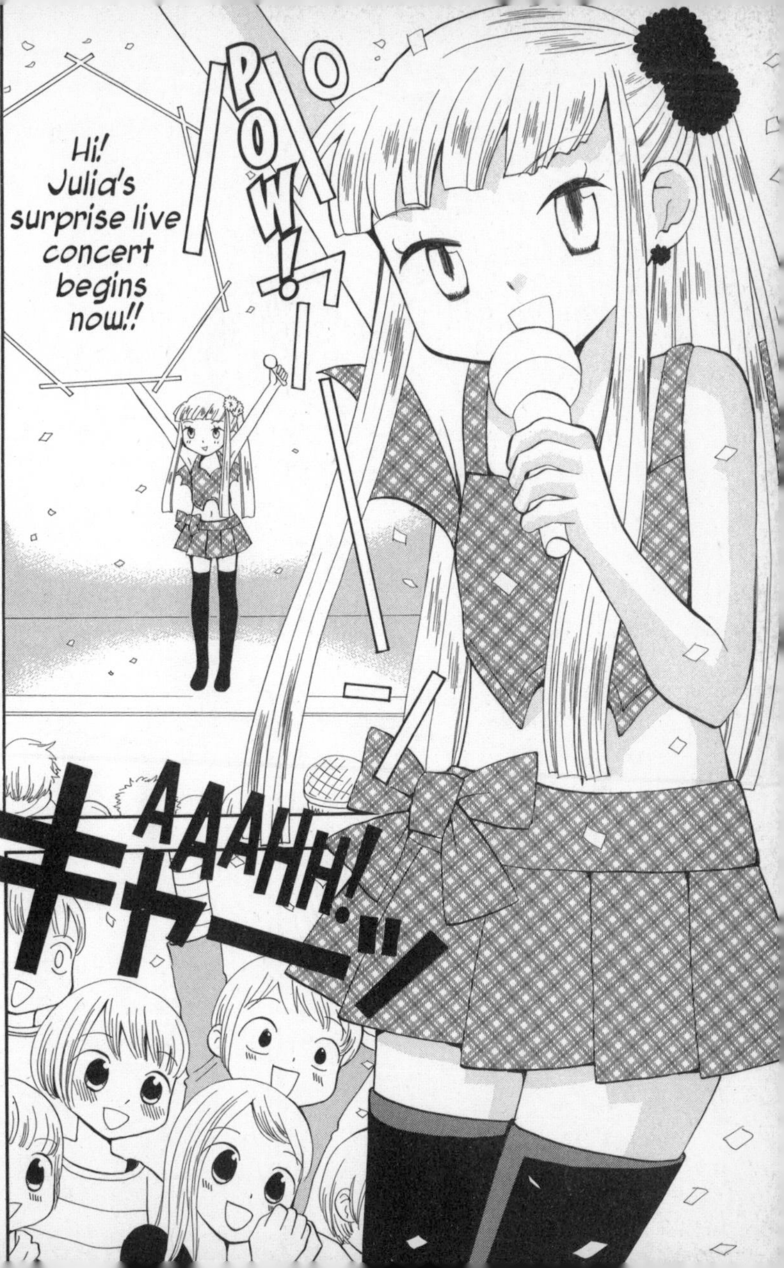
POW!
Hi! Julia's surprise live concert begins now!!
AAAHH!

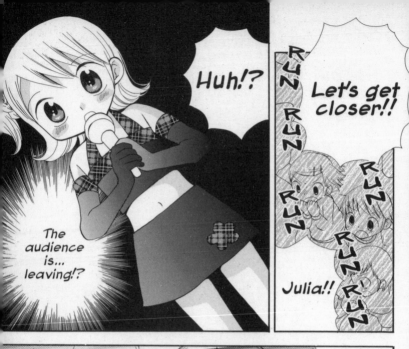

Huh!?

Let's get closer!!

RUN RUN RUN RUN RUN RUN RUN RUN RUN

Julia!!

The audience is... leaving!?

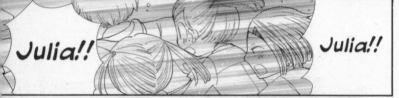

Julia!!

Julia!!

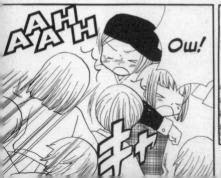

AAH AAH

Ow!

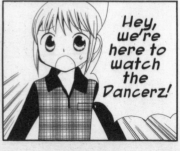

Hey, we're here to watch the Dancerz!

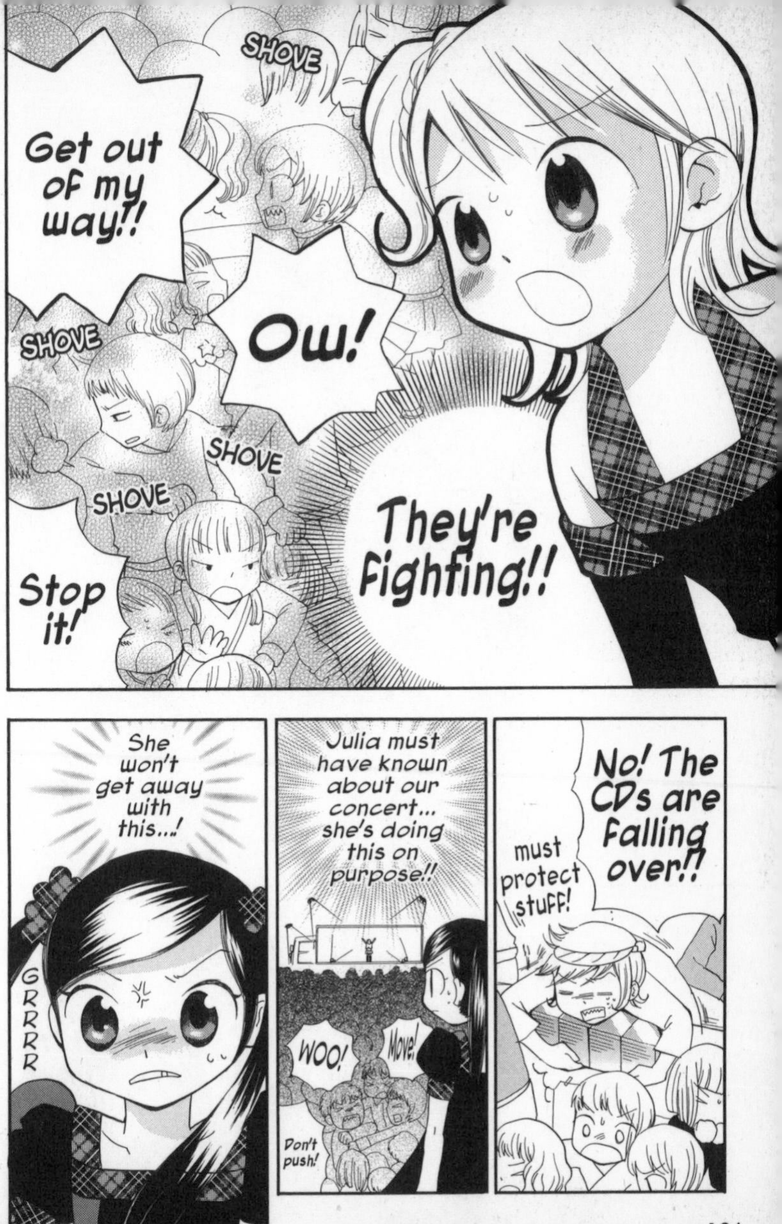
SHOVE
Get out of my way!!
Ow!
SHOVE
They're fighting!!
SHOVE
SHOVE
Stop it!
No! The CDs are falling over!!
must protect stuff!
Julia must have known about our concert... she's doing this on purpose!!
Move!
WOO!
Don't push!
She won't get away with this...!
GRRRR

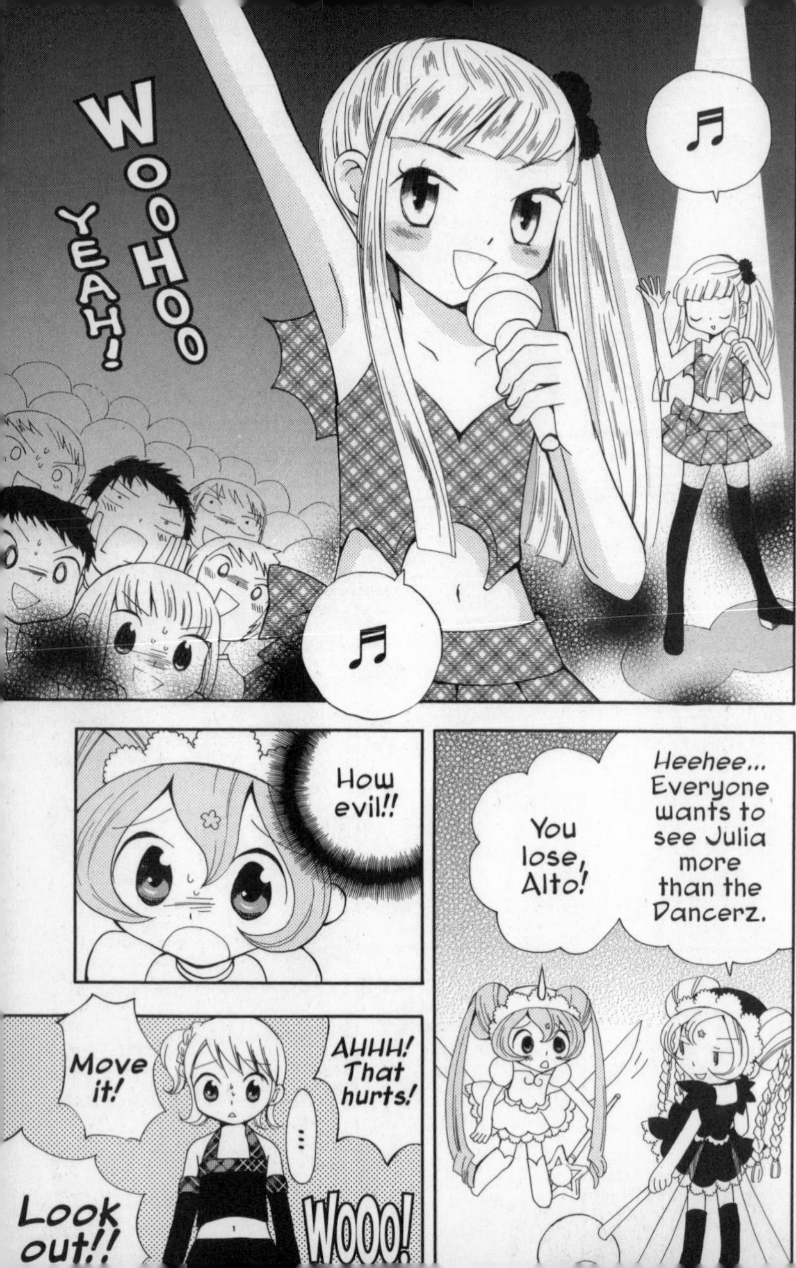

♬
WOOHOO YEAH!
♬
Heehee... Everyone wants to see Julia more than the Dancerz.
You lose, Alto!
How evil!!
AHHH! That hurts!
...
Move it!
WOOO!
Look out!!

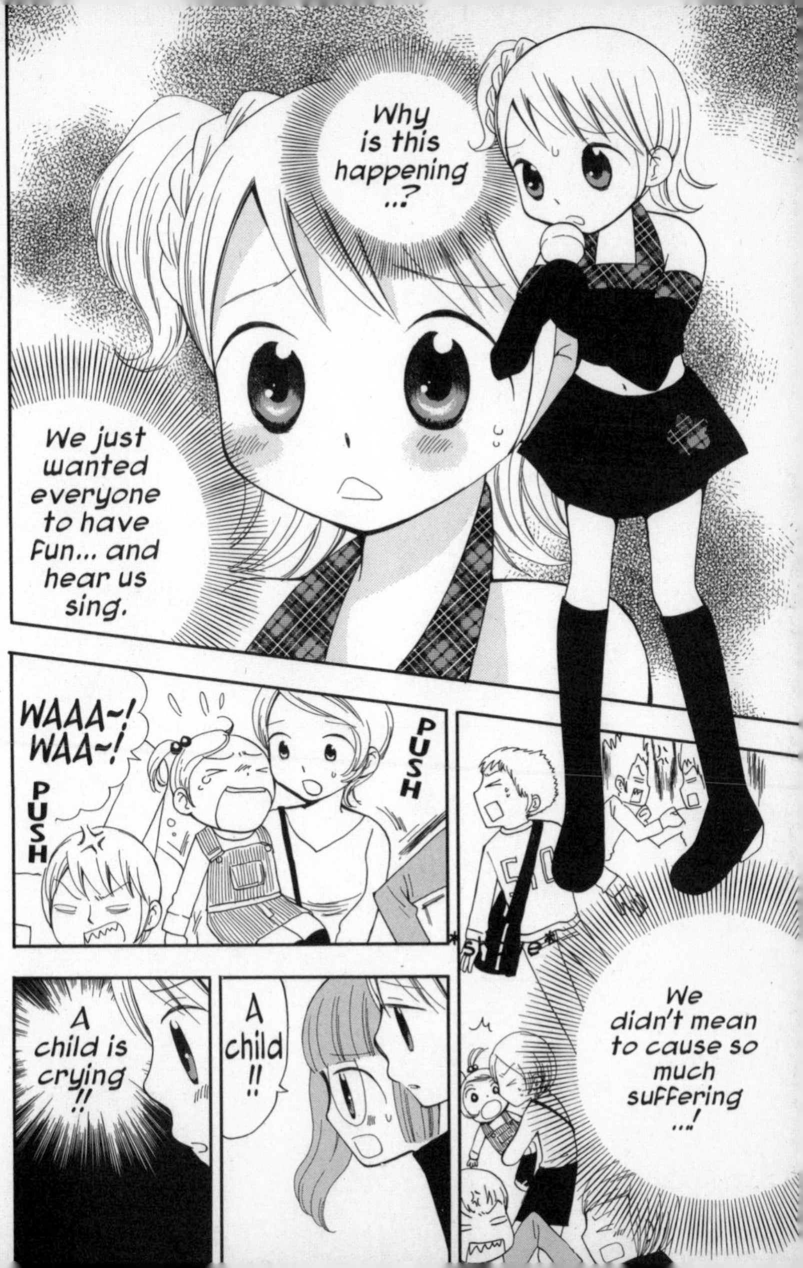
Why is this happening...?
We just wanted everyone to have fun... and hear us sing.
PUSH
WAAA~! WAA~!
PUSH
We didn't mean to cause so much suffering...!
A child!!
A child is crying!!

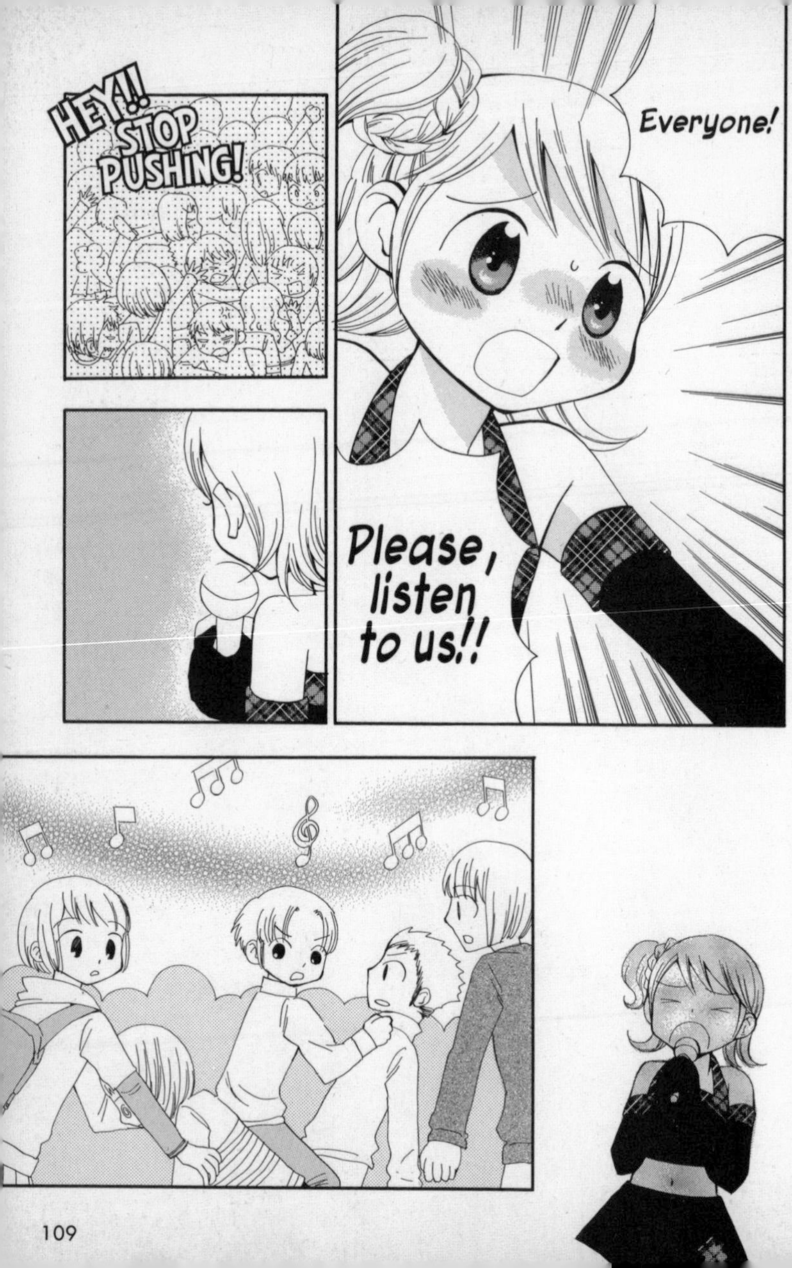
Everyone!
Please, listen to us!!
HEY!! STOP PUSHING!

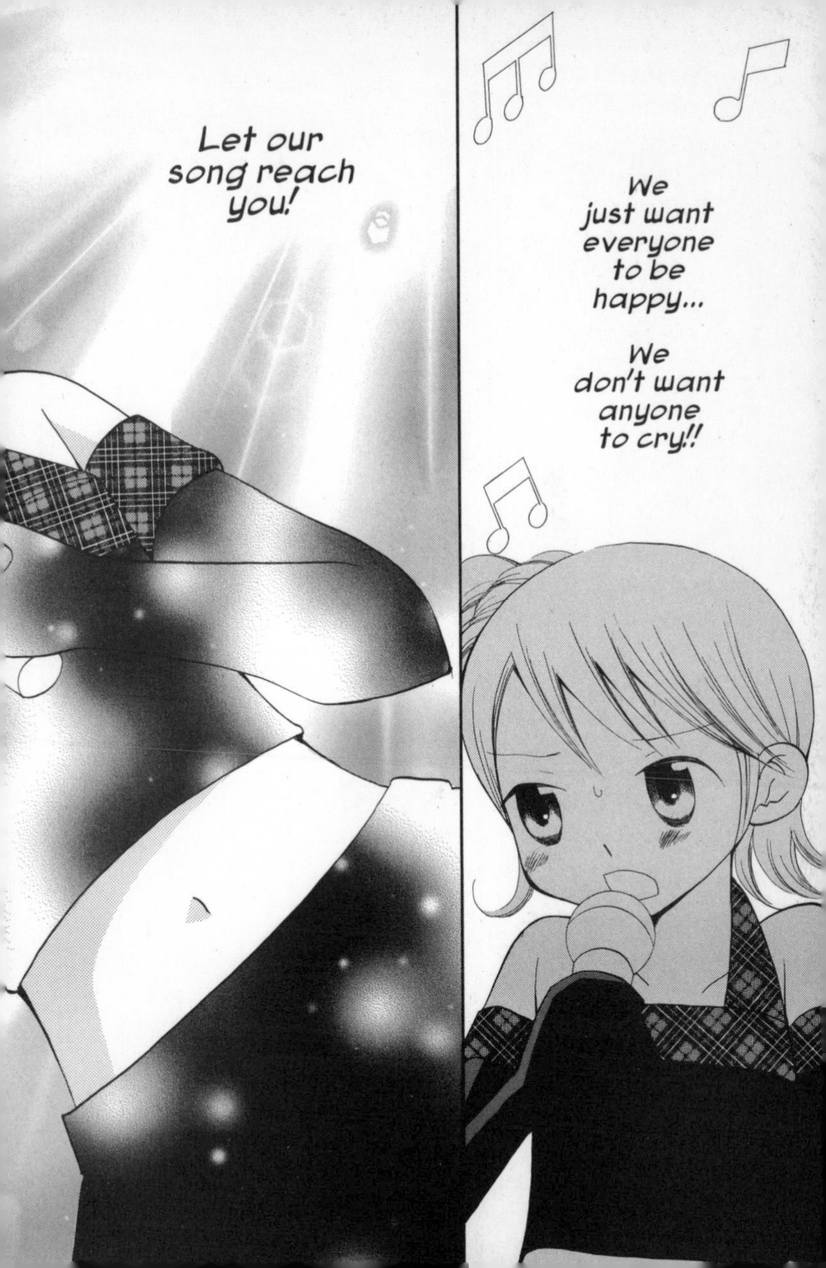
We just want everyone to be happy...
We don't want anyone to cry!!
Let our song reach you!

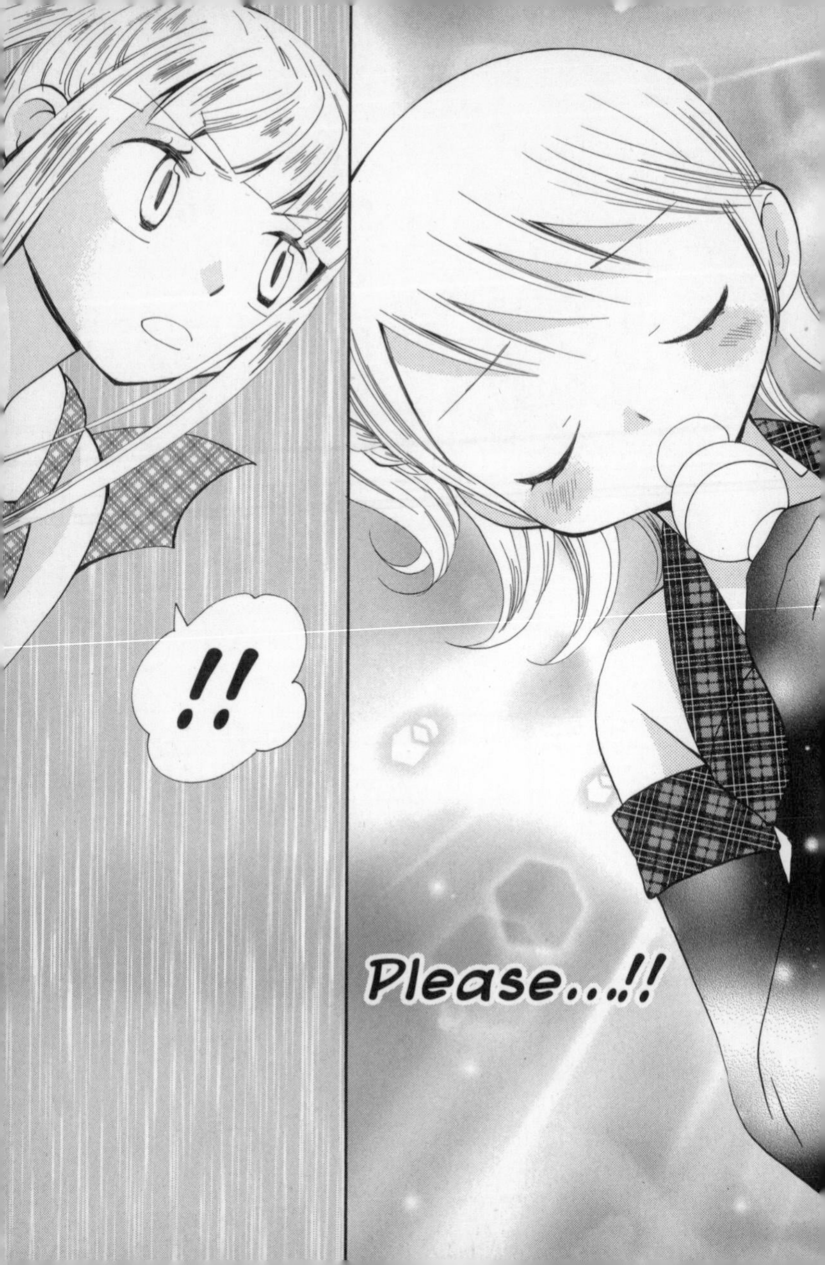
Please...!!
!!

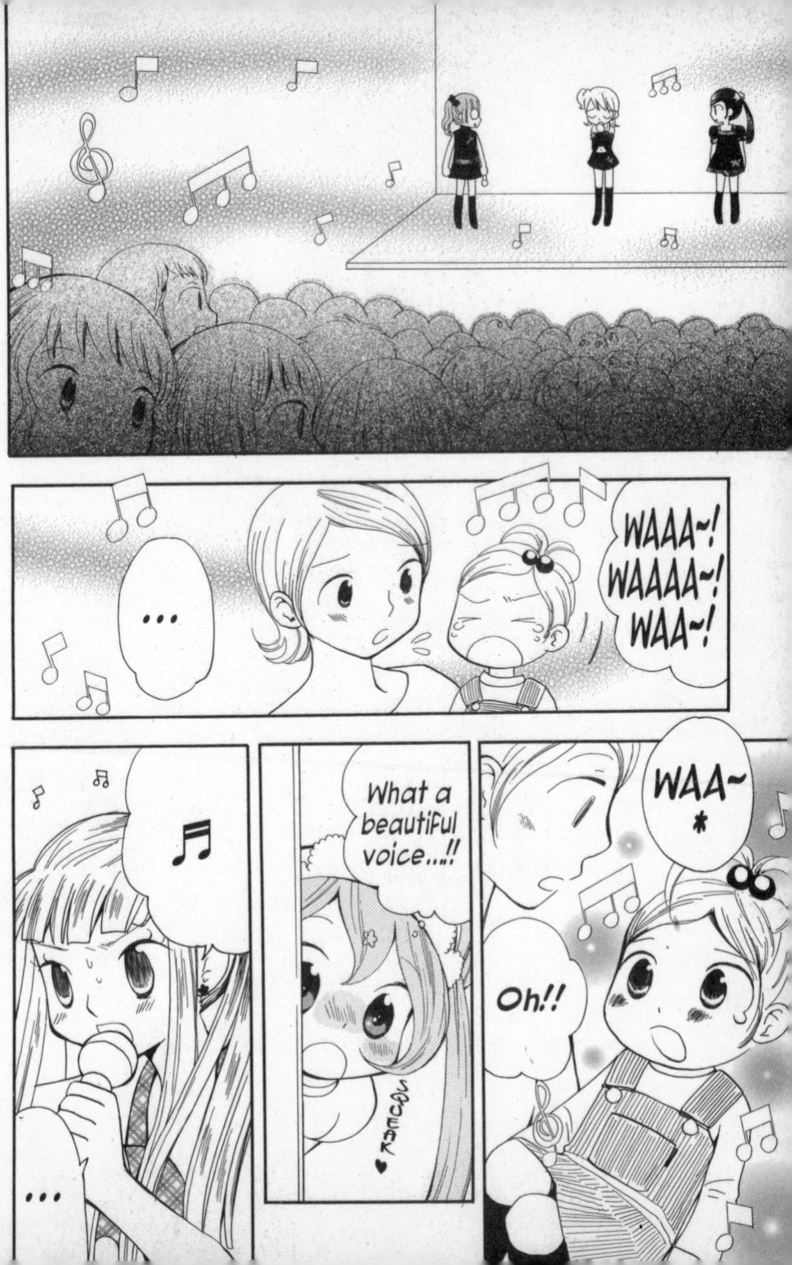
WAAA~! WAAAA~! WAA~!
...
WAA~ *
Oh!!
What a beautiful voice...!!
SQUEAK ♥
...

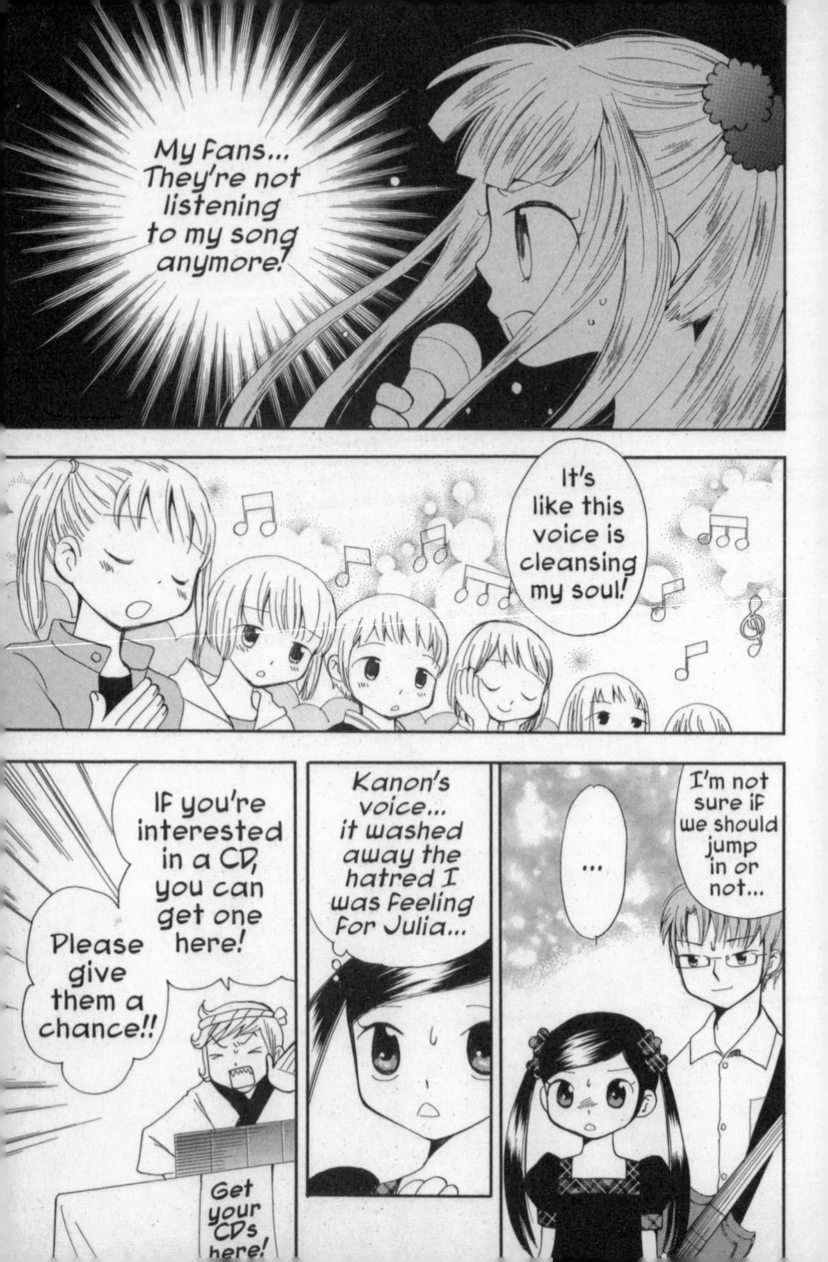
My fans... They're not listening to my song anymore!
It's like this voice is cleansing my soul!
I'm not sure if we should jump in or not...
...
Kanon's voice... it washed away the hatred I was feeling for Julia...
If you're interested in a CD, you can get one here!
Please give them a chance!!
Get your CDs here!

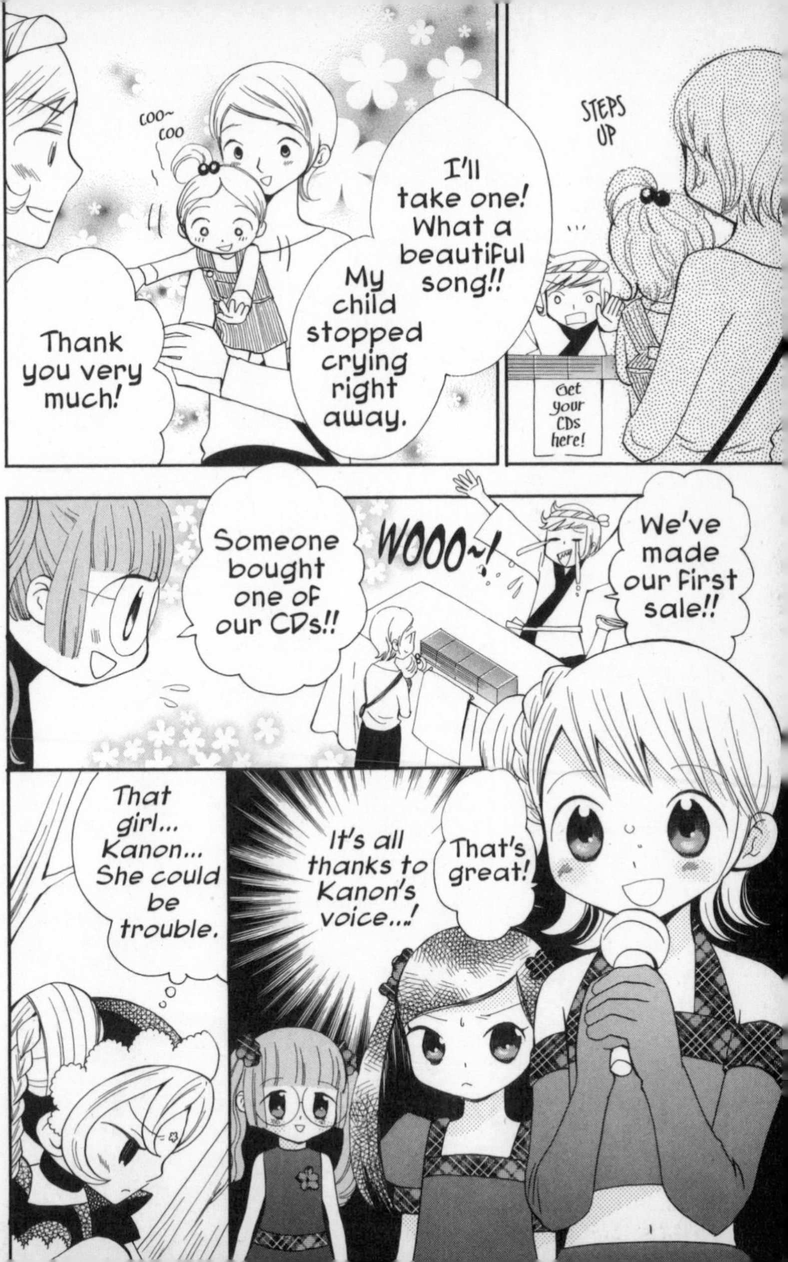
STEPS UP
...
Get your CDs here!
I'll take one! What a beautiful song!!
My child stopped crying right away.
COO~ COO
Thank you very much!
We've made our first sale!!
WOOO~!
Someone bought one of our CDs!!
That's great!
It's all thanks to Kanon's voice...!
That girl... Kanon... She could be trouble.

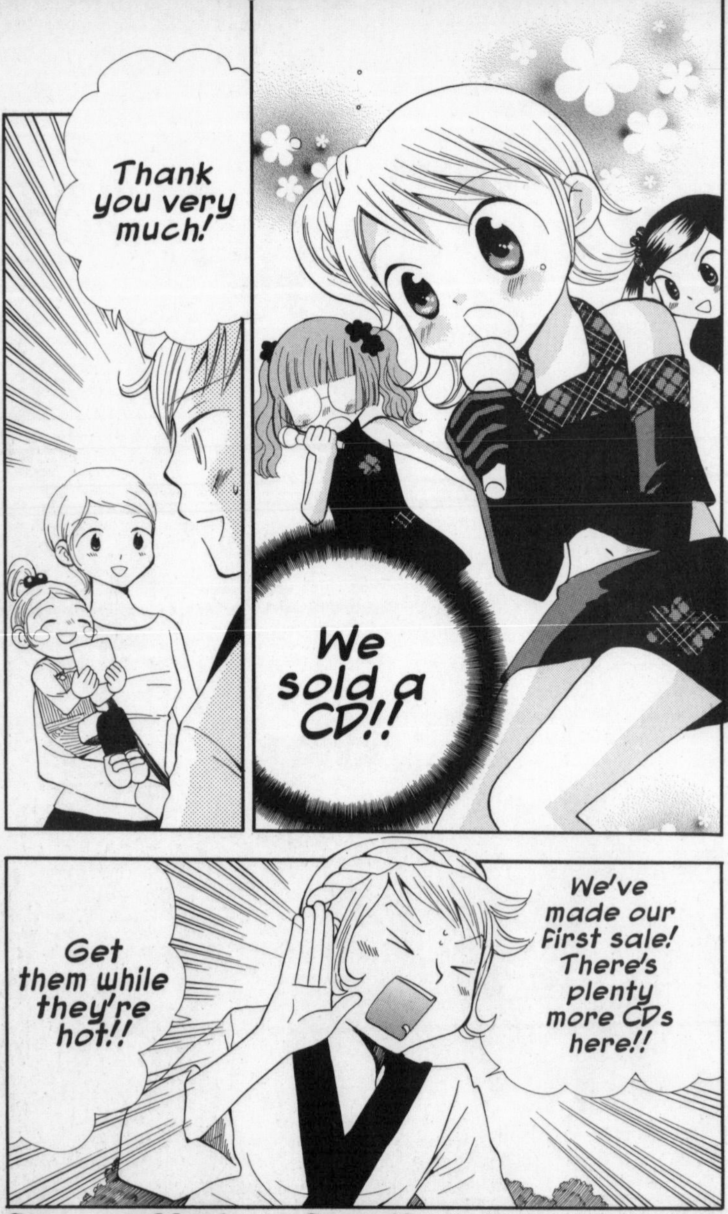
We sold a CD!!
Thank you very much!
We've made our first sale! There's plenty more CDs here!!
Get them while they're hot!!

Stage 18 Magic on Stage!?

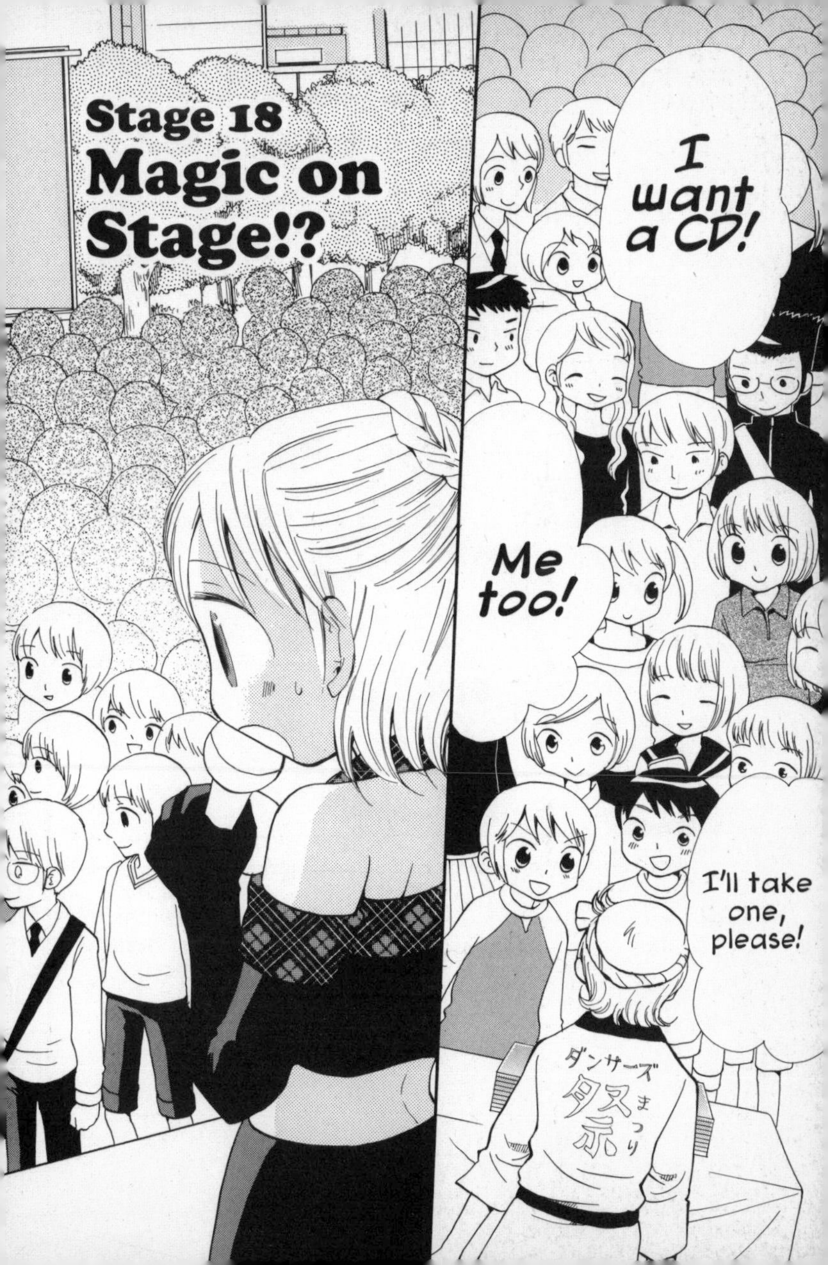
I want a CD!
Me too!
I'll take one, please!
ダンサーズ
まつり
Stage 18
Magic on Stage!?

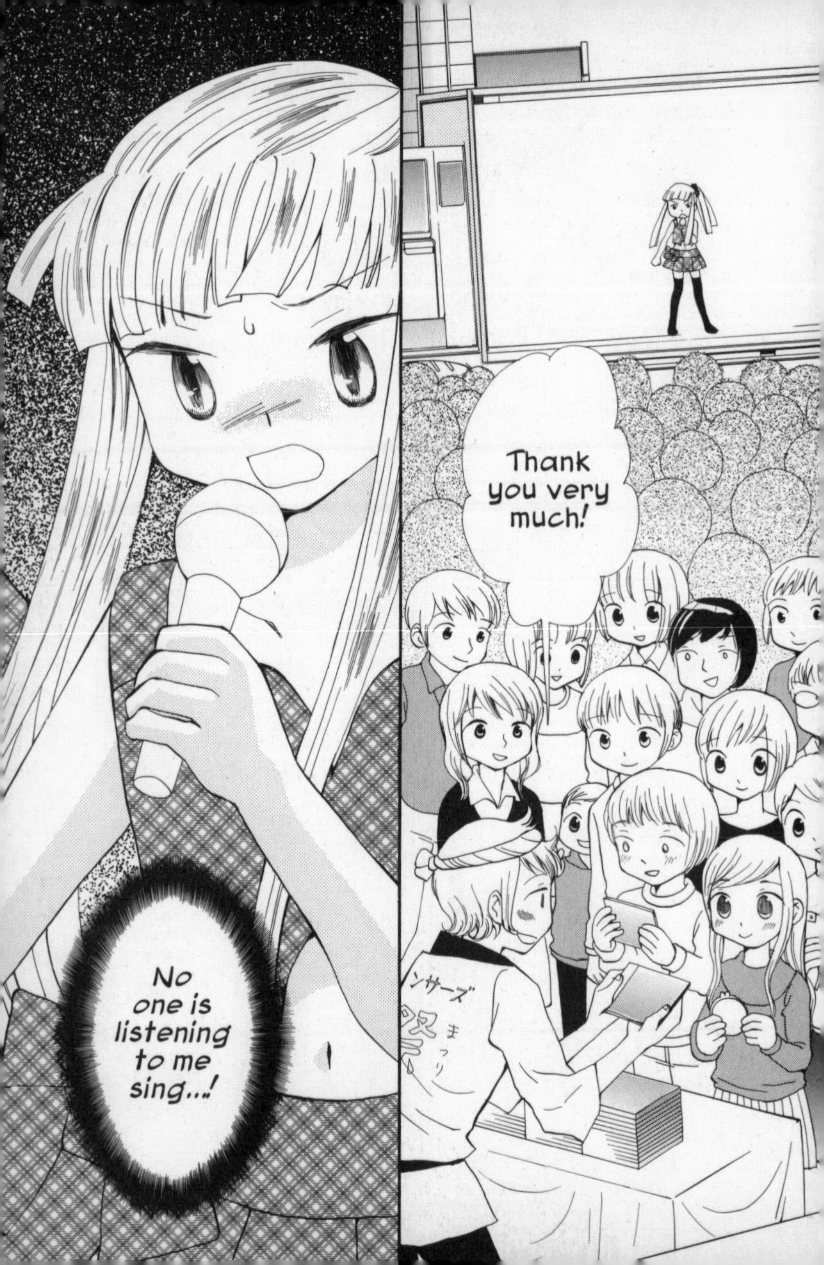
Thank you very much!
ンサーズ
祭 まつり
No one is listening to me sing...!

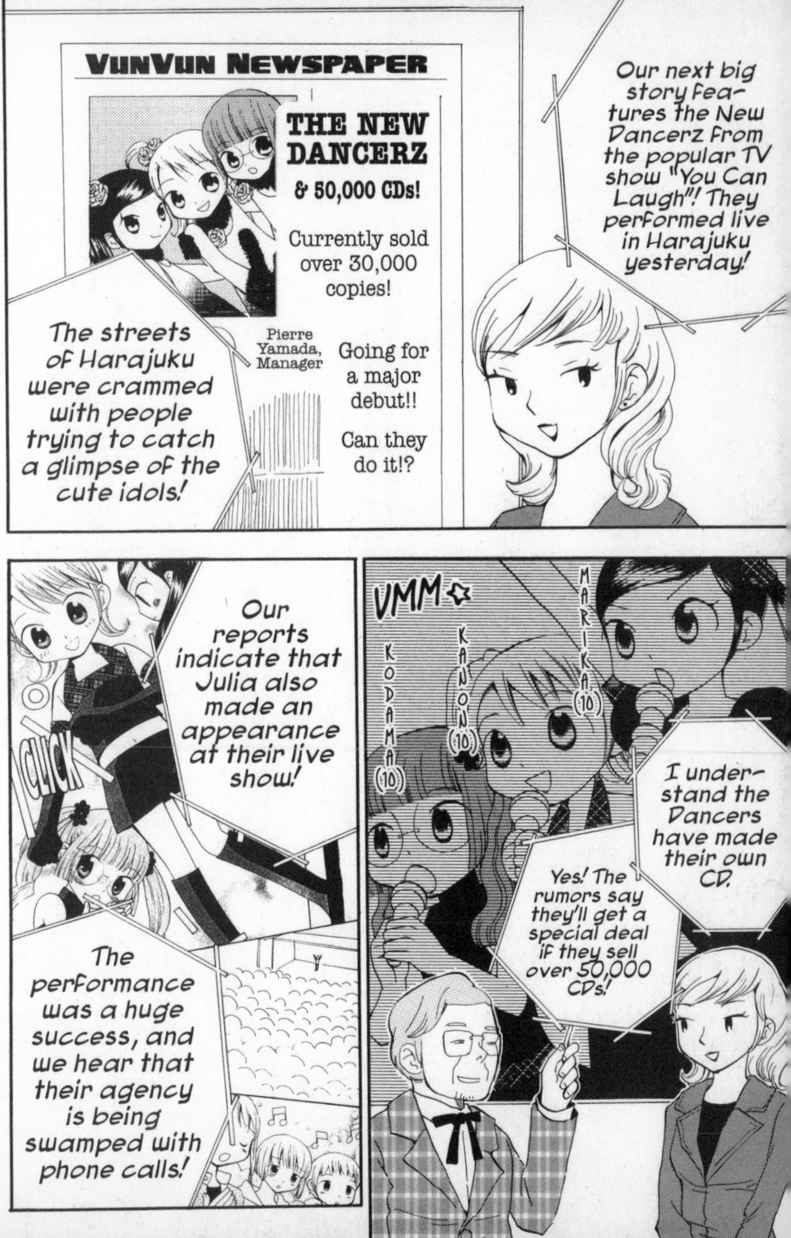
Our next big story features the New Dancerz from the popular TV show "You Can Laugh"! They performed live in Harajuku yesterday!
VUNVUN NEWSPAPER
THE NEW DANCERZ
& 50,000 CDs!
Currently sold over 30,000 copies!
Pierre Yamada, Manager
Going for a major debut!!
Can they do it!?
The streets of Harajuku were crammed with people trying to catch a glimpse of the cute idols!
MARIKA (10)
VMM
KANON (10)
KODAMA (10)
I understand the Dancers have made their own CD.
Yes! The rumors say they'll get a special deal if they sell over 50,000 CDs!
Our reports indicate that Julia also made an appearance at their live show!
CLICK
The performance was a huge success, and we hear that their agency is being swamped with phone calls!

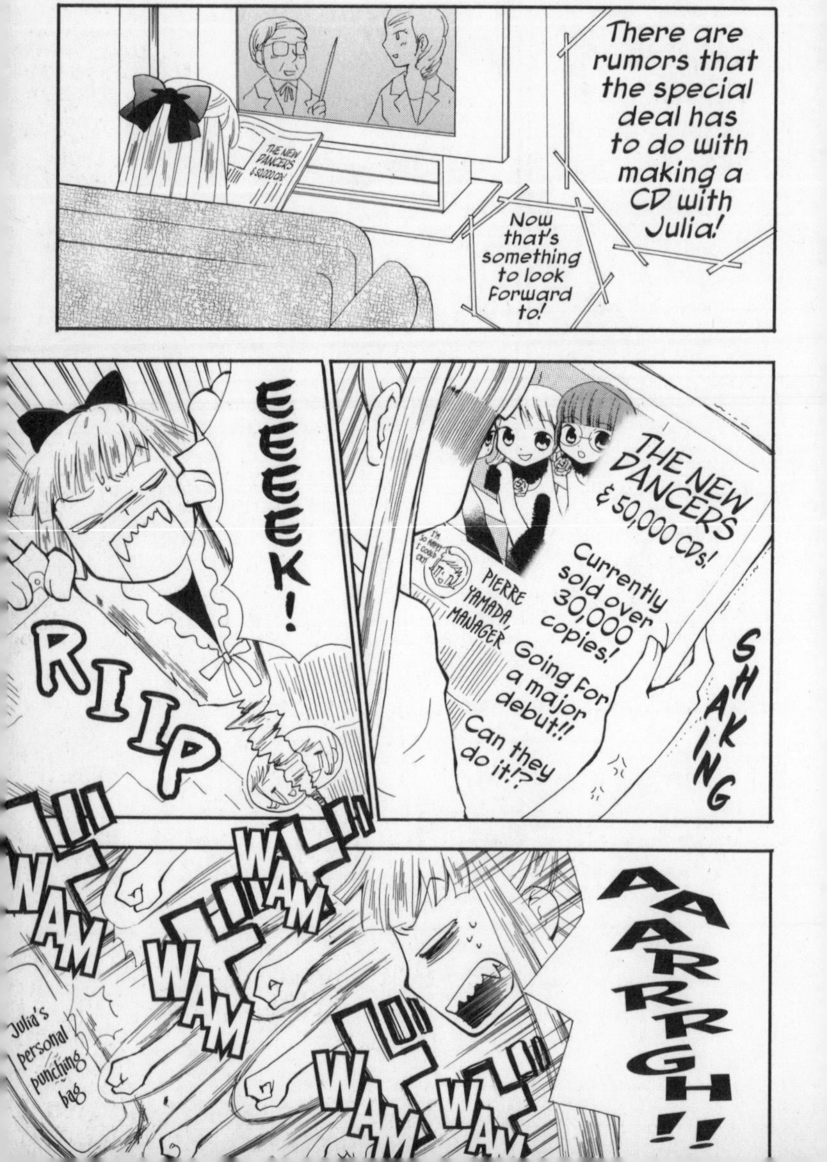
THE NEW DANCERS & 50,000 CDs!
There are rumors that the special deal has to do with making a CD with Julia!
Now that's something to look forward to!
THE NEW DANCERS & 50,000 CDs!
Currently sold over 30,000 copies!
I'M SO HAPPY I COULD CRY!
PIERRE YAMADA, MANAGER
Going for a major debut!!
Can they do it!?
SHAKING
EEEEEK!
RIIP
AAARRRGH!!
WAM
WAM
WAM
WAM
WAM
WAM
Julia's personal punching bag

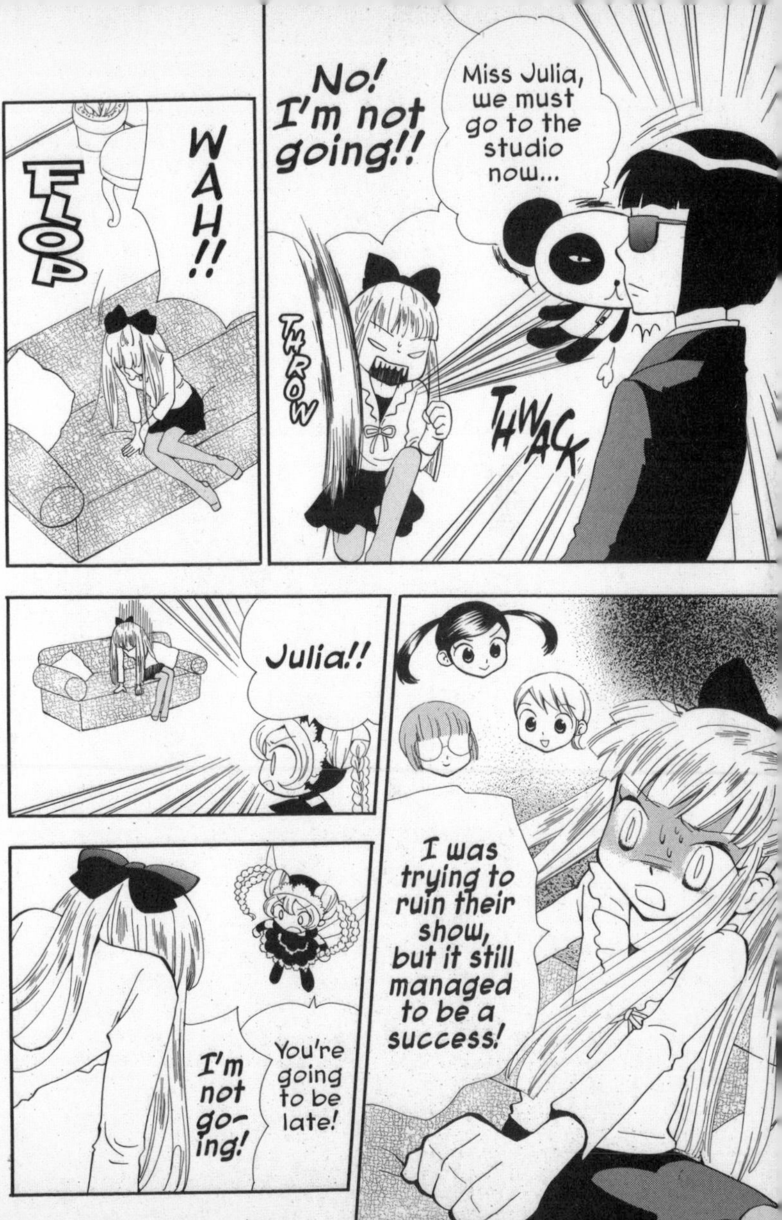
Miss Julia, we must go to the studio now...
No! I'm not going!!
THROW
THWACK
WAH!!
FLOP
I was trying to ruin their show, but it still managed to be a success!
Julia!!
You're going to be late!
I'm not go-ing!

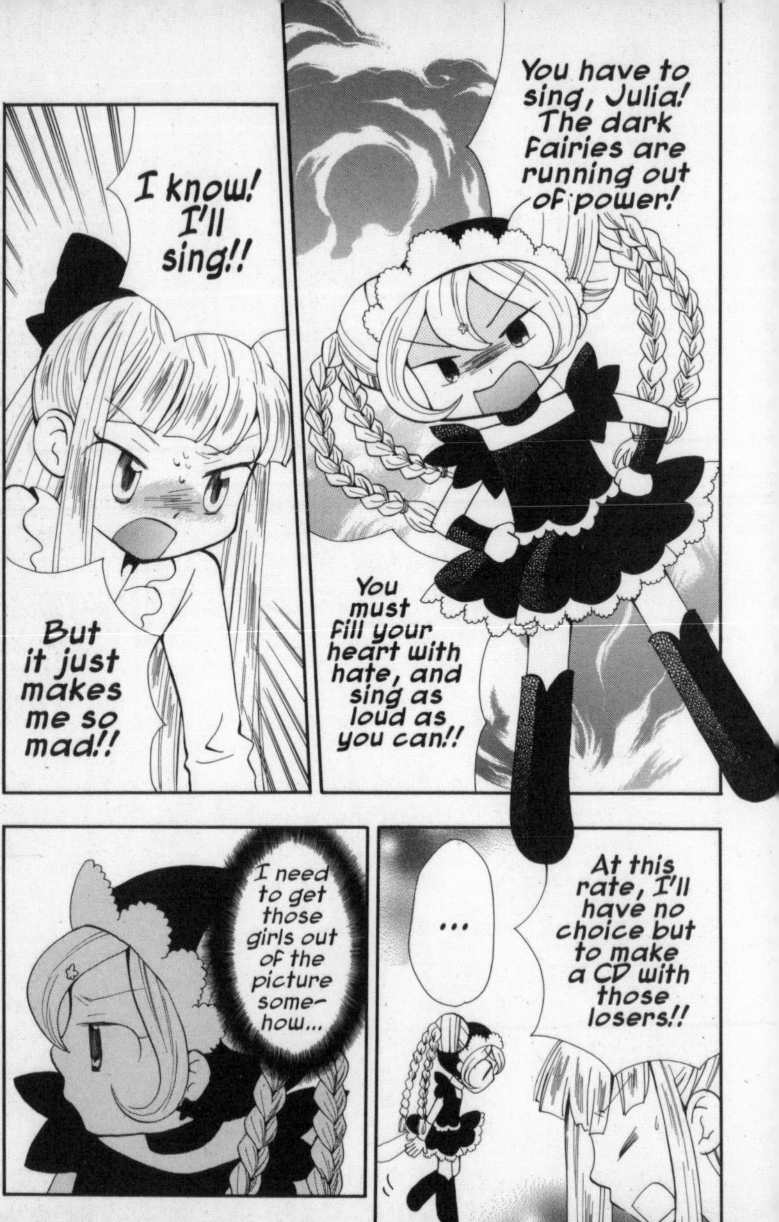
You have to sing, Julia! The dark fairies are running out of power!
You must fill your heart with hate, and sing as loud as you can!!
I know! I'll sing!!
But it just makes me so mad!!
At this rate, I'll have no choice but to make a CD with those losers!!
...
I need to get those girls out of the picture some-how...

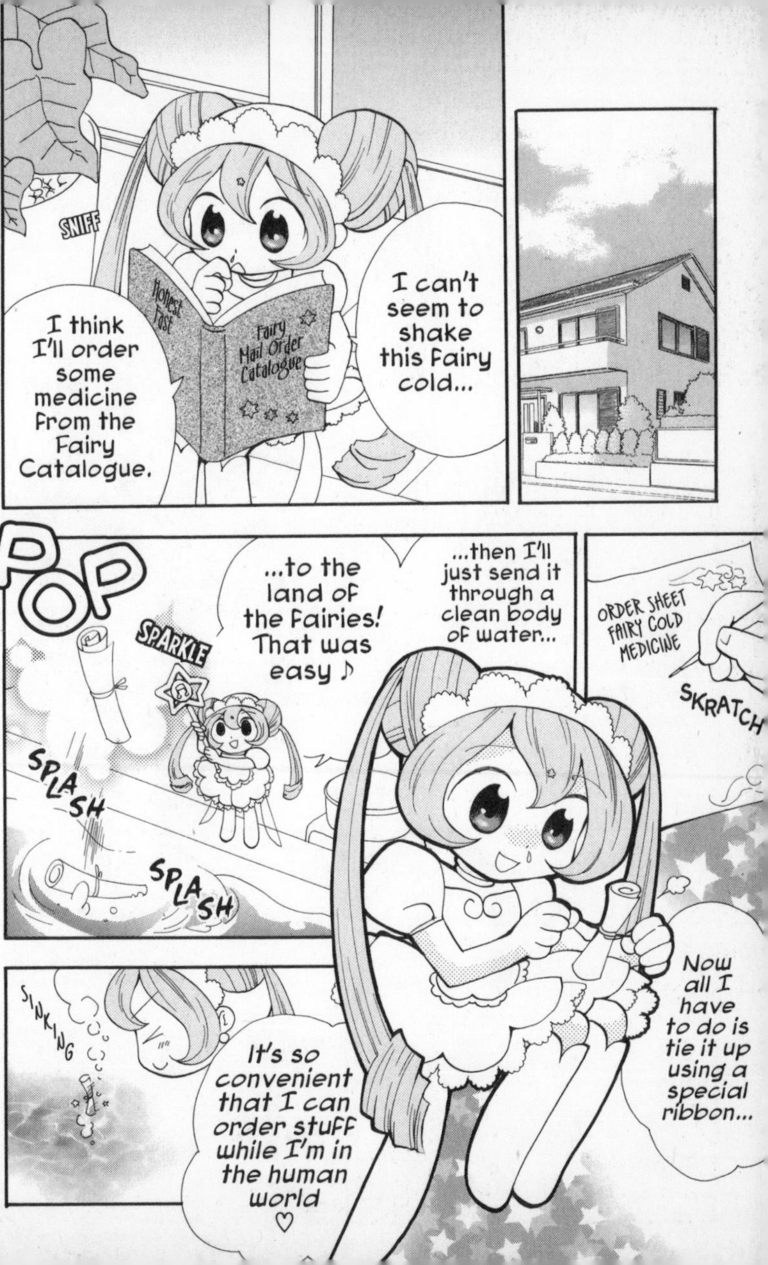

I can't seem to shake this fairy cold...
SNIFF
Honest Fast
Fairy Mail Order Catalogue
I think I'll order some medicine from the Fairy Catalogue.
ORDER SHEET FAIRY COLD MEDICINE
SKRATCH
Now all I have to do is tie it up using a special ribbon...
...then I'll just send it through a clean body of water...
POP
SPARKLE
SPLASH
SPLASH
...to the land of the fairies! That was easy ♪
SINKING
It's so convenient that I can order stuff while I'm in the human world ♡

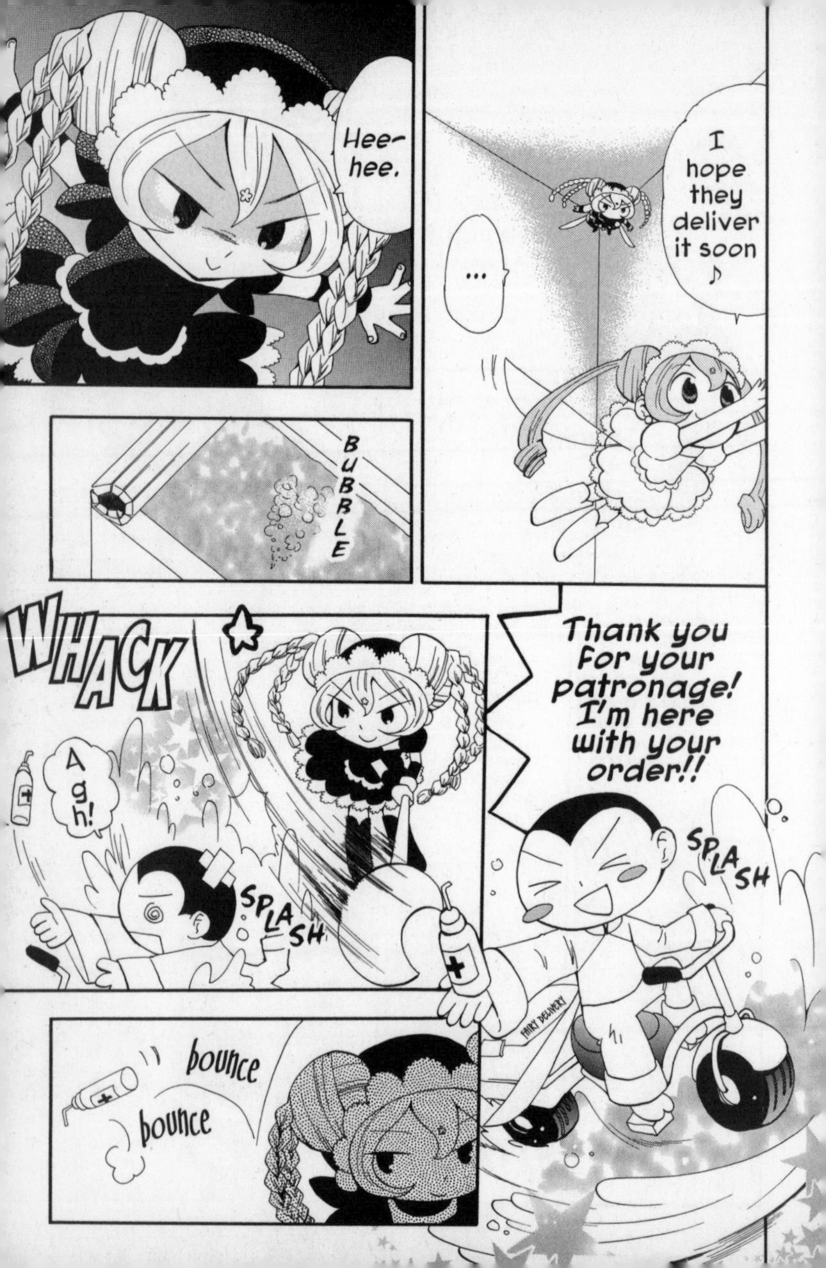
I hope they deliver it soon ♪
...
Hee-hee.
BUBBLE
Thank you for your patronage! I'm here with your order!!
SPLASH
WHACK
Agh!
SPLASH
bounce
bounce

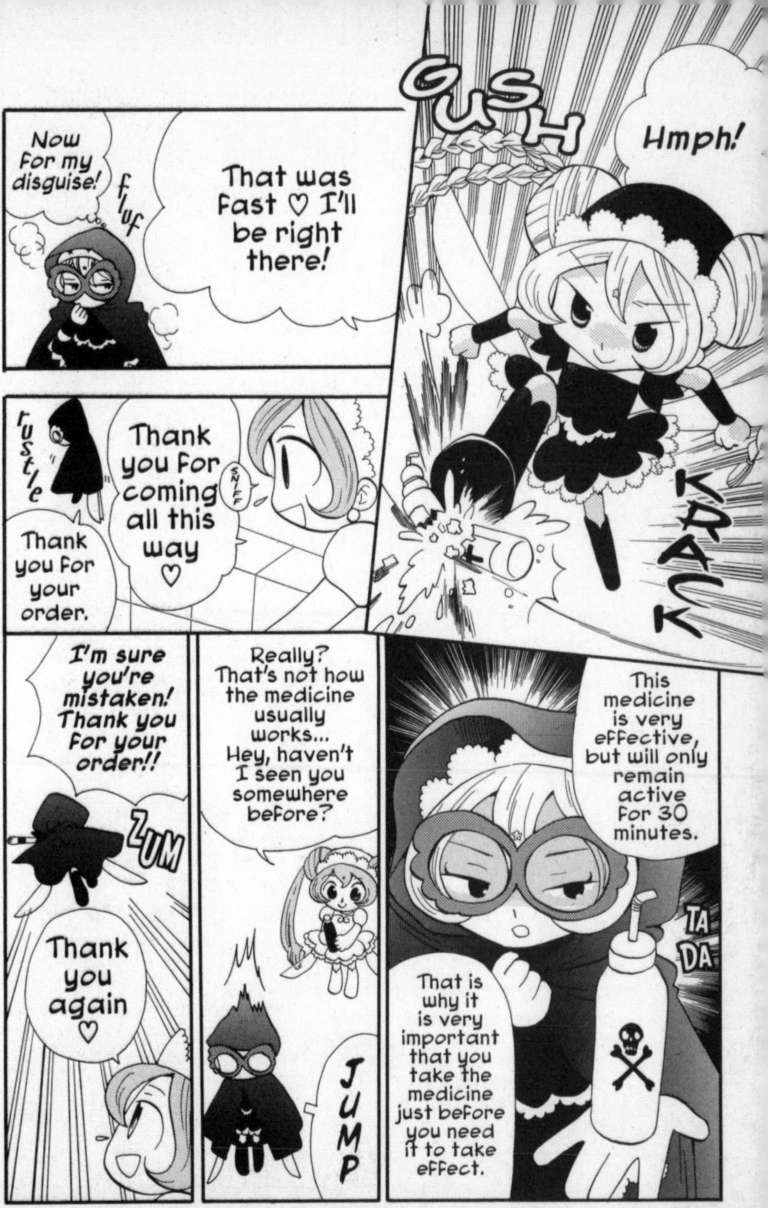
GUSH
Hmph!
KRACK
That was fast ♡ I'll be right there!
fluf
Now for my disguise!
Thank you for coming all this way ♡
SNIFF
rustle
Thank you for your order.
This medicine is very effective, but will only remain active for 30 minutes.
TA DA
That is why it is very important that you take the medicine just before you need it to take effect.
Really? That's not how the medicine usually works... Hey, haven't I seen you somewhere before?
JUMP
I'm sure you're mistaken! Thank you for your order!!
ZUM
Thank you again ♡

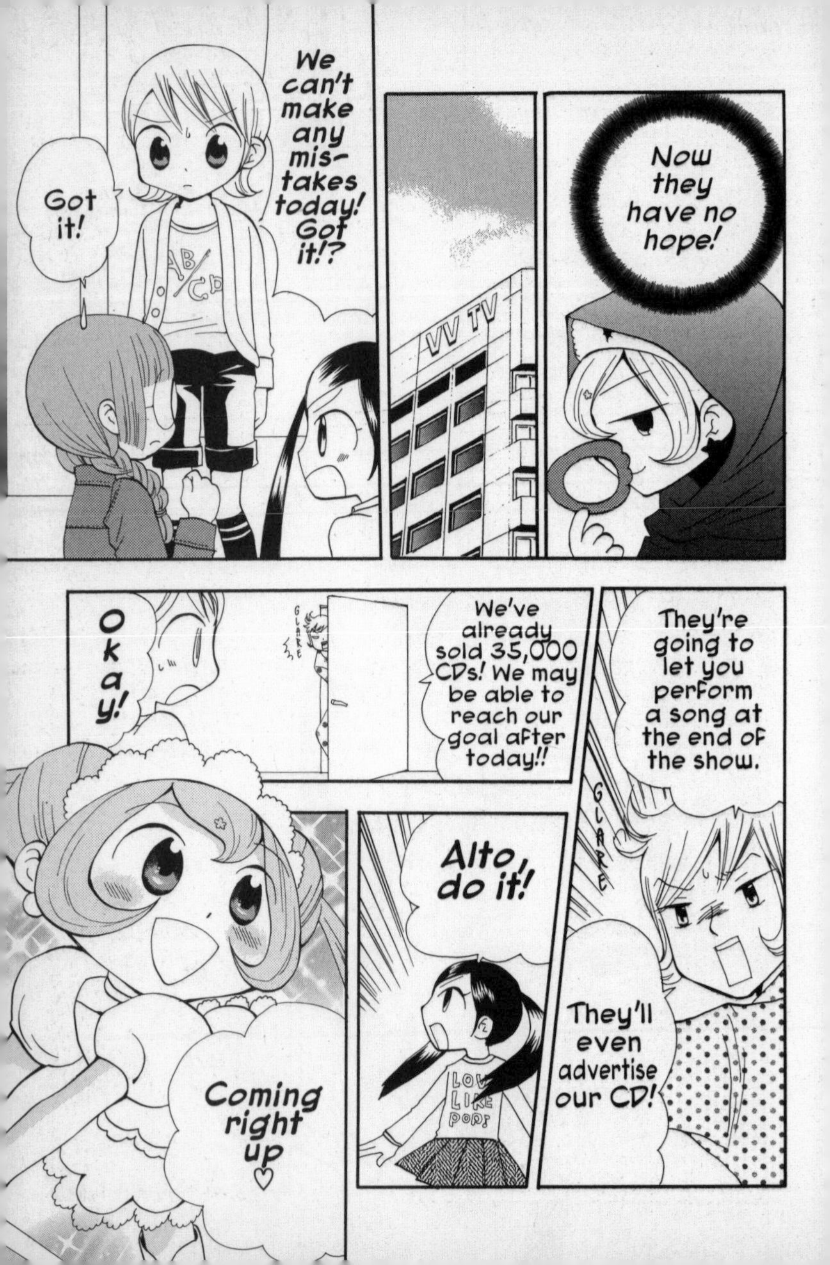
Now they have no hope!
VV TV
We can't make any mis-takes today! Got it!?
Got it!
They're going to let you perform a song at the end of the show.
GLARE
They'll even advertise our CD!
We've already sold 35,000 CDs! We may be able to reach our goal after today!!
GLARE
Okay!
Alto, do it!
Coming right up ♡

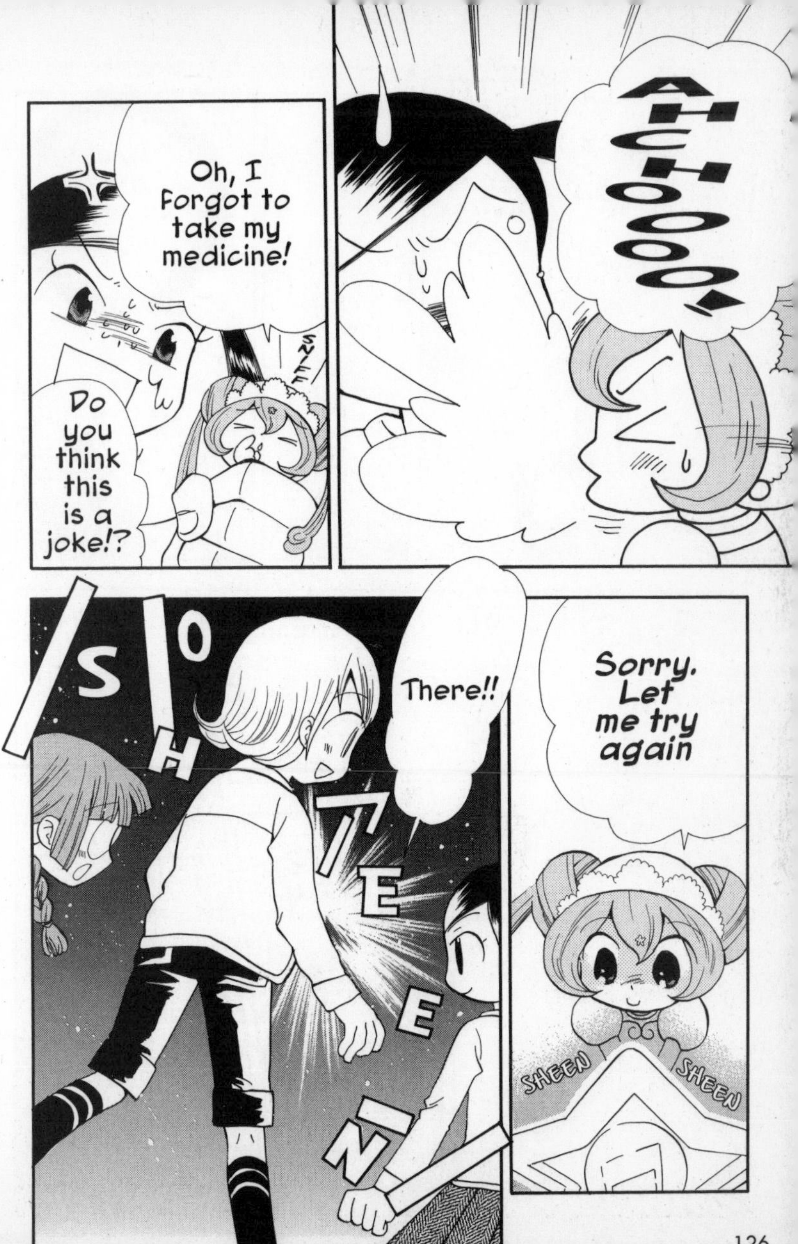

ACHOOOOO!
Oh, I forgot to take my medicine!
SNIFF
Do you think this is a joke!?
Sorry. Let me try again
SHEEN
SHEEN
There!!

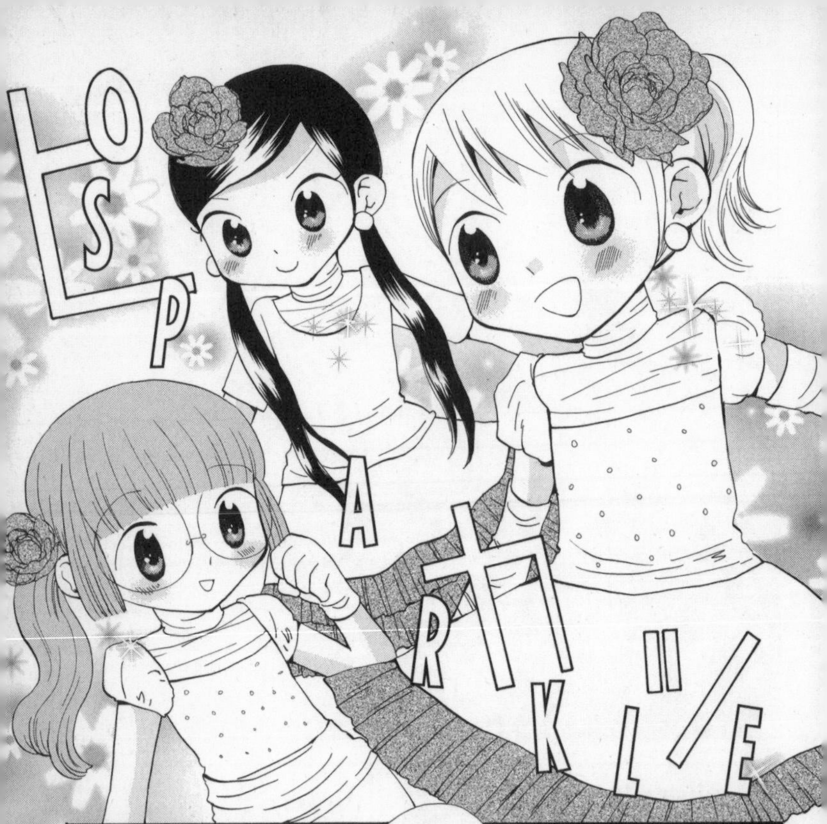
SPARKLE

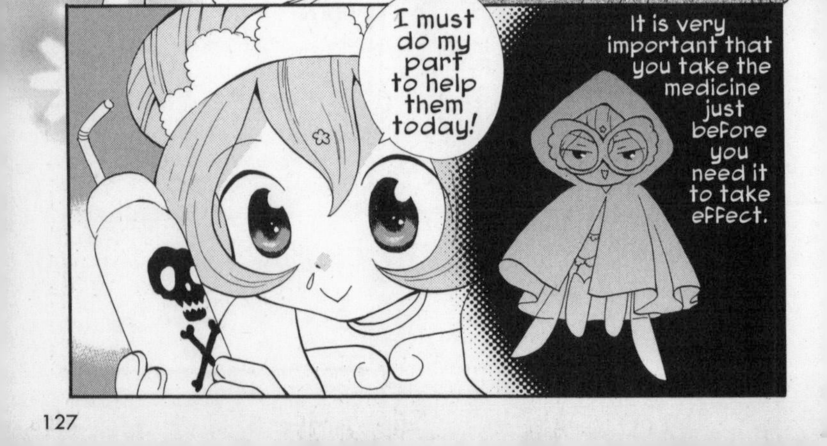
It is very important that you take the medicine just before you need it to take effect.
I must do my part to help them today!

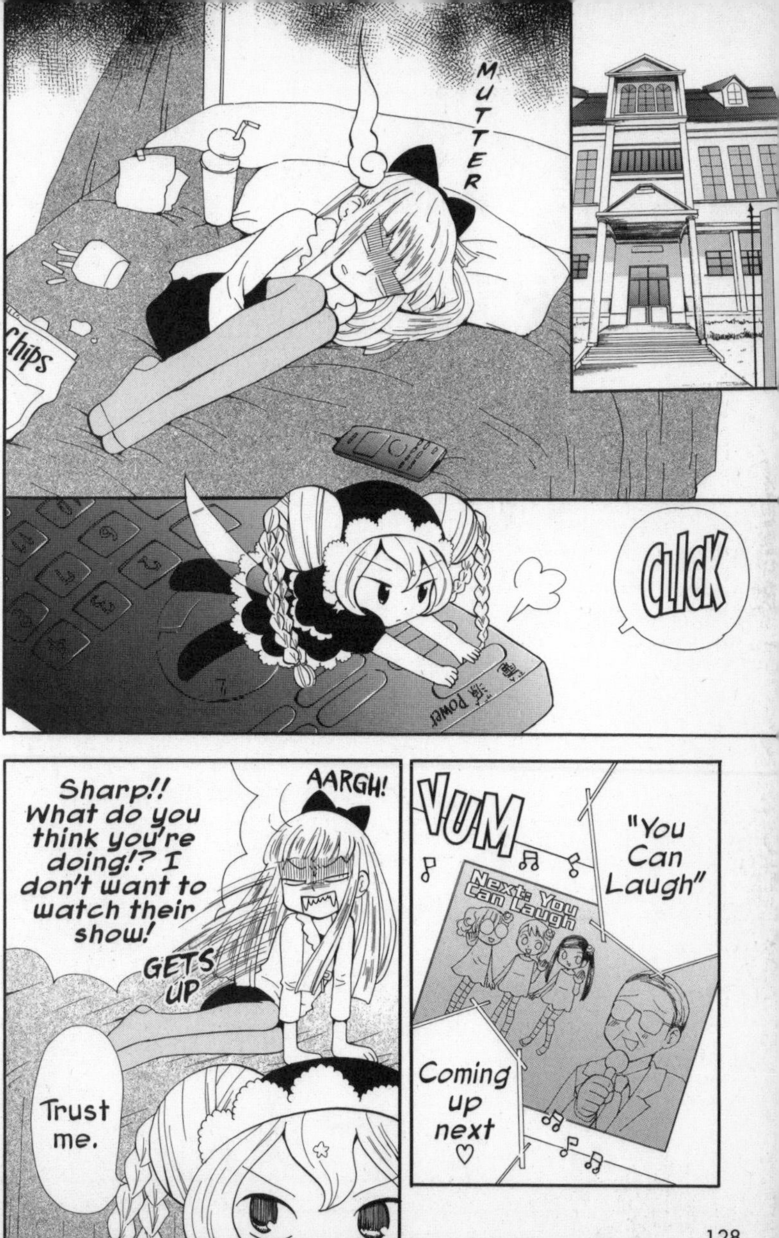
MUTTER
Chips
CLICK
Power
VUM
"You Can Laugh"
Next: You Can Laugh
Coming up next ♡
AARGH!
Sharp!! What do you think you're doing!? I don't want to watch their show!
GETS UP
Trust me.

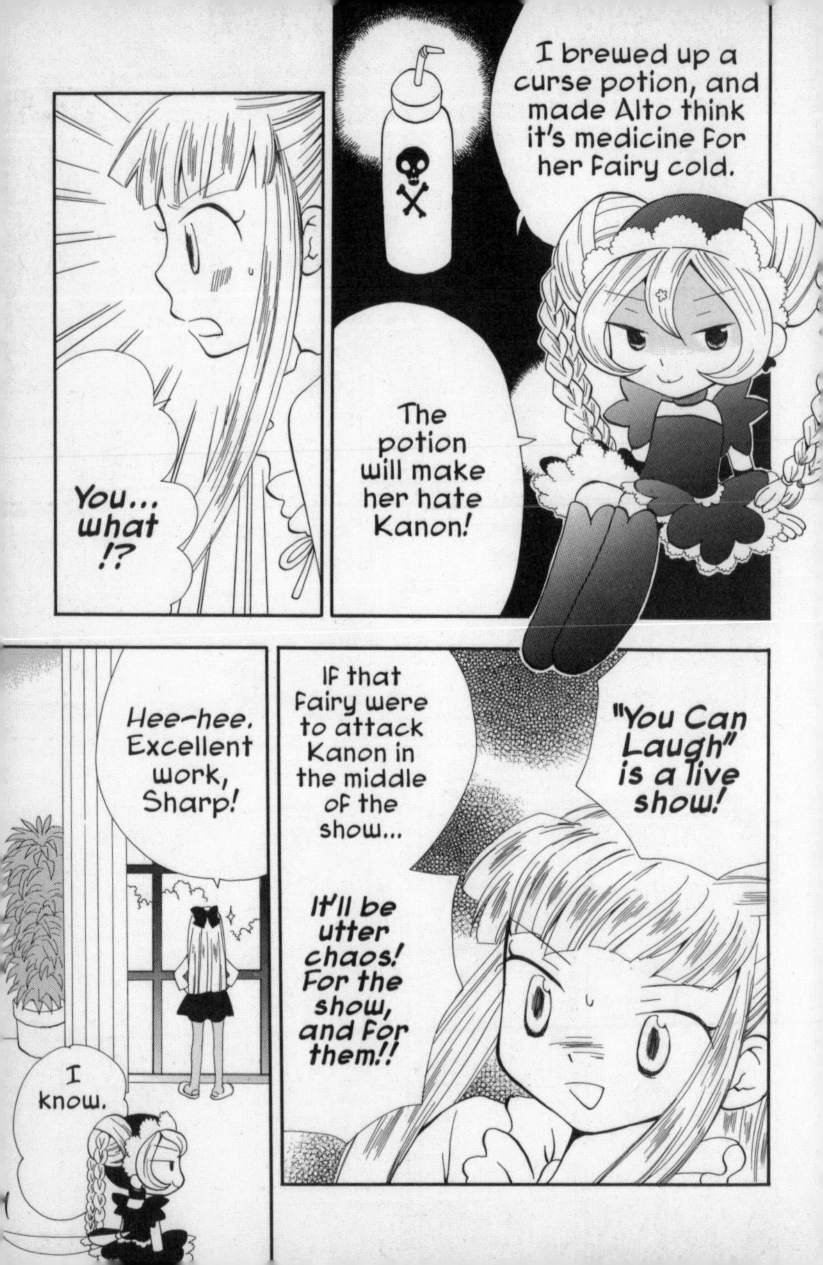
I brewed up a curse potion, and made Alto think it's medicine for her fairy cold.
The potion will make her hate Kanon!
You... what!?
"You Can Laugh" is a live show!
If that fairy were to attack Kanon in the middle of the show...
It'll be utter chaos! For the show, and for them!!
Hee-hee. Excellent work, Sharp!
I know.

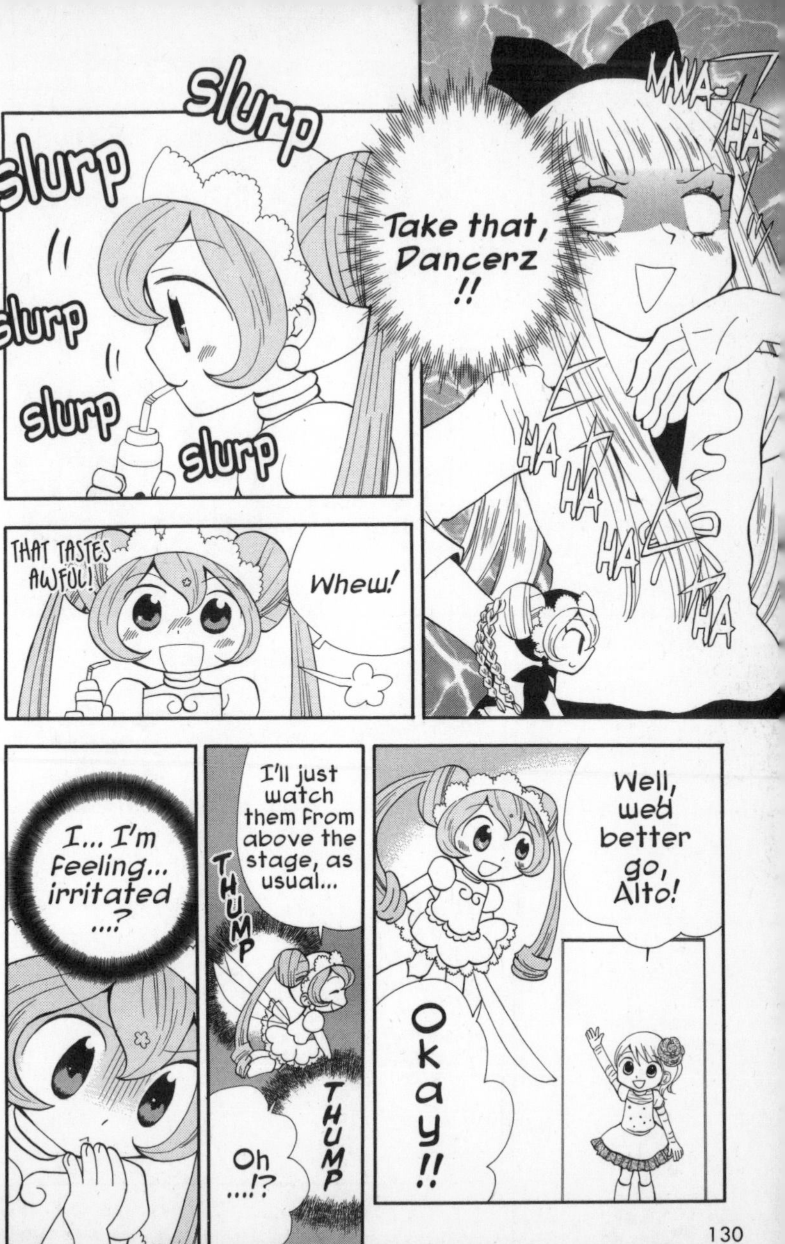
MWA-HA HA
Take that, Dancerz!!
HA HA HA HA HA
slurp
slurp
slurp
slurp
slurp
THAT TASTES AWFUL!
Whew!
Well, we'd better go, Alto!
Okay!!
I'll just watch them from above the stage, as usual...
THUMP
Oh...!?
THUMP
I... I'm feeling... irritated...?

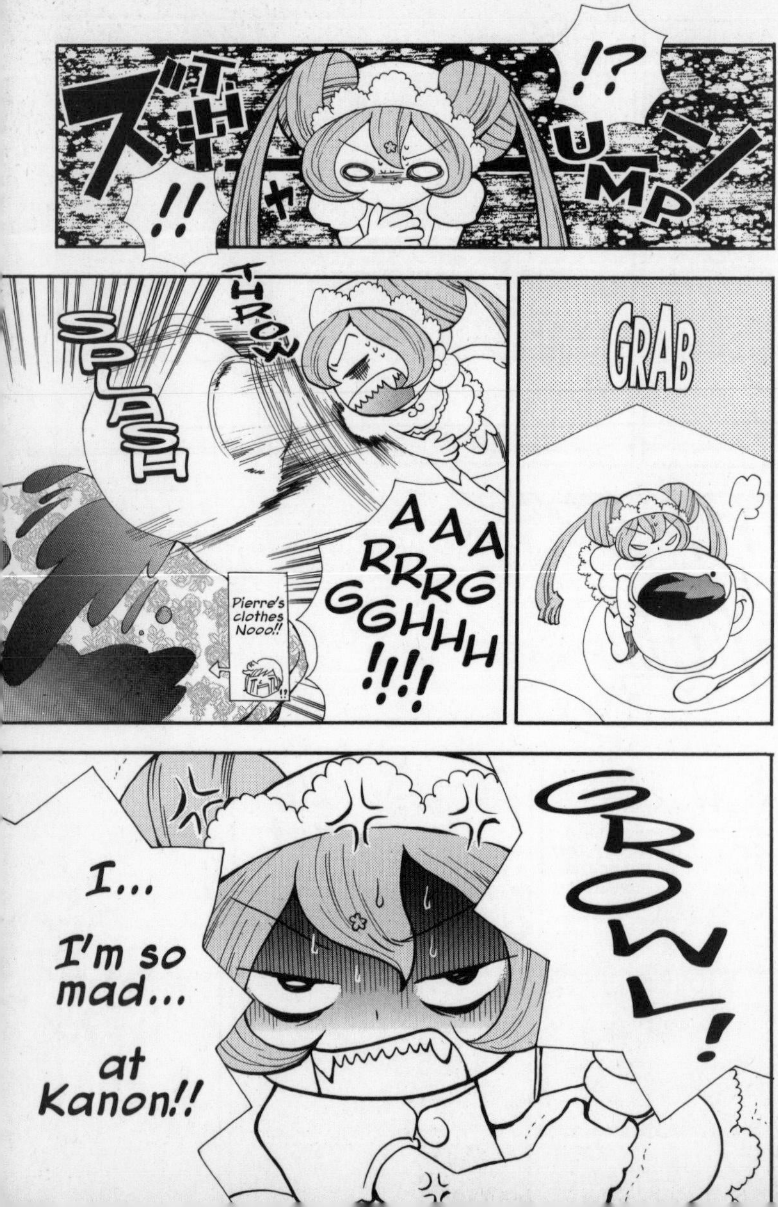

!?
THUMP
!!
GRAB
THROW
SPLASH
AAARRRRGGHHHH!!!!
Pierre's clothes Nooo!!
!?
GROWL!
I... I'm so mad... at Kanon!!

Read this way

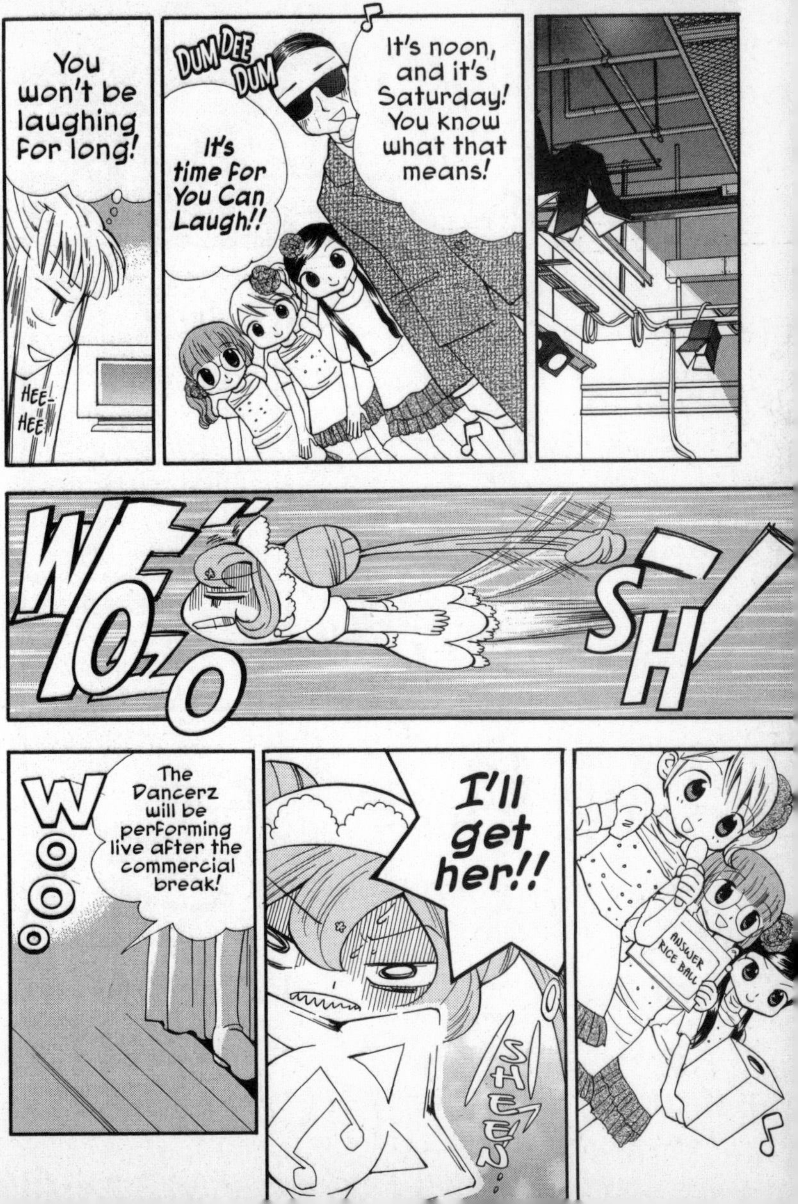
DUM DEE DUM
It's noon, and it's Saturday! You know what that means!
It's time for You Can Laugh!!
You won't be laughing for long!
HEE-HEE
WHOOOSH
ANSWER RICE BALL
I'll get her!!
SHEEN
The Dancerz will be performing live after the commercial break!
WOOOO

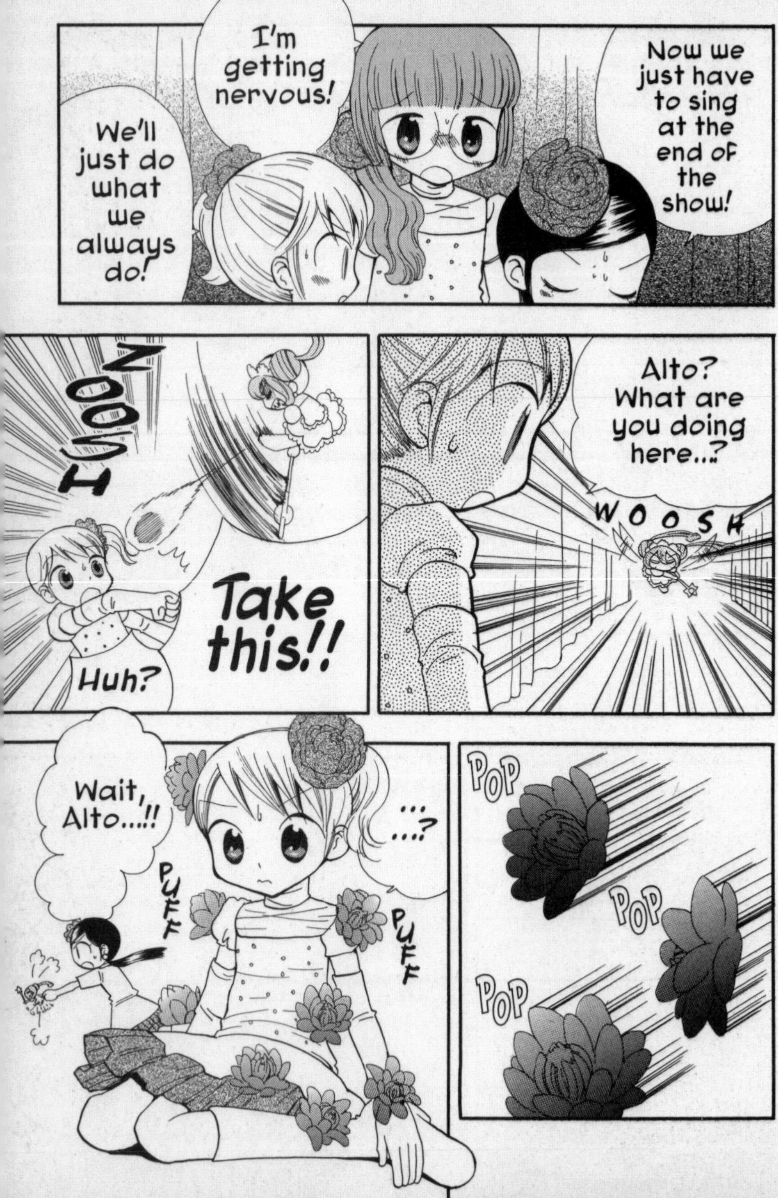

Now we just have to sing at the end of the show!
I'm getting nervous!
We'll just do what we always do!
Alto? What are you doing here...?
WOOSH
ZOOSH
Take this!!
Huh?
POP
POP
POP
...? ...?
PUFF
Wait, Alto...!!
PUFF

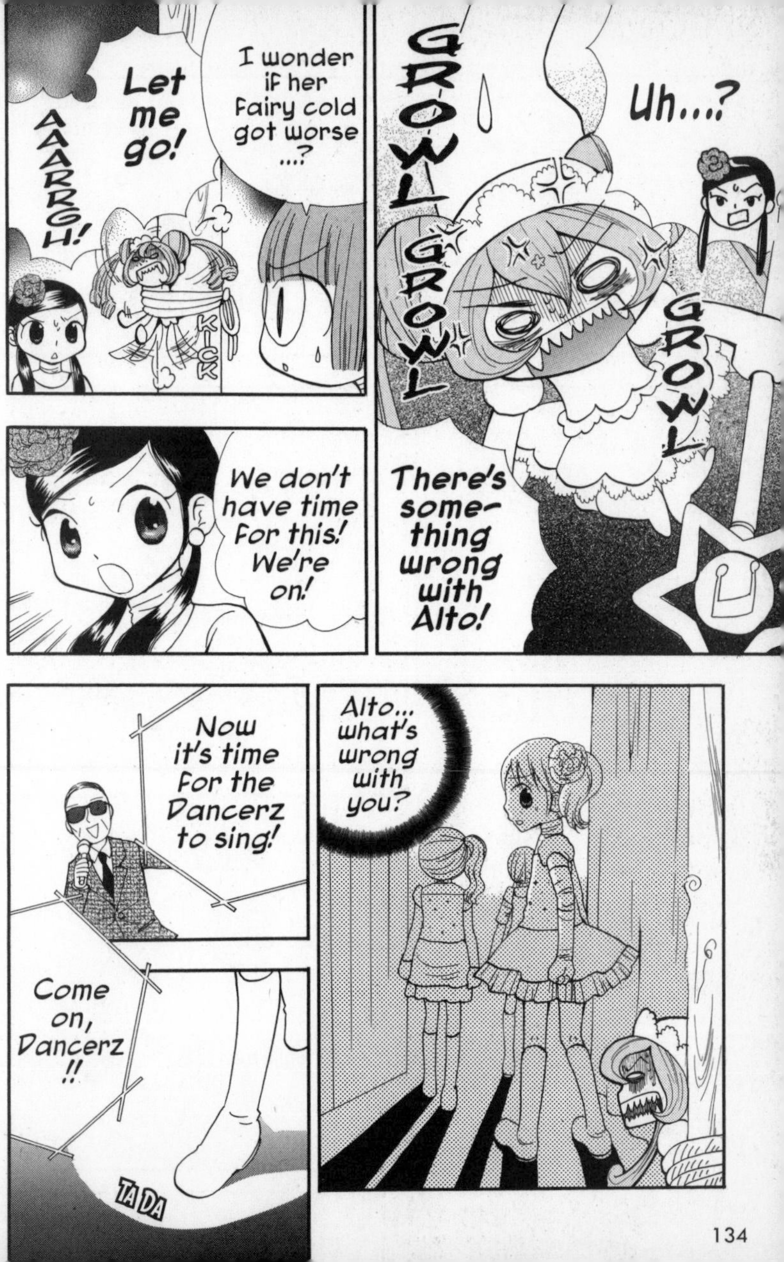
Uh...?
GROWL
GROWL
GROWL
There's some-thing wrong with Alto!
I wonder if her fairy cold got worse ...?
Let me go!
AAAARRGH!
KICK
We don't have time for this! We're on!
Alto... what's wrong with you?
Now it's time for the Dancerz to sing!
Come on, Dancerz !!
TA DA

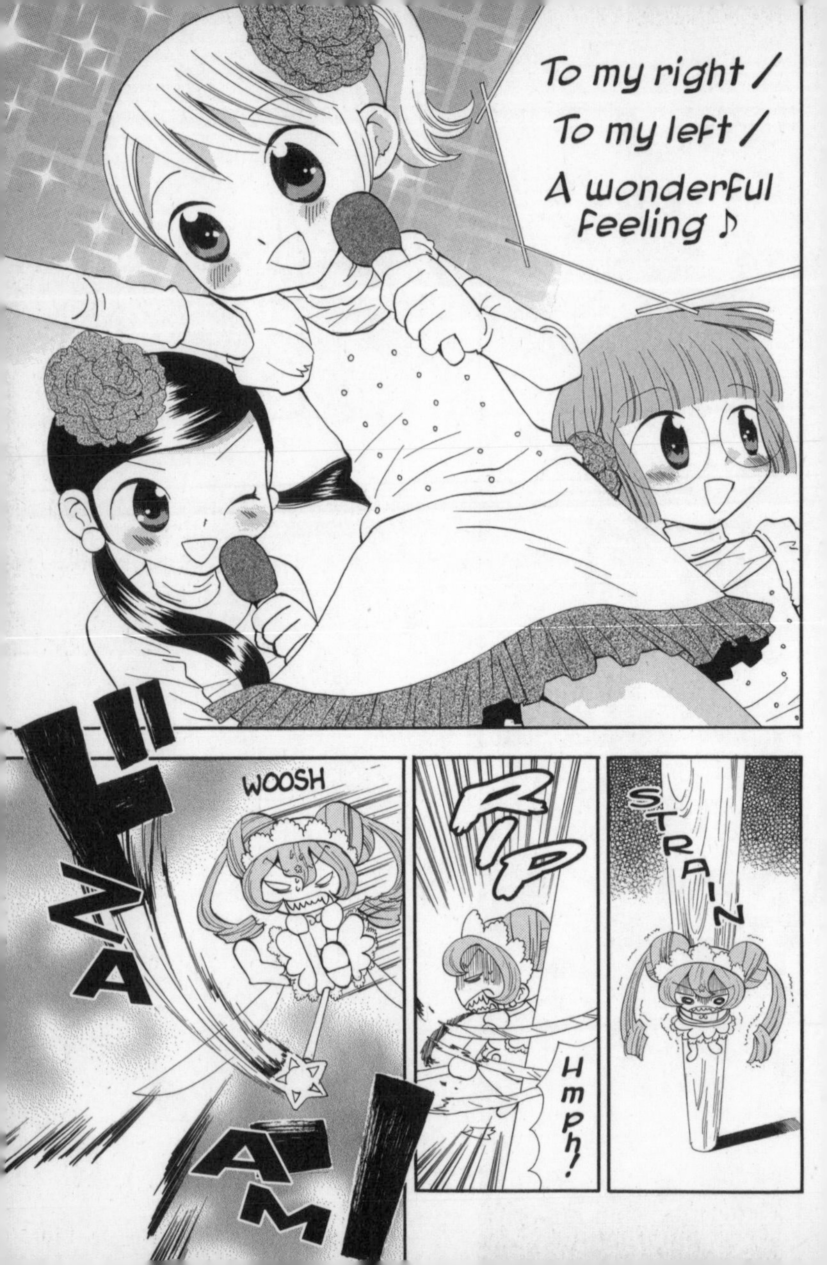
To my right /
To my left /
A wonderful feeling ♪
STRAIN
RIP
Hmph!
WOOSH

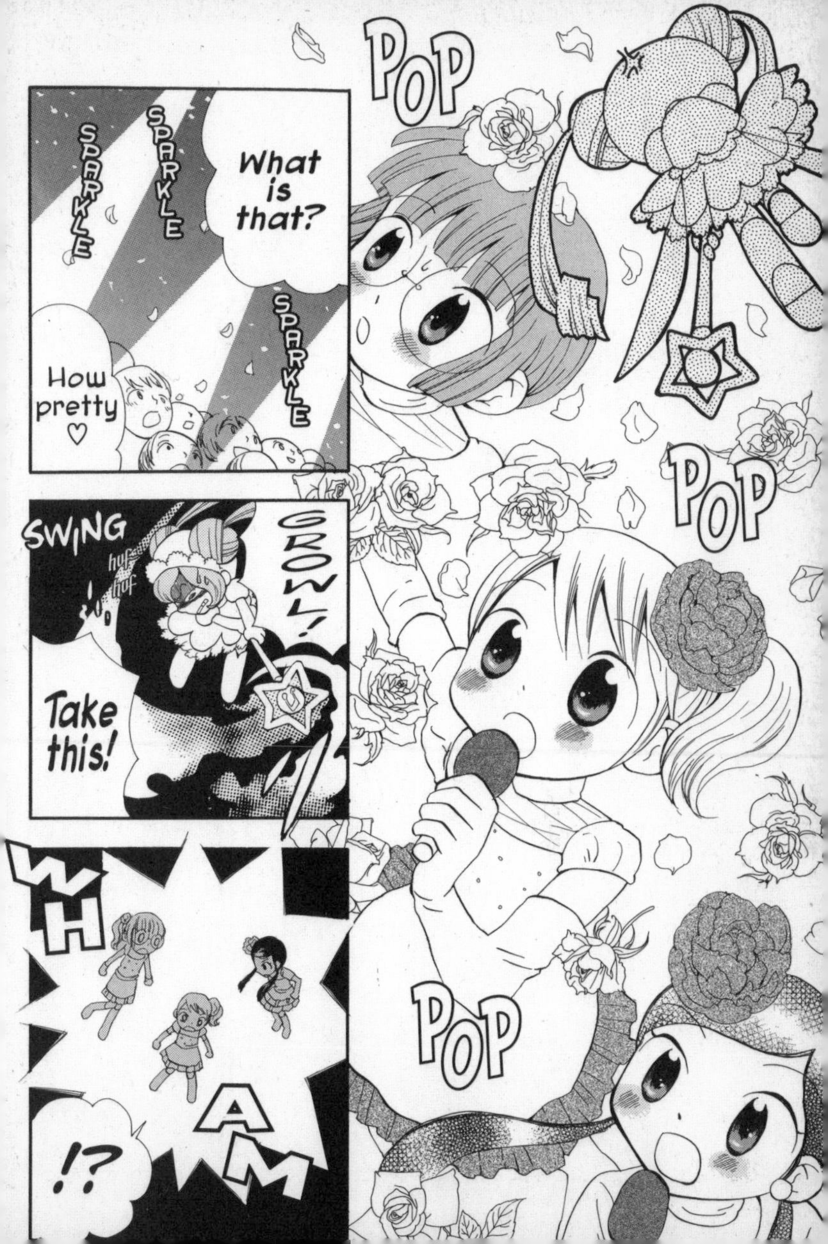
POP
POP
POP
What is that?
SPARKLE
SPARKLE
SPARKLE
How pretty ♡
GROWL!
SWING
huf huf
Take this!
WHAM
!?

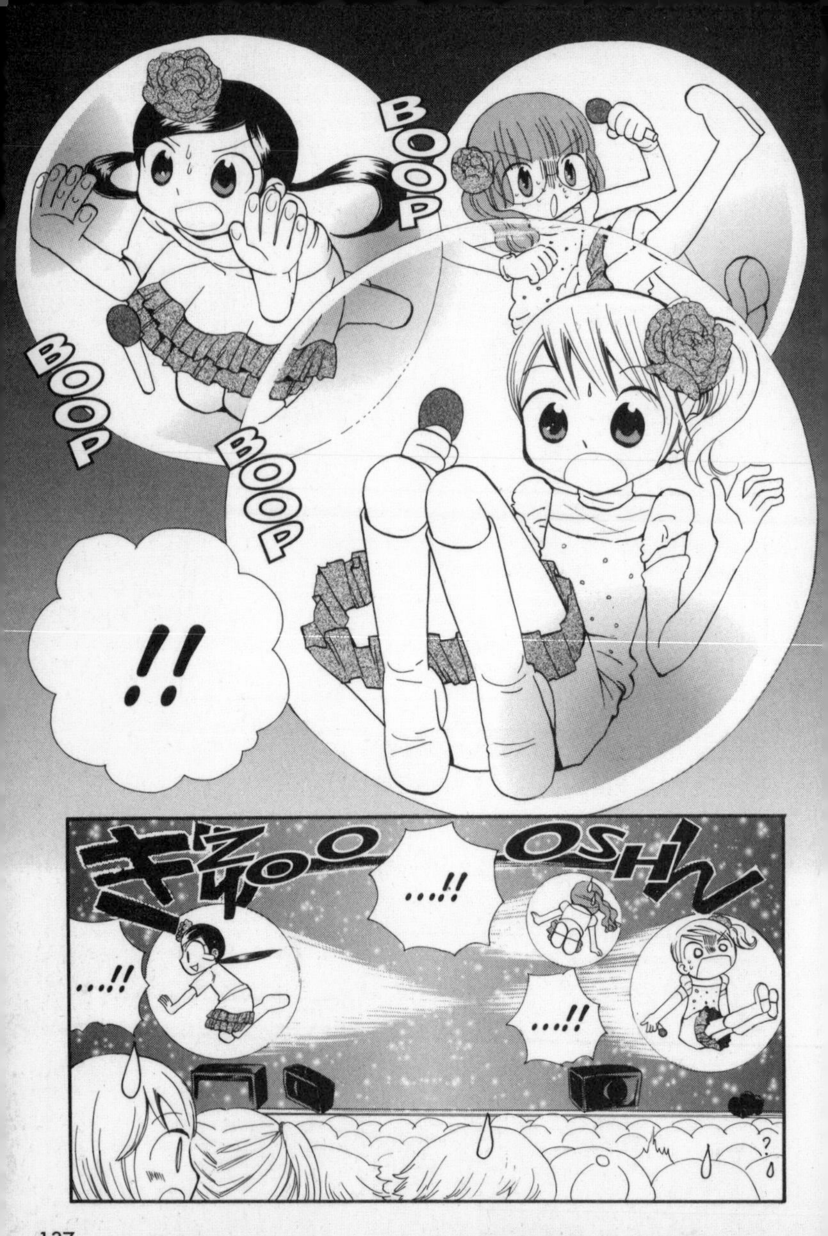
BOOP
BOOP
BOOP
!!
...!!
...!!
...!!

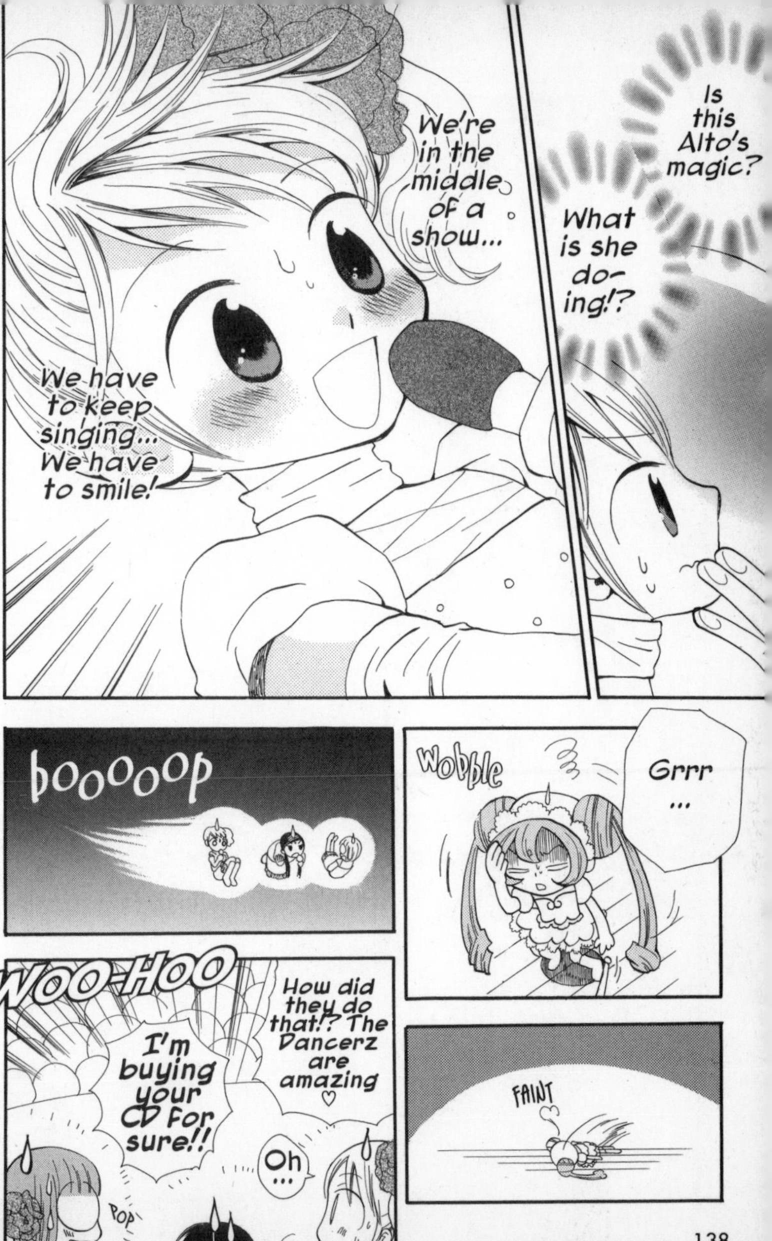
Is this Alto's magic?
What is she do-ing!?
We're in the middle of a show...
We have to keep singing... We have to smile!
Grrr ...
wobble
booooop
FAINT
WOO-HOO
How did they do that!? The Dancerz are amazing ♡
I'm buying your CD for sure!!
Oh ...
POP

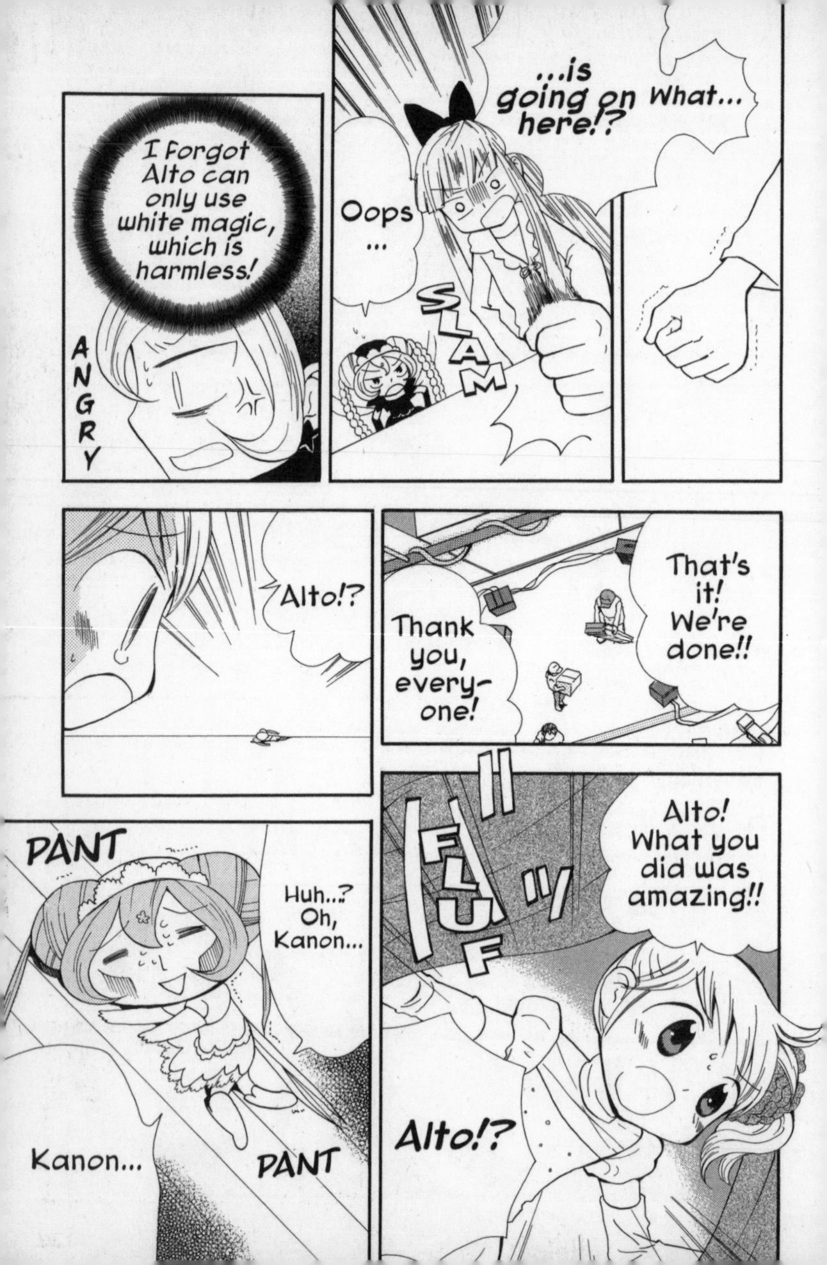

What...
...is going on here!?
Oops ...
SLAM
I forgot Alto can only use white magic, which is harmless!
ANGRY
That's it! We're done!!
Thank you, every-one!
Alto!?
Alto! What you did was amazing!!
FLUF
Alto!?
PANT
Huh...? Oh, Kanon...
Kanon...
PANT

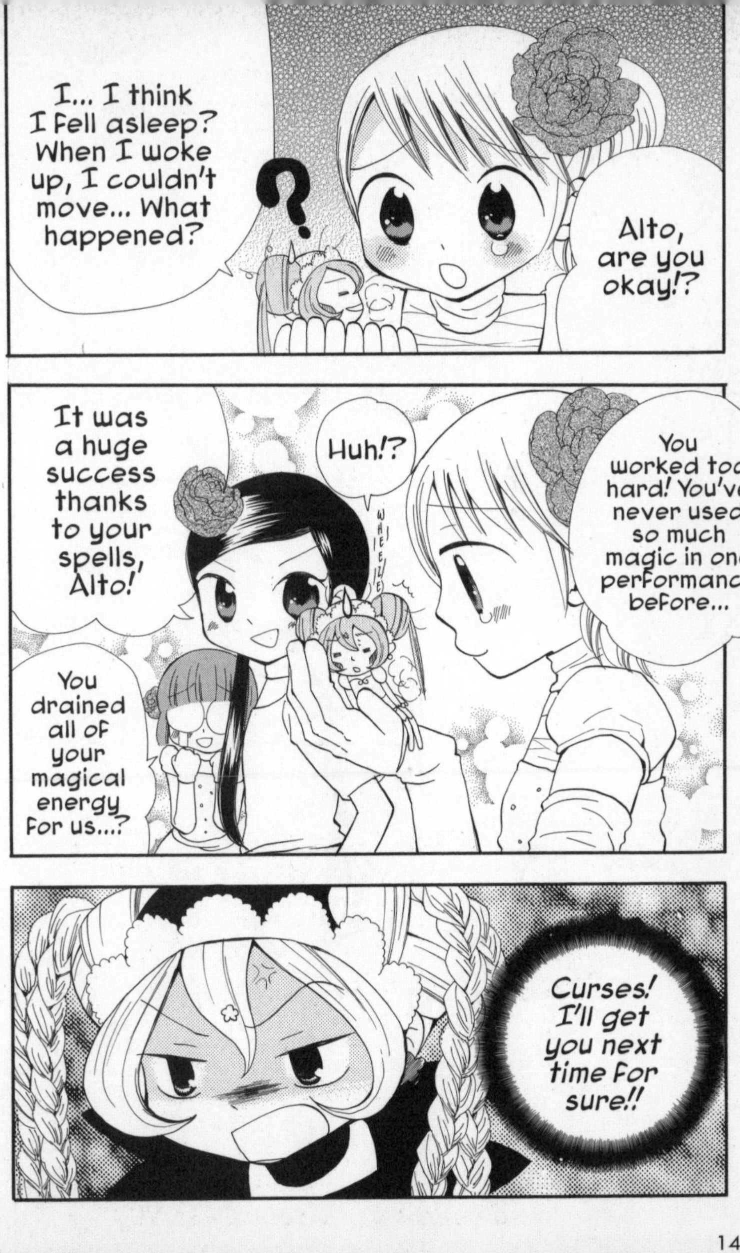
Alto, are you okay!?
I... I think I fell asleep? When I woke up, I couldn't move... What happened?
You worked too hard! You've never used so much magic in one performance before...
Huh!?
WHEEZE
It was a huge success thanks to your spells, Alto!
You drained all of your magical energy for us...?
Curses! I'll get you next time for sure!!

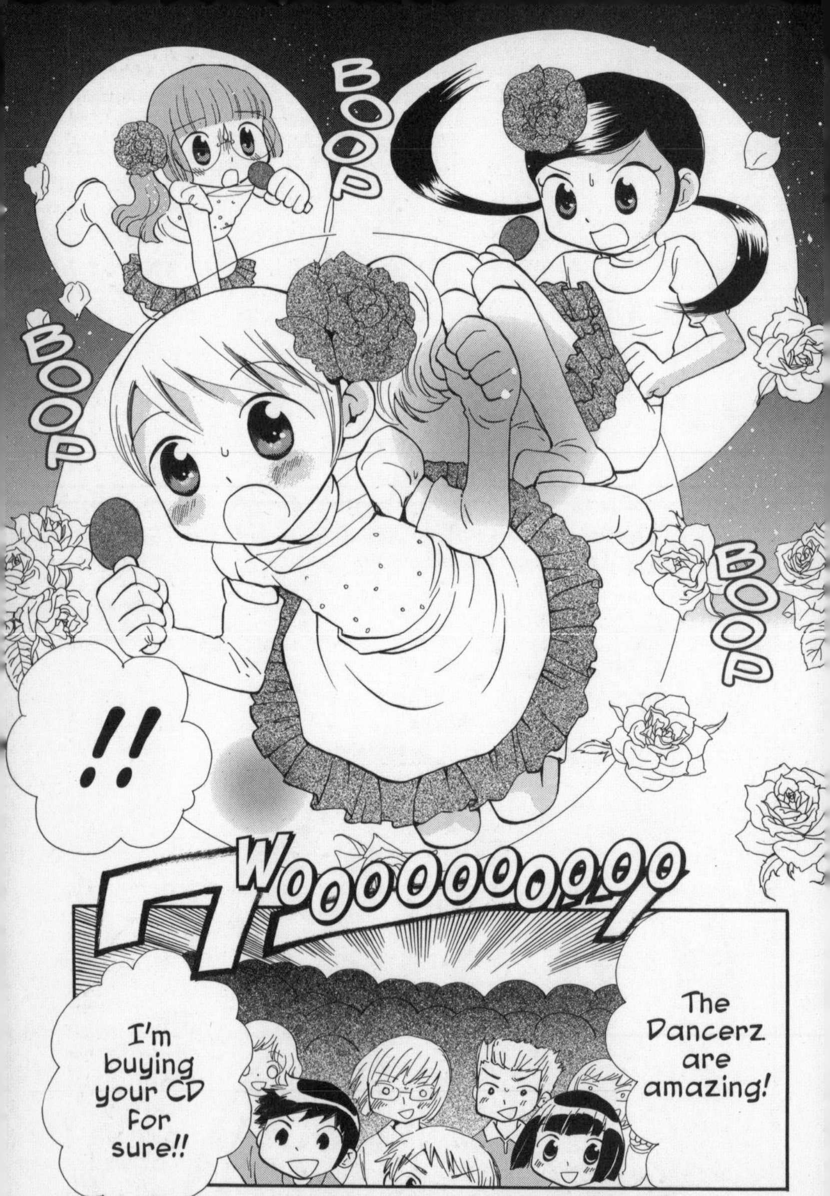
BOOP BOOP
BOOP BOOP
BOOP BOOP
!!
WOOOOOOOOOO
The Dancerz are amazing!
I'm buying your CD for sure!!

Stage 19 Uncertainty

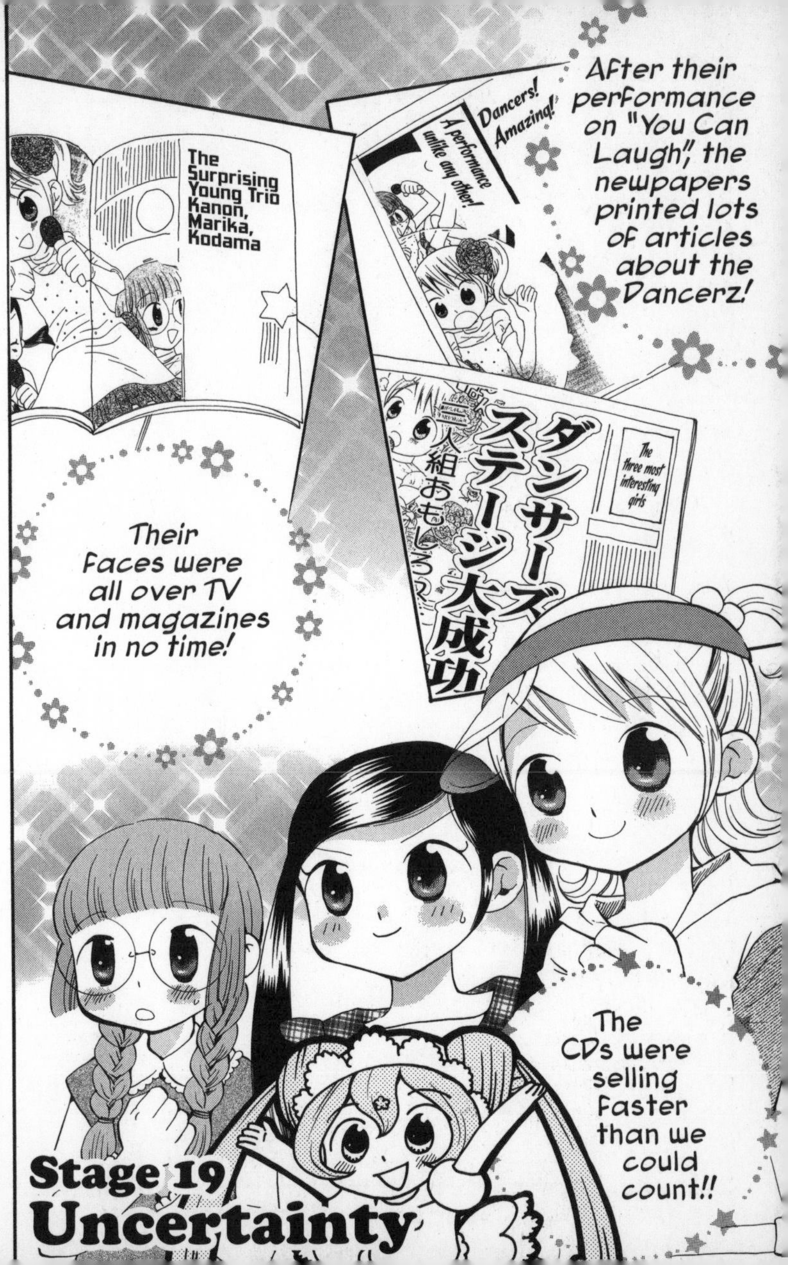
After their performance on "You Can Laugh", the newpapers printed lots of articles about the Dancerz!
Dancers! Amazing!
A performance unlike any other!
The Surprising Young Trio Kanon, Marika, Kodama
ダンサーズステージ大成功
The three most interesting girls
Their faces were all over TV and magazines in no time!
The CDs were selling faster than we could count!!
Stage 19
Uncertainty

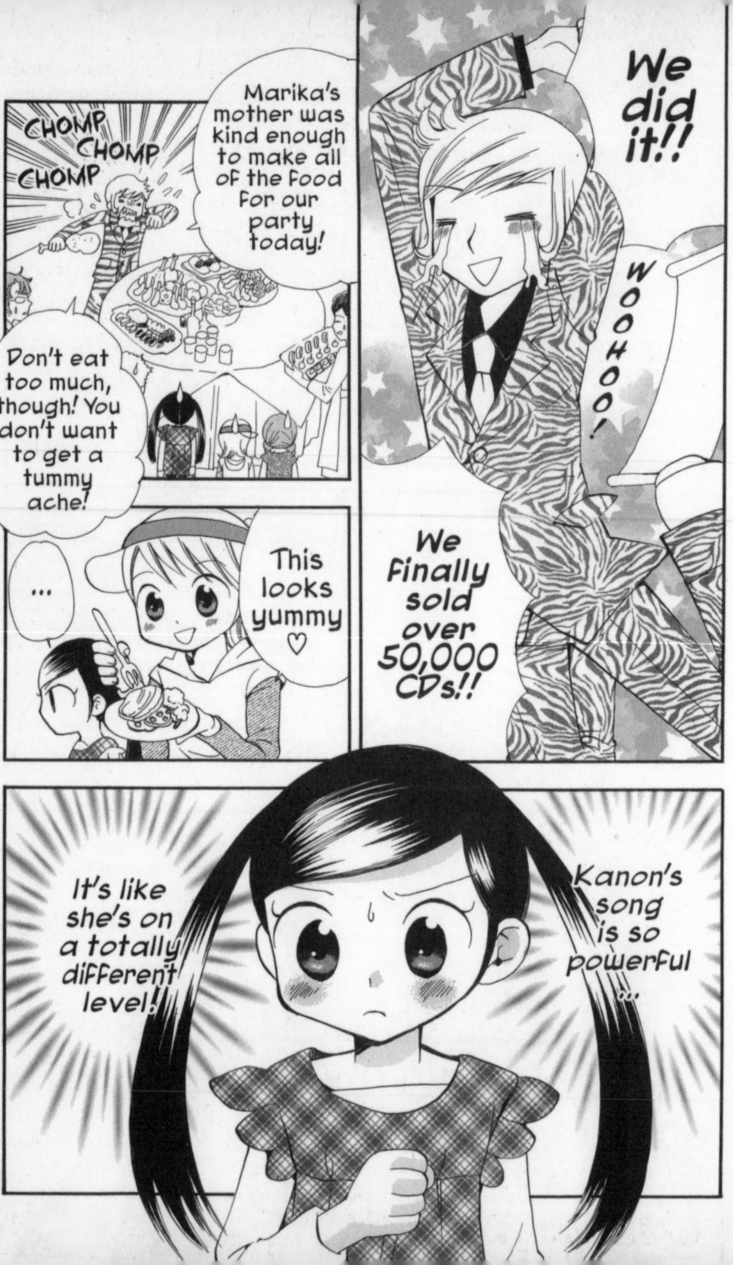
We did it!!
WOOHOO!
We finally sold over 50,000 CDs!!
Marika's mother was kind enough to make all of the food for our party today!
CHOMP CHOMP CHOMP
Don't eat too much, though! You don't want to get a tummy ache!
This looks yummy ♡
...
Kanon's song is so powerful...
It's like she's on a totally different level!

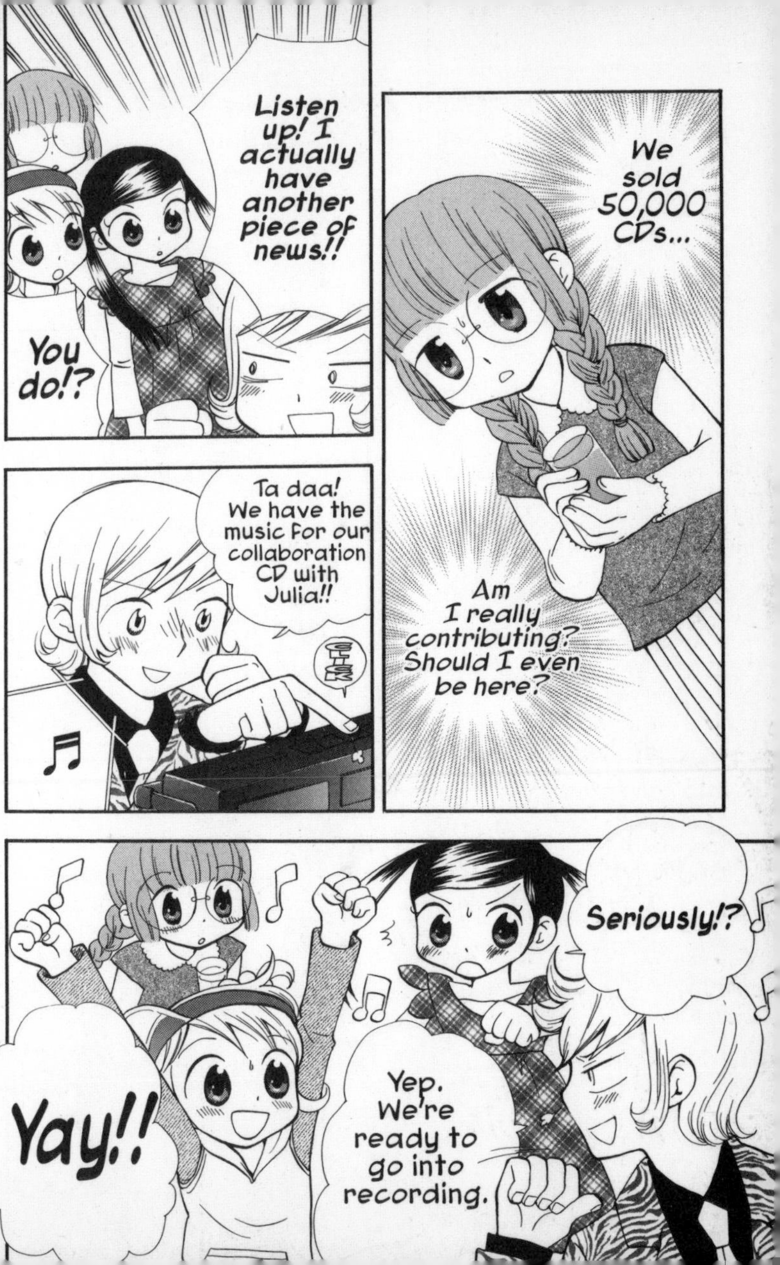
We sold 50,000 CDs...
Am I really contributing? Should I even be here?
Listen up! I actually have another piece of news!!
You do!?
Ta daa! We have the music for our collaboration CD with Julia!!
CLICK
Seriously!?
Yep. We're ready to go into recording.
Yay!!

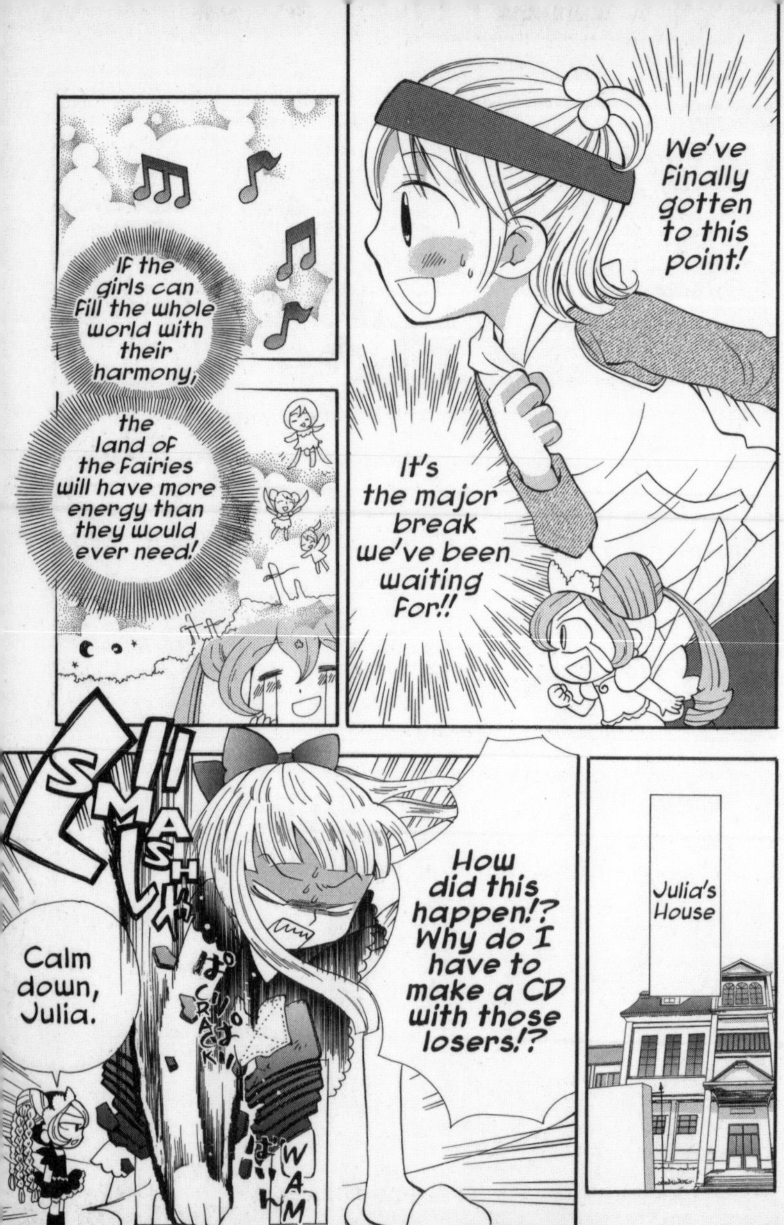
We've finally gotten to this point!
It's the major break we've been waiting for!!
If the girls can fill the whole world with their harmony,
the land of the fairies will have more energy than they would ever need!
Julia's House
How did this happen!? Why do I have to make a CD with those losers!?
SMASH
CRACK
WAM
Calm down, Julia.

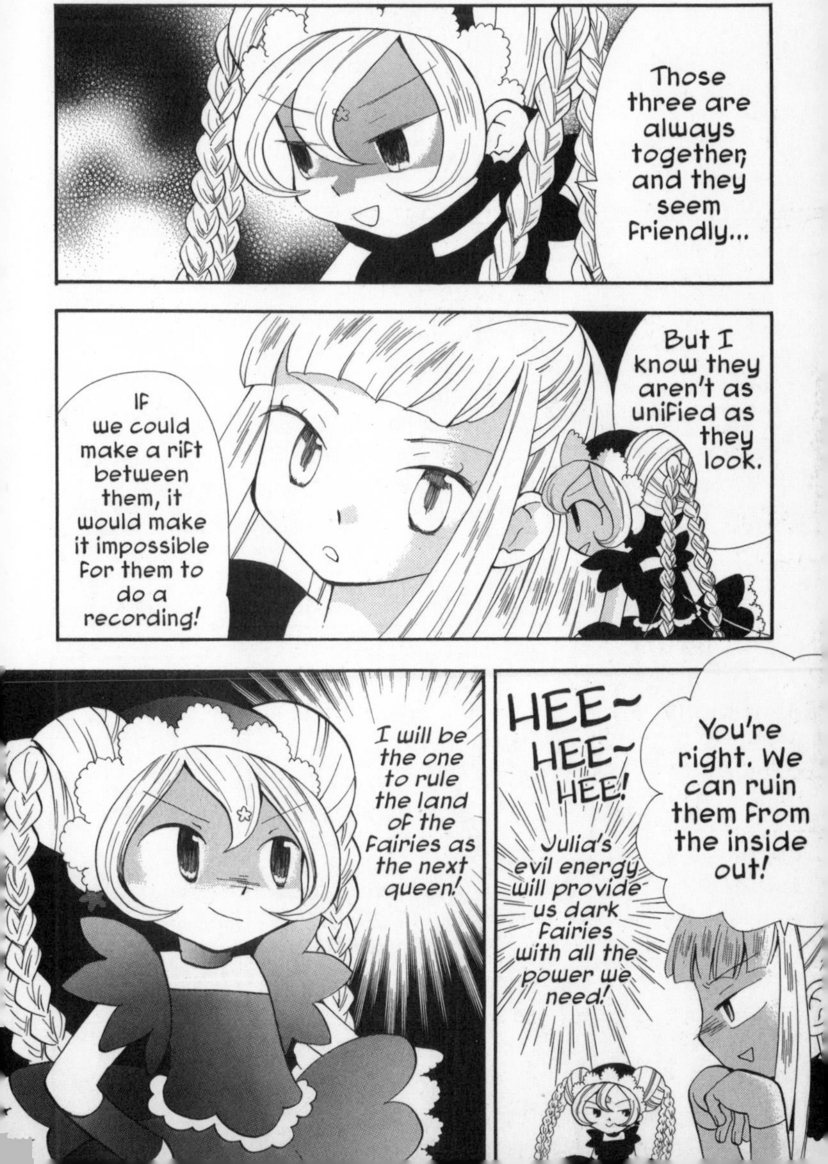
Those three are always together, and they seem friendly...
But I know they aren't as unified as they look.
If we could make a rift between them, it would make it impossible for them to do a recording!
You're right. We can ruin them from the inside out!
HEE~ HEE~ HEE!
Julia's evil energy will provide us dark fairies with all the power we need!
I will be the one to rule the land of the fairies as the next queen!

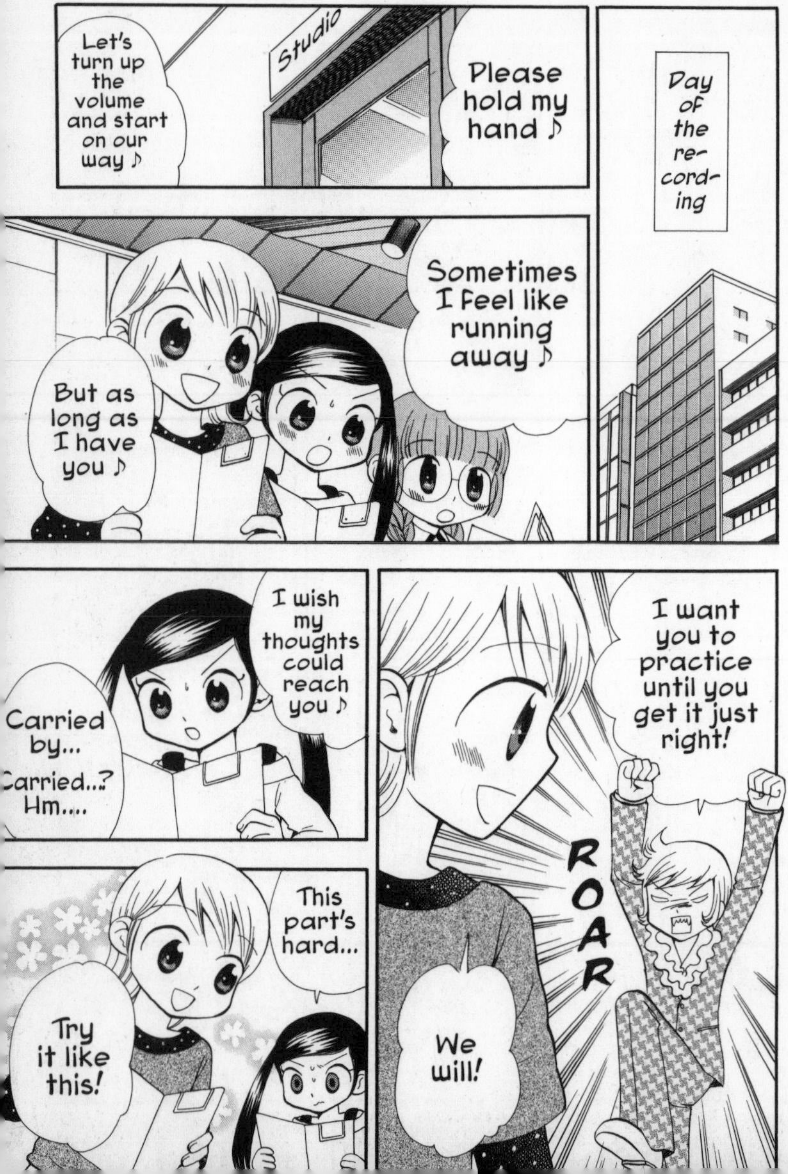
Day of the re-cording
Studio
Please hold my hand ♪
Let's turn up the volume and start on our way ♪
Sometimes I feel like running away ♪
But as long as I have you ♪
I want you to practice until you get it just right!
ROAR
We will!
I wish my thoughts could reach you ♪
Carried by...
Carried...? Hm....
This part's hard...
Try it like this!

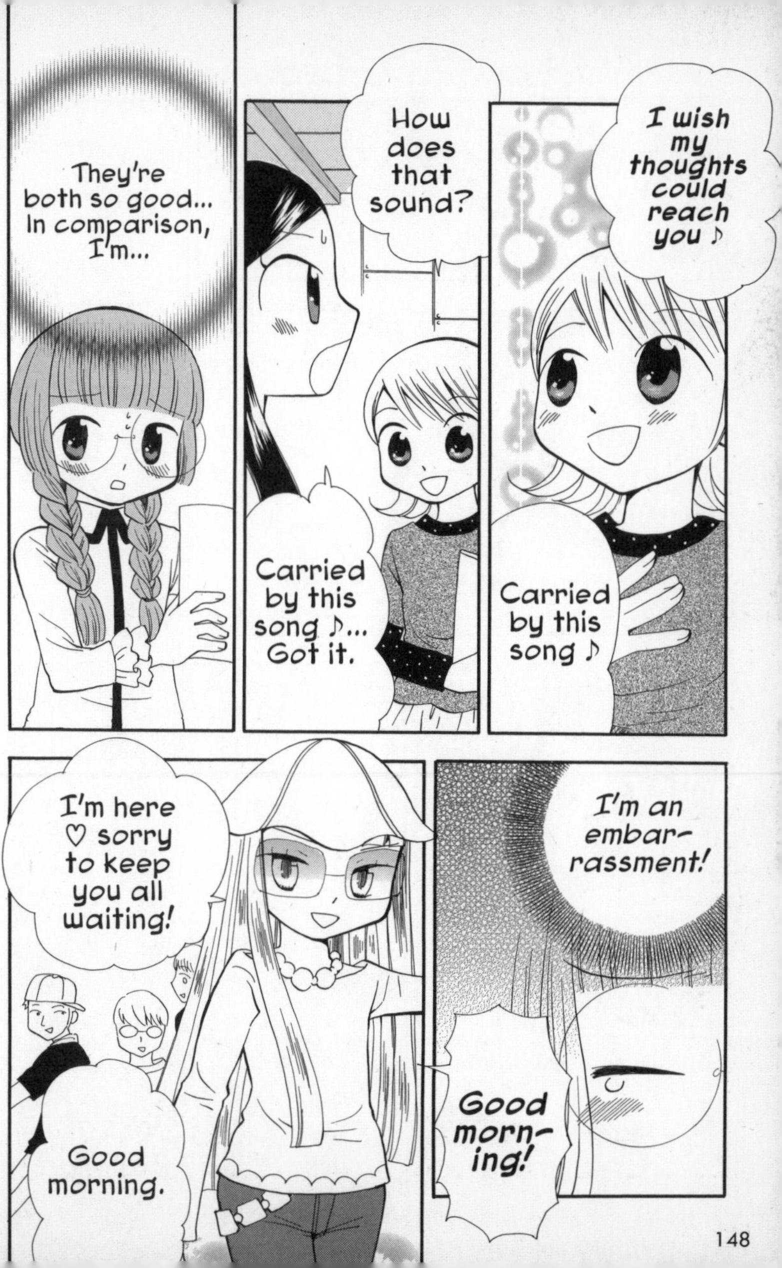
I wish my thoughts could reach you ♪
Carried by this song ♪
How does that sound?
Carried by this song ♪... Got it.
They're both so good... In comparison, I'm...
I'm an embarrassment!
Good morning!
I'm here ♡ sorry to keep you all waiting!
Good morning.

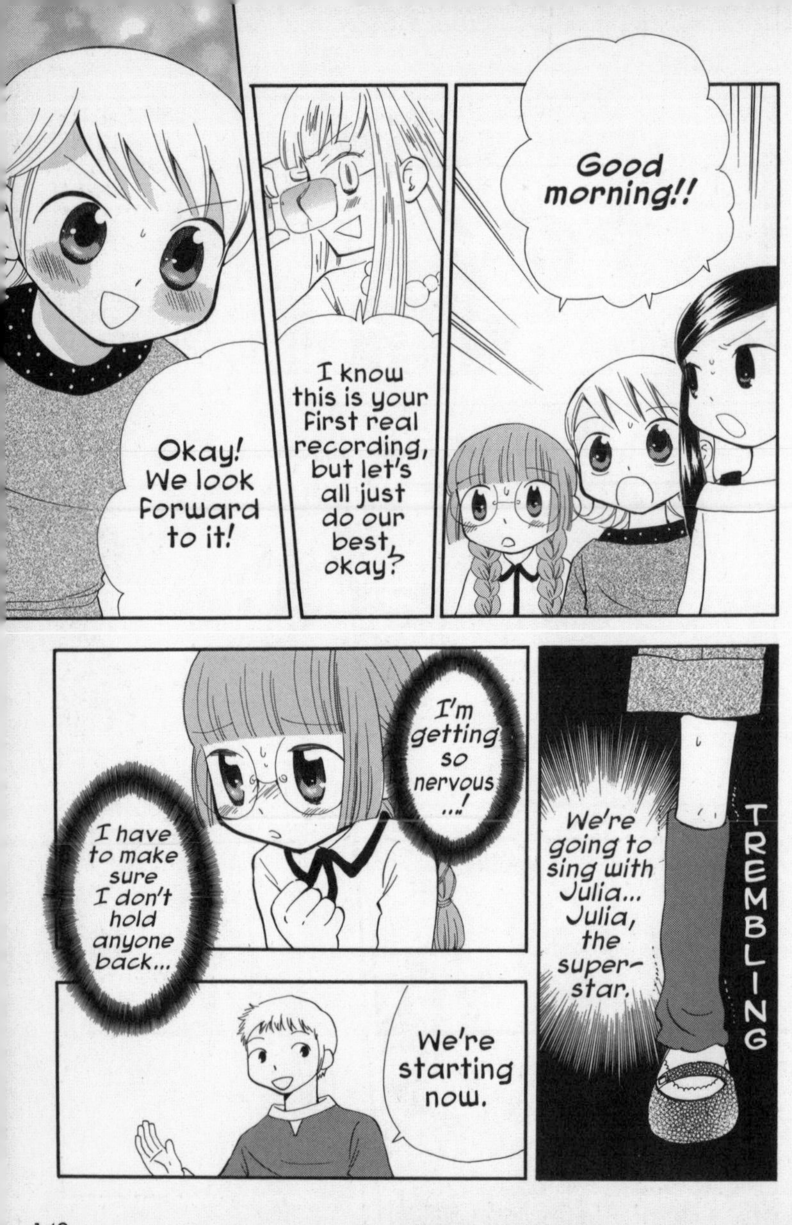
Good morning!!
I know this is your first real recording, but let's all just do our best, okay?
Okay! We look forward to it!
We're going to sing with Julia... Julia, the superstar.
TREMBLING
I'm getting so nervous...!
I have to make sure I don't hold anyone back...
We're starting now.

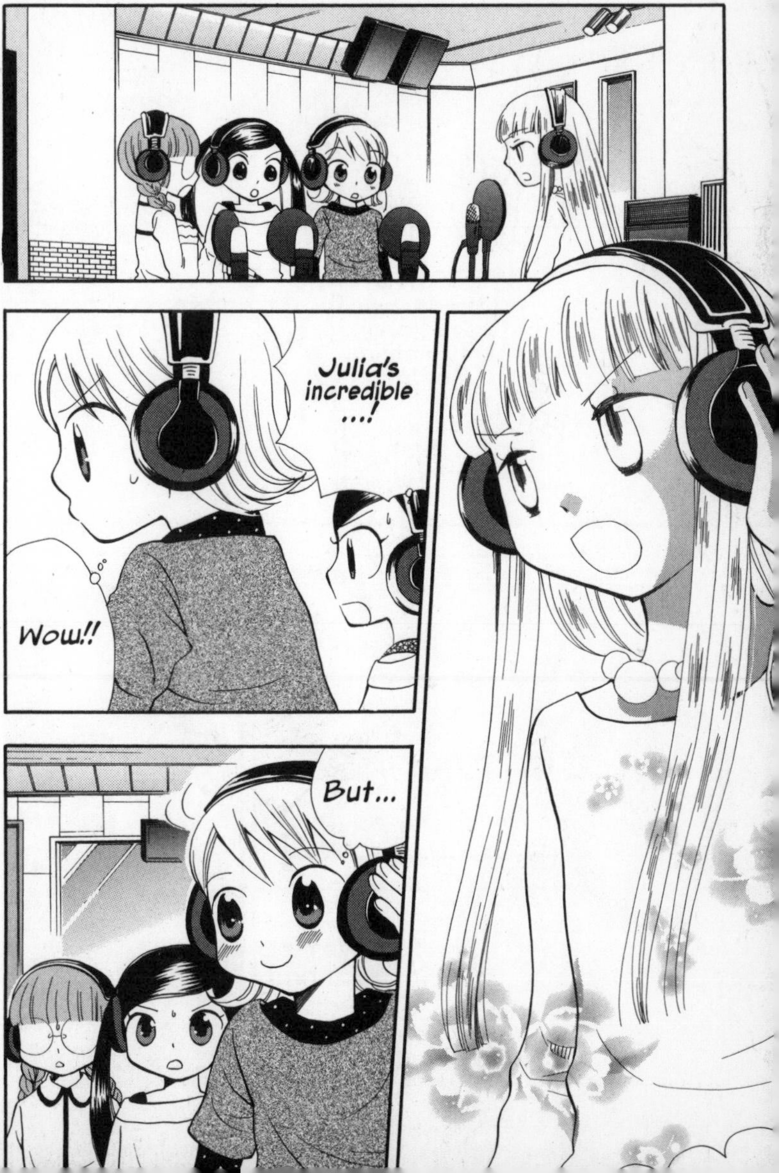
Julia's incredible ....!
Wow!!
But...

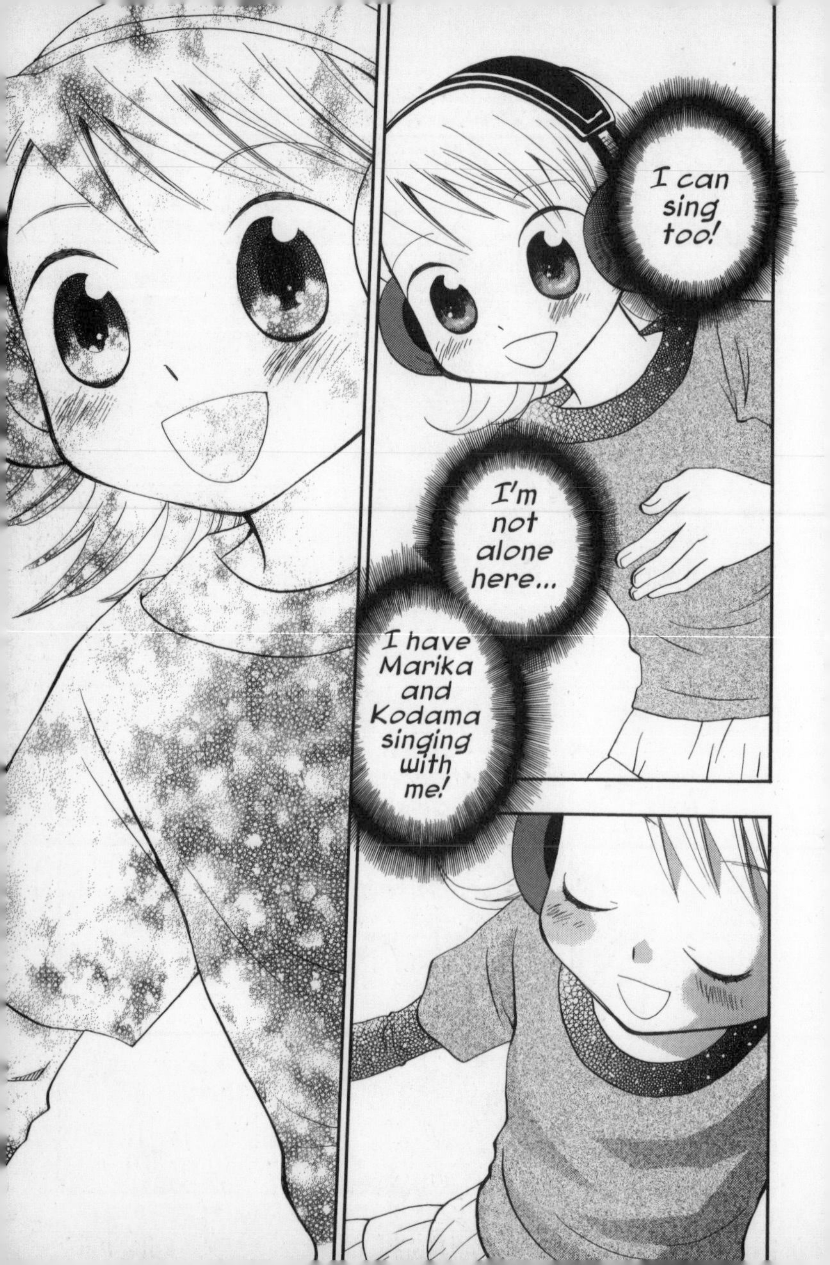
I can sing too!
I'm not alone here...
I have Marika and Kodama singing with me!

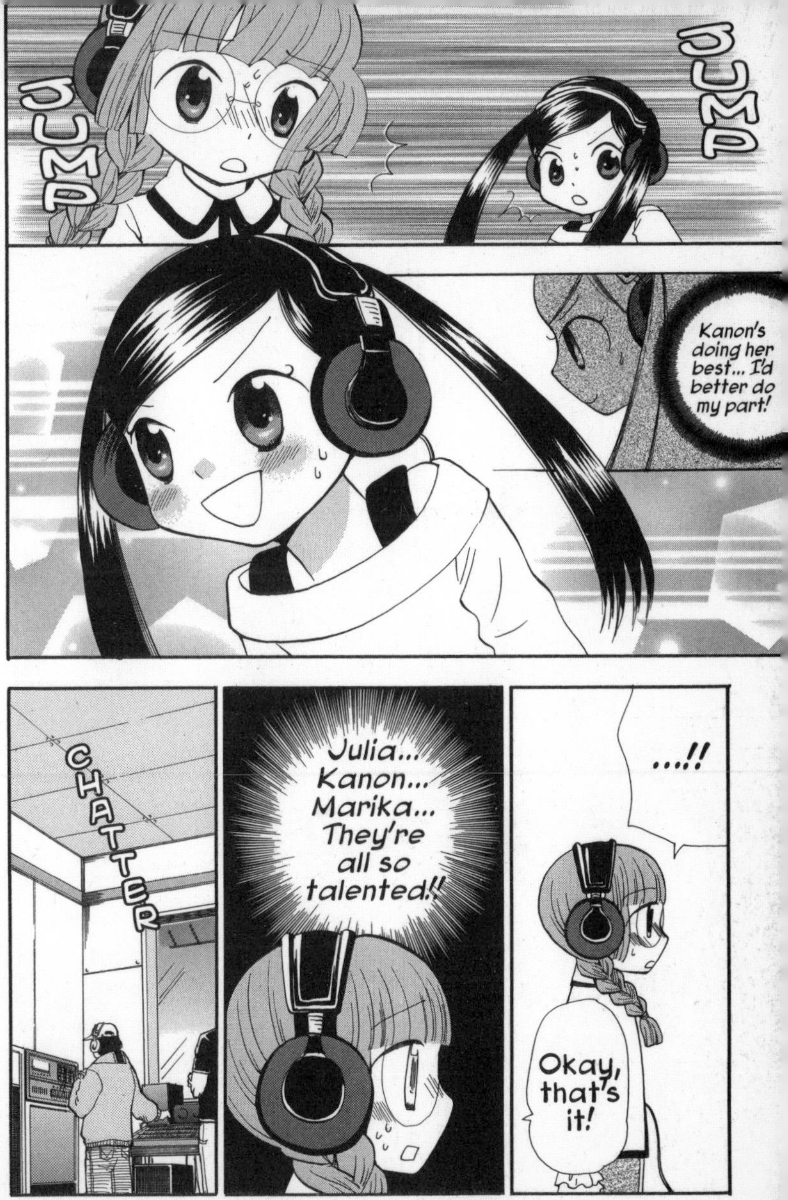
JUMP
JUMP
Kanon's doing her best... I'd better do my part!
...!!
Okay, that's it!
Julia... Kanon... Marika... They're all so talented!!
CHATTER

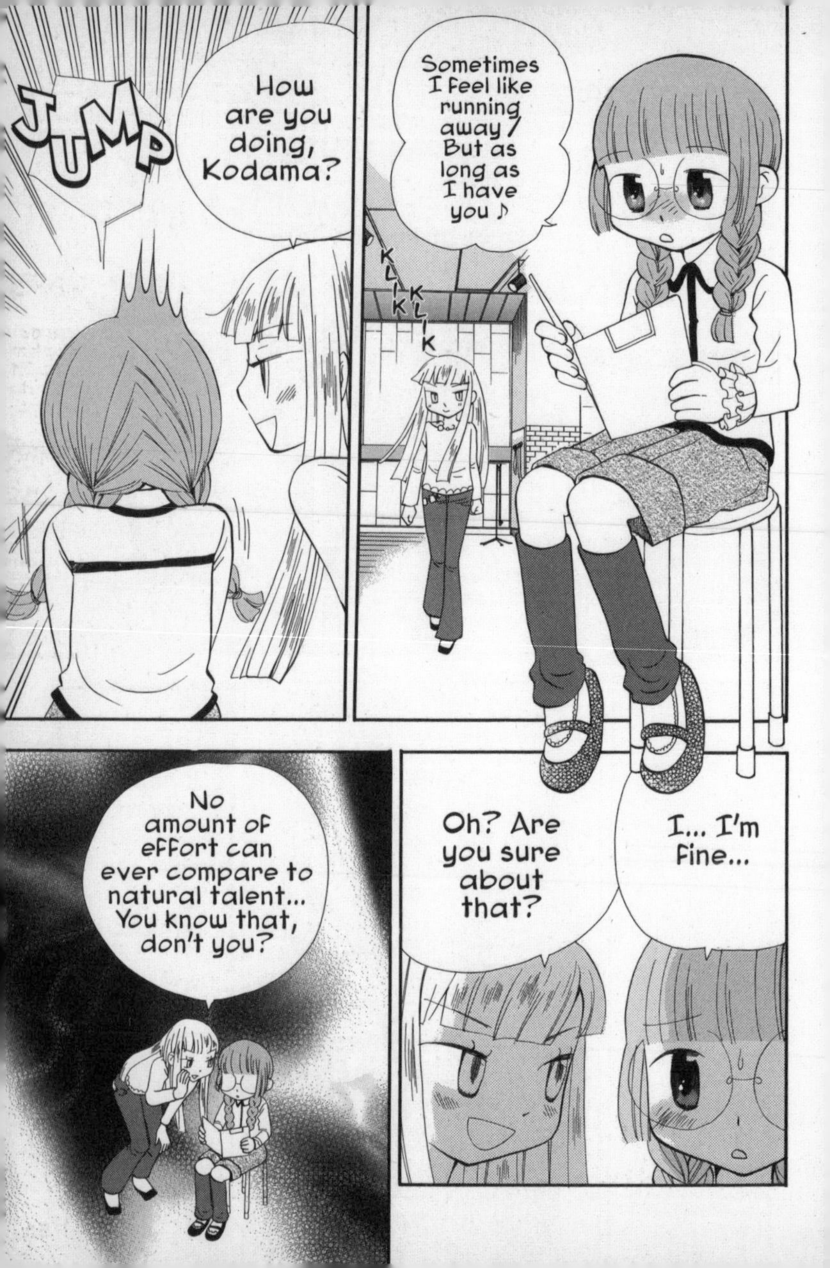
Sometimes I feel like running away / But as long as I have you ♪
KLIK KLIK
How are you doing, Kodama?
JUMP
I... I'm fine...
Oh? Are you sure about that?
No amount of effort can ever compare to natural talent... You know that, don't you?

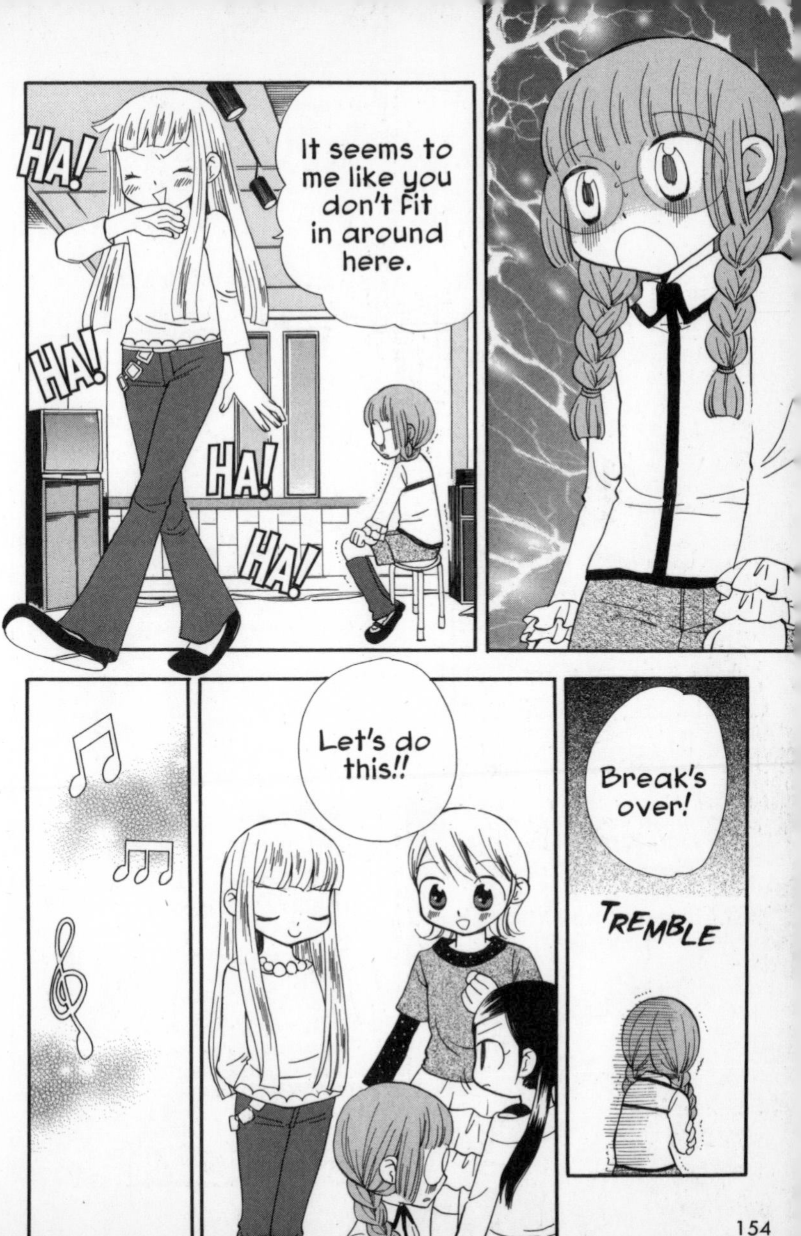
HA!
HA!
HA!
HA!
It seems to me like you don't fit in around here.
Break's over!
TREMBLE
Let's do this!!

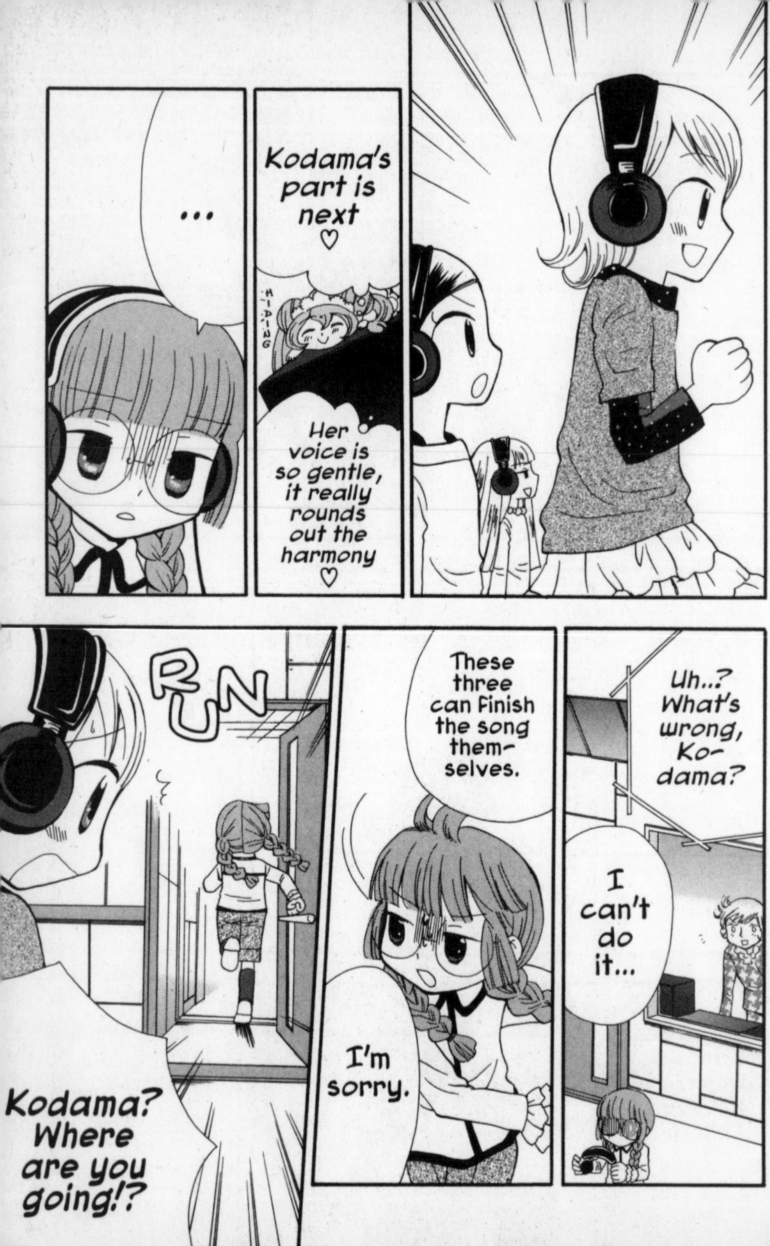
Kodama's part is next ♡
H-I-D-I-N-G
Her voice is so gentle, it really rounds out the harmony ♡
...
Uh..? What's wrong, Ko-dama?
I can't do it...
These three can finish the song them-selves.
I'm sorry.
RUN
Kodama? Where are you going!?

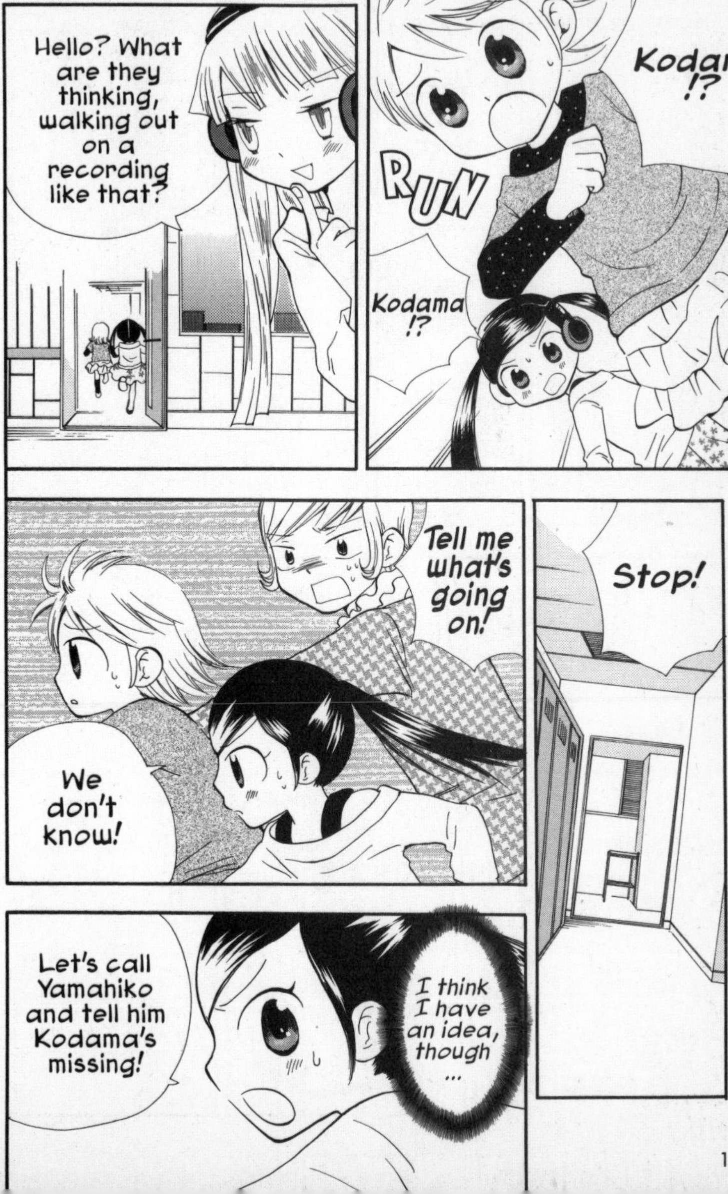
Kodama !?
RUN
Kodama !?
Hello? What are they thinking, walking out on a recording like that?
Stop!
Tell me what's going on!
We don't know!
I think I have an idea, though ...
Let's call Yamahiko and tell him Kodama's missing!

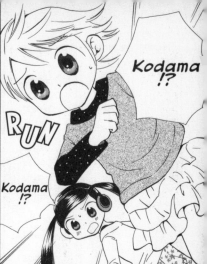

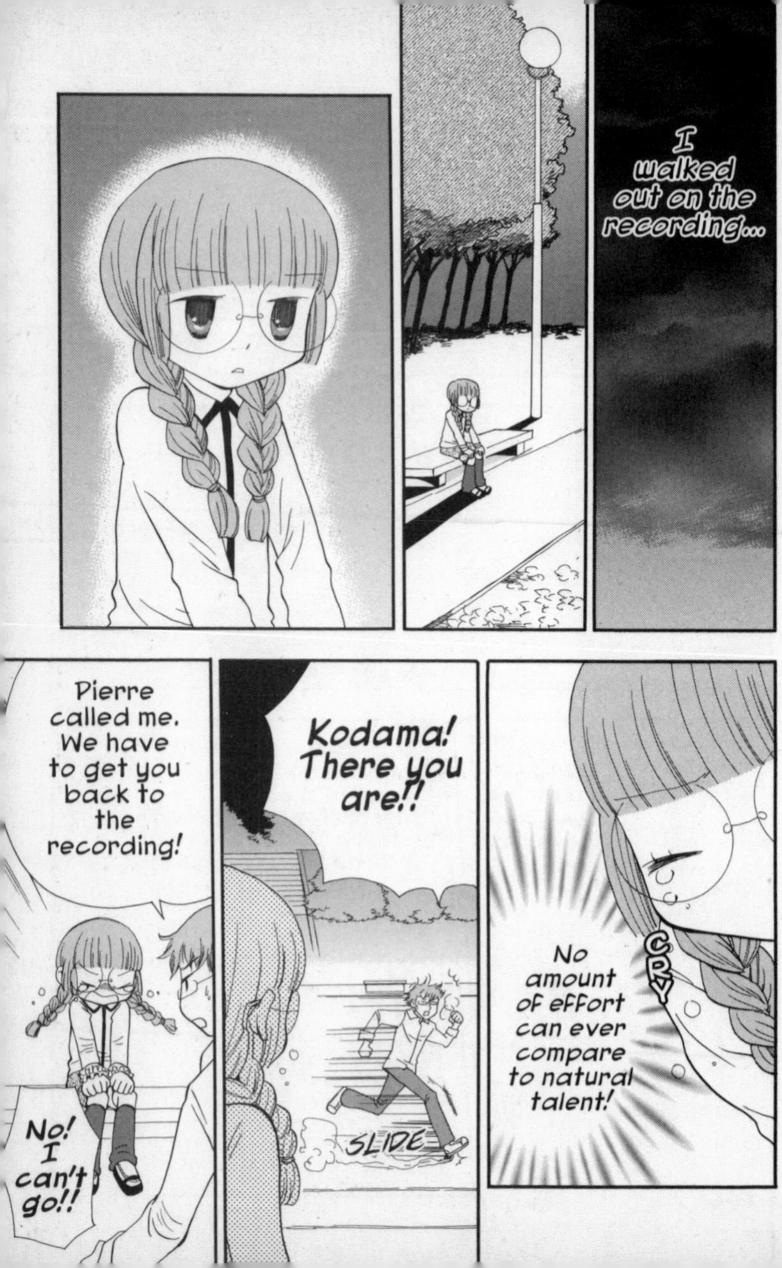
I walked out on the recording...
CRY
No amount of effort can ever compare to natural talent!
Kodama! There you are!!
SLIDE
Pierre called me. We have to get you back to the recording!
No! I can't go!!

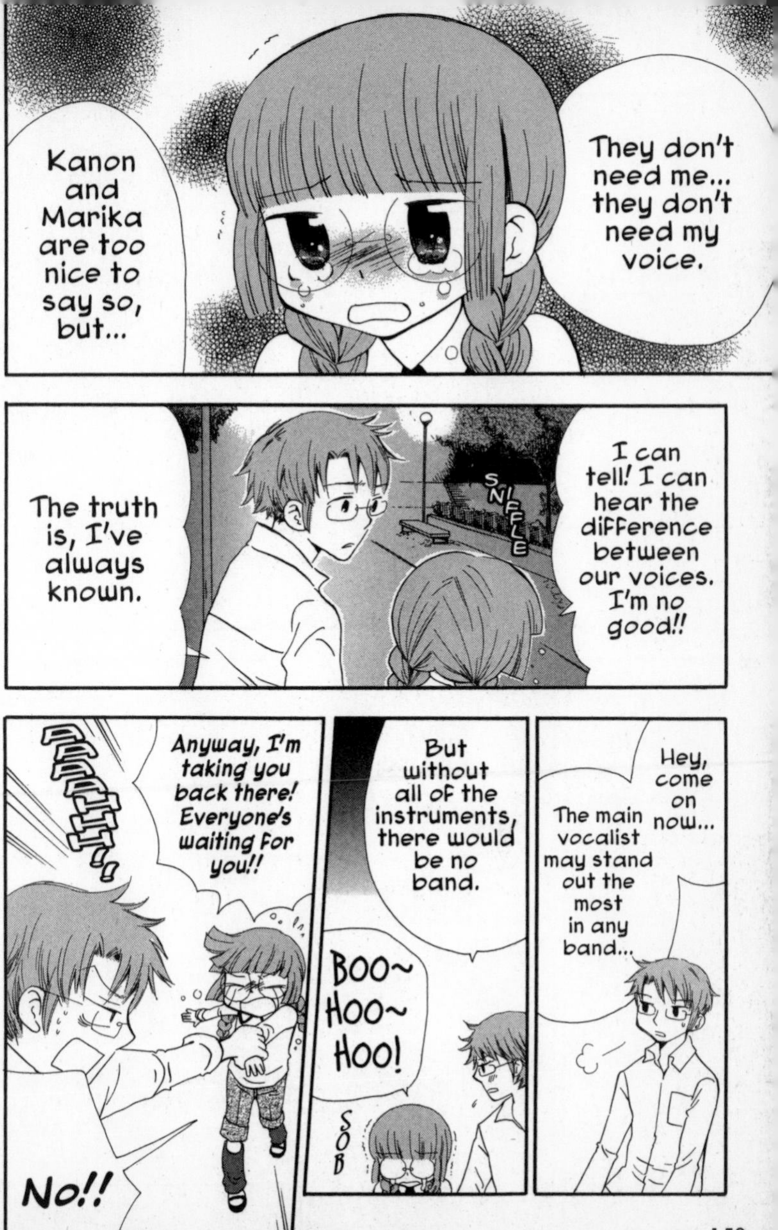

They don't need me... they don't need my voice.
Kanon and Marika are too nice to say so, but...
I can tell! I can hear the difference between our voices. I'm no good!!
SNIFFLE
The truth is, I've always known.
Hey, come on now...
The main vocalist may stand out the most in any band...
But without all of the instruments, there would be no band.
BOO~ HOO~ HOO!
SOB
Anyway, I'm taking you back there! Everyone's waiting for you!!
No!!

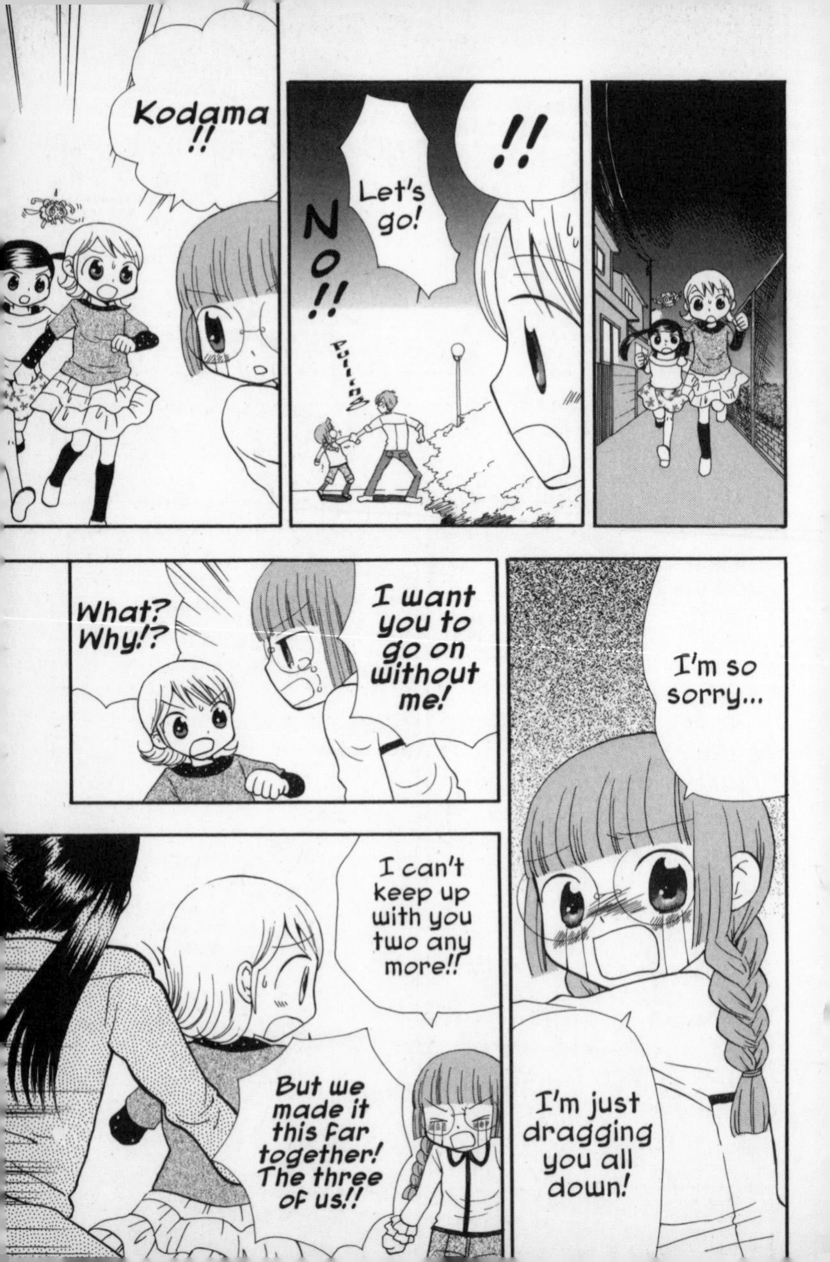
!!
Let's go!
NO!!
Pulling
Kodama !!
I'm so sorry...
I'm just dragging you all down!
I want you to go on without me!
What? Why!?
I can't keep up with you two any more!!
But we made it this far together! The three of us!!

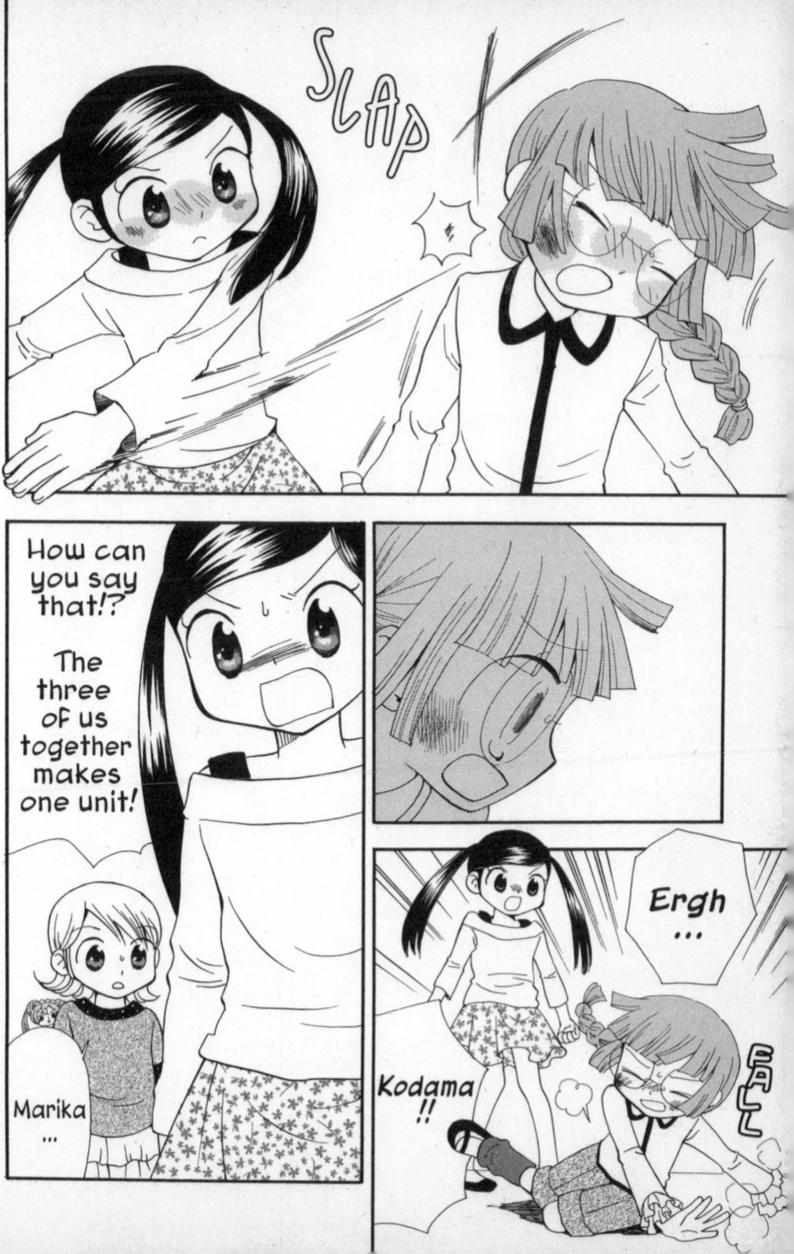
SLAP
Ergh ...
FALL
Kodama !!
How can you say that!?
The three of us together makes one unit!
Marika ...

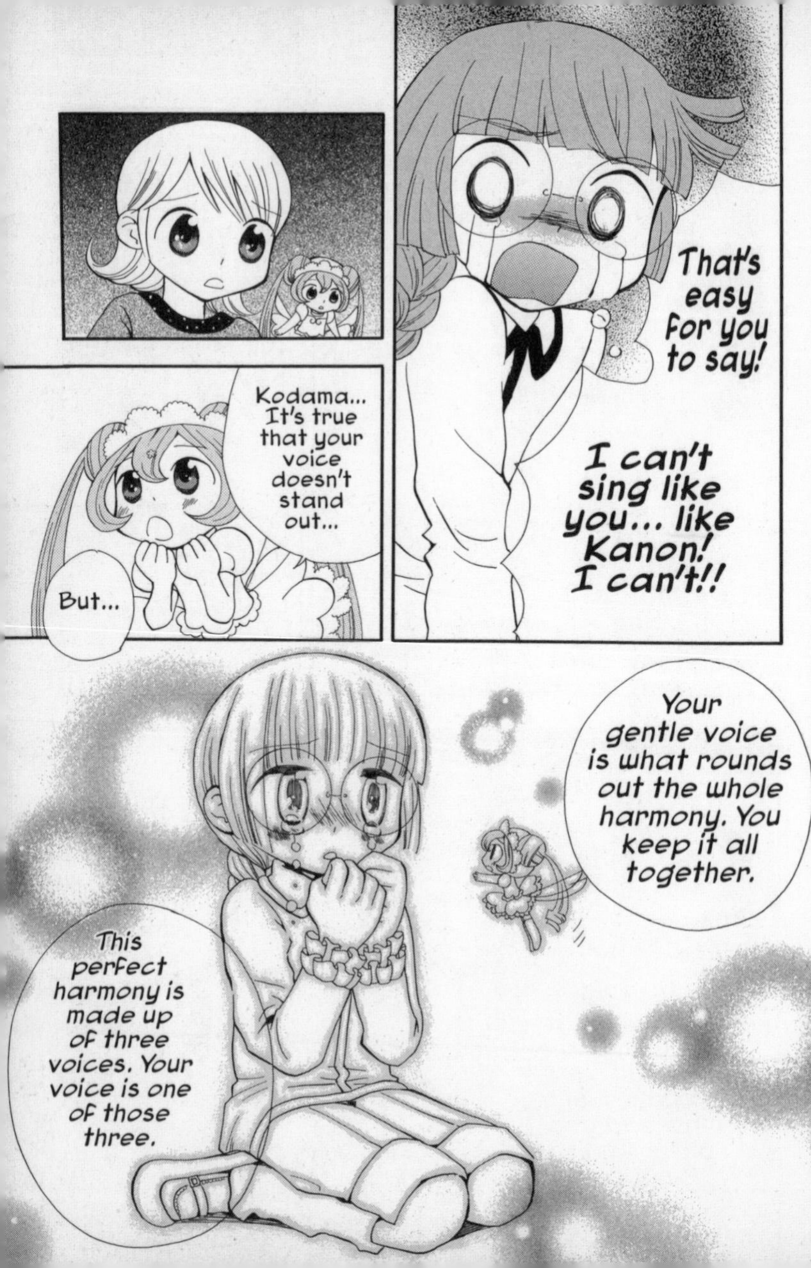
That's easy for you to say!
I can't sing like you... like Kanon! I can't!!
Kodama... It's true that your voice doesn't stand out...
But...
Your gentle voice is what rounds out the whole harmony. You keep it all together.
This perfect harmony is made up of three voices. Your voice is one of those three.

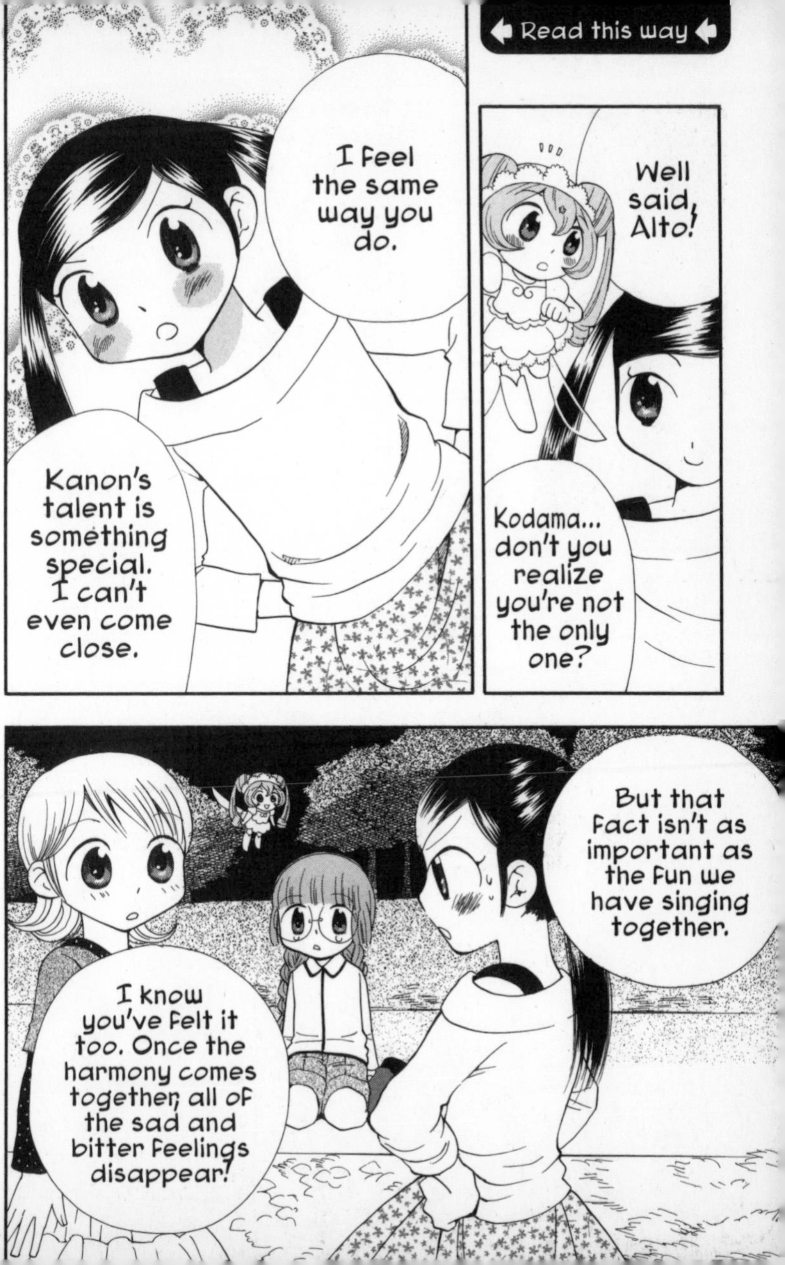
Read this way
Well said, Alto!
Kodama... don't you realize you're not the only one?
I feel the same way you do.
Kanon's talent is something special. I can't even come close.
But that fact isn't as important as the fun we have singing together.
I know you've felt it too. Once the harmony comes together, all of the sad and bitter feelings disappear!

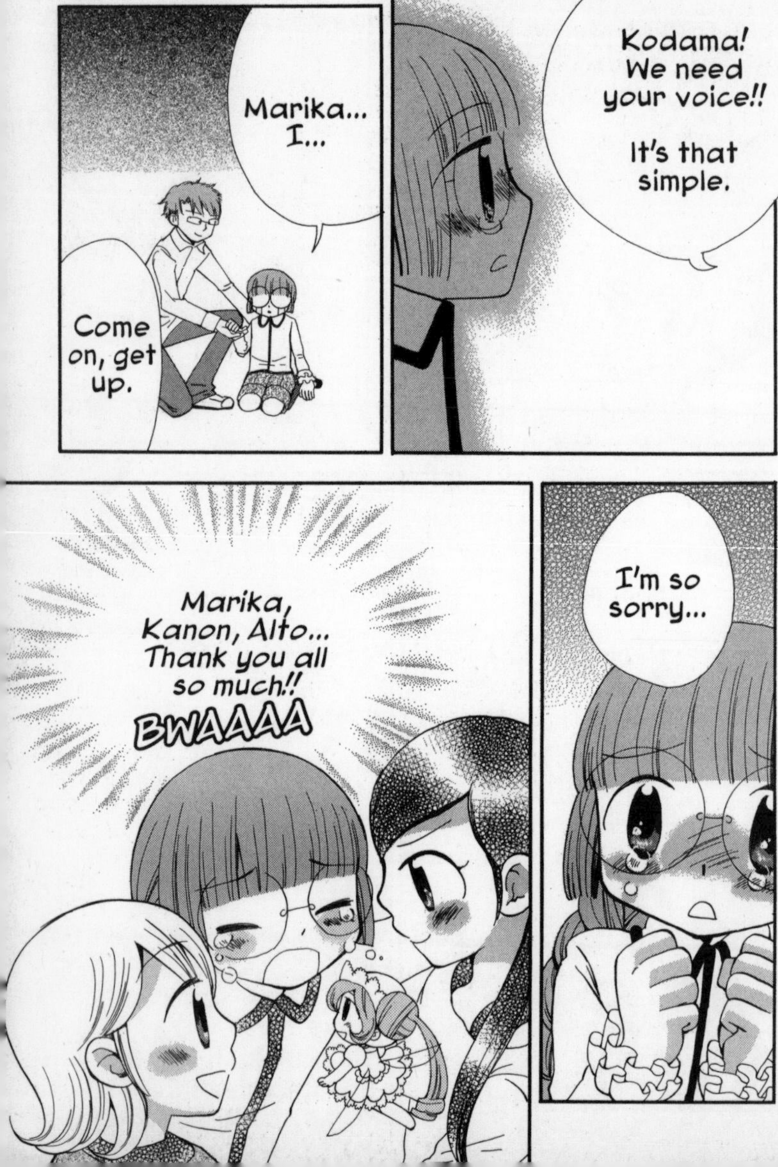
Kodama! We need your voice!!
It's that simple.
Marika... I...
Come on, get up.
I'm so sorry...
Marika, Kanon, Alto... Thank you all so much!!
BWAAAA

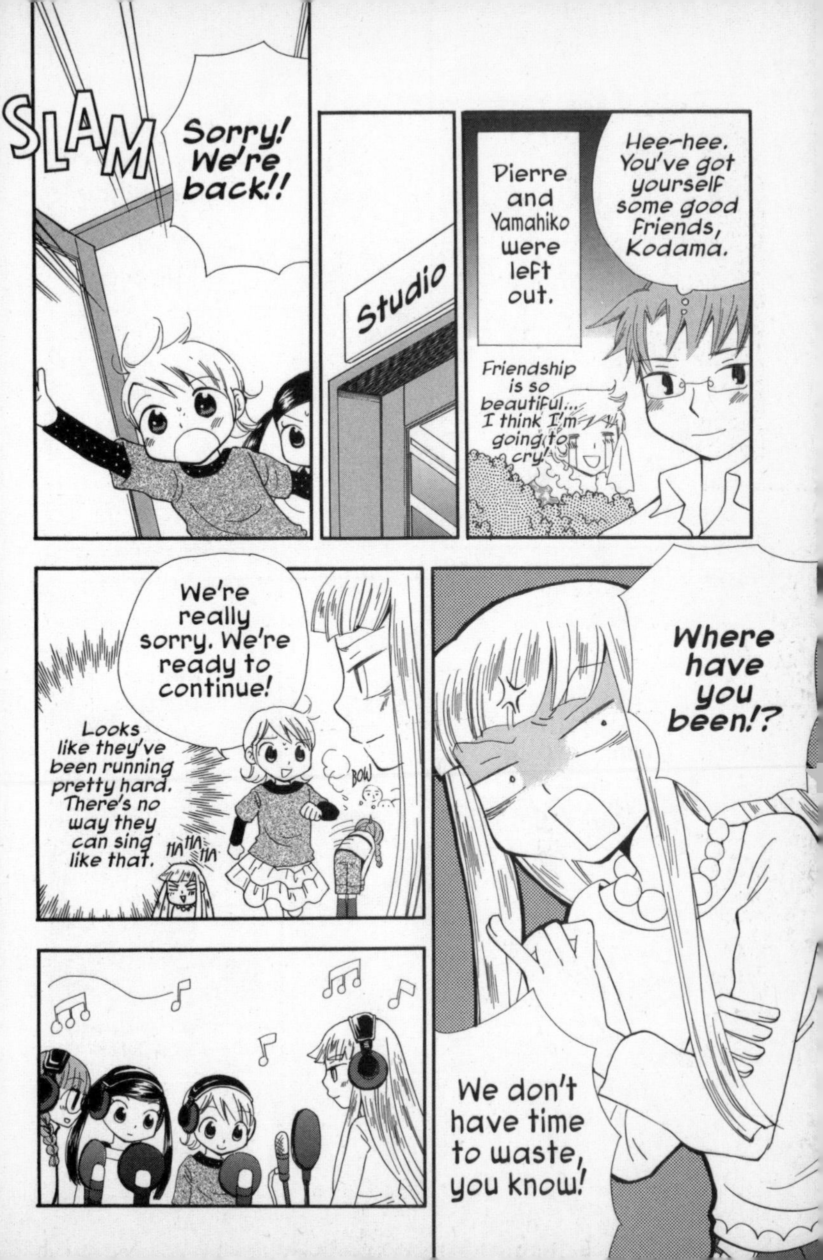
Hee-hee. You've got yourself some good friends, Kodama.
Pierre and Yamahiko were left out.
Friendship is so beautiful... I think I'm going to cry!
Studio
SLAM
Sorry! We're back!!
Where have you been!?
We don't have time to waste, you know!
We're really sorry. We're ready to continue!
BOW
Looks like they've been running pretty hard. There's no way they can sing like that.
HA HA HA

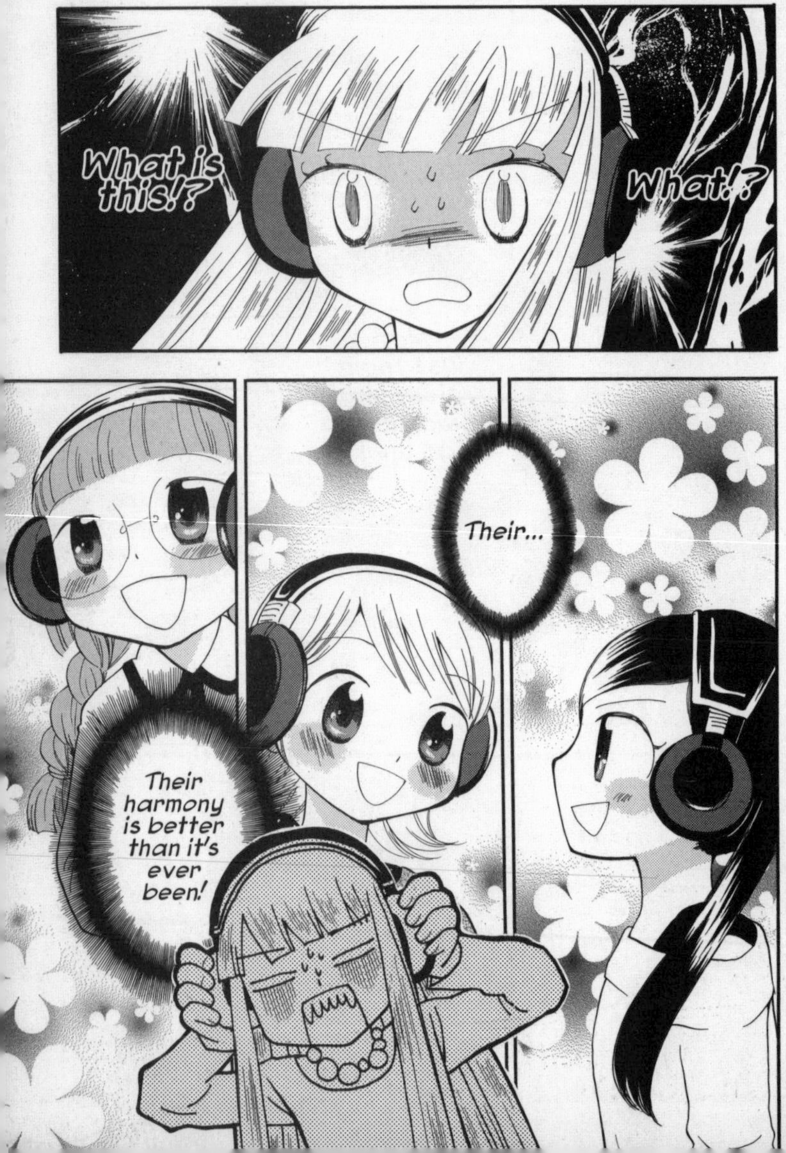
What!?
What is this!?
Their...
Their harmony is better than it's ever been!

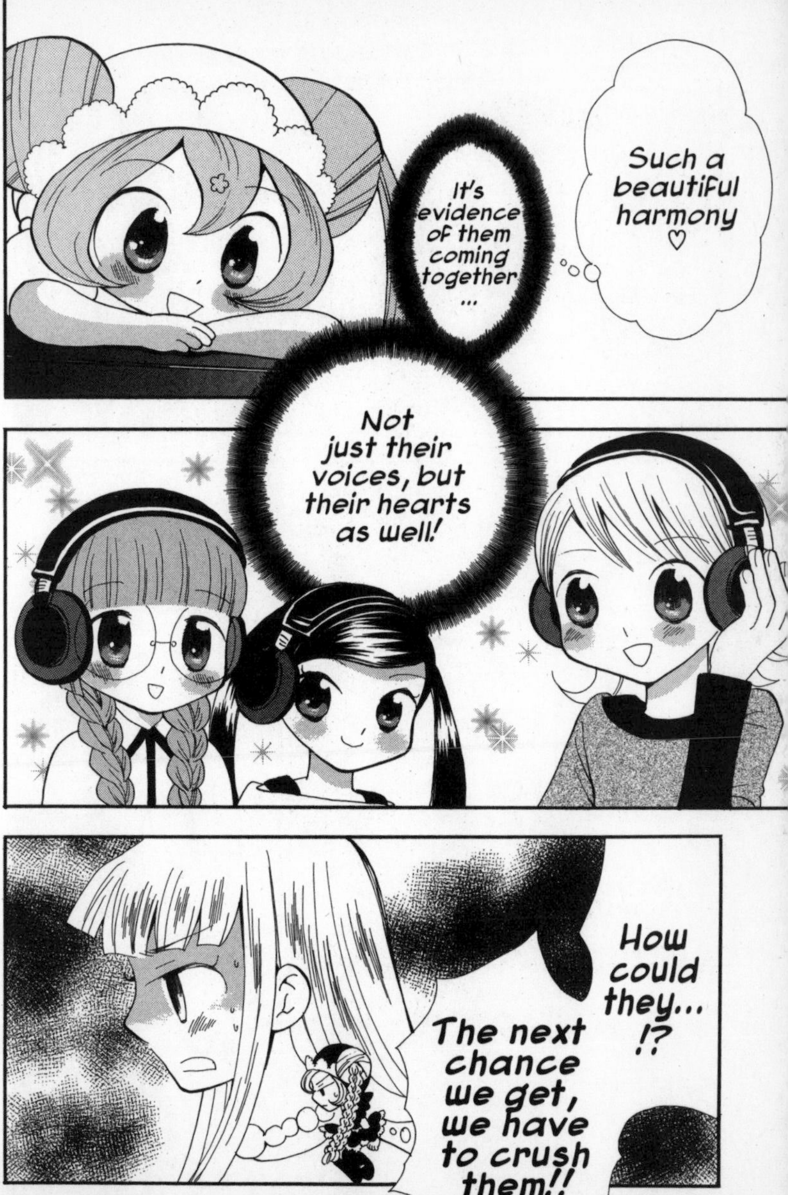
Such a beautiful harmony ♡
It's evidence of them coming together ...
Not just their voices, but their hearts as well!
How could they... !?
The next chance we get, we have to crush them!!

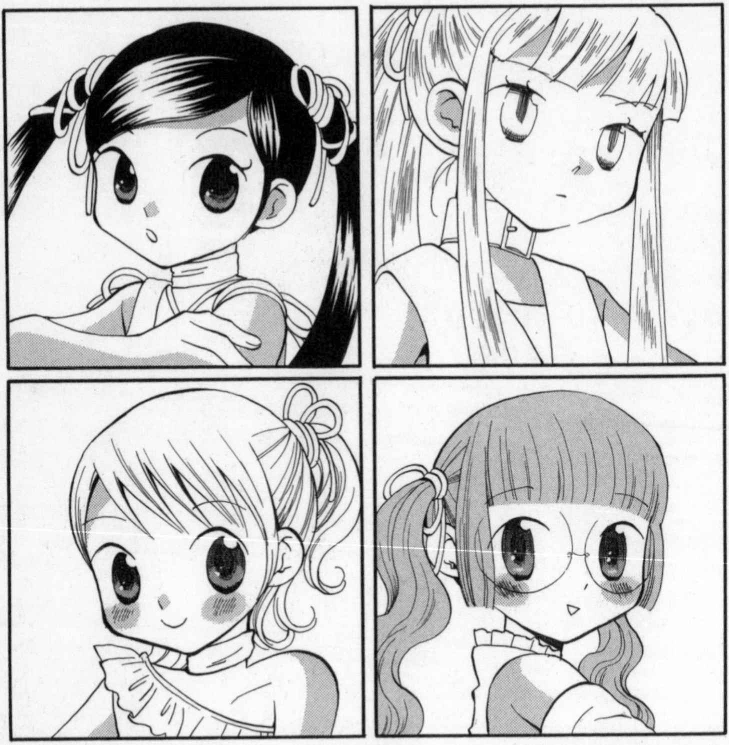

Stage 20
Hearts Linked by Song

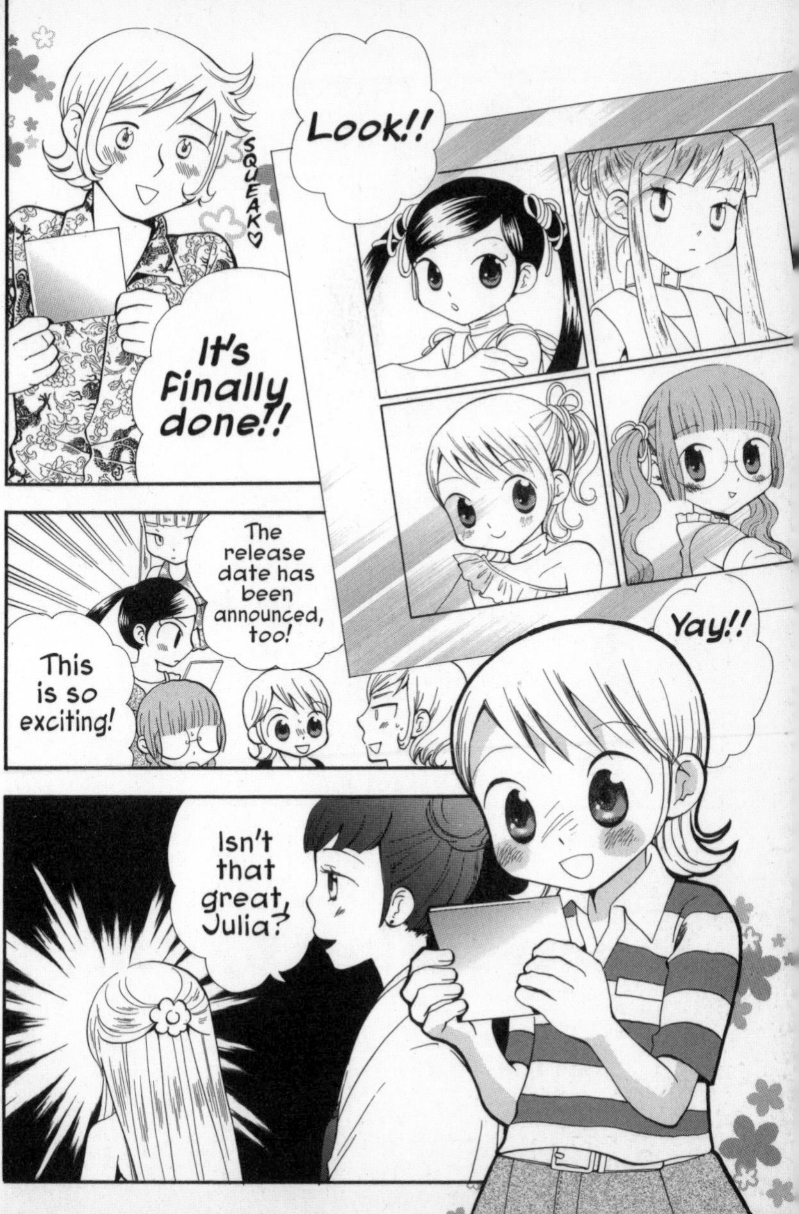
Look!!
SQUEAK♡
It's finally done!!
Yay!!
The release date has been announced, too!
This is so exciting!
Isn't that great, Julia?

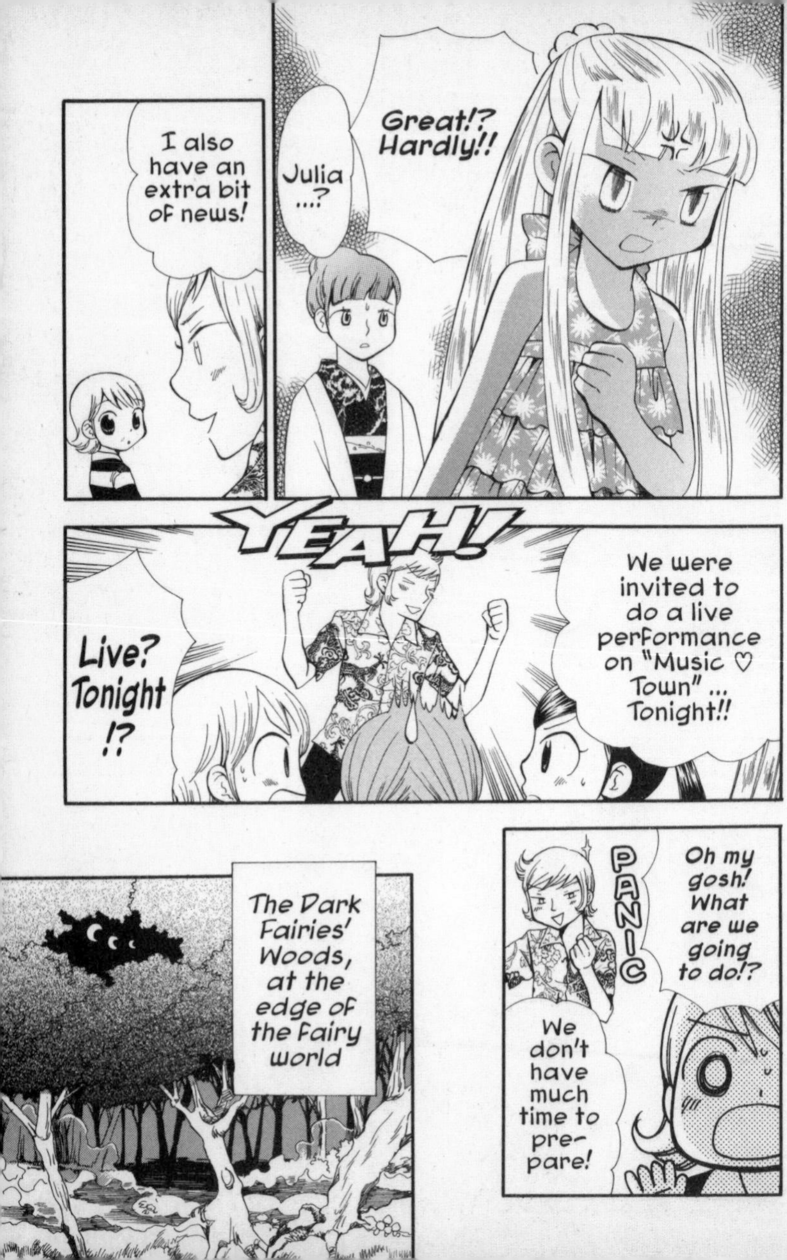
Great!? Hardly!!
Julia ...?
I also have an extra bit of news!
YEAH!
We were invited to do a live performance on "Music ♡ Town" ... Tonight!!
Live? Tonight !?
PANIC
Oh my gosh! What are we going to do!?
We don't have much time to pre-pare!
The Dark Fairies' Woods, at the edge of the fairy world

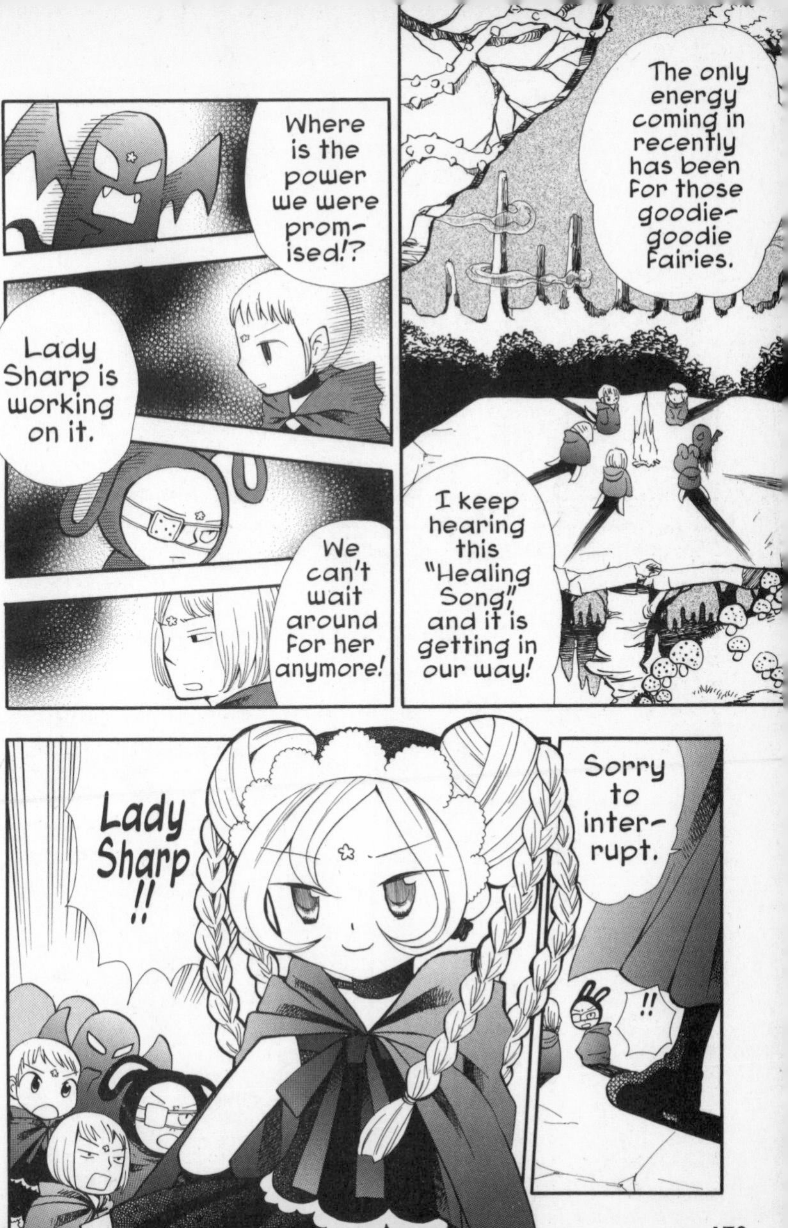
The only energy coming in recently has been for those goodie-goodie fairies.
I keep hearing this "Healing Song," and it is getting in our way!
Where is the power we were promised!?
Lady Sharp is working on it.
We can't wait around for her anymore!
Sorry to interrupt.
!!
Lady Sharp!!

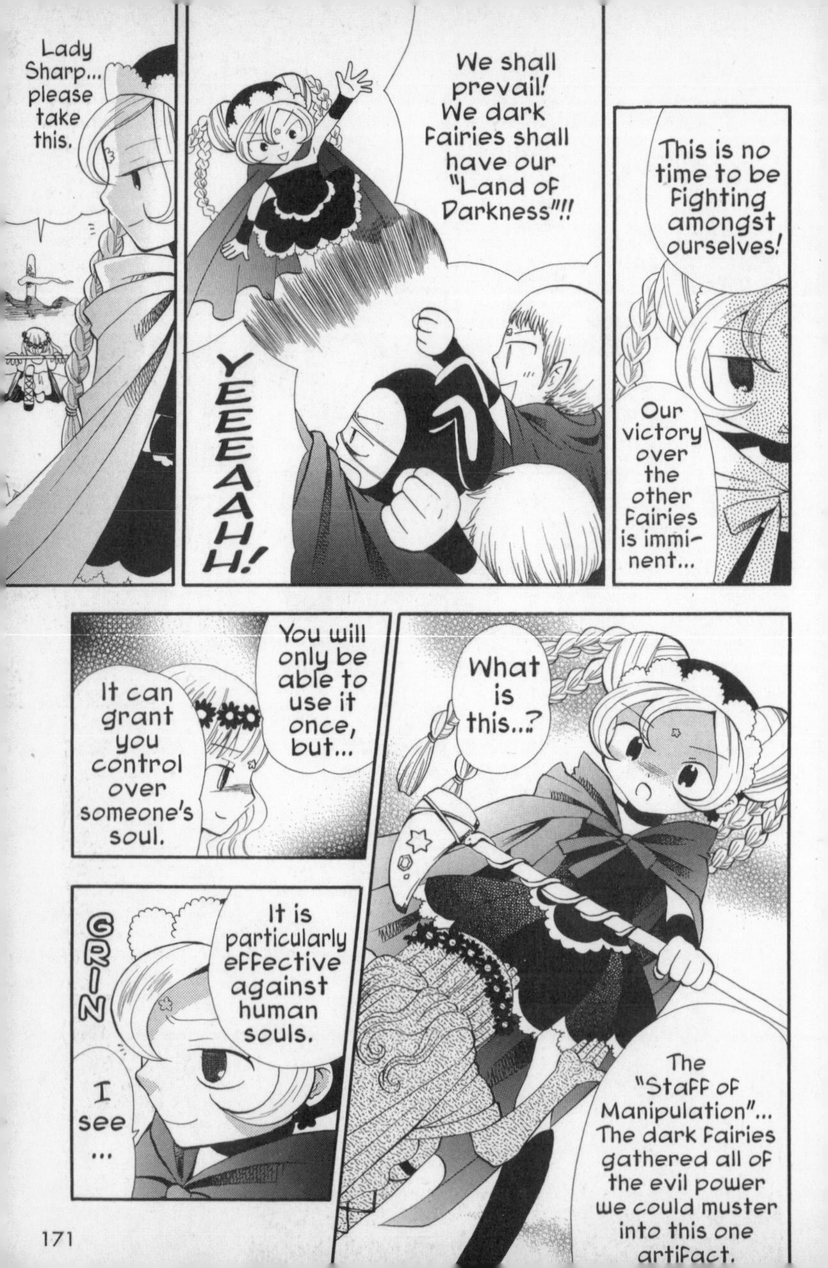
This is no time to be fighting amongst ourselves!
Our victory over the other fairies is immi-nent...
We shall prevail! We dark fairies shall have our "Land of Darkness"!!
YEEEAAHH!
Lady Sharp... please take this.
What is this..?
The "Staff of Manipulation"... The dark fairies gathered all of the evil power we could muster into this one artifact.
You will only be able to use it once, but...
It can grant you control over someone's soul.
It is particularly effective against human souls.
GRIN
I see...

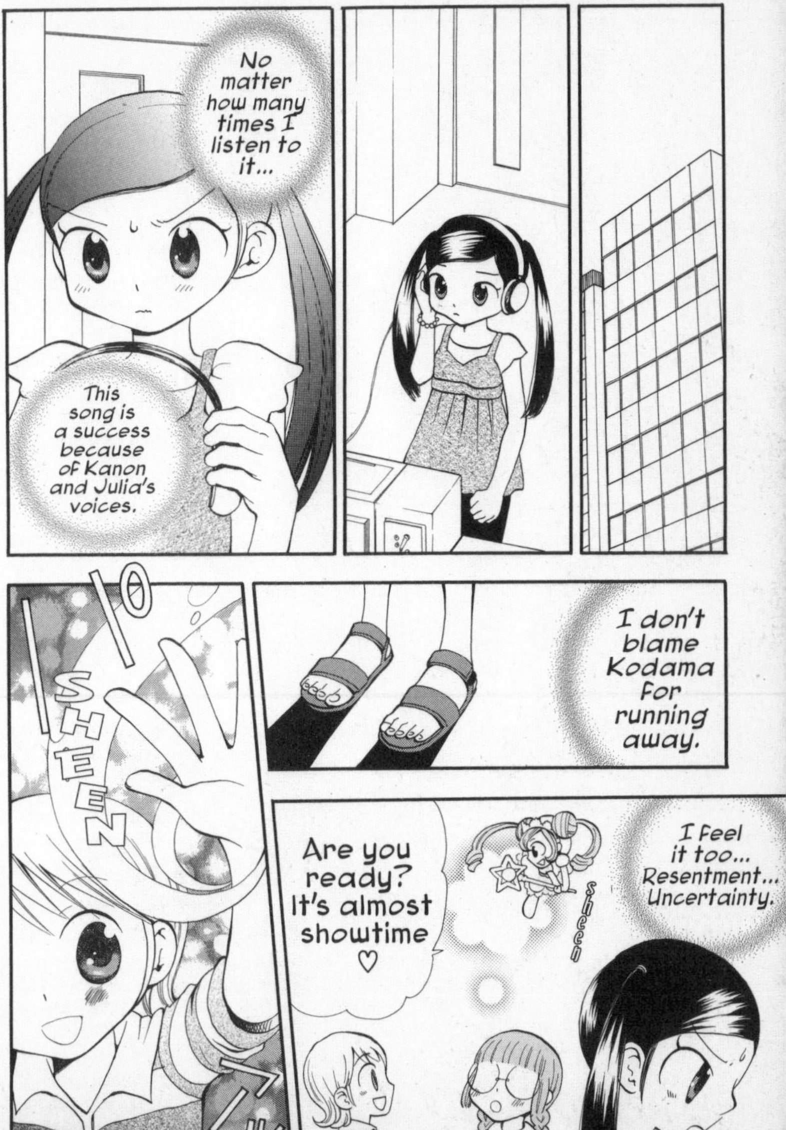
No matter how many times I listen to it...
This song is a success because of Kanon and Julia's voices.
I don't blame Kodama for running away.
I feel it too... Resentment... Uncertainty.
sheen
Are you ready? It's almost showtime ♡
SHEEN

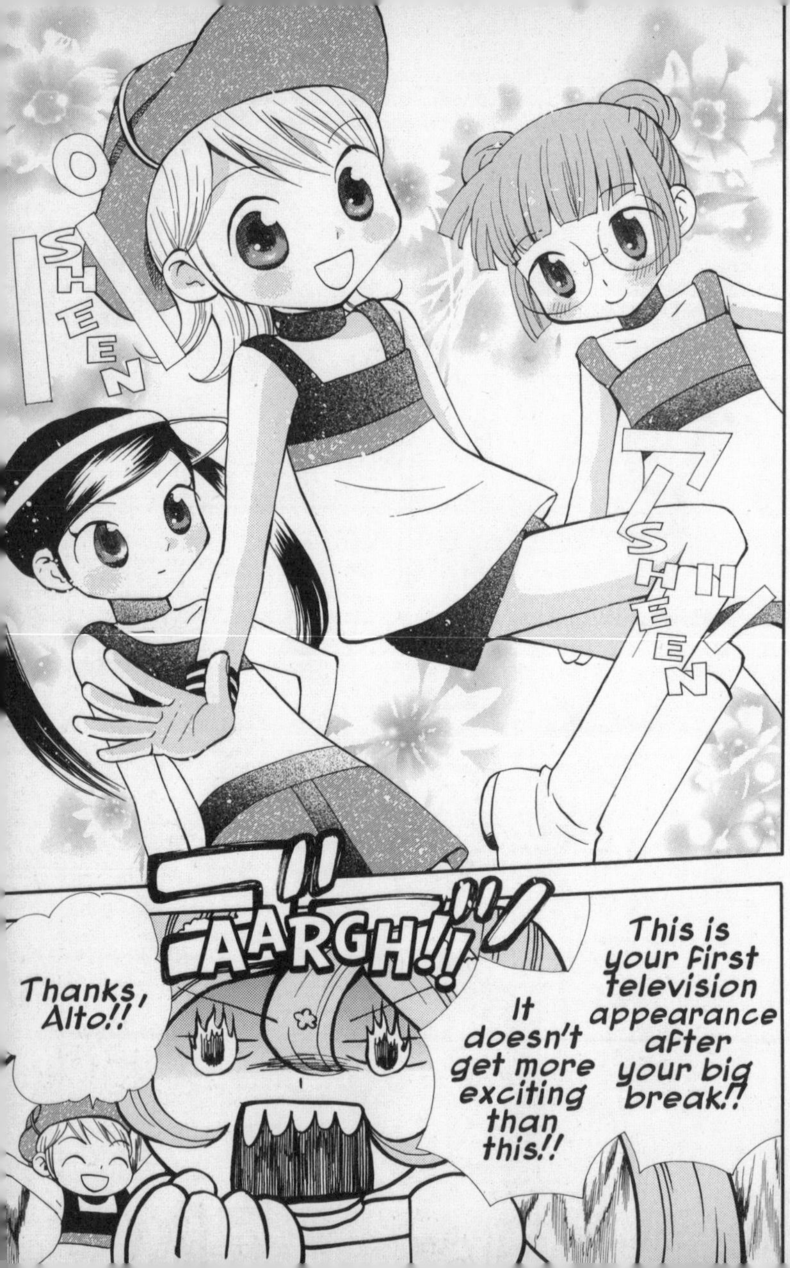
SHEEN
SHIIEEN
This is your first television appearance after your big break!!
It doesn't get more exciting than this!!
AARGH!!!
Thanks, Alto!!

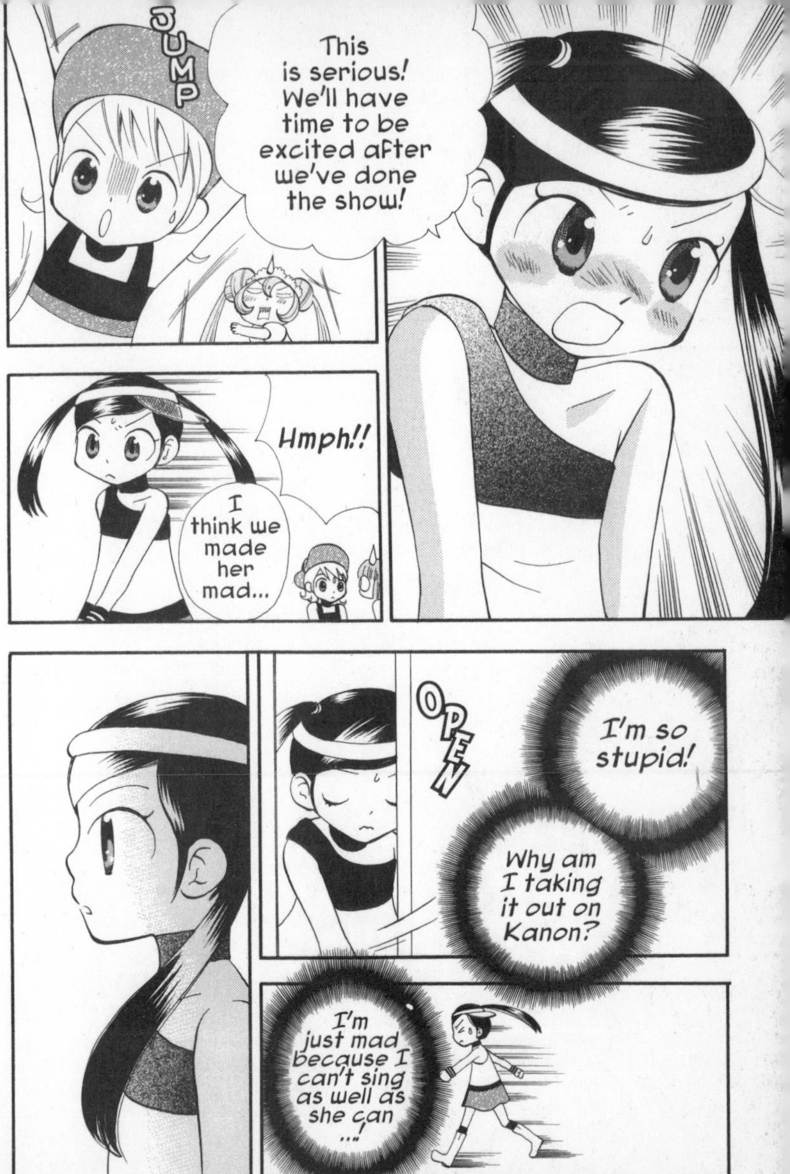
This is serious! We'll have time to be excited after we've done the show!
JUMP
Hmph!!
I think we made her mad...
OPEN
I'm so stupid!
Why am I taking it out on Kanon?
I'm just mad because I can't sing as well as she can ...!

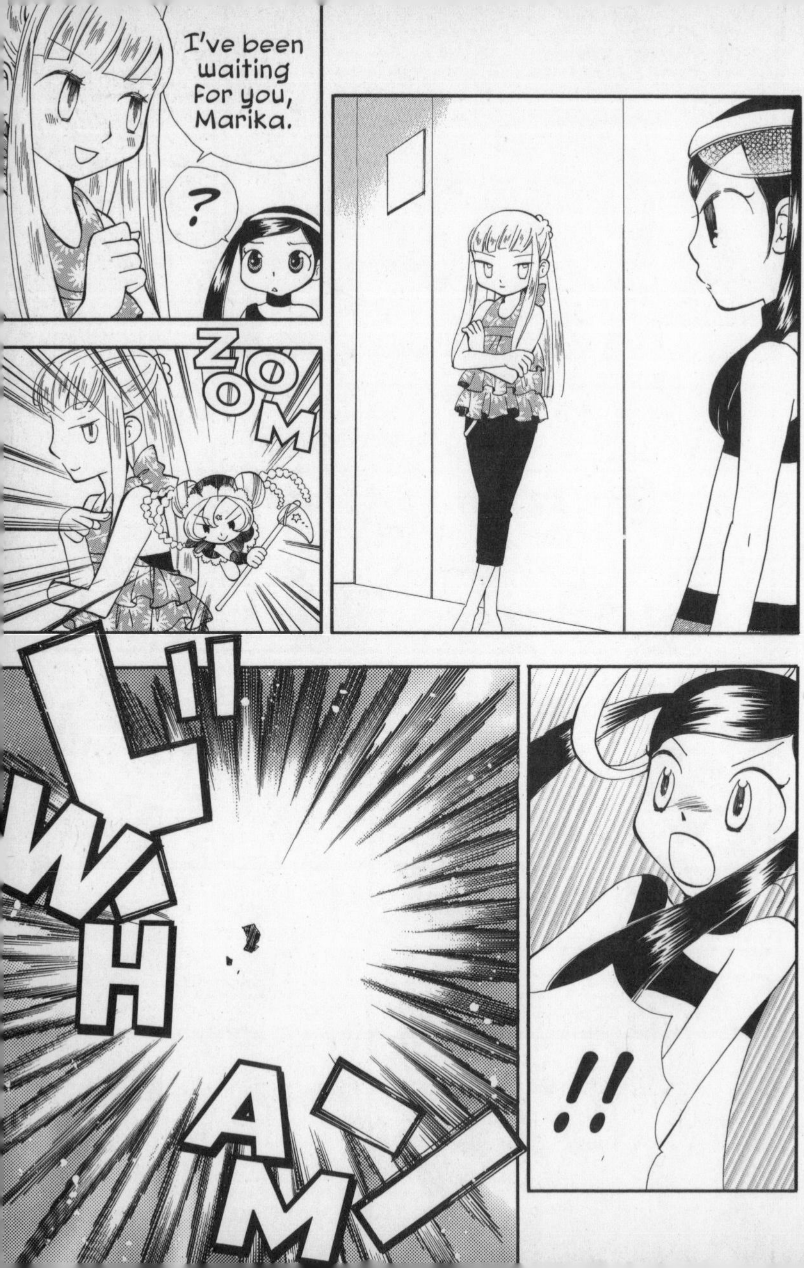
I've been waiting for you, Marika.
?
ZOOM
!!
WHAM!

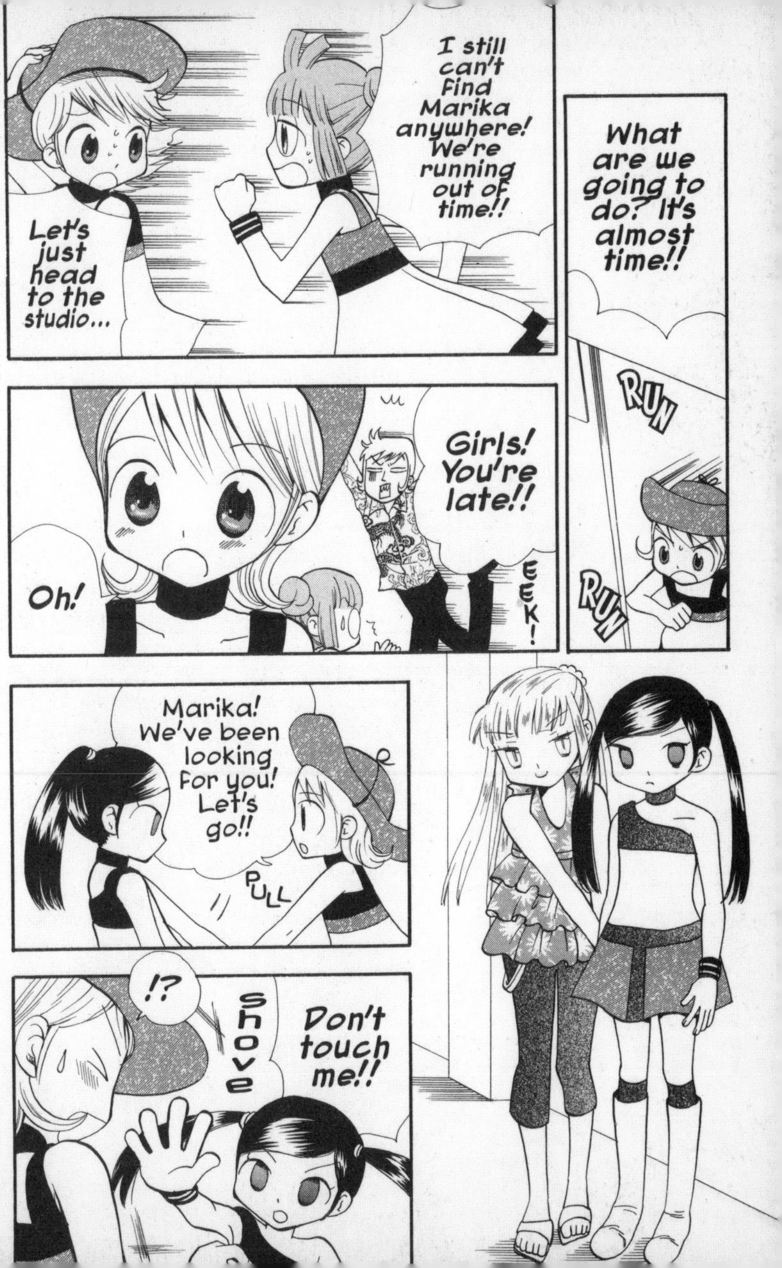
What are we going to do? It's almost time!!
RUN
RUN
I still can't find Marika anywhere! We're running out of time!!
Let's just head to the studio...
Girls! You're late!!
EEK!
Oh!
Marika! We've been looking for you! Let's go!!
PULL
!?
Don't touch me!!
shove

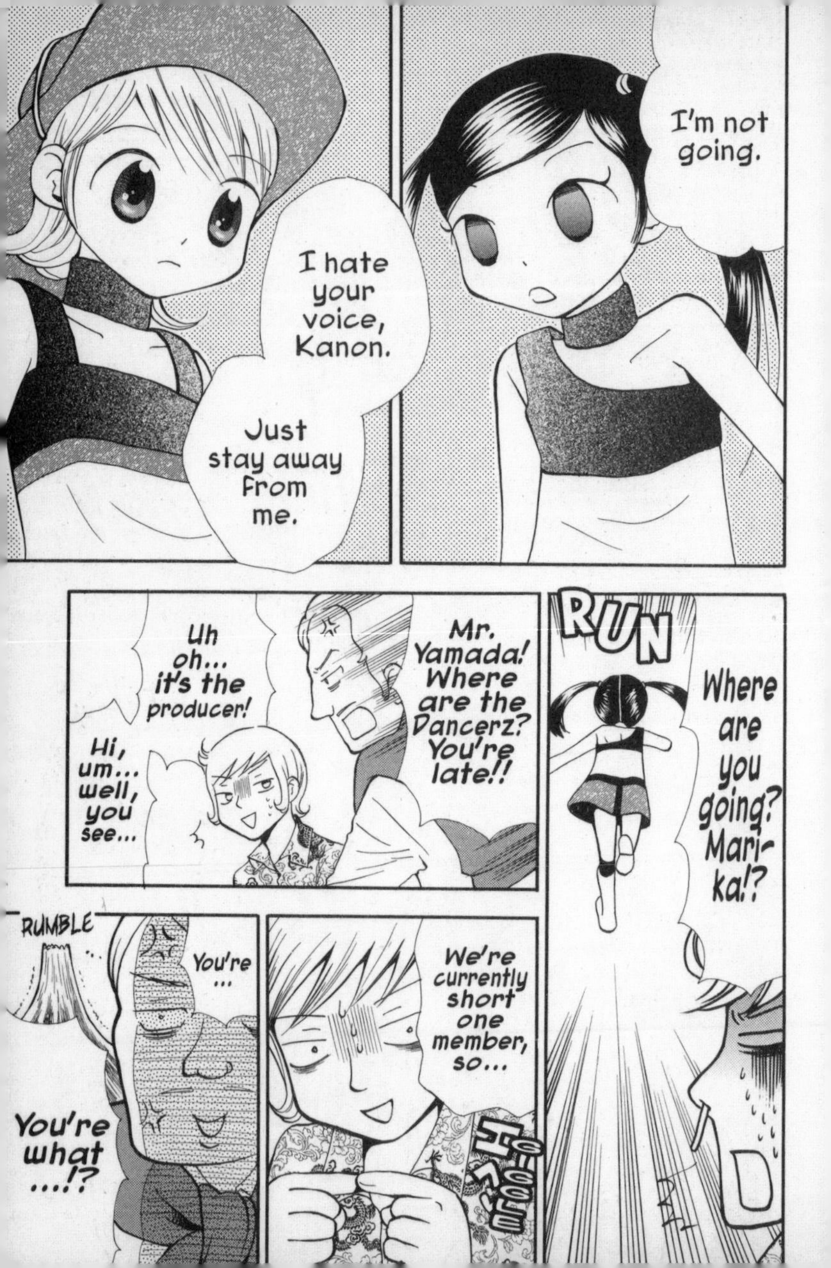
I'm not going.
I hate your voice, Kanon.
Just stay away from me.
RUN
Where are you going? Mari-ka!?
Mr. Yamada! Where are the Dancerz? You're late!!
Uh oh... it's the producer!
Hi, um... well, you see...
We're currently short one member, so...
GIGGLE
RUMBLE
You're ...
You're what ...!?

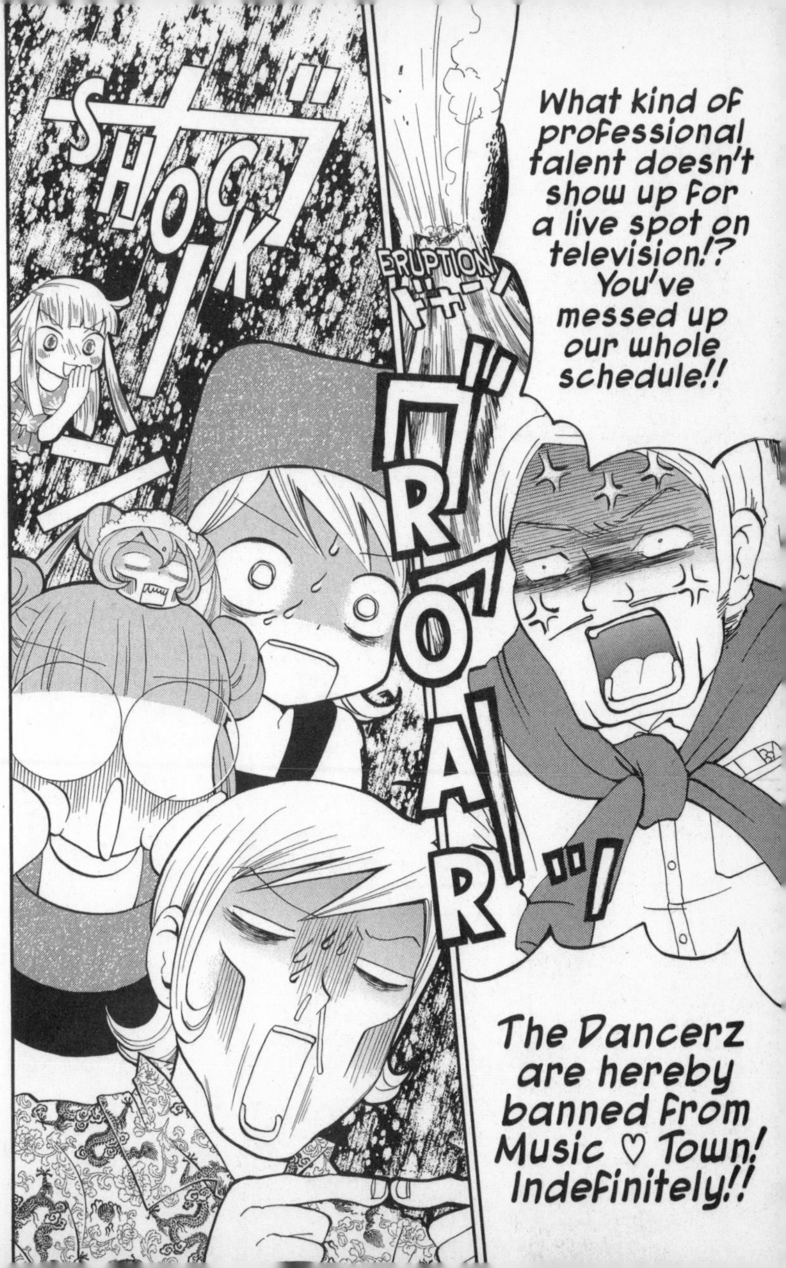
What kind of professional talent doesn't show up for a live spot on television!? You've messed up our whole schedule!!
ERUPTION
ROAR!
SHOCK
The Dancerz are hereby banned from Music ♡ Town! Indefinitely!!

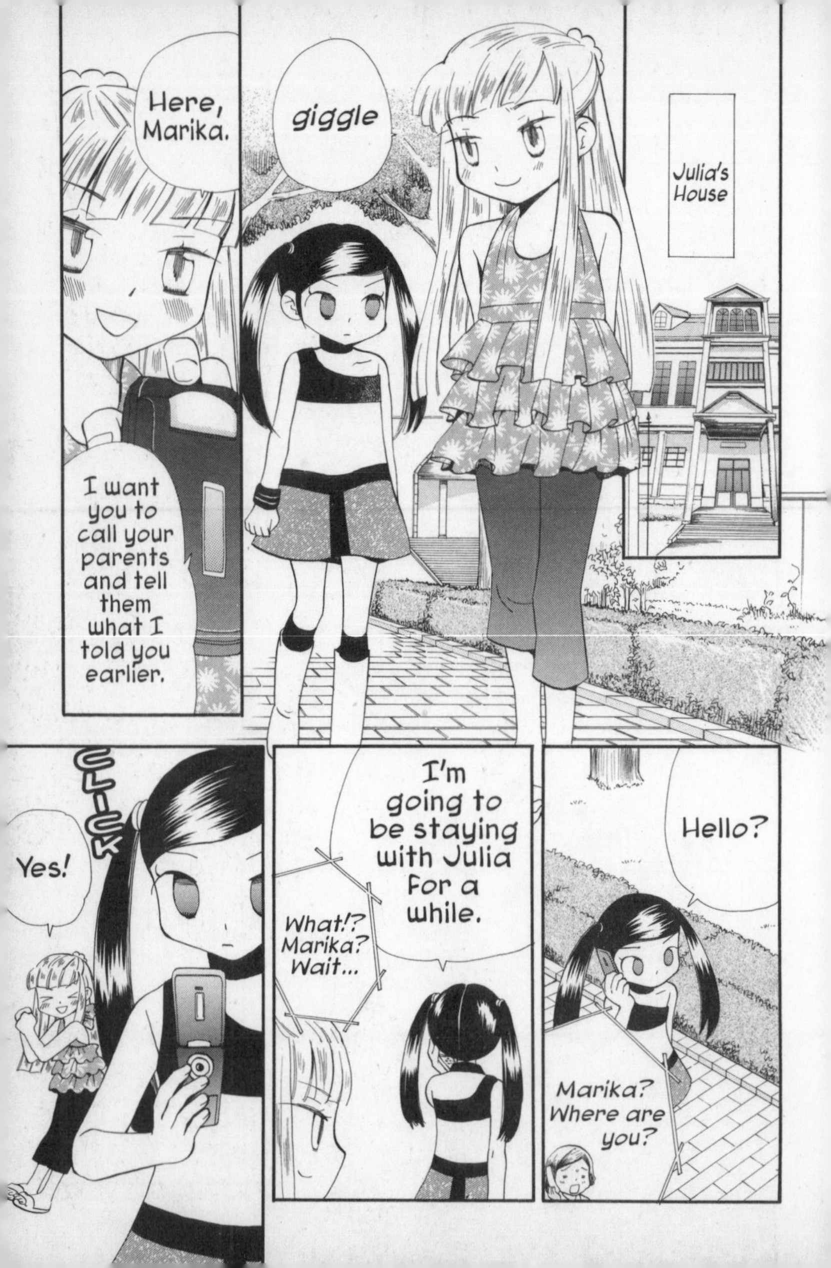
Julia's House
giggle
Here, Marika.
I want you to call your parents and tell them what I told you earlier.
Hello?
Marika? Where are you?
I'm going to be staying with Julia for a while.
What!? Marika? Wait...
CLICK
Yes!

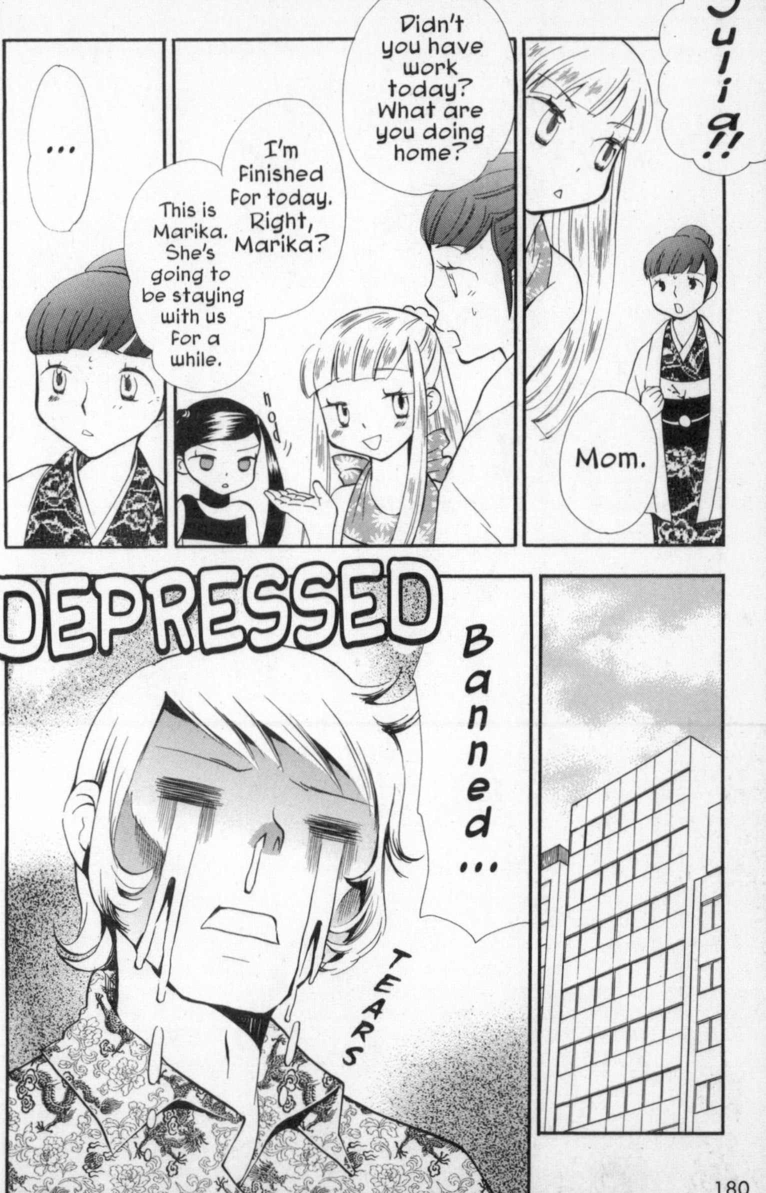
Julia!!
Mom.
Didn't you have work today? What are you doing home?
I'm finished for today. Right, Marika?
This is Marika. She's going to be staying with us for a while.
nod
...
DEPRESSED
Banned...
TEARS

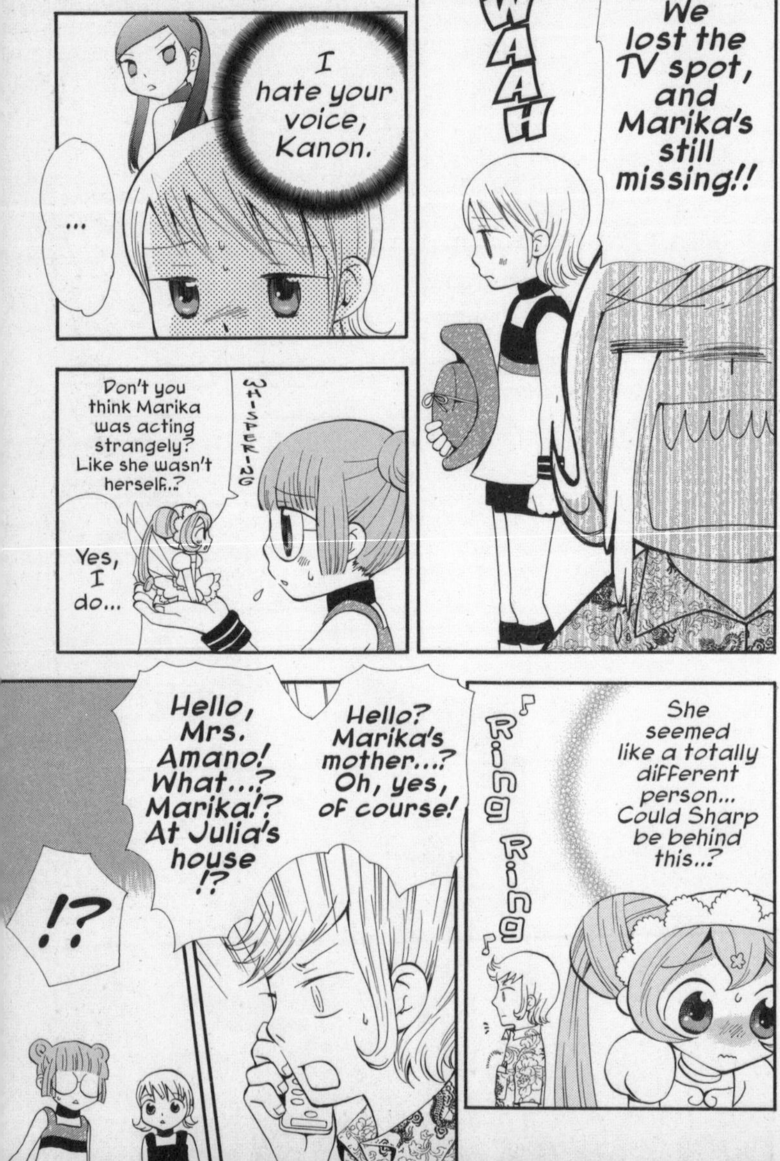
BWAAH
We lost the TV spot, and Marika's still missing!!
I hate your voice, Kanon.
...
WHISPERING
Don't you think Marika was acting strangely? Like she wasn't herself..?
Yes, I do...
She seemed like a totally different person... Could Sharp be behind this..?
Ring Ring
Hello? Marika's mother...? Oh, yes, of course!
Hello, Mrs. Amano! What...? Marika!? At Julia's house!?
!?

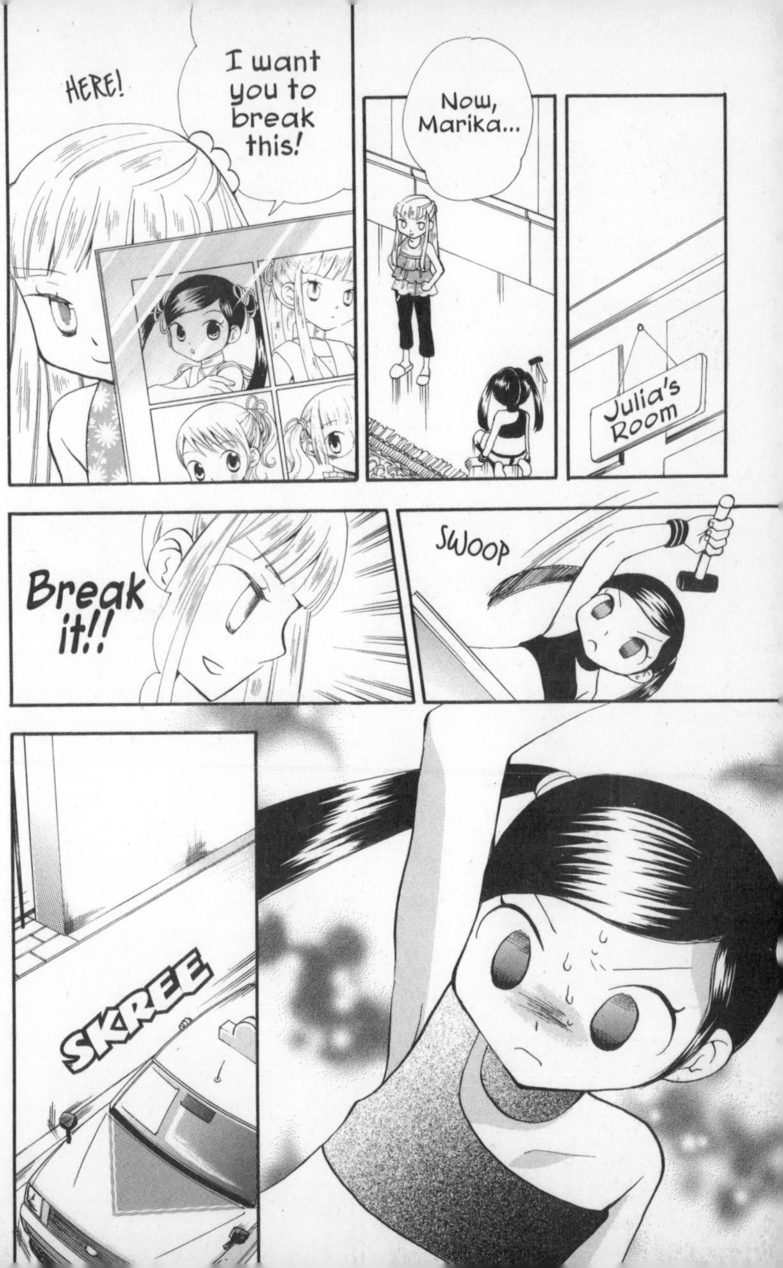
Julia's Room
Now, Marika...
I want you to break this!
HERE!
SWOOP
Break it!!
SKREE

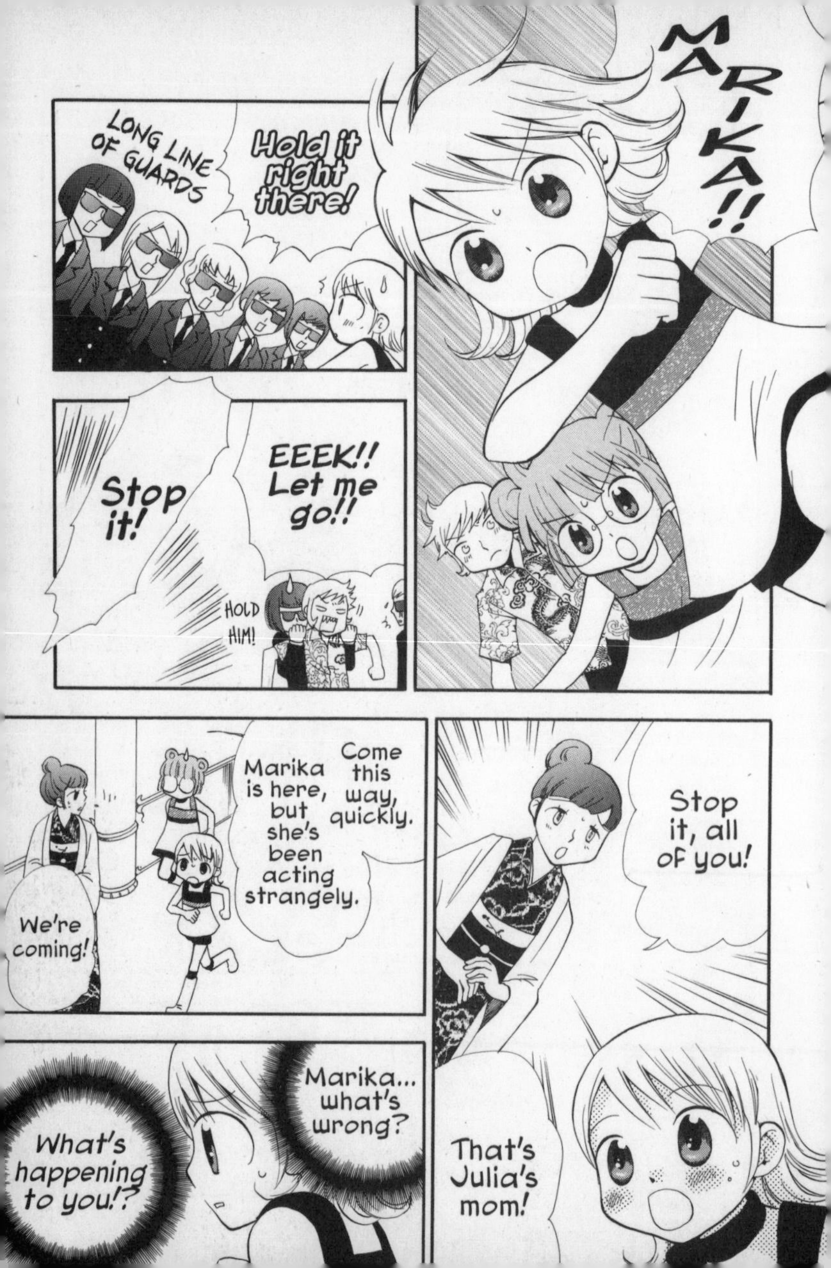
MARIKA!!
Hold it right there!
LONG LINE OF GUARDS
EEEK!! Let me go!!
Stop it!
HOLD HIM!
Stop it, all of you!
Come this way, quickly.
Marika is here, but she's been acting strangely.
We're coming!
That's Julia's mom!
Marika... what's wrong?
What's happening to you!?

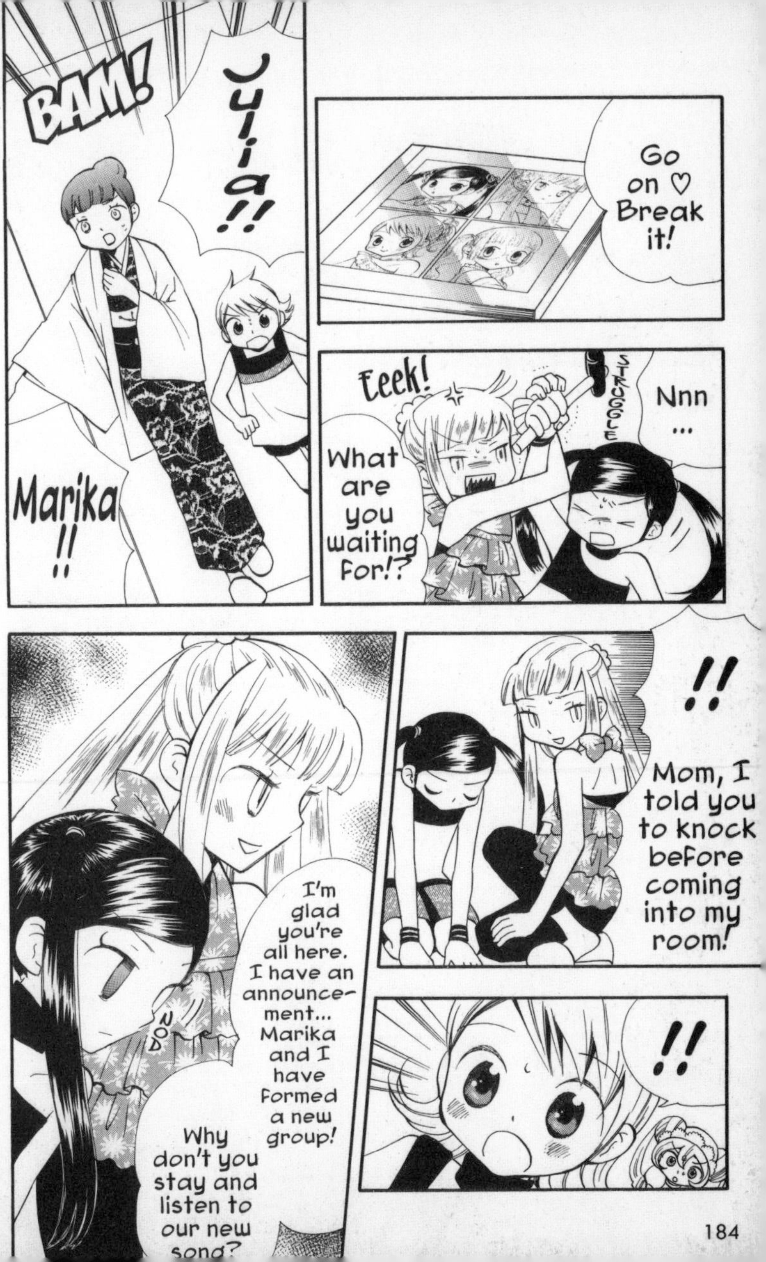
Go on ♡ Break it!
Nnn ...
STRUGGLE
Eeek!
What are you waiting for!?
Julia!!
BAM!
Marika !!
!!
Mom, I told you to knock before coming into my room!
!!
I'm glad you're all here. I have an announcement... Marika and I have formed a new group!
NOD
Why don't you stay and listen to our new song?

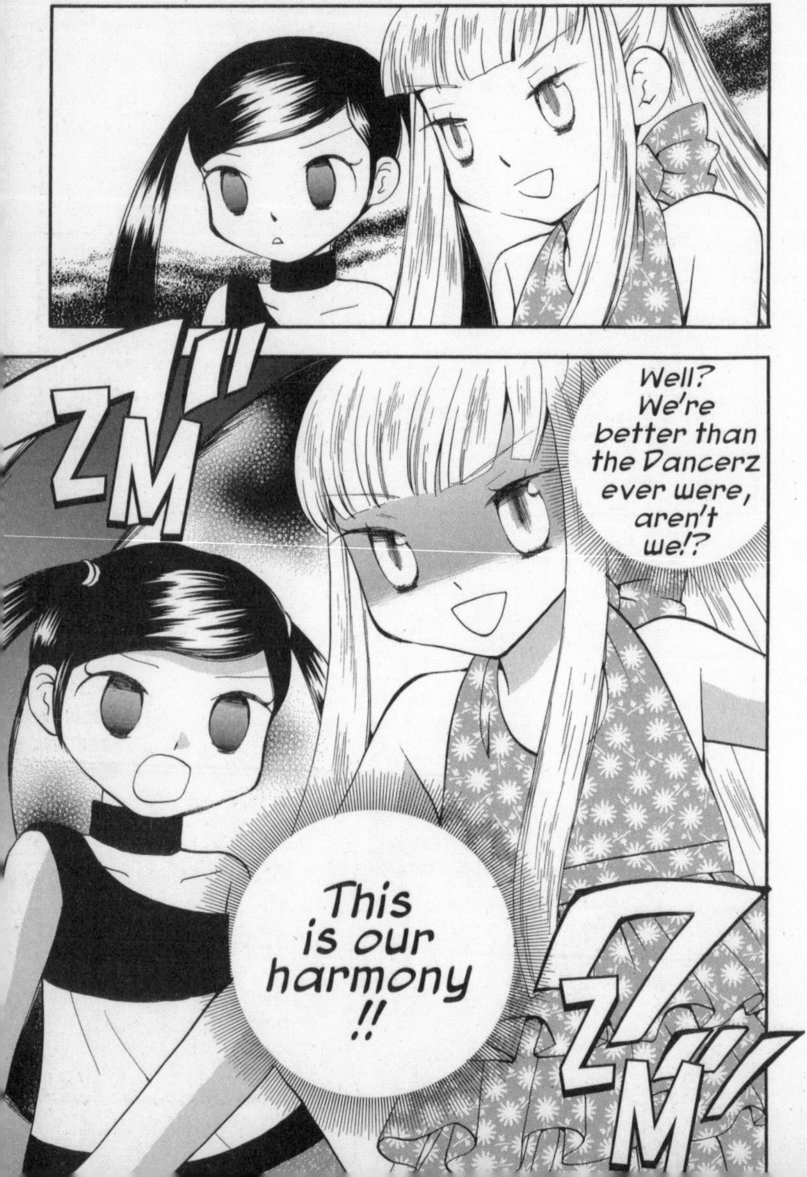
Well? We're better than the Dancerz ever were, aren't we!?
ZM
This is our harmony !!
ZZM

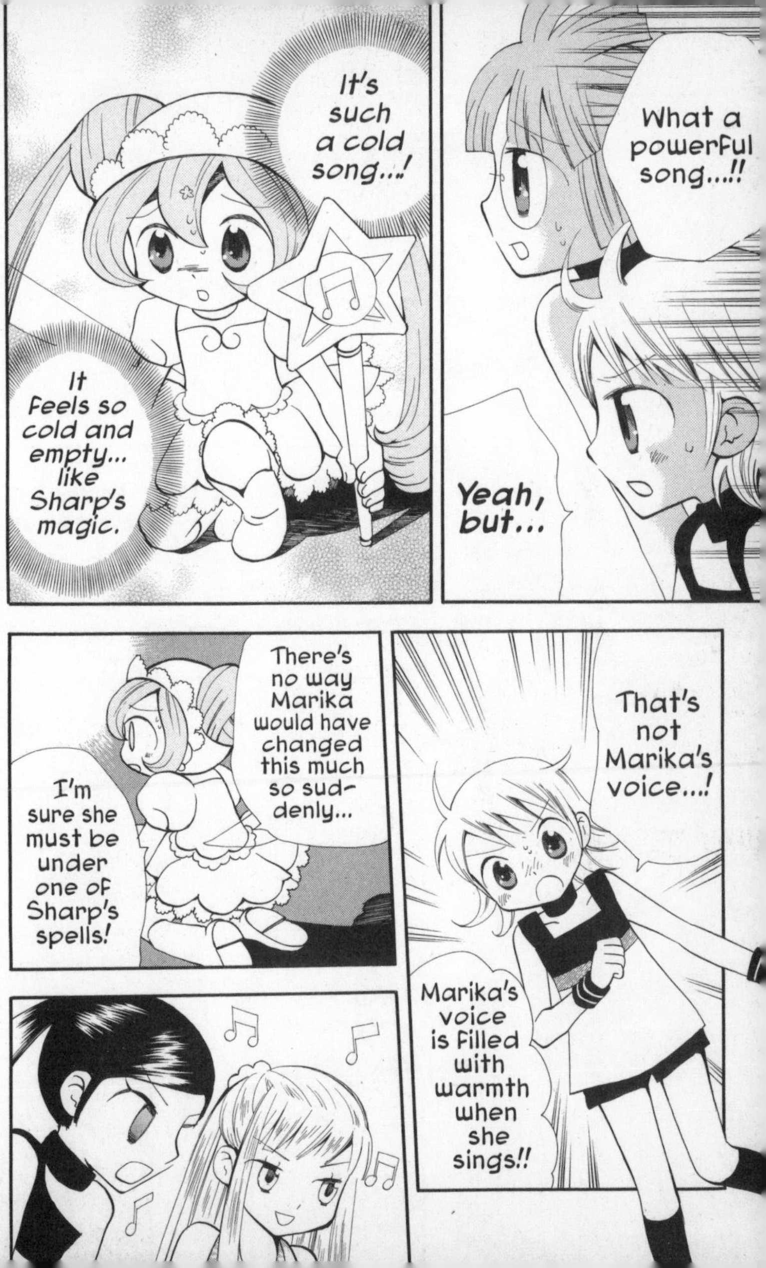
What a powerful song...!!
Yeah, but...
It's such a cold song...!
It feels so cold and empty... like Sharp's magic.
That's not Marika's voice...!
Marika's voice is filled with warmth when she sings!!
There's no way Marika would have changed this much so sud-denly...
I'm sure she must be under one of Sharp's spells!

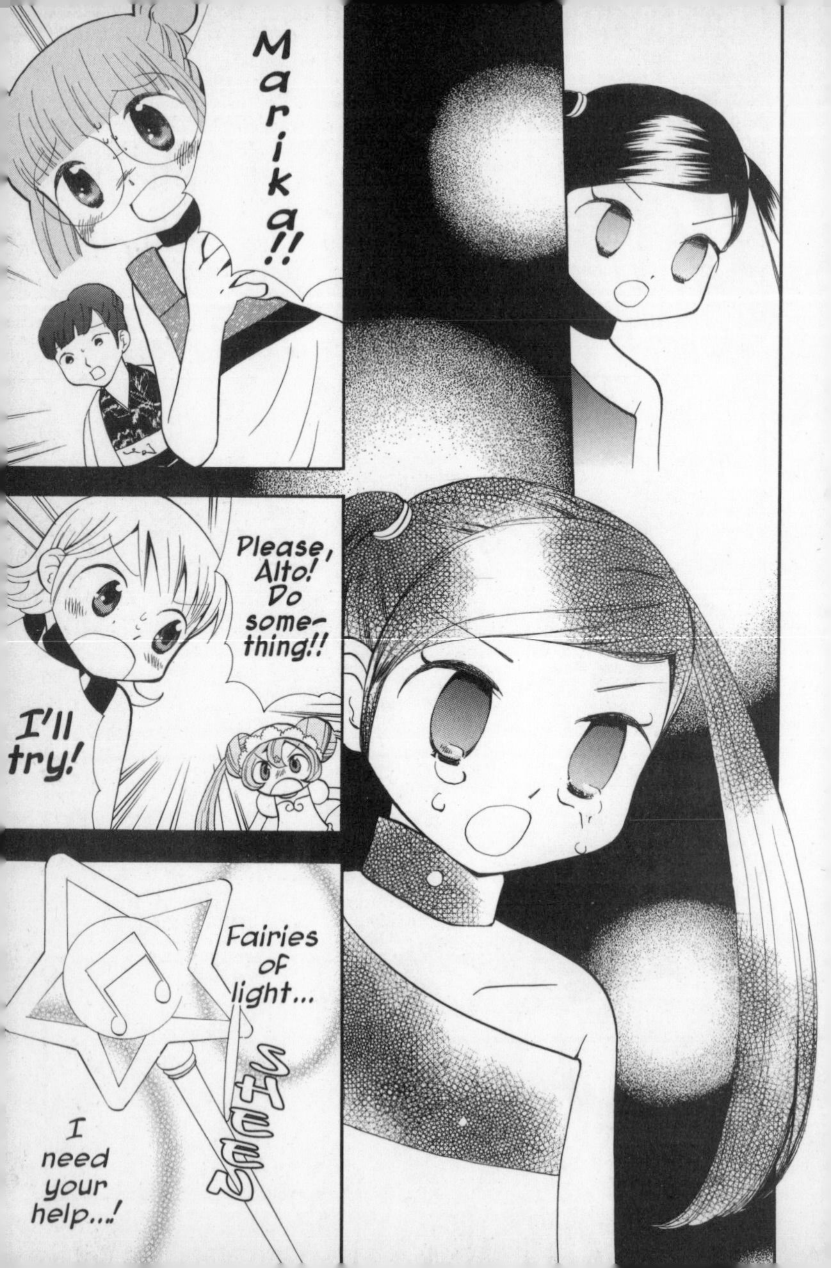
Marika!!
Please, Alto! Do some-thing!!
I'll try!
Fairies of light...
SHEEN
I need your help...!

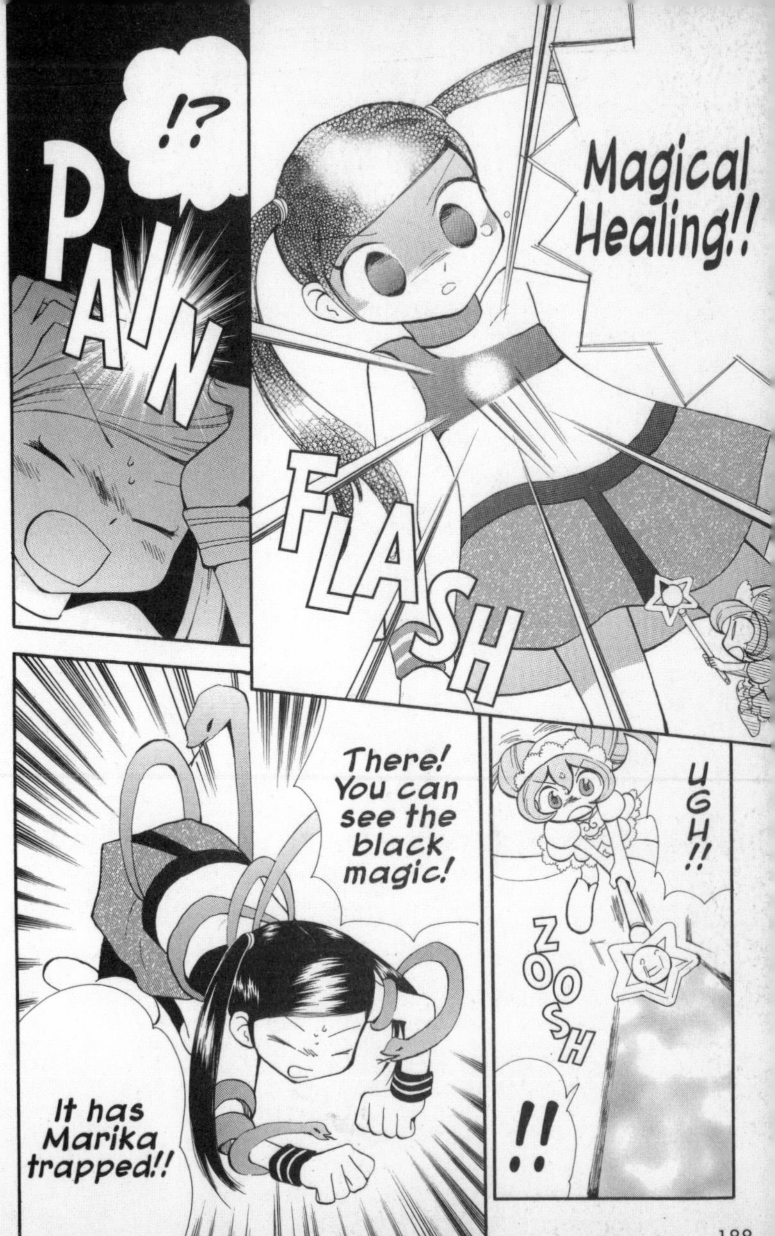
Magical Healing!!
FLASH
!?
PAIN
UGH!!
ZOOSH
!!
There! You can see the black magic!
It has Marika trapped!!

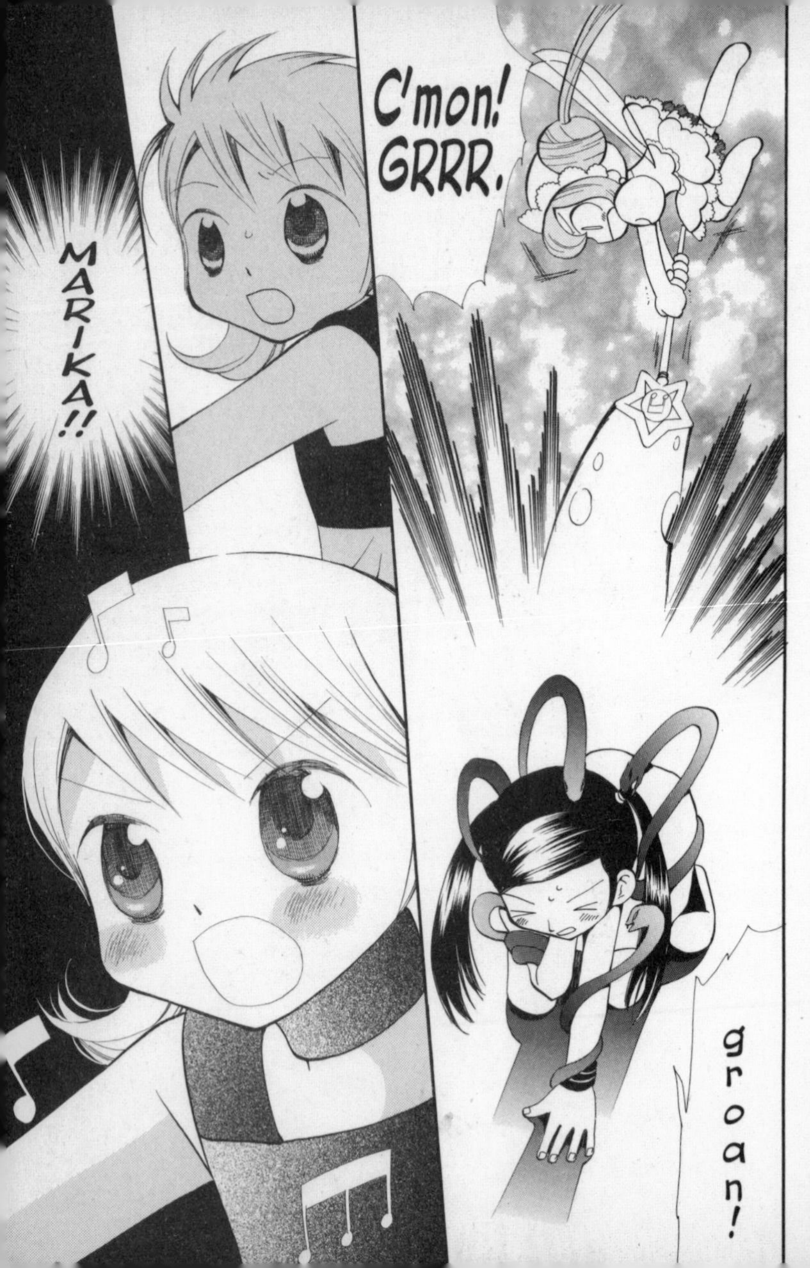
C'mon! GRRR.
MARIKA!!
groan!

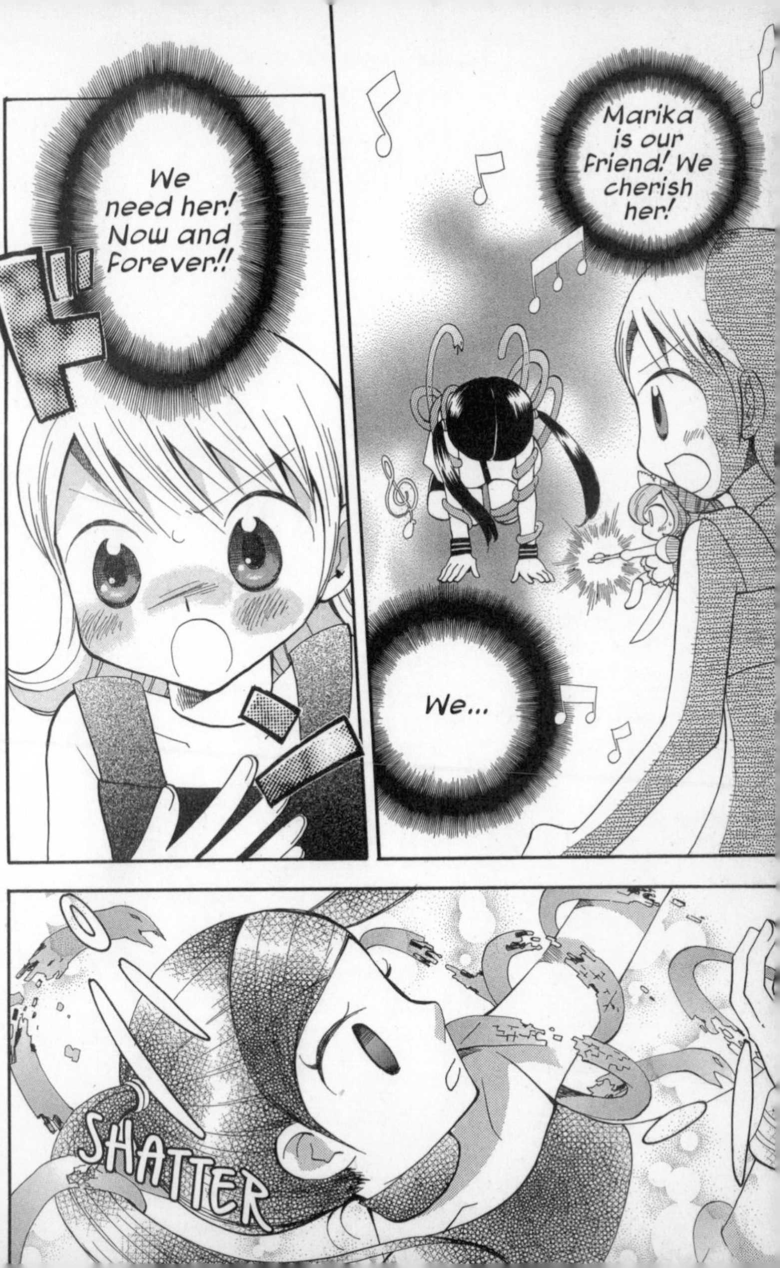
Marika is our friend! We cherish her!
We...
We need her! Now and forever!!
SHATTER

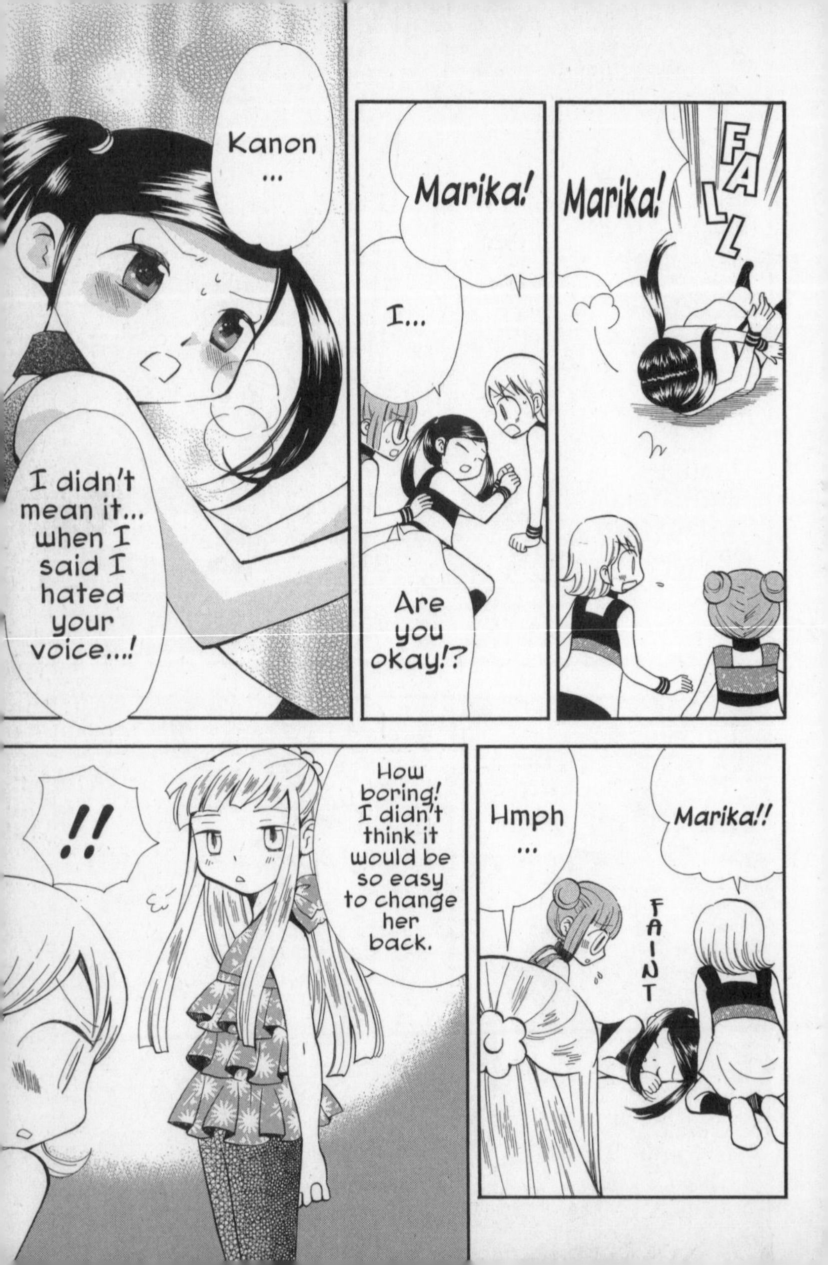

FALL
Marika!
Marika!
I...
Are you okay!?
Kanon ...
I didn't mean it... when I said I hated your voice...!
Marika!!
Hmph ...
FAINT
How boring! I didn't think it would be so easy to change her back.
!!

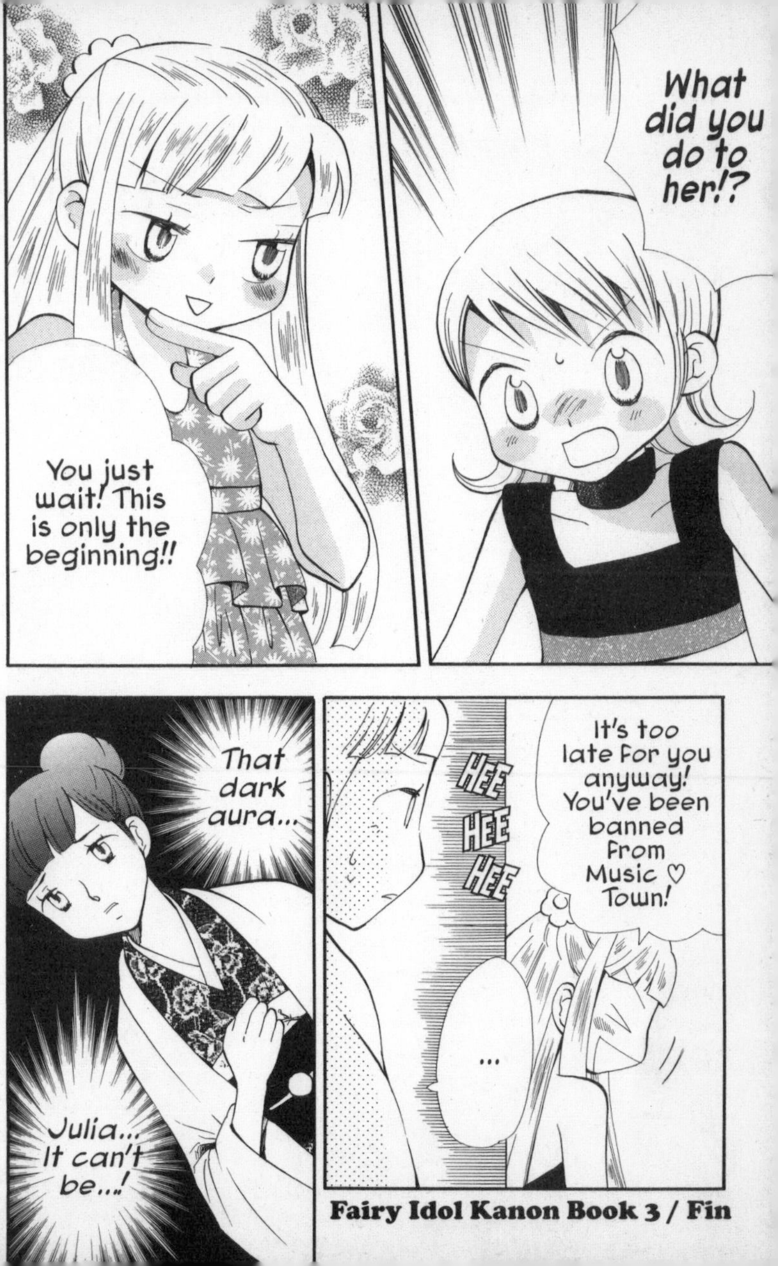
What did you do to her!?
You just wait! This is only the beginning!!
It's too late for you anyway! You've been banned from Music ♡ Town!
HEE HEE HEE
...
That dark aura...
Julia... It can't be...!

Fairy Idol Kanon Book 3 / Fin

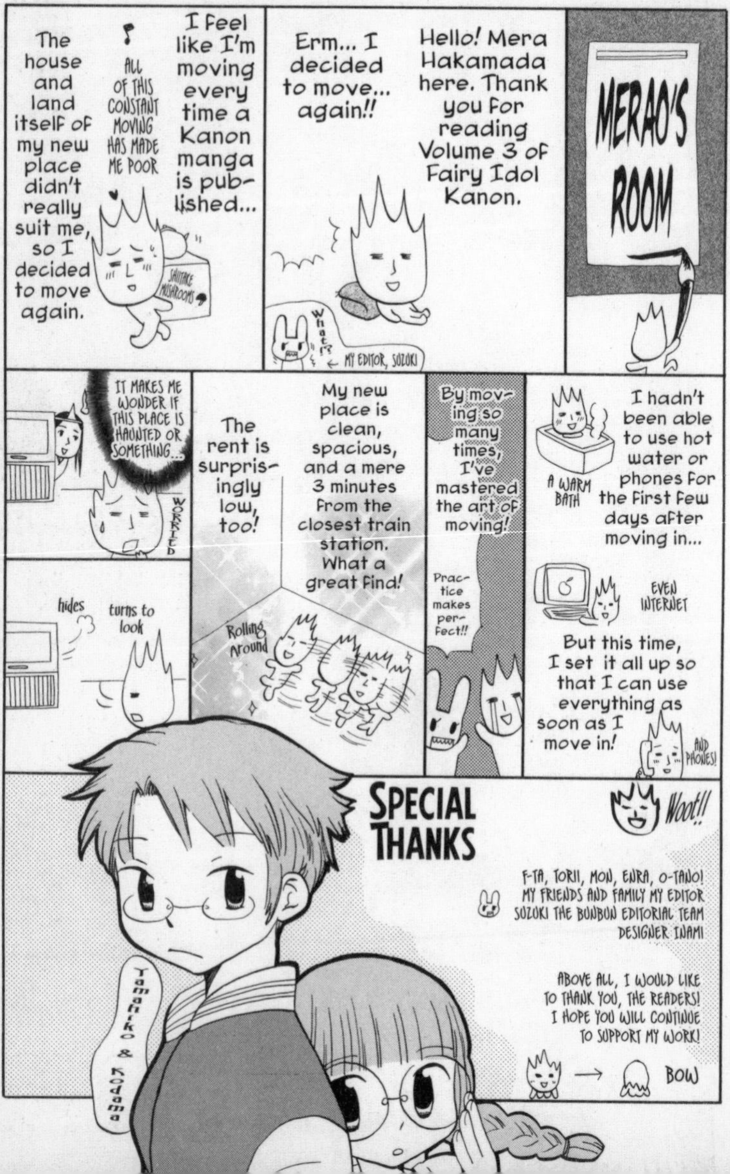
MERAO'S ROOM
Hello! Mera Hakamada here. Thank you for reading Volume 3 of Fairy Idol Kanon.
Erm... I decided to move... again!!
What!?
MY EDITOR, SUZUKI
I feel like I'm moving every time a Kanon manga is published...
ALL OF THIS CONSTANT MOVING HAS MADE ME POOR
The house and land itself of my new place didn't really suit me, so I decided to move again.
SHIITAKE MUSHROOMS
I hadn't been able to use hot water or phones for the first few days after moving in...
A WARM BATH
EVEN INTERNET
But this time, I set it all up so that I can use everything as soon as I move in!
AND PHONES!
By moving so many times, I've mastered the art of moving!
Practice makes perfect!!
My new place is clean, spacious, and a mere 3 minutes from the closest train station. What a great find!
The rent is surprisingly low, too!
Rolling Around
IT MAKES ME WONDER IF THIS PLACE IS HAUNTED OR SOMETHING...
WORRIED
turns to look
hides
SPECIAL THANKS
Woot!!
F-TA, TORII, MON, ENRA, O-TANO! MY FRIENDS AND FAMILY MY EDITOR SUZUKI THE BUNBUN EDITORIAL TEAM DESIGNER INAMI
ABOVE ALL, I WOULD LIKE TO THANK YOU, THE READERS! I HOPE YOU WILL CONTINUE TO SUPPORT MY WORK!
BOW
Tamahiko & Kodama

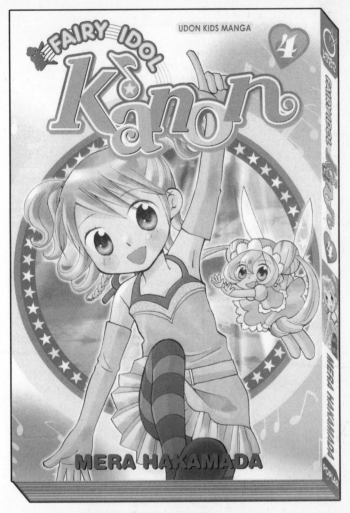

FAIRY IDOL KANON Vol.4
ISBN: 978-1-897376-92-8

Coming May 2010

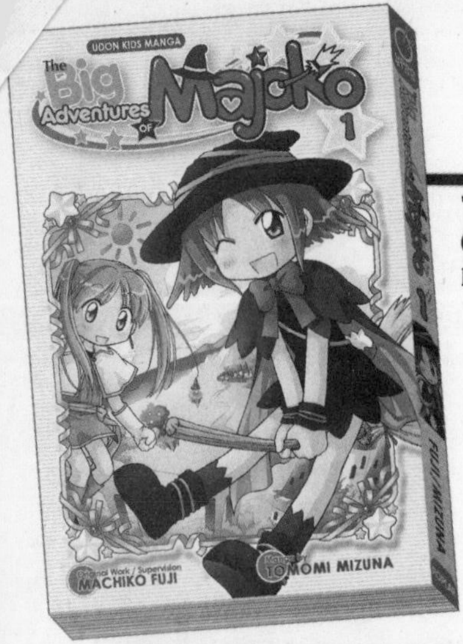
UDON KIDS MANGA
The Big Adventures of Majoko
1
Original Work / Supervision
MACHIKO FUJI
Manga by
TOMOMI MIZUNA
FUJI / MIZUNA

THE BIG ADVENTURES OF MAJOKO Vol.1

ISBN: 978-1-897376-81-2

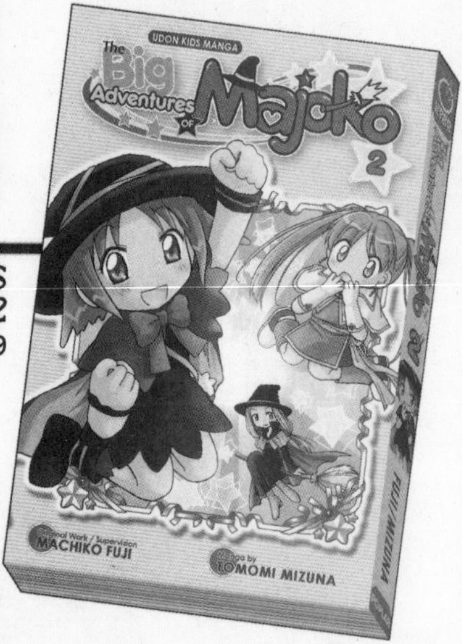
UDON KIDS MANGA
The Big Adventures of Majoko
2
Original Work / Supervision
MACHIKO FUJI
Manga by
TOMOMI MIZUNA
FUJI / MIZUNA

THE BIG ADVENTURES OF MAJOKO Vol.2

ISBN:978-1-897376-82-9

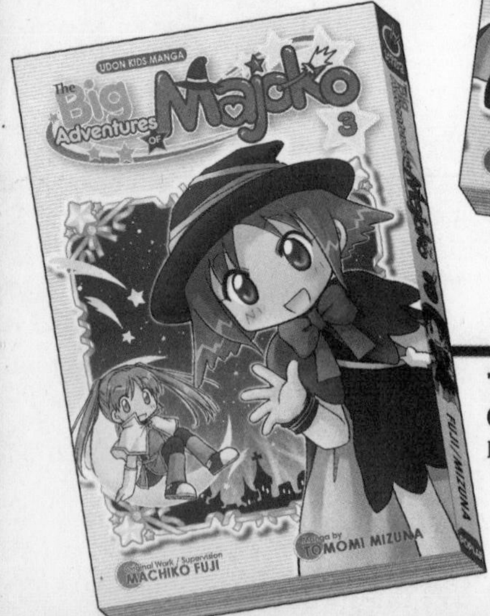
UDON KIDS MANGA
The Big Adventures of Majoko
3
Original Work / Supervision
MACHIKO FUJI
Manga by
TOMOMI MIZUNA
FUJI / MIZUNA

THE BIG ADVENTURES OF MAJOKO Vol.3

ISBN: 978-1-897376-83-6

THE GALAXY HAS SOME NEW BEST FRIENDS!

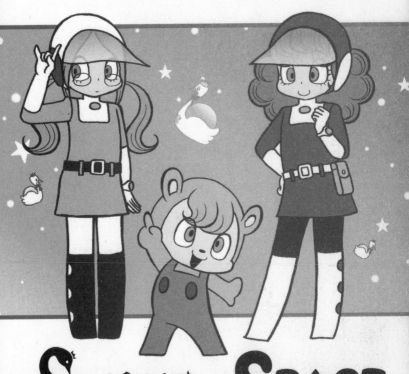

SWANS in SPACE

SCI-FI ADVENTURES FOR GIRLS!

SWANS IN SPACE Vol. 1
ISBN: 978-1-897376-93-5

COMING SOON:

SWANS in SPACE

VOLUME 2

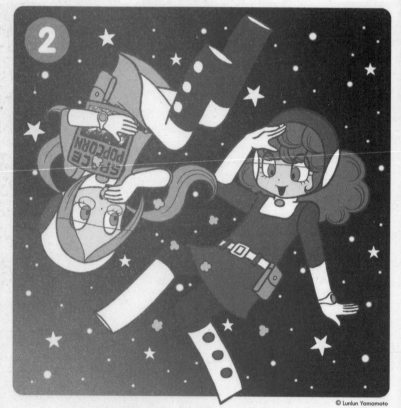

© Lunlun Yamamoto

ARRIVING JANUARY 2010

SWANS IN SPACE Vol.2
ISBN: 978-1-897376-94-2

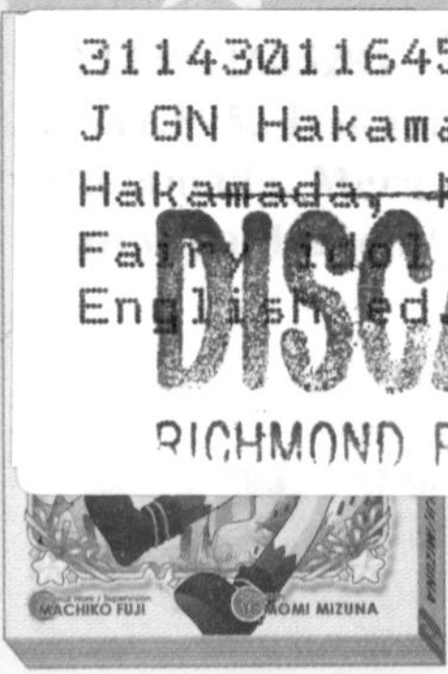
MACHIKO FUJI

THE BIG ADVENTURES OF MAJOKO

Vol.1
ISBN: 978-1-897376-81-2

Vol.2
ISBN: 978-1-897376-82-9

Vol.3
ISBN: 978-1-897376-83-6

Vol.4 *(March 2010)*
ISBN: 978-1-897376-84-3

Vol.5 *(June 2010)*
ISBN: 978-1-897376-85-0

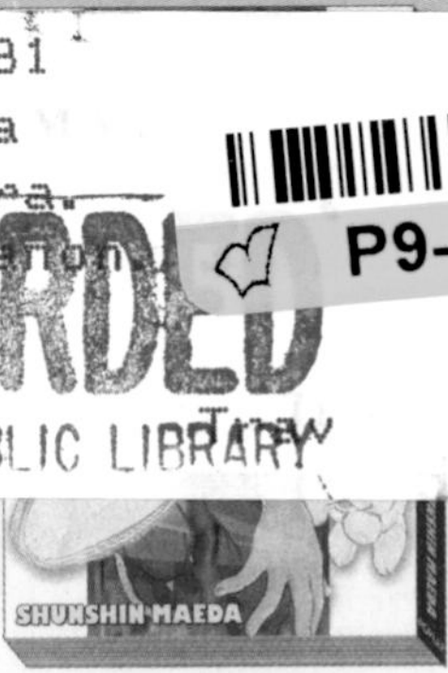
SHUNSHIN MAEDA

NINJA BASEBALL KYUMA

Vol.1
ISBN: 978-1-897376-86-7

Vol.2
ISBN: 978-1-897376-87-4

Vol.3*(Mar 2010)*
ISBN: 978-1-897376-88-1

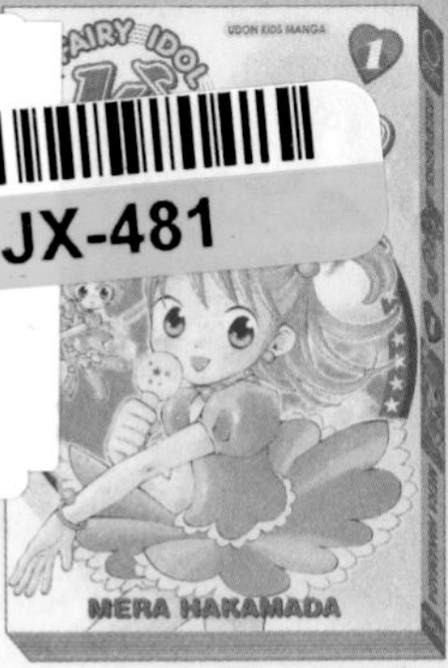
UDON KIDS MANGA
FAIRY IDOL
1
MERA HAKAMADA

FAIRY IDOL KANON

Vol.1
ISBN: 978-1-897376-89-8

Vol.2
ISBN: 978-1-897376-90-4

Vol.3 *(February 2010)*
ISBN: 978-1-897376-91-1

Vol.4 *(May 2010)*
ISBN: 978-1-897376-92-8

SWANS IN SPACE

Vol.1
ISBN: 978-1-897376-93-5

Vol.2
ISBN: 978-1-897376-94-2

Vol.3 *(April 2010)*
ISBN: 978-1-897376-95-9

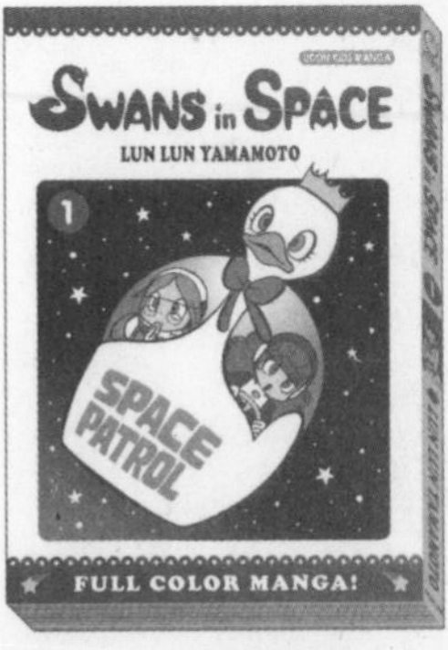
UDON KIDS MANGA
SWANS in SPACE
LUN LUN YAMAMOTO
1
SPACE PATROL
FULL COLOR MANGA!

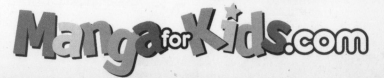

MangaforKids.com